DARE TO DIE

GARETH O'CALLAGHAN

Best wishes

Gareth O'Callaghan

W0006088

POOLBEG

All characters in this publication are fictitious and any resemblance to real persons, living or dead, is purely coincidental.

Published 1996 by
Poolbeg Press Ltd,
123 Baldoyle Industrial Estate,
Dublin 13, Ireland

© Gareth O'Callaghan 1996

The moral right of the author has been asserted.

A catalogue record for this book is available from the British Library.

ISBN 1 85371 635 9

Cover design by Poolbeg Group Services Ltd
Set by Poolbeg Group Services Ltd in Janson Text 10.5/13.5
Printed and bound in Great Britain by
Cox & Wyman Ltd, Reading, Berks.

Acknowledgements

Writing is an enigma. I know that now. I could never have imagined how reclusive an existence it can be. Nor could I have understood the fulfilment that it brings with its accomplishments. My special thanks to a small group of dedicated people; friends I have leaned on over the last two years.

My wife, Jacqui, for all her love and support. My greatest critic and strongest supporter.

My mother, Eileen, and Kathleen for the Novenas.

My father, Joe, for never letting me settle for second best.

To Paul Williams, the country's finest criminologist and investigative reporter. He's the bravest man I know.

To Fergus Gibson, for the good news I needed to hear every Monday afternoon.

To Kate Cruise O'Brien, my editor and friend. Her passion for literature, and her interest in my work, has taught me so much in such a short time.

To Philip MacDermott, Nicole Hodson, Paula Campbell and all the team at Poolbeg Press for a job well done and beautifully executed.

To all my friends and colleagues at RTE.

To all those who helped tirelessly with relevant suggestions and who wish to remain anonymous.

And finally, to a few special friends who never seem to get thanked: Don Baker, Mary Black, John McKenna, Jim Daly, Kevin Rowland, Tony McCarthy, Dicey and Carol Hanna.

To Jacqui, Kerri and Katie,

with all my love

"Imagination is more important than knowledge."

Albert Einstein

Chapter One

Dún Laoghaire, Dublin. 8.30 pm.

"Ma, will you watch where you're waving that umbrella or you'll take me eye out! I don't know why we couldn't have waited in that pub across the road."

"And what? Give your father ideas? I want him to be sober when he drops me up to the ladies' club later on. Now, have you got your ticket, love?" her mother asked.

"Jesus, Ma, for the hundredth time, the answer is *yes*!" Jamie yelled. "You'd better go before we all get pneumonia."

"Now, promise me you'll get an early night tomorrow night. Otherwise you'll be getting run down."

"Ma, I'm able to mind myself."

"Lisa, go back up to the van and keep an eye on your father. I don't want him slipping off for a couple of quick ones while we're not looking. I just want to say goodbye to your sister. There's a good girl."

"Ma, I hate when you say goodbye. Anyway, you shouldn't keep treating her like a twelve-year-old. And

1

as for me da, he's probably afraid that the van'll be stolen."

"*Stolen?*" she shrieked. "You'd want to leave a few thousand pound in cash on the front seat before anyone'd be interested in stealing that heap."

"What time is it?" Jamie checked her watch. "Jesus, it's nearly quarter to nine. Here, Ma, I have to go." She threw her arms firmly around her mother. "I'll miss you."

"Jamie, when are you ever going to find him?" she whispered.

Jamie drew back. "Find who?"

"A decent man who'll treat you properly, that's who. Someone who *really* likes you."

"Who knows, Ma? Maybe I've found him," she replied nonchalantly.

Her mother straigtened up. "That half-baked *shite*?"

Jamie had never heard her mother use such language. "*Mammy!*"

"Well . . . what else did you expect me to say? I swear to God, Jamie, if he as much as lays a finger on you, I'll . . . "

"Save it, Ma. I'm going to miss the boat."

"Well," she persisted, "you haven't answered my question. If he really loved you, you wouldn't miss me at all. And that's the way God meant it to be. That's all I want for you, love . . . to be happy. And *he'll* never make you happy. Don't ever think for a minute that he will. And if he ever asks you to marry him, which I can't see happening, I'll . . . "

"I *am* happy, Mam." Jamie threw her eyes up to heaven. "*You* wouldn't be happy if I arrived home with Johnny Depp."

"Johnny *who*?"

"It doesn't matter. Anyway, sure you've never met him so how would you know whether he can make me happy or not?"

"Never *met* him? I've never even heard of him!"

"*Tommy*, Ma, not *Johnny*!"

"Oh, *him*!" she growled. "Look Jamie," she persisted, "we've had this argument before. I just don't like the sound of him and I've never ever been wrong, have I?" She pulled a tissue from her coat sleeve and rubbed her eyes. "Oh God, I hate this. I always swear I'm not going to cry. And I always end up with big red swollen eyes." She blew her nose hard. "When are you ever gonna get a job at home? Or at least a job that you could fly back to. This place is perishing!"

"Ma, I told you, there were no flights left. And, anyway, I do have a good job."

"*At that radio station?*" she shrilled. "I don't know. I do have a queer feeling about all them showbiz people. Their feet aren't on the ground at all, if you ask me."

"For God's sake, Ma, will you keep your voice down. Listen, I'll ring you tomorrow, all right?" Jamie threw her bag across her shoulder and kissed her mother goodbye. She could feel her own tears well up as the older woman started to go to pieces. Best get out of here.

"Make sure you write," her mother shouted.

"Ma, I'm only a phone call away. An hour on the plane."

"Well, call me old-fashioned. It'd be nice to get a letter from my daughter now and again. I don't know why I learned you to write." Her chattering voice faded into the distance.

When Jamie looked back again, Lisa, her sister, was helping her mother to keep her umbrella the right side out as they pushed their way through the wind and rain back towards the van. Oh God, why? she wondered.

* * *

It was as rough as a rugby scrum. The car ferry had been at sea for an hour and passengers were dropping like flies. Frank McCabe sat slumped in his seat and cursed himself for not taking the plane to Heathrow instead. The weather was definitely getting worse, whatever the voice on the intercom said. He pressed his hand and forehead against the cold, damp window and scanned the darkness for a light or two.

A young boy sat across the aisle staring at Frank. He stuffed sweets, which he took from different bags, into his mouth. Occasionally, he'd make an effort to speak.

"Mammy, I feel sick," he blurted. He got no reaction from his mother who snored blissfully.

"Have some more orange and you'll be all right," his father mumbled.

The young boy promptly took a large slug from the

open bottle. His mouth was big enough to play the trumpet. Frank smiled at him. The child reacted by opening his mouth to show off the gooey mixture that he'd packed into the small space available. A bag of cold chips and a half-eaten burger sat on the table in front of him. Frank held his stomach and closed his eyes for a moment.

"Mammy, I feel sick." The boy pulled at his mother's sleeve and stuffed another toffee bar into his gob.

"Here." His father gestured to a packet of sweets. "Have another Freshie. And wipe your mouth."

"Mammy!" the boy pleaded with the snoring heap that lay sprawled across two seats in front of him. Frank moved his belongings closer to him and closed his eyes again.

"Mammy!" There was a loud cough and all hell broke loose. The father looked over the top of his magazine to find his clothes had turned psychedelic. He reacted like a champion pole-vaulter!

"Ah, Jesus, Mary! I thought *you* were keeping an eye on him!" He held his hands in the air as if about to give a religious blessing.

The woman opened her eyes. "Oh, Jesus, Mary and Joseph, you poor boy."

The child swayed from side to side. "Mammy, look!"

"It's all right, love." The woman grabbed a magazine that lay on the table in front of her. She leaned across the table and wiped the young boy's pullover.

"What are you doing? That's this week's *Buy and Sell*. I only bought it tonight!" The husband grabbed the magazine. "You can clean him with something else."

"*I* can clean him? *You* were the one who bought him all that crap. I knew this would happen." She settled back into her seat. "Well, you can clean him up. They're the only trousers he has with him. And they have to last him the week!"

"And what about me?" The middle-aged man pointed to *his* trousers. "How am I going to get these clean for your sister's wedding in the morning?" He eased his way delicately out of the seat. "I told you I never wanted to come in the first place. This is the effect your sister has on me. Something awful always happens when we're going to meet her. I always said she was bad luck," the man muttered.

"My sister? How dare you! As for that bitch of a sister of yours. She's never out of our house. Living on me lip day and night. A mouth like Gerry Ryan's. Tell her something and the whole parish knows in ten minutes!"

"Well, that's 'cos you invite her in in the first place, isn't it? Between the two of youse, I don't know how me bloody nerves haven't killed me by now!"

The woman closed her eyes and ignored him. He kept on. "Have y'ever asked yourself why this is your sister's fifth husband?"

Silence. Heads popped up randomly. Everyone within hearing distance was now leaning out into the aisles to get a better look.

"I'll tell you why! Because none of those other bastards were good enough for her. That's why!" She closed her eyes again. "I should've come on me own."

The father gently helped the young boy out into the aisle. He seemed to be in a hypnotic trance.

"Well, I'm going to the bar to get drunk!"

"So, what's new," the woman muttered.

The man stood up straight and looked around at the huge crowd who were gripped now by the car ferry soap drama. He nodded his head back in his wife's direction. "Isn't that just lovely coming from the boy's mother." He walked slowly down the aisle trying to conceal the front of his white trousers. "Lovely. Just fucking lovely," he muttered under his breath. "Come on, son. Daddy will get you a drink. Would you like a bottle of Coke?"

"Daddy."

"Yes, son?"

"I want Mammy."

"Don't worry, son. Daddy will look after you. We'll see your Mammy in Holyhead. That's if she doesn't fall overboard first."

The two casualties shuffled towards the door.

At last, silence.

Being single had its advantages, Frank pondered. He shifted around uneasily, trying to figure out who the shipping company had in mind when they designed these seats. Obviously, arses were the furthest things from their minds! If only he'd got on board earlier, he'd probably have got one of the posh armchairs in the video lounge. How was it that the ship always looked beautiful for the first part of the journey and resembled a bombsite on arrival?

He thought about taking out his guitar and playing a few ballads to cheer up the small crowd sitting around him. But the notion of another spoilt kid throwing up all over his pride and joy quickly put him off the idea. They were due to dock in Holyhead around midnight for the four-hour train journey to Euston, London. But, in these conditions, God knows what time they'd get there.

The bell sounded on the intercom. "Would Captain Van Dyke please report to the bridge. Captain Van Dyke to the bridge. Urgently, please."

Great, Frank thought. No bloody captain. That's all we need!

Brendan, his brother, had driven him to Dublin that night for the ferry journey. They'd kept the radio turned up all the way from West Cork, in the hope that the sailing would be cancelled due to bad weather. The notion of an extra night at home was very appealing. He hated going back. But a delay wouldn't have been such a good idea. His interview for the position of manager of the Clover Tap was for nine the following morning. He'd decided against taking the new hovercraft to Wales after a couple of the lads at home told him that it was like being tied to an ironing board and dragged across the Irish Sea.

Jesus, don't let me be late, he thought to himself.

He looked at his watch. Quarter past ten. Still another three hours in this squeaky tub. Frank had lost count of the trips he'd made on the ferry from Dublin to Holyhead. Each time, he swore it would be his last. It wasn't so bad on a quiet evening, or the odd time a group of the lads would take advantage of the return sailing on Good Friday to have a few pints and a singsong. The day return was always a bit of *craic*, he thought. It was a different story on a night like this. Wall-to-wall passengers, packed in like sardines.

He was trying to get comfortable when, all of a sudden, he spotted her. She'd propped herself up against the side of the lounge area, directly in front of him. She looked stunning even if she was about to throw up. Frank McCabe had just come face to face with his secret dreamboat. The girl with the unpronounceable Irish name who read *Nuacht* on RTE television. He'd spent years trying to pronounce it and recently came as close as he was ever going to get: Moira Ni Goira! Not too far off. Good enough for when her name came up in conversation in Molloy's pub on a Friday night. As soon as the news logo appeared on the pub screen at twenty-five past six, the entire bar would fall quiet out of tradition and respect. Frank would gaze and admire. The news bulletin became a love-feast and Frank a lovelorn suitor. Mr Molloy often remarked that the reaction was similar to the effect that Lotto balls dropping into a numerical sequence would have on most other men. Frank reminded Molloy that the sight of Charlie Haughey had a similar effect on *him*.

He was right. She had the most beautiful lips in the whole world: full and thick and round. He marvelled at how she always managed to get them around all those *focals* and *fadas*. What a woman! Tonight, however, she looked a bit green. Frank debated whether this was due to the rough sea or a lack of make-up. He'd read in a magazine that television stars wear a lot of make-up to hide the wrinkles caused by excessive drinking. The high life took its toll on these high-flyers. Everyone knew that they were out all hours of the day and night. Eating, drinking and celebrating. The life of a superstar. And now, here he was, only feet away from his idol. He could tell by looking at her that she wasn't a big drinker. Maybe the odd spritzer after the news. He'd put his guitar carefully on the seat directly opposite him, as he always did. That way, he could invite someone to sit down provided she was a fine thing. None finer than Moira Ni Goira. This was his big chance.

He knew that if he stared at her long enough, she was sure to look over. Then he could offer her the seat. After that the sky was the limit.

Jesus, he thought, what if she talks in Irish all the time? Then I'm rightly stumped. He could see she was on the verge of passing out. No surprise really. The boat was stuffed to capacity. It was hard to breathe with the heavy tobacco smoke.

He was about to stand up and walk over to her when a voice said, "Excuse me, you wouldn't just keep an eye on those while I go to the loo?" Frank looked up at the stranger and a small case hit him a smack in the head.

"Oh, sorry!"

As Frank rubbed his head, he took a good look at

her. She was blonde with short hair and very good-looking. She wore a heavy blue sweater and tight blue jeans revealing a perfect bottom. Frank disliked tiny bottoms. But he equally disliked giant arses. "Course I will, they're grand there," he quickly answered wondering where the words came from. "By the way, before you go," he said in his deep Cork accent, "could you tell us what's the Irish for 'would you like to sit down opposite me'?"

The girl's face lit up. She seemed amused. "Are you for real? I speak English! Thanks for the seat. I'll be back in a second!"

Ah shag it, now what? he thought to himself. He looked over in Moira Ni Goira's direction. As if to add insult to injury, some businessman in a suit and a pair of John Lennon glasses had just offered her a seat. I bet that'll be an interesting conversation, he pondered to himself. Ah hello. You're the woman off the telly. Any news? Eh eh? Do you get it? . . . Any news? Boring oul' shite. I bet she's heard that one a million times. While Frank watched Moira Ni Goira, he didn't notice the fair-haired stranger sit down opposite him.

"Thanks again for the seat." She reached into one of her bags, took out a Walkman and untangled the cables. "Are you on your own?"

Now there's a question! No woman had been that direct in years. Not since the days he drove in Dublin as a van driver for Buckley's Bread. On the other hand, maybe she was just being friendly. "Yeah. Well sort of, like," he stuttered.

"Are you learning to speak Irish?" She sat back in her seat.

"Eh, no I'm not," he replied, craning his neck to see how Moira was getting on with her friend in the pin-stripes. "Why d'ya ask?"

"Well, because you asked me what's the Irish for 'do you want a seat'?"

Frank laughed uneasily. "No, I did not. I said if it wasn't for the Irish, you'd never get a seat."

She gave him an odd look.

He'd managed to get out of that one nicely. It was time to change the line of conversation. "Are you going to London?" Frank tried to look interested.

"Yeah. I work there. This is my first Christmas home in four years. My ma nearly died when I surprised them on Christmas Eve. I walked in while they were having their tea. 'How are you? I said. My mother threw her arms around me and asked if I was pregnant." She laughed. "My boyfriend gave me a present of a few bob. Too lazy to go out and buy me a present."

"Did he not come home with you?"

"*Him* . . . come to Dublin? You must be joking. Anyway, he hates the Irish."

"Where's he from?"

The young woman seemed a little uneasy. "London. Why?"

"It just seems strange that he's going out with an Irish woman and he hates Irish people."

"He *is* strange." She pressed the *play* button on her Walkman.

"What does he work at?"

12

"Good question," she chuntered cynically, adjusting the earpieces. "I suppose you could say that he works for himself."

"Self-employed?"

"No, just pure fucking selfish, actually." She fiddled with the volume switch.

Frank was astonished at the brusque comeback. He waited before asking. "What is he?"

She'd closed her eyes and, obviously unaware of his question, started humming along to the song.

Frank continued to give her the once-over. No shortage of good looks, he thought. Late twenties, he reckoned.

She opened her eyes. "He's a cop!" she blurted out dramatically.

It came quite unexpectedly. Frank had forgotten the question. "What?"

"You asked me what he was? I'm telling you. He's a cop."

"Where?"

"London."

"Good job." Frank wasn't sure of what else to say. "At least now I know who to go to if I need to get any fines quashed," he jested.

She looked at him glumly. "God, you know if I start laughing I think I might never stop."

"Sorry," Frank said awkwardly.

She smiled. "*I'm* sorry. I shouldn't be so sarcastic. It's just that . . . " She stopped herself short and looked deep into Frank's eyes. It was as if she was really trying hard to say something. "What?"

She shrugged her shoulders. "Nothing." She shifted around the seat and took off the headset. "Did you ever hear the expression 'the right hand's never sure what the left hand's holding'? Well, that's Tommy. Every woman's worst nightmare."

"Are you afraid of him?"

"Are you afraid of the dark?"

"Then why do you stay with him if he doesn't like you?"

"Oh, he likes me all right. At least, he seems to. He's good to me."

"Compared to what?"

She smiled. "Tell me all about you. You're not from Dublin."

Frank shook his head. "Cork."

"Married?" she asked inquisitively.

"I suppose you could say I haven't let myself go . . . yet," he replied complacently.

They both laughed.

"No one will have me!"

"Ah, let's take out the violin," she mocked.

"So are you going out with this beetle-crusher for long?"

"Who?"

"Your policeman boyfriend."

She sighed. "Too long."

"Well, he must be doing something right if you've stayed together for . . . " Frank waited.

"Three years," she moaned.

"Jesus, three *years*? I'm lucky if I can survive three weeks!"

"Yeah, well, I suppose I *am* lucky." She lit up a cigarette and placed the headset back around her neck. "At least, I don't have to see him that often."

Frank was confused. "Well, surely if you've been going out together for three years, you have to bump into each other at some stage."

"Oh, we *do*! When you're living together in a small, two-bed apartment, it's difficult avoiding each other. But we just . . . do our own thing, I suppose."

Frank could feel that his friendly curiosity was about as welcome as a stray dog with rabies. "But surely, if you don't get on with each other . . . I mean, you're not married or anything . . . unless you're . . . "

"Pregnant?" She took a long drag from the cigarette. "Was that what you were going to say?" The smoke gushed from the side of her mouth in a long discharge. She shivered. "Jesus, don't mention the war." She collected herself calmly again. "No, I'm not pregnant."

"Sorry."

"You should have been a cop yourself. Nice line in questioning. And to think that I could have missed all this if I hadn't got my flight times mixed up. This could be my lucky night."

"I didn't mean to seem so nosey. You just seemed a bit . . . "

"Pissed off?" she spouted. "Yeah, I'm feeling pretty pissed off all right. I always end up asking myself why I'm going back after all the times I promise myself that this will be the last time."

"So . . . you secretly *do* love him, then."

"I think I used to love him once. That was a long time ago. Now, we just survive."

"I can't say I like the sound of this bloke."

"You don't want to know Tommy. Everyone who's got to know him has been used for something dire. You seem too nice for that."

"So you're telling me he wouldn't like me."

"Oh, he'd probably like you all right . . . provided you're not Irish, or Jewish, or black or Pakistani, or poor, rich, homeless, helpless, influential, pathetic. The list goes on. But then Tommy thinks everyone is pathetic, except him of course." Jamie shrugged her shoulders. "God, why am I telling you all this?"

"Because maybe I care."

"*Care?* You've only just met me. I'm going to the bar." She stood up.

Frank looked across at the young boy stuffing the contents of a bag of popcorn into his mouth. His father looked eagerly at the six full beer cans on the table in front of him. "Jesus, even the thought of drinking that stuff," he sighed.

"I'd say everyone on the boat feels the same way."

"Can you blame them?" Frank looked up at the forlorn-looking stranger standing opposite. "You'd swear we were at a funeral."

"Not far off, if you ask me."

"I think you could do with a bit of cheering up."

"I think that might need some divine inspiration."

Frank perked up. "No better person."

"Who?" she asked.

"Me!"

"What do you do?"

"I'm the Catholic Bishop of Watford Gap." He grinned.

"Come *off* it! I mean, I don't believe . . . " She paused and nodded at his khaki-brownish jacket and jeans. She sat back into her seat.

"What? Oh, *these*?" he declared, looking down at his casual wear. "Well, you don't expect me to wear all that heavy gear on a trip like this. Anyway, I'd have every oul' one and statue-kisser within a forty-yard radius looking for absolution." He looked around and discreetly blessed himself. "What about you?"

"*Me?*" She choked. "I suppose a few months . . . maybe, eh, a year." She thought to herself. "Midnight Mass, eh, two years ago?"

"*What?*"

"Confession," she muttered.

Frank smiled. "No, I meant what do you do for a living?"

"Oh!" She smiled with relief. "I'm personal assistant to the boss of a radio station in London." She waited as if for blessed approval.

Frank nodded slowly. "Marvellous. A bit like my own job really."

Jamie was completely addle-brained at this stage. "How could my job be like your job?"

"All to do with the business of communications, my dear. Intercourse, you know?"

Jamie coughed. "Really?" She could feel herself blushing. "I'm going up the bar. You don't mind me having a drink, do you?" She still couldn't make this individual out at all. Sitting opposite him had seemed like a good idea. Now, she wasn't sure.

He shook his head. "Not in the slightest." He searched in his pocket and pulled out a ten-pound note. "You wouldn't bring me back a small snifter, would you?"

"A *what*?"

"Paddy and white," he mumbled. "No ice." He winked at her.

Jamie was disconcerted. "Here, I'll get the first round." She made a quick exit.

"Excuse me," Frank called to the young boy's father who was sitting across the narrow aisle.

The man took a few moments to focus. "Are you talking to me?" he slurred in a flat Dublin accent.

Frank nodded. "Listen," he said prudently, "when the young woman who was sitting there a minute ago comes back, would you do me a big favour?"

The man cautiously drew all his beer cans in close to him and put his arm around them. "Wha'?" he droned.

"Would you lean across to me and say out loud, 'excuse me, but aren't you Bishop McCabe who confirmed my son?'" Frank waited for the answer.

The man thought for a moment. Then, with all the drunken strength he could muster, he nodded three times. "No problem. Bishop McCann."

"*McCabe!*"

"McCabe. No problem."

Jamie eased her way back into her seat and put the drinks down carefully in front of her. "Paddy and white for yourself." She sat down. "I got a couple of these," she said pointing to the Heineken bottles. "I hope you don't mind. It's just that it's ten deep at the bar."

"Not at all. Cheers!" Frank raised his glass and carefully clinked it against a bottle of lager.

"Here, you, McCann!" The drunk man stood up.

McCabe! It dawned on Frank that his plan might not have been such a jammy idea after all. He glanced nervously across at the swaying figure who was pointing at him.

"Aren't you Bishop McCabe," he slurred.

Heads popped up randomly as silence fell across the lounge.

Frank tried to signal a negative plea.

Jamie looked at him waiting for his next move.

It was all too late.

"You're Bishop McCabe who molested my son. I'm going to sue you, you bastard!"

* * *

"Here," she beckoned, "have another one." Jamie placed a large Scotch and ice in front of Frank. "Do you feel any better?" She started to laugh again.

"For God's sake, *please*, don't keep laughing," implored Frank.

"Well, at least we were able to move seats." Jamie muttered. "Serves you right for trying to fool me. *Bishop* McCabe, my arse."

"Well, at least it took your mind off that dashing boyfriend of yours."

Jamie nodded. "Yeah, I suppose you're right. Still, I suppose you would make a fine-looking bishop."

"Bit late for flattery."

"Never too late."

"What did you say earlier about mixing up your flights?"

"Ah, I was meant to be on the quarter to six flight last night," Jamie replied. "Of course mastermind here thought it was quarter *past* six. They could've let me through if they really wanted to. Typical security heads. Give them a cap and a badge and they think they're running the bloody country. Must remember to flash a bit of thigh next time. Do you ever go clubbing?"

"Sorry?"

"Nightclubs. In London?"

Frank shook his head. "Not my scene." He sipped his drink. "They're rip-off joints. Anyway, I'm normally too shagged, eh sorry, tired. Only fit for the nest by that time. Why do you ask?"

"Ah, nothing. It's just that *he's* a doorman up at Gino's . . . off-duty, of course. I just thought that maybe you might have run into him if you went there."

"Never mind your boyfriend, I wouldn't recognise Gino if he came up and kissed me."

Jamie laughed. "Gino's is a *club*, not a *bloke*!"

"Just shows you how much of an electrifying social calendar I've got going for myself!" He smiled. "Do you go there yourself?"

"Are you joking? With *him* on the door? No way.

I'm more into a good book and a quiet drink these days. Anyway, he wouldn't be too happy if he thought I was out enjoying myself." She closed her eyes. "I'm sorry, I don't mean to keep bringing him up."

Frank smiled. He was glad she'd missed her flight. As she closed her eyes, he took time to study her. He could never understand the appeal these huge London clubs had for people. They were always packed with posers who spent the entire night watching each other suspiciously. When they spoke, their mouths were full of marbles. It beat him how they could afford the extortionate prices they paid for cheap wine and champagne. He was a pint of stout man, and always felt that when you had enough, you just threw the head back and looked for a bright, white exit sign. Plain and simple. A bit like himself.

Jamie didn't seem to fit into that scene at all.

Frank glanced at his watch. Quarter past twelve. The boat should almost be in now. His next mission was to get a seat on the train beside Moira Ni Goira for the long journey to London. Just think, then he could tell the lads in Molloy's that he had spent a night with his favourite newscaster. And without a word of a lie.

* * *

It had been Frank McCabe's burning ambition as a young boy to grow up and marry his mother. Born in Glandore in west Cork, he hated school and told her that he wanted to leave when he was seven. He decided to become the man of the house at the age of ten, mainly because he seemed to be the only man around when his mother wanted odd jobs done. He left school at the first available opportunity and worked on a local farm for twenty quid a week, milking cows and shovelling shite. Every Friday at half past six, despite his mother's objections, he'd hand twelve pounds fifty to her, and tell her he was depositing the rest of the money in a Post Office account which didn't exist. She never suspected what was really going on. In fact, he used to leg it round to Donovan's supermarket for a few bottles of cider. Then he'd head for his pal Mike Brady's house where they spent hours watching rally videos.

Frank had one, and only one, passion in life. Rallying. The highlight of the year for Frank, for as long as he could remember, was the Cork 20 International Rally. He watched the most powerful cars in Europe jump narrow bridges and approach hairpin bends at well over a hundred miles an hour. He remembered one driver who told him that the experience was better than sex. He couldn't really argue. His hero was Austin McHale. When he'd get home from Mike's house, the adrenalin would still be rushing. He'd disguise the smell of the drink by saying it was a side-effect of his Ventolin inhaler, which he took for his asthma. His mother was convinced the asthma attacks were brought on by the sight of fast cars. Frank decided not to argue the point. That way, the local off-licence wouldn't go to the wall.

Frank went to England to look for work. Up to

that, he had been a driver for Buckley's Bread, delivering locally to foodstores and restaurants. He was fired. His dismissal was a sore point. He swore that someone swiped his placard while he took a short break from picket duty. When he returned, it never occurred to him to check the placard whose message should have read *Official Dispute on Here*. Instead, as he watched with horror a special report on the nine o'clock news on TV that night, his placard read *Billy Buckley is a bollocks!* His boss, Billy Buckley, saw it. So did over a million viewers. His friends thought it was hilarious. Billy Buckley didn't. Luckily, his mother was at her weekly ICA meeting. She only heard later that her son stole the show on the news that night. She was raging that she'd missed him. Frank told her the following week that he'd been offered a job in London as a barman at the Metropole Hotel. Nothing could have been further from the truth, but to tell her anything else would have broken her heart. It was the first time he'd seen his mother cry. On the other hand, she was proud that her son had got himself a good job in a posh hotel.

He'd never been to London before that. Come to think of it, he'd never been anywhere outside of Ireland. The night before he left, he called around to Mike Brady's to borrow a couple of rally videos and throw down a couple of flagons. The two lads made a pact that they would buy their own Mark II Escort within two years, get a bit of sponsorship from Donovan's supermarket – God knows Donovan owed it to them – and do a couple of rallies. Mike was a mechanic in the local garage. A good one at that. So that would save them money. The conversation went on long after midnight. Frank was about to go when Mike's sister walked in. Frank always had a soft spot for Marie Brady. A soft spot was an understatement. More like a marshy bog. He'd known her for as long as he'd known Mike. And Frank made a New Year's resolution every year that he'd get around to asking her out. But Frank was shy. He was never any good with the punchy chat-up lines. He'd never forget the kick he got one night at the disco in O'Dea's when he asked a girl if she'd like to go outside. For two weeks, he thought he was pissing broken glass.

He never thought Marie was interested in him until that last night at home. She put her head on his shoulder and her arms around his neck and told him she'd miss him. Then she planted a smacker on his lips. When he held her, he realised that she wasn't wearing a bra. This was an outstanding memory for Frank. It struck him that rally drivers overestimated their motor sport. He'd settle for a night in by the fire with Marie Brady anyday.

* * *

He still wished it was yesterday. No more pussy-footing around. He should have swept Marie off her feet. Maybe even taken her with him. As for that bad bastard she married, he'd hit her once too often. The straw that broke the camel's back came late one night when he arrived in drunk as a skunk. He threw her a

24

dig from behind while she was eight months pregnant. She lost the baby and almost died herself. She needed twelve pints of blood and a month in hospital. After a six-month-long nightmare, she went home to her mother. Frank knew he could have made her happy but he just wasn't the marrying type. Or so he thought.

He looked around the ship. Most of the passengers had crashed out. One poor bloke in the corner was just about flying the flag and having a serious problem remembering the fourth verse of "The Town I Loved So Well". Each time he forgot the words, he went back to the line "In my memory, I will always see the gas yard wall!" Frank smiled. He still got a large lump in his throat when the ferry pulled away from the harbour wall at Dún Laoghaire. But he wasn't one to show his feelings, particularly when it came to women. The only time he cried was on hearing the news that Mike had been killed on his way home from Dublin late one evening. He had just dropped his fiancée back to work in the city. The oncoming truck was definitely to blame. The father of the offending driver was a bigwig Inspector at Dublin Castle. The garda report stated that Mike had been driving recklessly.

"Bastards," Frank muttered.

"Sorry?" asked Jamie.

"Oh, nothing," replied Frank.

"Who are bastards?" she asked, a curious smile on her face.

"Ah, the cops. That's who!" Mike's accident was the last thing he wanted to discuss.

"What cops?" She leant forward on the table top like a counsellor trying to tease out a painful story.

"The British cops. Sure look what they did to the Birmingham Six. That could have been you or me," he replied. Tough as he was, the thoughts of home and the memories that raced through his head brought out a real moody streak in him. He enjoyed nothing more than to reminisce on the ol' times over a few pints in Molloys. But the memories became unbearable each time he had to take the ferry back to England. It was almost as if all his ghosts of Christmas past were sitting around him. Unbearable because, only a few hours ago, he was laughing at what Willie O'Connell had picked up for his son's birthday.

He paid one hundred and sixty quid for an old Lada and thought he'd nailed the bargain of the century. Willie presented young Sean with the keys in Molloy's that night and told him the car was around the back. Sean was gone forty minutes. One of the lads suggested that maybe he'd taken it out for a cut around the old disused quarry.

Sean arrived back. "I can't find it," he said, obviously trying to embarrass his father. "What make is it?"

"It's the green one beside the jacks door," Willie said, trying to hide the mortification.

"That's right," shouted Owny Flynn, half pissed. "Green inside, 'cos the grass hasn't been cut for two years."

The roars of laughter could be heard in the garda station four doors away. So much so, that within ten minutes, the squad car arrived to see what the disturbance was. They left with tears of laughter running down their faces, but not before one of them cautioned poor Willie.

"Now, Mr O'Connell, we take a very dim view of this sort of behaviour," the garda said, looking quite serious. "You know what riding a fat woman and driving a Lada have in common, don't you?" he asked, staring into Willie's eyes.

"No, Guard," Willie replied anxiously, looking visibly uneasy.

"Well, I'm about to tell you. They're both great fun till your friends catch you!" The entire pub collapsed with laughter. Willie was so annoyed that he almost hit the garda. He picked up his cap and stormed out of the pub.

Frank sat there on the creaky seat laughing to himself. I wonder what they're all doing now. Probably down in Molloy's. Lucky bastards, he thought to himself.

Homesickness, as it inevitably does, led to bitterness. Men were being laid off the building sites in the late eighties, due to the sick state of an unpredictable economy. This left many of Frank's colleagues in very distressful circumstances. No work meant no money. The little they could claim on social security, they spent in the pubs. As a result, they became totally reliant on a system they despised. Others had no entitlements. Frank was determined not to join them. He worked his way, in between random construction jobs, through four pubs in London, all

Irish related. The pub work wasn't well paid but it became more consistent and reliable. The hours were long and the work relentless. But he enjoyed the company of Irish people, most of whom he could relate to. He despised the attitude of the Irish government to their emigrants. He knew it was unreasonable of him to expect them to bring twenty million expatriates home. There was no work and where would they put them all? That wasn't the point. Most paddies that Frank talked to in Britain thought that Irish government ministers were slumming it in handy jobs. They read reports prepared by civil servants, opened supermarkets and exhibitions, cuddled babies and, at the end of the day, got a lift to the local in the state car and talked shite to their constituents.

Frank knew that it couldn't be that easy. If it was, he would be Taoiseach. He'd taken an interest in politics as soon as he arrived in England. He'd been there now, on and off, for twelve years. Five building sites, or was it six? The M25 for two years, industrial security and pub work. He'd lost count at this stage. He still ended up at home after each job. It was comforting to know that home was handy to get to.

* * *

He should have had a couple of pints to help him relax. But he was afraid they'd smell it off his breath at the interview later that morning. People were beginning to move around. They collected coats and cases and woke little children.

Thanks be to Jesus, Frank thought. Next time I'm definitely taking the new City Jet. He noticed that the girl opposite was studying him. "Is your fella meeting you off the boat?" he asked.

"I hope not. It's a long drive back to London from Holyhead." She smiled apprehensively.

He heard the familiar screech and hollow thud as the ship made contact with the wall of the pier. Not a moment too soon, he thought.

* * *

Maida Vale, London. 12.30 am.

The tiny device was identical to a drinking straw. As masterful as the all-embracing eye of the housefly. As insignificant as a discarded matchstick. Moving discreetly from side to side beneath the front door, it scanned the interior of the small, cramped flat. Outside, two heavily armed men crouched down over a small black and white monitor, as the miniscule camera lens gave them an ant's-eye view of the two dimly-lit rooms inside.

One of the men raised his hand and opened it wide.

"Five," grunted the second.

"Two in the front, three in the back."

The details were passed along a human chain of armed personnel, each one clutching a firearm against his bulky bullet-proof vest.

"Ramrod!" The man wearing the baseball cap gestured to two others who were holding a heavy black pipe, similar to the butt-end of a street light. They raised it to chest level and took up position directly outside the front door. Two more, each carrying a Heckler and Koch MP5 submachine-gun, squatted behind the giant metal pounder. Two others hunched below a window to the right of the door, cradling their lethal hand weapons. A lone dark figure, wearing a black beret, squatted on a flat roof, less than twenty metres away. The powerful infrared aim of his HKL33 rifle pointed down on to the back of one of the felons inside. A tenth of a second was all it would take to pepper his heart. The tall, leading figure looked around at his tightly-bunched team. "OK?"

They nodded in unison. Weapons were perched aloft. Breathing momentarily halted. And uncompromising silence. Their dark, imposing figures just about visible by the luminous letters on the back of each battle vest: police.

"Let's do it!"

The miniature camera was pulled back from under the door. A large, black plastic bag was thrown around the monitor kit and pushed out of the way.

"On the count of five. Ready?"

The two men were already swinging the giant hammer in a gentle to and fro motion, rapidly gaining momentum and muscle.

" . . . *three, two* . . . " The two men allowed themselves to be propelled forward behind the unstoppable charge of the huge iron battering-ram. " . . . *one!*" The beam smashed through the dingy, wooden door with the force of a small explosion. As the rod dropped to the floor, crashing through floorboards, the room was filled with an air of unnerving unexpectancy.

"*Armed police. Nobody moves!*"

The young athletic-looking officer surged forward, skipping and shuffling stealthily, past one stranger, obviously a watchguard, his hands high in the air, through the small kitchen into the spacious living-room. "*Hit the deck. Hands behind your heads. Move a muscle and I'll blow your fucking brains out!*" Moving and turning all the time, never stopping once, he swung around as a bald, black man was raising a shiny pistol towards him. "*Drop it, fucker!*"

The crack of gunfire was almost instantaneous. The would-be attacker was thrown backwards as his own gun discharged into the air, his arms outstretched, over the long table. Just for a moment, the young officer's eyes came to rest on the plastic bags full of white powder which were now strewn all over the floor and furniture. Not now, he thought. He pointed the Browning 9mm semi-automatic pistol at the whimpering Asian whose hands were shaking wildly. "*Get them up . . . higher!*"

"Don't shoot me, sir, please."

"*On the floor, fast!*"

"Please, don't shoot me. My children will be orphans. Their mother is dead. Now they will have no father."

"Where *you're* going, pal, your kids will be lucky to recognise you the next time they see you!" A hard kick to the groin sent the man down quickly and effectively. "No more kids for a while, mate!"

"Everyone OK?" The charged voice came from the other room.

"Yes, sir. Just fine. One down. One history." His eyes flickered from side to side. The weapon between his hands glided like a periscope, scanning for the third scumbag.

The toilet flushed.

The officer ran in the direction of the bathroom. He turned the handle. Locked. He pointed his gun at the door lock. Reinforcing his grip on the handle, he pulled the trigger twice. Half the door was blown apart. The bathroom was empty. Sachets of white powder bobbed up and down on the heavy waterline of the stuffed toilet bowl. The window was open.

The clumsy bullet-proof vest made a hasty exit through the small space impossible. As he swung down from the fire escape ladder, he could see the man he wanted, clearly unaware that he was running into a dead-end alleyway. There was no way he was going to scale the twenty-foot-high wall on his own. The officer could catch his breath.

The villain tried to toss a large black bin-liner over the wall. He grunted each time he threw it skywards.

"*Game's up, mate,*" the officer shouted in a rough, tacky east London accent. He pointed the gun and cocked it. "Now, step back from the wall and pass me the bag with your right hand, slowly . . . like a good boy." Police sirens wailed in the distance. Not much time, he thought. "D'you hear me, you horrible little shit?"

The yobbo froze.

"Now don't make me repeat myself, please." The

sirens were getting closer. Just as the officer was about to look around, he sensed movement. His assailant had spun around and was raising a sawn-off shotgun. A volley of gunfire followed. His attacker fell backwards into a small rubbish skip. Banknotes from the burst sack blew across his limp body. The officer holstered his weapon and picked up the sack. He removed his leather glove and cautiously dug his hand into the bulky weight. Money. Tons of it. In fact, more money that he'd ever seen in his life.

"Are you all right, son?"

The officer, visibly sweating, swung around, going instinctively for his gun.

"Easy, son. It's me, Jimmy Grant." He edged towards the young nervous cop, slowly putting his own weapon away. "Is he dead?"

"Think so."

The older cop reached into the skip. He felt below the jawbone for a pulse. He nodded. "Fairly dead all right." He looked at the sawn-off shotgun lying beside him. "Nasty piece of filth, that." He pinched the nozzle. "It's cold." He looked menacingly at the young cop. "This weapon hasn't been fired, son." He picked it up and smelled the barrel. "Why'd you have to fill him with so many holes?"

"I didn't want to take any chances, sir. I wasn't sure what he was going to pull on me. As soon as I saw the handle, I opened up." He took hold of the offending weapon and examined it closely.

"Made to kill big time, those things." The older man was looking more suspiciously at the body now.

"I wasn't too sure if he was on his own, sir."

"But you knew there were only five of them, son. I thought you knew we had the other four." He shrugged his shoulders. "It doesn't really matter, anyway. The bastard deserved what he got. What's in the bag?"

He hesitated. "Eh, money."

"Here, I'll take that. Forensics will want to check it." The older man held out his hand.

"Why?"

"*What?*"

"Well, I mean . . . no one knows we have it."

It didn't sink in for a few seconds. Then, "What are you saying, you stupid *wanker*?" Jimmy Grant roared.

"I'm saying I think we should keep the money. Why don't we *both* keep the money, Jim?"

"Because I'm saying *no*! I might have done a bit of duckin' an' divin' in my time but not any more. Anyway son, this job's far too big to be turning it into a cosy scam. There's likely to be a hundred grand in there. They're going to want to know where it went." He held out his hand and beckoned with his fingers. "Come on, give me the bag, son, and we'll forget all about it. Come on, we're all tired. It's been a long few days. I'll buy you a pint."

"I'm sick of handing it over all the fucking time, Jim. Why not let's just hold on to this one? Just this once. What d'you say?"

"'Cos it don't work like that, lad. Not any more. Not since Operation Wideboy. You know that. Now come on."

"Sorry, Jim. It's time you were getting on home. *Now!*"

The older man shook his head condemningly and turned his back. "It's not going to work, son. You'll see. And I'm not going to be there to cover for you." He started to walk away half-heartedly.

"Dead right." the young officer muttered.

The crack of gunfire from the sawn-off seemed to reverberate around the long alleyway forever. Then silence. Then sirens.

Chapter Two

The ferry port in Holyhead is a bleak little spot even during good weather. During the month of January, it's hell on earth. Frank could never understand why people rushed to get off the boat. It was too late for it to sink! Anyway, the train would be late as usual. He sauntered down the sloped ramp towards the red and green channels. Someone had recently decided to add a blue channel. It was obvious to Frank that most people hadn't the faintest idea what this new door was for and, for that matter, didn't care. He hadn't even bothered to read the small print below the sign himself. He looked around for his female companion. All he could see was a seething mass of boat-weary passengers. It reminded him of TV news reports of war-torn refugees being evacuated from a blitzed city. It was a ridiculous hour of the morning to be travelling anywhere. No one seemed to know where they were going and yet everyone was walking in the same direction.

There's a woman on a walking-stick, he thought. I bet they stop her.

Sure enough, she was taken aside. Frank watched from the back of the queue. He clenched his teeth with anger when he saw her reach for identification.

One of the officers opened her case.

Frank pushed through the queue until he was beside the woman. "Hang on. What's the problem?" he asked.

"I'm sorry, sir. Could you please take your place in the queue and we'll get to you in a moment?" the baldy man with the beer belly asked brusquely.

"Why are you questioning the old woman?" Frank spoke the same way he did when the shutters were thrown down in the Marine on a Saturday night. "Can't you see she's getting upset?"

"Are you related to this lady, sir?" asked the policeman who looked like Charles Bronson.

"I don't see why that's any of your business," Frank roared. "If I was related to her, I'd give you a good hiding for a start!"

The words were out before he had time to realise what the consequences of a statement like this could be. Passengers all the way down both queues almost climbed over each other to get a good look at the aggro up ahead. Frank had no sooner finished when the two officers had him by the arms. They were polite enough when they asked him to accompany them to the interview room but he knew he didn't have much of a say in the matter. As he turned to look for some support from the crowd, he felt the grip on his arms tighten uncomfortably.

"Here, pal, not so tight!" The two officers ignored

him. He tried to pull them to a standstill in the hope that they might sort out the small misunderstanding there and then. At least, there was little they could do to him in full view of the shocked crowd. He looked back towards the elderly woman. A group of uniformed officers surrounded her.

"Come on now, sir. That's it." They jolted his arms forward. "Just keep moving. Good boy."

Frank was annoyed and scared. Annoyed because no one had called him a boy since he was thirteen years old. And scared because he didn't know what was going to happen once he was taken beyond the door.

"Listen. You'll have to let me go! What about me train?" he insisted. "I have an interview in the morning." They ignored him. "Did you hear me? I'm going to miss my train!"

"You'll just have to get the next one, sir. Won't you?" the pot-bellied man said casually as he pulled a chair back from the table. The other officer kicked the door closed and pushed Frank around to the front of the seat. "Sit down!"

Frank could tell that manners had gone out the window now that they were alone with him. The two men left the room without saying anything. The door slammed so hard that Frank jumped to attention. He noticed that there was no handle on his side.

No handle on the inside of the door. Why? Because this was an interrogation room. A room for interrogating crime suspects. A single, bright fluorescent light hung from the ceiling. There were no windows, just that single light. Frank sat down at the bare table again. He searched in his pockets for identification. He had a cheque book and a pack of playing cards. Not much help. The door opened again and the two men entered with a third man whom Frank hadn't seen before. He looked at his watch. It was five to two.

"I was just wondering if I could get my train now . . . please?" Frank hated grovelling to these people but he felt it might be the best policy.

The man he'd never seen before smiled. "Well mate, it's not quite that simple." He sat down in front of Frank while the other two leaned against the walls with their hands in their pockets. "Cigarette?" He threw a box of Major on to the table.

"I don't smoke."

"What's your name?"

"Frank McCabe. What's yours?"

The officer ignored the question as he made notes on a blank sheet of paper. "What's brought you to the United Kingdom?"

"Sorry?"

"England!" the copper shouted. "Why have you come to England?"

"To work! Why?" Frank was getting tired of this charade. "For Christ's sake, it's not Moscow!"

"Mr McCabe, this is a little more serious than you seem to realise. You have already obstructed two British Transport police officers carrying out their duties. That in itself is a pretty serious offence." Frank couldn't take his eyes off the officer's baby moustache. He hated moustaches, especially small wispy ones. He reckoned that growing a moustache was one way that some men overcame inadequacies. He often wondered if they tickled a woman when she kissed one.

"What's so funny, Mr McCabe?" the officer asked.

"Nothing! Can I go for my train now?" Frank asked.

"We'd like to ask you a few more questions." The man in the chair put his pen on the table and sat back. "Is this your first time in the United Kingdom?"

"Why?"

"Just answer the question, sir. Is this your first time to visit the United Kingdom?"

"No." Frank glanced at his watch. Five past two. "I've worked on and off for about twelve years in and around London. Mainly in the construction trade."

"A brickie," one of the men mumbled. The other two laughed snidely.

"Foreman, actually." Frank looked the main officer straight in the eyes.

"Have you a criminal record?" one of the men leaning against the wall asked sternly.

"Of course not!" Frank wondered if his reckless driving offence in West Cork some years back would constitute a criminal record in Britain. He decided to say nothing.

"Good then. You don't mind just hanging on for a while till we check our central records, do you, Mr McCabe?" The man opposite him stood up and gathered the manilla folder and pages together. The other men stubbed out their cigarettes on the table top. Frank coughed.

40

The man who had asked all the questions turned to Frank. "I'd offer you a cup of tea, mate, only we're a bit short of teabags, I'm afraid!"

The men sniggered as they left the room.

"What about my train?" Frank shouted. He stood up to catch the door before it slammed shut. Bang. Too late.

Frank sat down. His legs were weak. His mind spewed out questions quicker than he could answer them. What was going to happen to him? Maybe he could make a run for it the next time they opened the door? No. He couldn't do that! Sure, then, he'd look as if he really did have something sinister to hide. They'd probably shoot him. Or worse still, set the dogs on him. He hated dogs. Alsatians! Anyway, where was he going to run to?

Jesus Christ, he thought. Calm down. There's been a mistake. They've got you mixed up with someone else they've been trying to nab. They'll let you away in a few minutes. He was beginning to shiver violently. The clock on the wall had stopped at quarter past four. He jumped when he saw the time. Then he looked at his own watch and realised it was only twenty past two. He hugged his shoulders. He wasn't cold. Yet he couldn't stop shaking. Nerves. Don't be stupid, he thought. What have I to be nervous about? Get a grip.

He had given up all hope of catching the train. He didn't care. He wanted out. Just as he was about to knock on the door, the three officers returned. This time, all three of them sat down opposite Frank.

"Now, Mr McCabe, we're sorry for keeping you."

The moustached officer placed his file in front of him on the table and slowly opened it. He glanced at a typed document and handed it to Frank. "We'd like you to sign it just there at the bottom of the page!"

Frank's face froze with terror. He had read all about this sort of carry-on. Wasn't this how they convicted the Birmingham Six and the Guildford Four? By forcing them to sign false confessions? By catching them at their lowest ebb, when they'd have agreed to anything in return for five minutes sleep. After *they'd* threatened the lives of their families and friends? Frank placed his hands on the table and folded his arms. "I'm not signing it." He sat back in the chair.

"What did you just say?" The officer looked across at his two colleagues.

"I'm not signing some stupid made-up confession. I have the right to remain silent until my solicitor is present." Frank stood up. "I'd like to be legally represented before this nonsense continues!"

By now all three officers were smiling. "What are you talking about?" the officer in charge asked in a flat cockney accent.

"Under the Prevention Against Terrorism Act, you are only permitted to hold me for seventy-two hours. Then you have to charge me or release me immediately!" Frank looked at the three men. "What are you going to charge me with?"

"What's all this 'right to remain silent' stuff, eh? What do *you* know about the PTA then, Mr McCabe?" The questioning officer leant across the table and lit a cigarette.

"I know what my rights are!" Frank banged his fist on the table.

"So maybe you *are* hiding something, you crafty little paddy, eh?" The officer picked up the yellow sheet of paper. "Do you know what this is then, mate?"

"What?" Frank gave a large gulp.

"It's a form to say that we gave you your coat back!" The officer laughed. "You're free to go, mate. Sign the form and you get your jacket back. We wouldn't want you to catch a cold on a night like this now, would we, boys?" He turned to his accomplices.

"No sir!" they chanted.

Frank stood up and pushed the chair back with his legs.

"Now, we've 'ad a talk with your wife and she tells us that you're on your way to London to host a benefit concert for the homeless. So, because of the type of blokes we are, we've decided to let you go without any further questions." The copper pinched Frank's cheek. "Fancy that then, eh, a benefit concert for the homeless? What a guy. A real decent Mister Charity, boys. That's what we 'ave on our 'ands. A gift from Almighty God, if you don't mind! Here's your jacket." He threw the coat at Frank. "You're a lucky bloke, Mr McCabe. See you again sometime!" He swung around and left the room.

Frank leapt forward to catch the door before it swung shut on him. He checked to make sure he had his bag, that his pockets were still intact, and headed for a small bench in the arrival terminal and sat down. He leaned down and put his head into his hands.

Who could he have called at that hour of the morning

for help? he thought. Who'd have believed him? Frank heard footsteps and looked up.

The officers who had questioned him were heading for the door marked EXIT. "Hey, Mister Charity!"

Frank focused his tired eyes on the small cop who was yelling at him.

"You're one lucky Tom-noddy, mate. She's a nice girl!" He threw his jacket over his shoulder and winked at Frank. They all laughed as they walked through the swing doors. Then silence.

He was about to put his head down again when he heard another voice.

"Aren't you getting the train?"

It was the girl who'd sat opposite him on the boat. "But the train's gone," Frank said wearily.

"No, it's not!" The woman came over and sat down beside him. "The engine wouldn't start. Or something like that. So they had to send to Crewe for another. We've been sitting down there for over an hour."

"So what brought you back up here?" Frank rubbed his eyes with his hand.

"Are you joking? I needed to get out for a breath of air. That train smells like a sewer! Anyway, I was looking round to see if I could find someone half decent to chat to." She put her hands in her pockets and waited.

"So?" Frank looked up at her.

"Well, you weren't on the train, so I decided to see if you were still up here!"

Frank took a deep breath and stood up. He bent down to pick up his bags.

"Here, I'll carry one of those." She picked up the guitar case. Normally, Frank would never let anyone carry his guitar. Right now though, he didn't give a damn.

"You wouldn't believe what I've just been through." He skulked along beside her as they moved towards the platform.

"First a bishop. Then a terrorist. I think I'd be inclined to believe anything at this stage."

"I got annoyed with those pigs because they were giving this old woman a hard time. And what do they do? They arrest me. Then they question me for an hour, as if I'm some sort of a threat to the public." Frank didn't notice the smile on her face.

"Then what?"

"Then what?" Frank repeated angrily. "Then they get me to sign this form. And then they say that they've been talking to my wife. My *wife*!" Frank was ranting. "Ha. My wife! I mean, I'm not even married." He paused. "Still, I hadn't a clue what was going on. But I guess I owe this *wife* of mine a big thank you."

"Don't mention it!" She kept walking, swinging the guitar case by her side.

"What d'you mean?" Frank stopped as they arrived at the edge of the railway platform.

"I said don't mention it! That was me! I told them I was your wife. I saw them taking you away after what had happened with the old woman. I reckoned that something daft was needed to get you off the hook. It worked, didn't it?" She pushed the guitar case through the door of the train and followed it on board.

Frank stood still, not quite able to believe what he had just heard.

The young woman turned around. "Well, are you getting on?"

He sat with his arms folded, hunched in the corner like a told-off child.

To say that Frank McCabe was devastated was an understatement. It was the closest he had come to doing a stretch in prison. Who was this mystery woman who'd saved his bacon? He remembered the young man and his elderly mother who'd been held captive by the police for nearly forty-eight hours. The man wasn't allowed to see his sick mother for the whole time. After their release, the poor woman had to be hospitalised. A shiver ran down Frank's spine.

An hour into the journey, the train stopped. Crewe junction.

Frank wiped the condensation off the window and peered out into the darkness. Typical pissy ol' night, he thought. He'd heard that this was where the drivers changed their shifts. He had also heard, from a well-sozzled Corkman one night, that the reason for such a long delay was very simple. The driver and the guard had to change the points on the main line themselves. This could take up to two hours. The poor man who told Frank the story was convinced that it was true. A crew change made more sense. But where was the crew tonight? Probably in the pub if they had any sense.

Still no sign of his friend. She'd dumped her bags opposite him as the train pulled out of Holyhead and headed off in the direction of the bar. He leaned over to get a closer look at the writing on the orange haversack. UP YOURS, it said. Frank smiled. Well that teaches you a lesson, he thought. He noticed the name on the bulky shoulder bag. *Jamie Carroll.* Must be her boyfriend's, Frank thought. Bit poofy for a bloke. Especially a cop. I wonder what his mates think when he arrives into the police station with that under his arm every morning! He did a side salute to the window and peered out into the darkness again. The train began to inch forward, shuddering and creaking, before breaking into a steady gallop.

"Are you sure you didn't want a drink?"

Frank looked up just as she sat down without spilling the four bottles of Heineken she was holding.

"No, not for me, thanks," he answered uneasily. "Bit late."

"Ah, go on. After what you've been through tonight, I'd say you could do with one." She pushed one of the bottles across the table. "I'd be on my ear if I drank them all. Anyway, typical, they'd no ice! So they're going to get warm if they're not drunk quickly."

Frank was parched. And to make matters worse, he'd bought twenty cigarettes before he'd boarded the train. He hadn't smoked in seven years but needed one badly after the incident with the police. "Ah sure, I may as well. Thanks." He picked up the drink. The lager roared down his throat. It tasted gorgeous.

"My Jesus, you're thirsty." She smiled as he put the near-empty bottle back on the table.

"Big swallow," Frank replied, trying to catch an

enormous belch before it reverberated round the carriage. Too late. It was a classic. He would have got a round of applause from the lads in Molloy's. "Excuse me," he whispered, trying to prevent an aftershock.

"Do you want me to get a doctor?" she asked. "I've seen people hospitalised for less. It's a good job that didn't come up during the interrogation." She put her feet up on the vacant seat beside her.

"I find the bottled beer a bit hard on the oul' stomach," Frank replied.

"Oh sure," she said. "I suppose you normally drink through a straw."

Frank smiled. "Thanks for what you did."

"No problem. You owe me a pint," she replied as she closed her eyes. Then, quite unexpectedly, she let out an unmerciful belch.

"Do you want me to get you an ambulance?" he asked sarcastically.

She looked mortified. Then she started to laugh. Between the belching and laughing, everyone in the carriage was now wide awake.

Frank stood up. "You'll have to excuse me. I've just met my wife," he said. With that, someone let out a belch, strong enough to cause a hernia. "Fair play," Frank shouted.

"I'm sorry?" came the reply as a priest peered out from behind the seat in front of them.

"Oh Jesus, I'm sorry, Father!" Frank dived back into his seat like a bold child.

They laughed hysterically until tears came to their eyes.

"You're not having much luck with the clergy tonight, are you?" she joked. She adjusted the couple of bags in front of her and tried to get comfortable.

She was both adorable and gorgeous. How come he'd only realised that now? Her face was warm, yet mysterious. Her eyes were the bluest he'd ever seen, despite her obvious tiredness. They seemed to sparkle more now than earlier in the journey. He felt as if he'd known her for years, not just hours. "Jesus, I'm shagged," he blurted. "Would you like a cigarette?" he asked, digging into his coat pocket.

"No, thanks," came the reply.

Frank lit up and went into a fit of coughing.

"What the hell were you playing at with those butchers in Holyhead anyway?" she asked.

"Ah . . . " he sighed. "It's bad enough when they pick on you or me. At least your nerves can cope! But that woman must have been in her eighties. The poor 'oul dear was petrified. I mean, do they realise what sort of a picture they paint for tourists coming into the country with these big hungry muck savages hanging around waiting to nab you when you get off the boat?"

"I thought *we* were the muck savages!"

"I suppose it'll give them something to talk about when they meet their mates in the pub tonight." Frank fumbled with his jacket again.

"I'm Jamie. Pleased to meet you." She stretched across the table. It was a good firm handshake. Frank liked that. If there was one thing that put Frank off someone, it was a wet-fish handshake.

"Same name as your boyfriend?" he asked, remembering the name he'd seen on her luggage.

"Who?" she enquired with a look of mock dismay. "My boyfriend? His name is Tommy. He wouldn't . . . " she stopped short and left it at that. "Whereabouts in Cork are you from?" she asked as she opened another bottle.

"Glandore. More west Cork than Cork," he replied quietly.

"What's the difference?"

"Quality of life, I suppose. The most beautiful scenery anywhere in the country. Where are you from yourself?"

"Artane. In Dublin. De'nortside, as they say. The most beautiful corporation houses in the country." She laughed as she shook her head from left to right. "Have you heard all the northside jokes?"

"No. But I'd say I'm about to." Frank grinned.

"What do call a northsider driving a sports car?" she asked.

"I don't know," replied Frank.

"A car thief!" Jamie flung herself back into the seat.

They both laughed heartily.

"Why do northside birds fly upside down?" came the next one.

"I don't know," replied Frank.

"So they can dump their load on the southside!" Jamie shrieked.

"When a northside girl is out with her boyfriend, what does she use for protection?"

Frank couldn't take his eyes off her lips. "I don't know."

"A bus shelter!" Jamie slapped the table top over and over again.

She had a great laugh and a lovely smile, Frank thought. It was a shame that her hair was so short. Still, she was great fun. She wasn't tall. But then she wasn't small. Her fair hair would look nice shoulder-length. She was well-proportioned. Frank liked voluptuous women. Big breasts and firm hips. He also loved a warm, outgoing personality. A bit like hers. He didn't know many Dublin women, apart from the few he'd worked with in the pub business down through the years.

"Well, Frank, has anyone ever told you that you're the spitting image of Elvis Presley?" she asked.

"You're not going to believe this, but you're the first!" Frank replied seriously. They both roared laughing. A few minutes' silence passed.

"How did you know my name?" he asked. He was serious now.

"How do you think?" she asked playfully.

"I haven't a clue." He was slightly put out by the way she stared at him.

"It was written on something you play with regularly," she teased. She put her hand up to her face and started giggling.

It was one thing being a bit smutty in the presence of the lads, but it was a bit much when it came from a complete stranger. And a strange woman at that.

"You've lost me," he said. "Come on. Where'd you see it?"

"On your guitar!" she goaded. "Where else do you think?"

Frank smiled as Jamie shoved another bottle of lager into his hand. "Jesus, I'd better not," he said hesitantly. "What time is it?"

"Ten past five." Jamie looked at her watch. Frank had never seen a watch so big in all his life.

"A bit short-sighted?" he suggested.

"Very smart," she said. "Very smart for a culchie."

"It's the fresh air," he snapped. He'd heard this one for more years than he could remember. He took the beer and sipped it. "No pollution where I come from!" he continued defiantly.

"Is it true what they say about country fellas?" she asked curiously. "That they're sexier than Dublin blokes?"

Frank choked on his mouthful of beer. How was he going to answer that one?

"Well?" she continued. "Are they?"

"What would you think?" he prompted as he peeled the green label off the beer bottle.

"Well, if I said they weren't, I'd be only hurting your feelings," she jibed. "And if I said they were, I'd be giving you a big head. Wouldn't I?"

Frank stood up. "*Me* to know, *you* to find out!" he whispered as he tapped his nose twice with his finger. He gave her a little wink. "I'm off to the boys' room. Where is it?" The lager was running through him. He wasn't sure whether the blue air had turned his cheeks a bright shade of red. He'd never spoken so frankly to a woman.

"*Me* to know, *you* to find out!" She winked back.

He sat on the toilet bowl in a blank stare. Twenty

past five. He never thought he'd end up feeling this way about a blank stranger. In less than half-an-hour they'd be arriving in Euston. Then, that'd be it. She'd head back home to her lover. He'd attend his job interview. His stomach was in a knot. She'd struck a chord somewhere deep down inside. All he knew right now was that wherever that precious chord was, it wanted to be picked up and played like an orchestra.

The rocking motion of the train had almost lulled him into a trance. It was only when someone tried to turn the handle to get in that he stood up.

Chapter Three

Jamie Carroll moved back to Dublin with her family shortly after the Birmingham pub bombings in 1974. Although she was only seven years old then, she could still remember the other children taunting her in the school yard. They cornered her in the small, benched shed while she ate her sandwich and drank her half bottle of milk. "You're an Irish pig, my daddy says," they shouted. "You killed our friend's mammy." Over and over. *"Pigs, pigs, pigs!"* they chanted. One of them grabbed the bottle of milk and splashed her uniform. Miss Timmons, her teacher, told her to come into the classroom and not to mind what the other children were saying. "None of this is your fault," she said. She was nice. She even spoke like her mammy and her nana.

Jamie was too young to understand the implications. Or the reasons. But not too young to remember her two older brothers being sent home from the school they all attended in Coventry, one with a black eye, the other with a bloody nose. Her mother told her that night that a crowd of bold men had broken the sitting-room window because they'd drunk too much.

Her father was forced to leave the local car factory where he worked as an electrician because of the threats from workmates who'd been his friends for years. When he reported this to his foreman, he was told that maybe they were right. He'd be better off out of the place for his own safety. A small group of Irish republican activists, claiming to be at war with Britain, had indiscriminately bombed two pubs. Some of the victims they had murdered were Irish. Where was the sense in that?

She remembered her mother wrapping her in a dressing-gown late one night and putting her into the back seat of the car beside her young sister, Lisa. Her father ran in and out of the house loading the boot with clothes and other things that her mother would call to him for from behind the car. Their next-door neighbour gave him a hand.

A man standing at his hall-door across the road shouted and waved his fist.

"Run, you green Fenian bastards!" he roared. "Run before I get a couple of the lads around and we'll hang all of you."

Her mother cried quietly. Her father shouted orders to his friend next door. Her two brothers read comics. Her father quickly jumped into the car and handed a set of keys to his friend.

"I'll call you when it's safe," the neighbour said to her dad. "Don't worry about a thing. I'll make sure nothing happens to the house."

He had an English accent and yet he wasn't annoyed with them like the other people. It was all too much to understand. She remembered people shouting as they drove up the street. Some of them leant out of bedroom windows, while others gathered in a small group on the corner close to their house. As the car passed the corner, Jamie recognised one of her best friends from school. As she waved to her, the young girl stuck out her tongue and gestured with two fingers. Jamie's dad told her to keep her head down. Someone threw a big stick and it hit the back window. Her mother cried louder. Her brothers read their comics. Her father shouted back at them. *"Bastards!"*

She remembered her father cursing the people who lived on their street. Twice, her mother told him not to drive so fast. A policeman on a big horse stopped their car near the entrance to their estate, close to where they all got the bus to school. She noticed that there was a big fire burning beside where her father went for a game of pool with his friends. A big crowd was breaking the windows. Her father asked the policeman to let him stay in the car because he was afraid of what might happen to him if the crowd recognised that he was Irish. Jamie remembered asking her mother what was wrong. One of her brothers told her to shut up. The policeman opened the door and dragged her daddy from the car.

Her daddy was shouting. "Stop, please, stop!" Then he got back into the car and rubbed his face. They drove away and there was silence.

She slept until they arrived at Liverpool. They

always took the Haversham car ferry, but not that night. That was the ferry that the men who planted the bombs were going to take when they were arrested. Her daddy knew two of the men and told her mammy it couldn't have been them as they were at home at the time the bombs were left primed to explode.

She was excited at the prospect of the boat journey. Her mother told her that Nana and Grandad would collect them when they arrived in Dublin. Daddy would have to go straight back to Coventry to collect more bits and pieces. Jamie had talked to Nana the night before on the phone. She told her that her mammy was letting her stay home from school for a while, and that she could stay up late and watch telly with her brothers, Seán and Barry, but she wasn't allowed to watch the news. Her baby sister, Lisa, would have to go to bed because she was only two. It was a seven-year-old's dream.

They never returned to Coventry. Her father brought over what was left in their house bit by bit. He got odd jobs, doing a bit of domestic plumbing and rewiring. Eventually, they were able to move out of their grandparents' house into a house their daddy got from the corporation.

She was a very quiet and subdued child. Her teacher often had to send for her mother. Why didn't Jamie do her homework? She was fascinated with the Irish tricolour, which appeared on every copy and schoolbook in her bag. As time went on, her deep hatred for the way Irish people were treated at the hands of the British down through the years made her more and more rebellious. Her mother noticed that she was different to her brothers and younger sister. Jamie loved reading while the others would play on the street. Her English teacher said that Jamie's brain was like a sponge. It soaked up everything she could get her hands on. She was first in the queue when the mobile library arrived at Northside shopping centre on Tuesday evenings, and always the last to leave. She volunteered at once when the position for editor of the school newspaper was advertised. Needless to say, she was a resounding success, though some of the teachers thought she'd made the newspaper a bit too militant. But then, of course, that was Jamie Carroll.

She lost her virginity at the age of sixteen to a lad who ran the local mobile shop. It happened one night after the disco in *Jets* nightclub beside the airport. Her father would have broken his legs if he'd found out. So she only told her younger sister Lisa. The twelve-year-old hadn't a clue what she was on about once she got beyond telling her about deep kissing.

Jamie couldn't figure out what all the hype was about. A quick ride with Derek Jones did not, despite all she had read, leave her in an unforgettable state of seventh heaven or with a mind-blowing, smouldering afterglow. More like a great big hickey below her left ear, one broken shoe heel and cabbage-coloured skid marks down the back of her faded blue Wrangler jacket from the spot in the grocery van that Derek chose as their love nest.

It was all over in a matter of minutes. Foreplay consisted of a quick grope in Derek's pocket for a condom one of his mates had given him. Hands, heavy breathing, heaving and gallons of saliva. She was trying to stop a brussels sprout from rolling into her bra which was already packed with two handfuls of tissues to give her that fuller, more impressive look, when Derek froze on top of her. His face turned a dark shade of red and his eyes bulged. She could see the veins standing out on the side of his neck. Jamie stared at him. No one had ever told her about this bit. Maybe he was having a heart attack. She tried to move, but found herself pinned between the carrots and the new potatoes; the sort her mother had just bought that morning. Derek released a loud, plaintive groan that seemed to come all the way from his toes. It was like the groan her grandad let out the night he died from cancer above in the hospital. Then her sex machine slumped down on top of her. The silence indicated that that was it. He seemed lifeless but he certainly wasn't dead. He rolled over and had a cigarette. Halfway through, he offered her a drag. She nodded her head. The two of them lay there side by side, surrounded by scattered vegetables and fruit staring at the roof of the van.

"Was it all right?" Jamie didn't take her eyes off the ceiling.

"Yeah. It was great!" Derek blew rings in his cigarette smoke.

"Where'd you learn to do that?"

"From videos the lads do get," he said smugly.

"I'd say you're a bit of a gigolo, Derek Jones." She thumped his shoulder.

"Like in the circus?"

Jamie tutted and threw her eyes up to heaven. "That's a *juggler*! Forget it. Do you know what I'd love?" Jamie leant on to her elbow and looked sexily at Derek.

"What?" Derek's eyes opened wide in anticipation of what was next on the menu.

Jamie looked into space and licked her bottom lip. "I'd love a Curly Wurly!"

"What?"

"A Curly Wurly. You have them on the top shelf!" She stood up and took the box of Curly Wurlys down. "D'you want one?" She held one out to Derek.

"No!" It was a clear sign to Derek that their night of passion had come to an end. He tried to manoeuvre his jeans back up to his waist without knocking over any more of his van's stock.

She always had a craving for chocolate and after all it was on the house tonight. They got some peculiar looks when they stepped out of the van which was parked at a bus stop. Six CIE workers were waiting for the ghost bus into the Summerhill depot, and one of them knew her father.

"Oh Jesus, there's that dirty oul' fucker Patsy Nolan!" Jamie whispered to Derek as she tried to straighten her skirt. Derek slammed the door and the two of them walked past the group of men. "How are you, Mr Nolan?" she said quickly.

"Good morning, Jamie," Mr Nolan answered disapprovingly. "Does your father know you're out so late?"

"Yeah. Why?" she replied bravely.

"Ah no reason. I'm sure he'd prefer you to be at home in your bed than in the back of Derek Jones's vegetable van." The other men laughed. He folded his arms and looked up the street at the approaching bus. "After he left me in Madigan's earlier tonight, he was on his way up to the disco to collect you!"

"Oh, *Jaysus*!" She didn't know whether to vomit or faint. Or both.

"Stacking the shelves for tomorrow, Derek, are we?" One of the other men laughed. "You'd want to oil them springs, son. They're a bit squeaky."

"Ah, fuck off!" Derek roared back over his shoulder as he put his arm around Jamie.

The bus pulled up and the men boarded. "Hey Jamie, is that the new look?" another of the men shouted as the bus pulled away.

"Oh Jesus." She looked down at her waist. "Me skirt's tucked into me fucking knickers!" Derek roared laughing.

Every dog in the area was barking. Lights were going on up and down the road. Eyes were peeping out under bedroom curtains to see what all the commotion was.

One window opened a couple of inches.

"If you don't shut the fuck up and get out of there, I'll call the law," a voice threatened.

"I bet you my da's got the police out looking for me."

"You'll be all right," Derek kept saying.

She expected Church Avenue to be lit up with

police cars. She reckoned that the local priest for whom her mother did housekeeping work for would be in the sitting-room, consoling her. Her sister would be on the phone to everyone in the class, bawling, while at the same time telling them that she now had the bedroom all to herself.

"Sweet Jesus," she thought to herself. "What'll happen when I walk in?"

They turned left into Church Avenue. There wasn't a sound.

"Maybe they're all out looking for me," she said quietly, close to tears.

"You'll be all right," came the reply.

"Are you a fucking parrot?" She looked at him. "Say 'you'll be all right' once more and I'll burst you! Go on. You better get out of here," she said.

He stopped.

She kept walking.

"I'll go in with you if you want?" he whispered.

Jamie shook her head from side to side as she broke into a dash. She knew that Derek Jones was as well-mannered as a cannibal and as romantic as a bitch in heat.

"Where's me goodnight kiss?" he shouted.

"You'll have lips like Mick Jagger's if me da gets his hands on you!"

Her father's van was in the drive. There wasn't a light on in the house.

"Oh Saint Anthony," she implored as she blessed herself and put her hand up to her heart. "Just get me out of this one and I swear I'll never do it again!"

She turned the key in the door. There was a deadly silence. She could hear her father snoring upstairs

"Jesus," she muttered, "you wouldn't want to be bleeding to death on this doorstep." She breathed a deep sigh of relief. She took off her shoes and tiptoed upstairs watching out for the creaky floorboards, numbers five and twelve. She crept into the pitch-black room.

"Where were you?" Her sister whispered sleepily. "It's ten to six!"

"I was staying over in Sharon's," Jamie replied quickly. "I couldn't sleep so I decided to walk home."

"Liar!" said Lisa. "You were with Derek Jones, I bet."

"Go to sleep!" Jamie dived in under the quilt.

There was a loud thump on the floor. Lisa reached out and switched on the bedside lamp.

"Jesus, Jamie!" Lisa put her hand up to her mouth. "An apple just rolled out of your knickers!"

"Go to sleep, Lisa!" Jamie grunted as she tried to stifle a laugh. "And turn out the light!"

"Jesus, I never thought you were such a slut!"

Jamie's head hit the pillow. That was close, she thought. She was going to have to wear one of her brother's polo neck jumpers for a couple of days. Just to hide the evidence.

* * *

Jamie had always found it difficult to hold down a job. She had an extremely low boredom threshold. She inevitably ended up telling the authorities how things should be run. This led to frequent arguments with employers. When she left the Loreto Convent on St Stephen's Green, she took a job as a checkout girl in Quinnsworth. But she lost the head one busy Saturday afternoon when a grumpy old bitch accused her of short-changing her by ten pounds. The manager reimbursed the elderly customer and then casually told Jamie that the tenner would come out of her wage packet. Considering that her take-home pay was forty-four pounds after tax and PRSI deductions, this was the straw that broke Jamie's back. She stood up from the cash register. She whipped off her lime-green overalls and shouted for the manager. As soon as she could see him coming down the aisle, she let rip.

"Mr Campbell," she shouted, "are you accusing me of robbing money?" Every checkout was ten deep with Saturday shoppers. She stood, hands on hips, waiting for a reply. "Well, are you?"

It was clear from his face that the manager was seething. He gritted his teeth as he tried to straighten the glasses on his nose. The last thing he needed was a noisy scene, and he knew that Jamie was well able to start one.

"We'll discuss this at half five, Jamie," he replied.

"Answer my question!" she shouted.

"It would appear that there's a small discrepancy involving a customer's change here," he explained as he approached her till. He was visibly embarrassed. Almost like a man who had been caught doing something naughty on *Candid Camera*. "It's a matter that will have to be sorted out in private later. You know the policy of this store, Miss Carroll. Now, back to work!" He glared at her.

She stared back defiantly and climbed out over the side of her checkout cubicle.

"Well, you know what you can do with your policy *and* your fucking job!" she roared.

An old woman used her trolley to push her way through to the front of one queue. "You tell him, love. The bastard!" she shouted. She put her handbag between her knees and started a slow handclap. Everyone joined in. The manager was getting angrier by the minute. The clapping stopped. There was a deadly silence all over the store. It was like a scene straight out of a bank robbery. Jamie Carroll was holding the manager to ransom. "You can shove it up your arse," she screamed as she headed for the main door.

"Staff aren't allowed to use the customer entrance." Mr Campbell tried to be as polite and restrained as his management course had taught him to be. "Miss Carroll, I'm not going to tell you again!"

Jamie swung around in the doorway, pointed her nose in the air and showed him her middle finger. "Well, I'm not *fucking staff* any more, am I?"

There was an almighty cheer as she kept on walking.

Chapter Four

The train was late into Euston. It was a bitter morning and still pitch dark. Frank looked away from the window and across at Jamie. She was still fast asleep. He thought he should wake her since the train was emptying out fairly quickly. He shook her arm.

"Hey, we're here," he whispered. No reaction. "Are you awake?" he asked, thinking to himself that it was a bit of a stupid question.

Suddenly, she sat bolt upright in the seat.

"Where are we?" she groaned, still half-conscious.

"We're here," Frank replied. "Back in London."

She slumped into her seat and dropped her head back on to the warm overcoat. Somehow, Frank had managed to sneak his jacket in between her head and the cold window while she was asleep. She could smell the aftershave from the collar which was just below her chin. It was nice. Not like the gear Tommy wore. She watched him as he stood out into the aisle. He put on his jacket and stretched his arms back out over his shoulders. Great body, she thought.

He took his bags down from the overhead shelf. "Are you right?" he asked.

"Sure, what's the rush?" Jamie replied.

She was right, Frank thought. Might as well sit down and get in a bit more chat. Too late. Jamie was on her feet and looking overhead for her bags. As she stretched to take hold of her luggage, Frank ran his eyes over her figure. Nice body, he thought. He reached up over her to prevent the baggage from tumbling down. Jamie fell back against his chest. Their eyes met. Frank thought about kissing her on the lips. They were only a fraction of an inch away from his. They seemed poised. Almost ready. She didn't move. Don't chance it, he thought.

"Here, I'll take the big one." He picked up a large bag and moved towards the nearest door.

A gentleman and a ride, she thought. She tried to remember where she had come across a combination like this before. Never.

Frank found himself hoping that she'd like to go for a bit of breakfast before heading off to wherever it was she was going.

They walked down the long platform slowly together. Frank had become quite attached to Jamie. Maybe it was like the way the Irish stick together when they're far from home. Even on package holidays to the continent, the first thing the Irish do is go looking for an Irish bar. He knew, though, that this was different. He looked up at the giant clock at the far end of the platform. Quarter to seven. Time was against him but he was enjoying the company and, more importantly, quietly scheming to himself. They'd been deep in conversation from the moment Jamie had come around. Frank talked while he tried to figure out ways of delaying the goodbyes. He reckoned that they had discussed more in that twenty minutes than they had during the entire train journey.

"Hey, Elvis!"

Frank spun around. Jamie looked back. A big black ticket inspector at the check-in booth smiled. "Hey man, I thought you said last time that you wasn't coming back to this place?"

Frank grinned from ear to ear. "Hey, Fats. I thought you said you were getting a job on the underground?"

"No way, man. It's way too dark for me down there. Sure I'm black enough as it is, man! Why, I has to keep smiling down there so's people can see me!"

Frank walked over to him and dropped his bag. They greeted each other with a handclasp and a big hug. Jamie could see them chatting from where she stood.

"You take it easy, Elvis," the inspector shouted.

"You too, Fats," Frank yelled back. "Drop in for a drink."

"You got it, man!"

Jamie was waiting for Frank at the side door to Euston. "I've gotta hear about this Elvis business," she said curiously.

Frank was still laughing to himself.

"It's weird. Everytime I go through this place, he's always checking tickets. He started calling me Elvis because of the guitar. An' I started calling him Fats, 'cos he looks like Fats Domino."

"Fats who?" asked Jamie.

"Fats Domino, the great rhythm and blues singer of the . . . ah, no one!" Frank knew by the way Jamie was looking round her that she wasn't even vaguely interested.

"So why Elvis?" she asked.

Frank blushed. "Because of a talent contest I won years ago."

"You entered as *Elvis*?" she screeched.

"It's a long story." There was no time left to be talking nonsense. Frank still needed to find out her address. "Listen, would you like to go for a bite to . . . " He was cut short in mid-sentence by the arrival of a smart-looking Golf GTi which pulled up alongside them at the side entrance to the station.

"Oh Jesus, there he is!" Jamie sounded shocked. "At least, I suppose now I won't have to get the bus!" She hesitated before opening the door. "I hope to see you again. You're a really nice fella."

Jamie opened the passenger door. A silent, frosty kiss was exchanged.

Frank didn't know which way to look.

"Frank, this is Tommy," Jamie shouted, as she battled to get her bags into the back seat. "Tommy, this is Frank. I met him on the boat."

"Pleased to meet you," Frank shouted. He stepped forward and held out his hand.

Tommy's poker-faced expression confirmed what Jamie had been saying earlier. He looked exhausted and spent.

Frank stood there on the kerb, wondering what was

the best thing to do. He felt like the loser in a game of musical chairs.

"Does your friend Paddy want a lift?" Tommy asked cheaply.

"It's Frank, not *Paddy*, smart arse!" snapped Jamie. "Can we drop you anywhere, Frank?" Jamie asked as she sat reluctantly into the passenger seat.

"No, thanks," Frank replied. He was delighted that she'd offered him a lift. "Sure I'm only around the corner." He knew that he should be moving off, but he wanted her to say goodbye first.

"OK." Jamie had hoped that he would take the lift. That way, Frank could get to know Tommy a little better. Perhaps then, they could exchange telephone numbers and make it all look very platonic and above-board.

"See you round." Frank turned on his heel and headed into the early morning mishmash of busy commuters. He waved and got swallowed up in the swarm.

Why did I have to be such a smart bitch? Jamie wondered as the car pulled out into the traffic. Her mother would love it if she arrived home with such a good-looking bloke. Come to think of it, she wouldn't mind arriving anywhere herself with such a good-looking bloke. And Irish into the bargain. She missed him already. She looked across at Tommy. So much for welcoming her home.

* * *

The morning headline caught his eye as he walked past the small paper kiosk.

70

Frank picked up a copy of *The Daily Mirror.* He handed a fifty-pence piece to the shivering woman behind the counter. As he turned to pick up his bag, he saw the small headline down the side of the front page. *FERRY WOMAN IN MYSTERIOUS DEATH.* His breathing slowed as he read the column.

A 63-year-old Irish woman collapsed and died late last night as she was being questioned by British transport police in Holyhead, north Wales. It is believed she was travelling on board the car ferry from Dublin. She was being detained for questioning shortly after the ship docked when she collapsed. A post mortem will be carried out this morning. A full investigation into the incident is being carried out by police in Holyhead.

"Jesus," he muttered. The same woman he'd tried to protect the previous night.

"God rest her poor soul," a voice mumbled.

Frank looked over the top of the paper. A small hunched man in a dirty-looking, badly stained full-length coat stood shivering in front of him. He looked as if he hadn't seen a bed or a decent meal in years. "Who?" Frank asked curiously.

"The poor woman off the boat. That's why I can never go back."

"Back where?"

"Back home. They'd never let me as far as the end of the platform. They don't even let me on the underground these days. They do have no heart. They're just animals fighting among themselves.

Looking for bait like us to pick on and kick around like a football," he continued.

Frank knew the accent but couldn't place it precisely. "Where are you from?"

"Skibbereen." He tipped his cap respectfully. "I haven't been back since I buried the Duchess."

"Duchess?"

He tipped his cap again. "My mother, Lord rest her."

"When did she die?"

The tramp scratched his stubbly chin as he swayed from side to side. The rotten smell of cheap wine cut its own steamy path through the crisp morning air. "I can't honestly remember. Fifteen years . . . maybe more. I still miss her."

"So why can't you go back?"

"Money, I suppose . . . "

"And?"

"And them . . . the authority. They do have no time for us whatsoever. I suppose I'd be better off dead." He ran the back of his hand under his red runny nose and sniffed loudly. "You couldn't spare fifty pence for a hot cup of tea, son, could you?"

"What's your name?"

"They call me Paddy. Paddy Last." He grinned. Most of his teeth were missing. The others were brown and rotten.

Frank took out his wallet. "Here's some money. Go and get yourself a good hot meal. Where do you live?"

"The *Morning Star*. It's a hostel. That's why they call me Paddy Last. 'Cos I'm always the last in every night and the last out every morning. But I don't feel too good about that place. I won't be hanging around after dark any more. Not up there. I saw one of their own do it, you know that?" He shrugged his shoulders and shivered violently. "I couldn't believe me eyes. And I've seen some strange things in my time."

Frank couldn't make any sense out of this. "In the hostel . . . who did what?"

"No, not in the hostel. In the back lane beside the hostel. Poor bloke didn't stand a chance. Shot him in the back. And him walking away. He was one of his own. And they're making the shaggin' murderer out to be some sort of a hero now. And that was *after* he'd shot the first bloke. The one who had the bag. Thought I was dreamin', so I did. Enough to make a lad give up the drink." He waved a bottle in a brown paper bag.

Frank checked his watch. "Here, listen, look after yourself. I have to go."

"Where are *you* from? I know that accent."

"Glandore," replied Frank.

"And who's your stock?"

"My mother's an O'Sullivan . . . my father's McCabe."

"Well, God bless them." He backed off. Other people were taking a wide berth to avoid this dirty creature.

Frank pulled a small diary out of his jacket. "Here, hang on a minute." He scribbled on a page of the diary. He ripped it out and handed it to him. "Here, that's where I work. If you're ever passing, drop in for a bowl of soup."

The old man pored over the details. "The blessings o' God on you, son, eh . . . Frank." He scrunched it up and rammed it into his pocket. "And *they're* suppose to be protecting us!" he continued. "Jesus, Mary and Joseph, the bang was something unmerciful. There were bits of the poor fellah all over the place. I didn't know which way to run. I decided to get out before half the force descended on the fuckin' place." The tramp realised that Frank was almost out of hearing distance. He took a fast swig from the bottle. "Twenty years." He paused and belched. "Maybe thirty. But, mark my words, I'll be going home next week." He looked down at his left hand. A twenty-pound note. *"Jesus Christ!"* The down-and-out was ecstatic. "The blessings o' God and his nearest an' dearest on you and your family, son."

"Good luck, Paddy Last." Frank smiled.

The old man swayed from side to side. "I'll raise a glass for you. You're a good lad. Bless you." He staggered off down the street.

Frank knew well where the money would be spent. Still, at least he's happy for a while, he thought. Dear God, don't ever let me end up in that state.

* * *

Rush hour traffic was hectic. Jamie pulled hard on her cigarette. Not even so much as a "how did you get on? How is your family? I must go home with you next time." But then, Tommy wasn't like that. He had his moments, but he was one of the boys.

He'd been with the London Metroplitan Police for nearly fifteen years. His colleagues called him "barrow-boy" because of his flat, cockney accent. Growing up in east London, Tommy had always been fascinated by the big criminals who made his patch one of the most notorious and, in a ludicrous sort of way, respected stamping-grounds in Britain. He used to tell the kids at school that he was Jimmy Frazier's messenger boy. Jimmy was one of London's arch-criminals in the sixties. A close friend of the Krays, the very mention of Frazier's name unwittingly sent tremors of heart-quake through even the toughest bullies. Kids who narked Tommy were reliably informed that "Mad" Mickey Pierce would be waiting for them outside the school gates after school. "Mad" Mickey had reputedly murdered half his class at a school reunion fifteen years previously. Why? "Because I never liked fuckin' swots!" He'd been out of prison now nearly two years. Word had it Tommy played pool with "Mad" Mickey after school!

Tommy was addicted to the TV detective series *The Sweeney* as a boy during the seventies. That was why he chose a career in the London police force. He thrived on violence. The total disregard for the law. The magnetic charm of fraud and corruption. He was a model cadet but the dark side never left him. Villains fascinated him. He always had that hankering in him to explore their minds and find out what made them tick.

His early days on the beat were spent close to his native Stepney in east London. Because he knew the cockney dialogue, and had a feel for the common 'duckin' an' divin'' of local thugs, his bosses felt he'd be useful in sourcing what bent deals might've been going down. Nothing could have been further from the truth.

During his two years in cockneydom, Tommy managed to build up and nurture an illegal trade so secretive and sophisticated that two of the city's most notorious gangland bosses suspected nothing strange. He made deals with touts. He organised back alley box-ups. He encouraged his colleagues to get involved in the odd scam. He was even known to be partial to the idea of swapping a sawn-off shotgun in the building society in Peckham for a pair of sawn-off jeans on a beach in Marbella the following Saturday. His bottom line to the local mob was simple: pay me or work for me! Without him, many of them would have got caught.

At the same time, he was nurturing a number of important connections within the force. As a result, he was promoted to the position of detective constable and assigned to the elite Drug Squad division based in New Scotland Yard. He became known around town as a crack cop . . . for more reasons than one. In the eyes of his peers, he was a dedicated officer, devoted to his work. He was devoted all right. But it was to another, more malignant, cause. Tommy's winning blueprint was his stealth. No one, not even Jamie, knew quite what he was like. His weakness was insatiable greed. "Everyone loves a bit of dirt!" he'd say. But a bit was never enough. People who dealt with him treated him with respect. But they knew Tommy Barrett was an evil bastard, not to be trusted under any circumstances.

Jamie often asked herself why she had gone out with Tommy for three years. He was fun in company and told some great jokes and stories about people. He was also extremely handsome. All her friends fancied him rotten. Tall, dark and good-looking, he kept himself extremely fit.

At home, she was lucky if she got a grunt out of him. And, when she did, it was normally the same old string of abuse that he always gave her; the house, the job, her hair, anything. Jamie reckoned that it was easier to let this relationship drag than to finish it. Anyway, she was afraid to think of how he might react if she told him that she'd had enough.

"Who's your man?" he asked without taking his eyes off the road.

"Just someone I met on the train!" Jamie took a long drag from the cigarette. "Why?"

"And on the boat?" he continued.

"Yeah. He offered me a seat," she answered. "Probably more than you'd do for a woman." She looked at him with a half grin.

"What's that supposed to mean?" He looked away from the traffic and stared at her.

Jamie knew that it was better to quit now than pay later. "How did you get on while I was away?" she asked quickly.

"Fine!" he replied drearily. That was the sum total of conversation.

The paper caught Jamie's eye. She stared at the main headline and then at Tommy. He didn't react. Her breathing became uneven as she read further into the front-page story. Her face froze. The murdered detective had been a good friend of both of them. Once, at a party, she'd confided in him about the state of their relationship and how she felt that Tommy was playing around behind her back. Jimmy Grant's advice made him a friend for life. Tears welled up in her eyes as she remembered how they danced together to a slow Beatles favourite of his.

"It's just not working. He doesn't give a fuck about me."

"Yes, he does. Maybe he has a funny way of showing it. Anyway, you could have the pick of any man in London if you really wanted to. In fact, do you know something? If I was a few years younger myself, I'd be fighting to get to the top of the queue." Jimmy gave her a gentle, reassuring hug.

Jamie smiled. "Get away. You're just saying that. Vera Grant's a very lucky woman."

"You know something, I've been telling her that for fifteen years."

They both laughed.

Jimmy looked at her, admiringly, without speaking.

"What are you thinking, Jimmy?" Jamie asked.

"Just that there's something very special about you, Jamie. I noticed it the first time I was introduced to you. You've got something that very few people have.

You have the gift to reach out and touch people in a special way. You make people's lives happier. Always remember, you're the power in this relationship. *He* needs *you*. *Always* remember that . . . "

Decent friends were hard to come by in a big city like London. In fact, Jimmy Grant was more than a friend. He was like a father to her, a great big cuddly teddy bear. She tried hard to stifle the tears. "It didn't happen, did it?" She squeezed her right eye closed as she read with her left. "What happened?" she whimpered.

Tommy's breathing quivered. "No one's very sure. He ran down this blind, dark alley after a con on his own. The guy had a shotgun. He . . . just blew Jimmy away."

Jamie sobbed. "Where were *you* when all this was going on?"

"About thirty feet behind him. I heard the crack of the shotgun as I got to the corner of the lane. Jimmy was lying face down. Still. The bloke pointed the gun at me. So, I . . . let him have everything I had."

"And why didn't you ring me?"

"How could I? You were on the boat."

Jamie wanted him to reach across and hold her hand. To hold her tightly. She needed to be held right now. To feel cushioned. Protected. She placed her hand on his leg. "Stop the car, please."

Tommy glanced across at her. He winced when he saw her tears. "I can't. It's the middle of rush hour, for God's sake!"

"This is *Jimmy*, not some stranger. *Our* Jimmy!" she implored, holding up the paper.

"I know," he replied calmly. "He *was* my partner."

She held a tissue to her nose. Tommy was cold. He didn't seem to give a damn. It was like a hideous nightmare. Maybe he was in shock, she thought. Yeah . . . maybe.

They were silent for the rest of the journey.

* * *

Frank managed the interview appointment by the skin of his teeth. He had to freshen up in the gents' toilets of a *MacDonald's* restaurant around the corner from Whitbread's huge offices. He got some funny looks from early morning diners who stepped into the bathroom only to find Frank naked from the waist up, shaving with one hand while putting on hair gel with the other. His suit looked as if a mechanic had serviced a car in it. He knew that packing it into his carrier bag and putting a pair of loafers on top of it was idiotic. But then, it hadn't seemed like a bad idea at the time. Most of the creases were down the back of the jacket. The front looked grand. His trousers were a different story. They had more lines and creases running up and down them than Limerick Junction. He'd hoped to get over to Ray's flat before the interview for a quick shower and a slice of toast, but he'd had to knock that on the head.

He'd known Ray for years. He'd worked on a few of the building sites with him. Frank had decided to tell Ray that he was going for the position of site foreman. Ray was an alcoholic, and Frank knew that the excitement caused by the news that his best friend might be handed the keys to his own pub would be enough to kill him. It would be like a child finding Cadbury's chocolate factory under the Christmas tree.

* * *

He wasn't a great man at interviews. Not that he had attended many of them. Usually, he was just told by the bar manager or site foreman that he was to start the following day. It had probably worked to his advantage that he had other things on his mind on the journey the night before. Not much time to think about what he might be asked. And the Clover Tap was an Irish pub through and through. It was also his local, years ago.

There was no one else there to be interviewed when he arrived. He broke out into a cold sweat. "Fuck! I'm late!" he whispered, as he stepped into the reception area, hoping that he had gone through the wrong door. No. This was the only door! He ran two fingers under the tight collar of the shirt trying to position the front under his Adam's apple which was screaming out for space. He hated wearing a suit. Weddings and funerals were the only occasions. Maybe he'd got the date wrong. Maybe he was late. Maybe he should have come yesterday. Why wasn't the place full of people? He walked over to the young girl who sat at the reception desk.

She put her phone down and smiled. "Can I help you, sir?"

"I have an appointment." Frank put both hands in his pockets.

"And the name?" She picked up the phone.

"The Clover Tap."

The receptionist nodded. "No, I mean *your* name."

"Oh, eh, Frank McCabe."

"All right, Mr McCabe, if you'd like to take a seat, somebody will be with you shortly."

He sat down on the leather couch and waited. As his hands shook and his knees knocked, his mind was locked on Jamie. Was there a hope of making contact with her again? Nothing serious like! He half smiled at the notion. He doubted it. London was a pretty big place. Still.

Come on, Frank. Focus on the business for a while, he told himself.

As he stared at the picture of two big frothy pints of Whitbread's ale on the wall in front of him, he didn't notice the lift door opening. A tall, leggy brunette in a short skirt came over to him. She held one side of her spectacles and eyed Frank up and down.

"Mr McCabe?" she enquired in a soft voice.

"Eh, it's a bit early for me!" he whispered. All he could see was legs. He looked up. "Oh eh, sorry. I was, em, just thinking."

"I know." The tall woman looked across at the picture on the wall. "Inviting. Aren't they?" She looked back down at Frank and adjusted the hem of her skirt.

"Very!" Frank kept his eyes firmly fixed on the picture of pints.

"If you'd like to follow me, Mr Bumpster will see you now." She turned and walked ahead of him, jiggling her bottom.

When they neared the office door, she stepped back to allow Frank to move ahead. Out of the blue, he felt it. Maybe he was wrong. No, there was no mistaking it. She had her hand on his arse. He jumped two steps ahead and swung around. "Steady," he quipped, as his hand came down on hers. "What's the story here?" he asked.

She removed her hand. "Your shirt's sticking out. Can't have you looking sloppy, Frank."

"Oh right, thanks." Frank fixed his shirt tail, half relieved and half disappointed.

"My name's Louise . . . with a *u*." She pouted her lips revealing one of the most gorgeous mouths he'd ever seen.

"Pleased to meet you, Louise . . . with a *u*. My name's Frank . . . with an *F*!"

The secretary looked him up and down. "I hope we'll be seeing more of each other, *Frank*." She turned slowly and left.

"I hope so too," Frank replied as he watched her walk slowly down the corridor. Yes, I hope so too, he thought.

He pushed open the door.

There were three brewery officials. The man in the middle reached across the table and shook Frank's hand.

"At long last we meet, Frank. Bumpster!" He let go of Frank's hand and sat down.

"I'm sorry?" Frank wasn't quite sure what he had just heard.

"I beg your pardon?" The man looked up at Frank over the edge of his horn-rimmed glasses.

"I didn't catch what the last thing you said was!"

"Oh, don't worry about it, Frank. Just nice to meet you at long last. I've heard quite a lot about you!" He smiled and glanced down at the papers in front of him.

"No, after that I mean!" Frank continued nervously. "Something about your bum being sore." He couldn't believe what he'd just said. The other two men put their hands up to their mouths to stifle their sniggering. The man in the middle stopped smiling. He didn't appear to be too impressed by Frank's question.

"*Bumpster!*" He took off his glasses. "That's my name. Nigel Bumpster!" He started to smile again. "Now, Frank. Have a seat, please!"

Frank sat down. He felt weak. *Frank McCabe is a prat!* was all that went through his head during the thirty-minute interview. However, it didn't seem to matter. Nor was the interview what he'd imagined. Not quite the Spanish inquisition; more an informal briefing and friendly discussion. Mr Bumpster was delighted that Frank had so much varied experience in the pub trade. He asked Frank how he would cope with the usual tricky situations: rowdy punters; football supporters; stag and hen parties; the loveable local who goes for it after a couple too many. Frank immediately thought of Ray. Mr Bumpster commended him on each of his carefully prepared answers. The other men nodded. In fact, they said nothing during the entire interview. Bumpster told Frank to expect a large number of brewery officials and invited guests at the relaunch. His office would look after the invitations. After that, it was all down to Frank.

"No problem, Mr Bumpster!"

They all seemed impressed by Frank's confidence.

Bumpster! Frank pondered to himself. I suppose it could be worse. His first name could be Billy! Frank stood to shake hands with Mr Bumpster.

"A pleasure again, Frank." The handshake signalled that a deal had been done. "Likewise, Billy!" Frank realised what he had just said. "Sorry, I mean Nigel." The four men all laughed. "A touch of first-night nerves!" Frank joked. "Do you mind me asking why there's no one else here for the interview?"

"Because we felt we didn't need to interview anyone else." The three men stared at Frank. "You're our man, Frank."

"I hope you're right," Frank replied quietly.

"Don't be silly, Frank!" Nigel retorted. "You can do it, man!" They all laughed again during the longest handshakes Frank had ever experienced. This was as challenging as arm wrestling, he thought. He threw his coat over his arm, turned and opened the door. As he stepped forward, he noticed three coats and three umbrellas hanging up in front of him. He realised that he'd just stepped into a small cloakroom instead of the main hallway.

"Wrong door, Frank!" Mr Bumpster roared in a childish excited voice. "Works every time, old boy!" His two assistants were doubled up. "Welcome to the A-Team, Frank McCabe!" Frank walked slowly towards the real door. It dawned on him that this was a form of company baptism. An *old boys' joke*! He smiled to himself. From what he could gather, they all thought the sun shone out of *his* arse! That was all that mattered.

The sun was shining as he stepped out on to Waterloo Road. He looked up at Capital Tower and breathed in the cold morning air. He was rather proud of his morning's achievements. So much so, that he said hello to almost everyone he passed on the way back into the city centre. A saunter up Oxford Street towards Piccadily Circus, he thought. Why not? He looked at his watch. Five to ten. Time for some proper breakfast.

* * *

Frank was given the keys three days later. The pub had been closed for three weeks for major renovations. Whitbread's, the owners, felt it would be better to close the doors and do a good job fast, rather than work around patrons who were trying to enjoy their drinks. Frank checked his watch and hung the giant set of keys beside the main cash register. He tried to calculate how much of his own hard-earned cash had been eaten up by this monster over the years. Maybe thousands. Surely more. He was distracted by what sounded like a grand piano being dragged from the lounge into the bar.

"Excuse me, mate! Where do you want this thing put?" one of the workmen asked. He was pulling a beautifully renovated 1950s Hornby juke-box. It must have been worth a small fortune.

"Jesus, lads, steady! That's not a stock car you're trying to push-start there!" Frank took his jacket off and hung it beside the keys. "You can leave it there. I'll sort her out later."

The lads headed back out by the cellar entrance for more furniture. Frank flicked through the music menu. "Three times a lady", "You're having my baby", "Everything I do, I do it for you". Well, shag them anyway! Frank thought. Not one single Elvis song. He'd soon fix that. He started to search down the front and around the back of the juke-box for the name of a supplier. There it was, just beside the selector button: *Musgold Suppliers*, Southend-on-Thames. Tel: 445 4454.

He picked up the private phone behind the bar. He couldn't understand how a big company involved in music nostalgia could forget to include Elvis Presley in their juke-box selection. All this new rave crap and grunge nonsense. They don't make them like they used to, he thought.

"Good morning, Musgold Suppliers. Can I help you?" a squeaky voice enquired.

"How are you? This is Frank McCabe from the Clover Tap in Highbury. We got one of those juke-boxes from you this morning and I'd like to talk to someone in charge there." Frank clicked into the authority mode. After all, he was the boss.

"What seems to be the problem, sir?" the girl continued in a "heard it all before" tone.

"Well you see, I've been a big fan of Elvis Presley for years. And I just noticed there's not one song of his on the menu," Frank continued in a matter-of-fact sort of way. "Is there a reason for this?"

There was a long pause on the other end of the line.

"Hello," Frank continued. "Can you hear me?"

"Sir, I'm sure you're not the first to be disappointed by a juke-box selection and I'm sure you won't be the last," she continued. "I'm sure if you mention your problem to the manager of the pub, he can get in touch with us directly. Then we can arrange to alter the sequence of songs at his request. Our selections are decided by stringent market research. Basically, what's there is what's popular, sir." Frank couldn't get a word in edgeways. "Anyway", she went on, "if you take *my* advice, you'll head down to your local job centre and try and *get a job*! After all, it is a bit early to be singing Elvis songs and drinking pints, *don't you think*!" She hung up.

Frank was flabbergasted. He was about to pick up the phone and give her a piece of his mind when his worst nightmare walked in off the street. Ray strolled in through the main door. He was obviously working somewhere locally and it was time to wet the whistle. Frank dived down the steps of the open cellar door at the end of the bar walk. He perched halfway down the ladder waiting anxiously to hear what was going to happen next.

"'Scuse me, mate, how's it goin'?" Ray roared in his loud Ardee accent at one of the lads behind the bar. "Give us a pint and a Paddy, please. What sandwiches have you got?"

Frank smiled. Some things never change, he thought. It was only twenty past midday. Ray was late. He must be slipping.

"Sorry, mate, we're closed," replied the electrician who was busy hanging a new lamp above one of the cash registers. "Official opening is next Friday night. Invitation only."

"Invitation, my arse," Ray barked. "I was drinking in this pub when you were counting your communion money. Mind you, looking at you now, you're probably still counting it."

Frank stayed motionless on the cellar steps. This was the crucial moment. Ray would either get up off the stool and leave, or insist, in his own inimitable way, on getting his pint. Frank breathed a deep sigh of relief. He could hear Ray's stool move back across the tiles.

"Who's the manager here, mate?" he enquired.

Frank could hear his heart beating twenty to the dozen.

"Dunno, mate," came the reply. "I'm only here for the day doing the electrics behind the bar."

Ray stormed out of the bar muttering every four-letter word he could think of.

It was three days away, but Frank had already begun to worry that Ray might try and gatecrash the official opening on Friday night. Frank pumped sweat as he thought of what might happen. Ray would find out who the new manager really was. Frank would never be forgiven for not telling him in the first place. And even if it was forgotten, he would never get Ray out of the pub. The drink was free for invited guests. He would think of something. The fact that Elvis was missing from the juke-box was causing him more of a headache.

He picked up the newspaper Ray had left behind on

the counter. *The Daily Star.* Much the same story on the front page. DETECTIVE GUNNED DOWN IN COLD BLOOD.

He read on.

A 42-year-old detective was shot dead early last night in a vicious attack during a north London drugs bust. Detective Sergeant James Grant, married with four children, was pursuing a well-known city drugs baron when he was gunned down in a dark alleyway at point-blank range from behind. The single shot to the back, fired from a lethal sawn-off shotgun, killed the police officer instantly. Grant's colleague, 34-year-old Detective Constable Thomas Barrett, shot dead his killer. The killing took place just off Hampton Green, in Maida Vale, north London, shortly after 7.30 last night.

Frank's eyes flitted between the main article and two photographs alongside the main headline. One was of the murdered detective. The other was of . . . the man Jamie had introduced Frank to before driving away earlier that morning. That was Tommy. Detective Constable Thomas Barrett of the London Metropolitan Drug Squad, to be precise. It was all beginning to come back to him now. The tramp at the paper kiosk. Paddy Last. The hostel in Maida Vale. Frank stared at the two photographs. But Paddy Last said the killer shot one of his own. The newspaper said that the young detective shot the killer. Frank was completely bewildered now. Maybe the tramp was talking total balls. But, on the other hand, he seemed to have got his location spot on. Then again, these poor blokes would say anything for a few quid.

Chapter Five

The day, by now, seemed like a complete blur. Jamie was glad to have the house to herself for the evening. She was well and truly shattered after the long trip. And deeply upset at the news of Jimmy's death. Part of her didn't want to be alone tonight. The other part was glad when Tommy went out to work shortly before nine. His bosses had told him to take time off after the traumatic attack on his colleague. Tommy explained that he felt he'd be better off engaging his mind with some demanding work.

As soon as he'd left the house, she locked up and got into the bath. She'd been dreaming of a long hot bath all day. She didn't know how she'd managed to put in the full eight hours at the job, but at least it was over now. The thought of Tommy under her feet all evening was too much for her, chopping and changing the television channels with the zapper, then trying to coax her out for a drink. She could just do her own thing. The added bonus was that he was working a week of nights.

She stretched out on the small couch, in her

towelling bathrobe, which she had swiped the year before from a hotel in Birmingham while on a computer training course, and sipped a cup of tea. Van Morrisson was playing on the CD unit. Her sister had let her borrow his "Greatest Hits" collection to take back with her. However, she wanted it back when she visited in March for the long Saint Patrick's weekend. She thumbed through the photographs of New Year's Eve in Madigan's. One of the best nights in years. All the girls were in great form. It was as if she'd never been away from home. She put them down and went back to the Patricia Scanlan novel she was reading.

No matter how hard she tried, she couldn't get comfortable. Nor could she concentrate. The couch was too small and too narrow. Tommy had promised that they'd go and have a look at some new furniture months ago, but he was in line for a transfer up north so that idea was quickly knocked on the head. She hummed along to the words of "Have I told you lately that I love you?" She looked over at the gas fire as the words "You filled my life with laughter, you could make it better," came pouring out of the speakers. And she smiled. She remembered Frank belched on the train and the way his face turned bright red. Then, she remembered waking up with her head on his jacket. She ran her hand gently over the side of her head which had lain on the jacket. What's he doing tonight? she wondered. Probably wrapped round his girlfriend. She was raging that she'd spent so much time asleep on the train. Couldn't be helped, she thought. By now, she was exhausted, but she wasn't tired. She felt uneasy.

Yet she had no energy or desire to do anything other than sit there. A limbo sensation, or lack of sensation, that drove her mad. Jimmy's death had shocked her enormously.

She went into the bedroom and pulled a chair over to the wardrobe. She still couldn't see over the top. She held the door with her right hand and felt around the flat, dusty top with her left. She took an old office document holder down and jumped off the chair.

As she did, a small tobacco wallet and a ragged brown envelope fell down on to the floor. Jamie looked at them curiously before picking them up. Tommy didn't smoke. The odd joint at a party, maybe. Certainly not a pipe. Anyway, no one except Jamie ever went near the top of the wardrobe. She picked the wallet up and opened it, careful not to spill the contents on her clean bedroom carpet. There was a small amount of musty tobacco inside. It must have been left behind after a party. She pulled her face away as the smell got up her nose. She hated pipes and cigars. She was about to close it again when she noticed a number of small sachets almost buried in the tobacco. Five. Maybe more. First she thought they were skins for "roll your own" cigarette smokers. But on closer examination, they looked more like small plastic sachets of salt. Or maybe powder. She held one up to her nose. A strange smell. She looked at the cover of the wallet. *Best before: Sept '94.* Maybe something from a case Tommy had been involved in, she thought. She looked at her fingertips. They were white. She cautiously ran the tip of her tongue across one of them. Salty and slightly fizzy. She felt a choking sensation and ran her tongue across the sleeve of her bathrobe. Jamie felt a cold shiver run up her spine. She put the sachets back into the envelope, careful not to spill any on the carpet. Her nose twitched. What was the smell? She sniffed the envelope. No. Definitely not that. It was a wet, smokey, almost fishy smell. She opened the door of the wardrobe fully. It was obvious that Tommy had been living alone for a couple of weeks. The wardrobe was like a bargain-basement. Clothes and shoes everywhere. She pulled back garments, layer by layer. Then the pong hit the back of her throat. She coughed and turned away. When she'd caught her breath, she carefully lifted the offending black binliner from the back of the wardrobe. Sweetest Jesus, what's he got in here? she asked herself. Keeping the bag at arm's length, she placed it carefully upright against a chair. It was littered with tiny holes. Each hole like a small burn mark. She delicately unknotted the top and peeped inside. Bundles of damp newspaper, from what she could see. Cop on, she muttered. It's hardly going to bite you. She plunged her hand slowly into the contents. It was paper, all right. Mostly damp. Maybe Tommy had used it to wrap the kitchen breakables before they'd moved into the more spacious house from their old cramped flat. But that was ages ago.

She tucked the cardboard box under her arm and dragged the clumpy binbag down the stairs behind her. Out onto the doorstep and into the bin. She was relieved that it was gone. She wasn't sure why.

She went back into the sitting-room and sat down on the rug in front of the fire. She carefully dusted off the top of the cardboard box and opened the flimsy lid. She smiled. There was a photograph of herself and Bryan Adams taken outside the Point after his concert three years before. Her best friend at home, Sheila, who took the photograph, was furious because Bryan didn't have time for one with her before he dived into the big black limousine and disappeared. There were old letters from her sister and Sheila, and a bundle of old Christmas cards from home. But they weren't what she was looking for.

She knew she had a big map of Ireland somewhere. Tommy had suggested the summer before that they tour Ireland for their holidays. Jamie was so excited that she asked her sister Lisa to send over a map. Naturally, Tommy changed his mind shortly afterwards and went off with his mates to see the English cricket team play in Australia. Selfish bastard, she thought. He's only interested when he wants a ride!

Any hope she had of finding the map was running out by the time all the nostalgia was scattered across the rug. Just as she was about to give up, she spotted it; still in the big envelope which Lisa had sent. She feverishly spread it out on the carpet. She had to find out where Glandore was. It might be a sort of bonding process. With her face only inches from the surface, and her eyes squinted, she slid her index finger across the map face from left to right. Donegal to Dungarvan. Bunbeg to Bantry Bay. What would her friends think if they could see her now, she thought. No thanks. Glanmire. Gleneely. Glanthaun. She couldn't believe that there were so many Glans and Glens! Glentown. Glandore. Yes. There it was! She tried to find somewhere she knew that was close by. Cork was fairly close. So was Clonakilty. Jamie had gone to the Gaeltacht which was only a few miles from Clonakilty. She'd only survived two days. Her mother was convinced that she spoke English in an effort to be expelled. Well, at least she knew a bit more about him.

Her mind was working overtime. Where did he work? What did he work at? Maybe he went to one of these Irish clubs she'd heard about. They weren't the trendiest of places. Country music and *ceilís*. Still, it was worth a shot. She wondered how many Irish clubs there were in London. Couldn't be many, she thought. But what if he wasn't interested? Then she'd look like a complete prat.

She put her head down on the map, closed her eyes and slept.

* * *

It was twenty past three in the morning. Wednesday or Thursday? Frank was so tired he'd lost count. It had been the longest day of his life and it was a long way from over. He was having terrible trouble regulating the pressure on the beer taps. He'd taken them apart and put all the pieces back together again. Then he discovered two small washers that didn't seem to belong anywhere.

He remembered that this had happened to Stevie Cullen at home during the Winter Stages Rally, a couple of years back. Stevie had no sponsors and a very small budget, so all the lads chipped in a few quid each and offered to help him look after his rally car on the day of the rally. It was an old Datsun 240J Stevie had bought from a Garda auction of stolen cars which had never been claimed by their rightful owners. Actually, if the truth was known, it had taken seven Garda auctions to get rid of it! One look at this geriatric heap and people thought that its original owner must have prayed that it *would* be stolen. Still, it wasn't to be sniffed at. As Stevie himself put it, at least he *had* a rally car. Motor sport experts mightn't have seen it as a very competitive rally car. But, at least, it was a rally car. Steve converted it to rally specification himself and entered every rally event in the calendar. The reason Stevie was able to afford to compete in so many events, Frank recalled, was because he never got further than a couple of hundred yards in each.

One of the lads had just replaced a large engine part, with only seconds left to go to the start of the next stage, when they all realised that there were two large screws left on the ground. A hasty decision had to be made. Stevie decided to take a chance and drive the car as it was. They could repair it later. Fifty yards up the hill there was a loud rattling noise and the engine fell out of the car, all over the road. There were bits of engine everywhere! Stevie was so embarrassed that he abandoned the car and legged it across a field. The humiliation stayed with him for years.

Frank scratched his head. He knew the washers had to go somewhere. What if the taps cracked on the night of the relaunch and soaked all the guests? He gave a nut a quick twist with a wrench and promptly got covered in half a gallon of brown ale. He was fit to be tied. He might as well have been lying under Stevie Cullen's rally car. His back ached and his sciatic nerve was killing him. He shouted to the other lads to call it a day. He couldn't even offer them a pint because the pressure system was still bunged up. They picked up their coats and tools and headed for the door in a fairly pissed-off state.

Silence for the first time in days. No drills. No shouting. No hassle. Frank sat up on a stool and surveyed his new domain. It was coming together nicely. So why wasn't he deliriously happy? He took a deep breath and sighed. All he could think of was a tramp and a cop and a murder. And then there was Jamie.

He knocked off the lights and, as he turned the key in the main door, promptly fell down the three steps leading up to the entrance. Right into the path of a policeman on the beat.

"Hello, hello, hello. Have we had one too many then, sir?" The copper nudged his helmet up over his forehead and looked at his watch.

"Eh, I run the pub and, eh, I like, forgot about the steps, Officer." Frank picked up his belongings and started to walk backwards.

"Straight home now, sir, or I'll have to organise you a lift."

"No problem, eh, goodnight." Frank turned and quickened his pace. He had a horrible feeling that the word *guilty* was written across his forehead. What a day, he thought. He still had the daunting task of looking over the guest list for Friday night's big bash and familiarising himself with the huge list of guests. He hadn't heard of half of them. Some were business heads. Others were from showbiz.

As he set the alarm and turned the key in the door of the flat, Frank wondered how it would all end.

* * *

Jamie was in the shower when Tommy arrived in from nightshift. He was always in bad form after a night's work. This morning, she reckoned, he'd be worse than ever. She could hear the door closing.

"I'm home," he called wearily.

"I'm in the shower. I'll be down in a minute." Jamie stood there and let the scorching hot water run down her. It was one of the nicest times of the day. She could hear him head into the bedroom.

"Do you need a lift?" he shouted.

"Wouldn't mind, why?" her hollow voice echoed in the bathroom.

"It's just that I've got to meet some people this morning at nine."

"For what?" she asked curiously.

"Ah, nothing much. Chance of an extra bit of security work. That's all."

Jamie turned off the shower and reached over to grab the towel. No towel. "Shit!"

"What's wrong?"

"Ah, I thought I had a towel. Will you get me one out of the hot press?"

"OK"

She could hear the door of the hot press opening. "Come on, Tommy, I'm freezing."

"Hold your horses." Tommy pulled back the shower curtain.

"Jesus, you gave me a fright." She threw her hands up. Although they'd lived together for over two years, there were still times when nudity felt uncomfortable. "Thanks." She covered herself with the towel. She looked up at Tommy. He was smiling as he looked her up and down.

"Don't cover yourself." He moved closer to her. "What would you say to me getting in there with you?"

"Get outta here, Tommy Barrett. It's ten past seven on a winter's morning. I've to be in work in an hour." Jamie dried herself. Tommy watched her.

"Why so early?"

"Because my boss is away and I'm running the show."

"Ah, come on. Ten minutes." He ran his fingers down her back as she dried her legs.

"Ten minutes!" Jamie smiled. "Why? What are we going to do for the other nine and a half?"

"Ah, fuck it. Suit yourself." Tommy stormed out of the bathroom.

Jamie sat down at the mirror and started applying her make-up. She could hear Tommy rummaging in the bedroom. "What are you doing?" she asked curiously. The thought of him at the wardrobe was making her uneasy.

"Looking for something!"

"I can *hear* that. Tell me what it is and I might have put it away." She could hear a chair being pulled across the room. He was looking for something on top of the wardrobe. Her heart was beating faster.

"It's a small plastic bag for holding tobacco."

Jamie eyes opened wide as she stopped putting on her lipstick. "Why, what was in it?" No answer. She dropped the lipstick holder and walked quickly into the bedroom. "Tommy."

"What?" He was rooting with both hands. Lifting things. Checking under papers. Opening suitcases.

"What was in it?" She waited for an answer.

He looked up at her, then went on searching. "Ah, just something I had to drop over to these fellas."

"Was it money?"

"No." He stood up and stared at her. "Why do you ask?"

"'Cos there was no money in it!"

"In what?" Tommy looked worried.

"In the tobacco pouch." Jamie opened the drawer beside the bed and took out the tobacco pouch. "Is this what you were looking for?"

"Where did you find it?"

"It was on top of the wardrobe."

"Oh, thank God." He laughed and ran his sleeve

across his forehead. "Jesus, you had me worried there for a minute." He stood there, took a deep breath and held out his hand.

"What is it?" she demanded.

"Just something I have to drop over to a couple of mates." He was stumbling. Lying. "Eh, it's Fred's. He left it here the other night."

"That's funny. I didn't smell any pipe smoke when I got in yesterday."

"I opened all the windows. You know how much I hate pipes."

"Why was it covered in dust?"

He swallowed hard.

"What's in the sachets inside?"

"Sachets? Eh, probably just salt or something."

"Oh yeah. Where were you then? *Pizza Hut?* Or maybe even *MacDonalds*."

"Don't try to be smart. It doesn't suit you." He sneered.

"What's in the sachets!" she shouted. "Drugs? It *is* drugs, isn't it?" Her voice trembled. She grabbed the wallet and poured the tobacco onto the floor, along with four small sachets. Then she threw the empty wallet back in his face. "You're bringing drugs into my house! How fucking dare you!"

"It's *not* drugs. Don't be so stupid!" he snapped.

"You think *I'm* stupid?" shouted Jamie.

He turned quickly and pulled back the wardrobe door. He instantly knew that something was missing. "Where is it?" he asked agitatedly.

"What?" Jamie cried.

"The *black bag*, for God's sake!"

She looked at him. "What was in *that*?" she screamed.

He grabbed her arm forcefully. *"Where is it?"* he roared. He was shaking violently now, sweating.

Jamie pulled her arm away and wiped her eye. "I threw it in the bin." The look of horror on his face appalled her.

"Threw it in the bin?"

Jamie started to cry. "Why? Tell me, please. What was in it?"

Tommy pushed her out of the way. He ran down the stairs, taking three and four steps at a time.

Jamie watched from upstairs as Tommy kicked the plastic bin over on to the footpath. He pulled out the last few sticky remnants of gunge that clogged the bottom of the container. *"Gone!"* he roared. *"It's gone!"*

"Of course it's gone," she shouted. "It was full of old newspapers."

He bounded back up the stairs with bloodcurdling energy. He grabbed her again and started to shake her. *"Old newspapers, hah!"* he scoffed abusively. He ran to the window of the bedroom and pulled back the curtains. "What time do they come at?"

"Who?"

"The *binmen*!"

"How do I know? Since they started collecting the bins at night . . . *I don't know*!"

He started to pace up and down, grunting and whimpering like a wild animal. "Where do they take it?"

"Take what?"

"*The fucking rubbish!*"

"I don't know," Jamie sobbed. She sat on the side of the bed and started to cry. "Please tell me, Tommy, what was in the bag?"

He stared at her, his eyes roaring red and tearful. "A dream," he rasped. "Now, thanks to you, it's become a nightmare." He grabbed his jacket and looked at his watch.

"Tommy, I don't know what's going on in our lives but I'm sick of all these bloody secrets you're keeping from me. All these mysterious people you go off and meet and never tell me about."

He ignored her. "Where do they take all the shit?" He caught her by the arm.

"I don't know," she sobbed. "Wherever *shit* normally goes, I suppose."

He ran down to the kitchen and thumped the table. "Jesus Christ," he roared in a rage.

"Tommy, what was in the black bag?" she called. "Please!" Silence. She followed him slowly into the kitchen. Tommy sat at the table with his head buried in his hands.

"Jesus, Jesus, let me think. Em, I'll have to tell them . . . No. I can't. I'll say I'm working. No. I can't do that." He ran his hands through his hair like a man possessed.

"*Who?*" Jamie pleaded. "*Who* will you tell?"

"Nobody!"

"You know something, Tommy," Jamie rubbed her nose with a tissue and sniffed, "I met you three years ago this week. And I still don't know you at all." She waited. "And I don't want any more of your moods or your storms or your little secret games."

"*Secret games!* Is that what you call it? *Secret games!* You don't know what you've just done." He gritted his teeth and stretched his lips back as he moved nearer to her.

"What was in the black bag?" she persisted.

"The black bag, the black bag," he repeated, over and over.

Her mouth dropped open. She stared at him. "How long has this been going on, Tommy?" She waited for an answer.

"How long has *what* been going on?" He was running around the kitchen like a madman.

"Tommy," she shouted. "Answer me."

"That's got nothing to do with you." He opened presses and banged them again. "I don't always ask you where you've been every time you go out. Do I?"

"*Tommy*," she roared. "Do you have any idea what all this is doing to us? You don't tell me anything any more. How am I meant to understand? How am I meant to be happy? I have a *right to know*! Maybe I can help. Are you in trouble? If you are, maybe we can both figure out a way to sort things out. I want to help you. Please?"

He swung around to face her. "Do you know something. You're more stupid than I ever imagined."

Jamie walked over to him. "*Me? Stupid?* Why are you doing this to me? Why are you treating me like shit?"

He stared out into the garden.

"Well?" She grabbed his arm. *"For God's sake, answer me!"*

He shook off her grip and stared into her eyes. She didn't like what she saw. It was a deep, dark evil look.

"Do you have any idea what you've just done? As a result of your stupidity, you may have just got me killed!"

Jamie looked at him. "It's over, Tommy." She looked him straight in the eyes. It was what he knew best. Her eyes filled with tears. "For so long, you've treated me like a fucking doormat. Someone to put you to bed when you come in pissed out of your mind. Someone to cook for you and wash your clothes. Someone you can just shag whenever you fancy it. Well, I've got news for you. This is the end of the road, Tommy. I'm fed up getting coffee and a slice of grief. I'm fed up of you terrorising me. You *really* scare me sometimes, do you know that? Then you don't talk to me for days on end. You seem to think it's OK to give fifty per cent. 'Buy her a rose and say sorry.' What do you take me for? I may never know what's going on in that devious little mind of yours. But, then again, maybe that's a good thing. At least, I won't have it on my conscience. When you do eventually get burnt, don't come looking for me to kiss it better. 'Cos I won't be here. I've had all I can take. No more, Tommy. You're not going to hurt me any more. It's finished between you and me!"

"What do you mean, *finished*?"

She could hear the usual mocking tone in his voice. *"Finished.* Exactly what it sounds like. I want you and everything to do with you out by the time I get home this evening. Otherwise, I'm going to call Inspector Reidy to find out exactly what's going on. If I can't find out, *he* will. Because you're not dragging *me* down with you, Tommy Barrett. This is my house. My *home*."

"*Your* house?"

"Yes, *my* house. I bought you out when you broke it off last year. Remember? The night you walked out? You said *she* was the one for you? How long did *that* one last for? *Two fucking weeks?* How could I have been so bloody stupid as to take you back? At least this time I'll know better. You're only a lodger, Tommy. Good for paying the mortgage, that's all. But don't you worry. I'll find someone else to pay the bills. Go back to your mother and see how long she'll put up with you!" Jamie stormed out of the kitchen in tears.

The front door slammed.

"*Bastard!*" She was alone.

Chapter Six

Jamie arrived bright and early at the main door of City Radio. She gave it a push. It was still locked. She checked her watch. Eight thirty-five. Still, she didn't mind being half an hour late. It was a rare occurrence. This morning was an exception.

Few people could say that they loved their jobs. Jamie did. It had a certain *je ne sais quoi* about it. She didn't have a clue what *je ne sais quoi* meant. But she'd heard a woman use it on David Darling's *Talk to the Doctor* slot one day when she was asked to describe a multiple orgasm. It sounded good.

Working at City Radio was more than just a job. And she was a part of it. Yes, she loved her job. She relished the glitzy side of the business. The chance to get closer to more stars than most people have had hot dinners.

People's perception of the radio business couldn't have been further from the truth, she knew. To the uneducated ear, it was a life of sex, drugs and rock and roll. A never-ending rollercoaster of fame and fortune. A license to print money.

If only, she thought. Jamie wasn't really cut out for the wild side of life. A bit of a Ted in younger life, she preferred her quiet local to the wine bars of the West End. After hours, she enjoyed the company of her close friends over a quiet drink or a video. During office hours, she was like an animated character in a children's cartoon. Showbiz was showbiz. No half measures. So much so that, rain or shine, she would stick on a pair of dark glasses each morning as she turned on to Tottenham Court Road. She got the odd look of admiration from lads walking in the opposite direction. She liked to think the glasses gave her that *mysterious* quality. And they did. On one occasion, one man walked straight into a lamppost because his head stayed in the wrong direction for too long.

But Jamie had one problem when it came to work. She could never be on time. This morning was different. She rapped on the glass door with her knuckles and looked up and down the street as she waited for a reply. Two men winked at her. She smiled back. Just then, she noticed an old man in a security uniform staring at her through the window.

"Here, open the door. I'm freezing." She shivered in her low-cut top and short skirt.

"We don't open till nine, luv," the small individual shouted from behind the door, his eyes firmly fixed on her shivering cleavage.

"I work here!" she mouthed. The keys turned in the door.

"Sorry, luv. I 'aven't seen you around here, that's all." He kept looking down. Jamie pushed past him.

"I'm not surprised, when you don't look at people's faces." She pulled her jacket lapels close together to cover her boobs. "I'm Jamie. Mr Pickering's PA. And my eyes aren't in my chest!" She walked quickly across the empty reception area.

"Oh, I always wear a vest. The wife wouldn't let me out without checking that it's on!"

Jamie looked back at the old man. She wasn't quite sure if what she'd heard was what he'd said. Some security, she thought. Like something out of *Dad's Army*. She pressed the button for the lift. *Bing!* The door opened. Her stop was the third floor.

She had often heard it said that most people would give their right arm to work at a radio station. It was an ambition that Jamie had harboured since she met Randy Phelan when she worked in Northside. He was Ireland's number one deejay and Jamie's favourite. "I wouldn't mind Phelan," was Randy's cheeky catchphrase. Jamie remembered the red faces in Loreto the day after Randy turned up for a fund-raising event arranged to save the school from closure. The mention in the evening paper read: *Sister Margaret was quoted as saying that "All the sisters in the convent here love Phelan. This is the best thing to happen to the nuns in over a hundred years!"*

He arrived at the supermarket to do a promotion for a new continental beer which had just arrived in Ireland. Mister Sex, as he became known, stood in the off-license for three hours handing out samples of the beer to shoppers. Jamie reckoned that he was having the odd tipple himself. By half one that afternoon, he was serenading the female customers with "Strangers in the Night". By quarter to three, he was telling everyone who passed by his stand as quickly as they could that "this piss would rot your guts." Later, with the help of his agent and a policeman, he left the shop by a back door, seriously ill.

Jamie remained a devoted fan. She loved his voice and especially his choice of music. Her bosses piped it throughout the supermarket at Northside, so she heard the whole show.

She was visiting her aunt in Luton when she heard the job vacancy for City Radio being advertised on the radio station's *Find a Job* slot.

Her mates couldn't believe it when she told them she had been called for the job as receptionist at the station. Management, she was told, had received thousands of applications for the position. Even she was surprised when she received a phone call from Ian Pickering, the managing director, that Saturday morning. She didn't know the name of a single celebrity on the schedule. However, it all worked to her advantage. Mr Pickering later told her at the Christmas party that she had been selected because of her cool-headed approach to the job. A job that required feet on the ground at all times. Jamie reckoned he also liked her legs, even if he was old enough to be her father. Jamie was flattered.

She was promoted to her current position as personal assistant to the managing director within a month of joining the station. She took to the job like a fish to water. She'd check her boss's schedule first thing. Then, after a cup of coffee and a quick phone call to Nikki, her best friend, she would set about organising promotional activities for the radio station. This included lining up guests for the morning chat show host, David Darling.

Jamie had heard about the ego problems that superstars suffered from. But here was one big terminally ill- ego. David's vanity left other household names in the shade. He annoyed her like a bad rash. Constantly asked her out. She declined gracefully each time. Lately, though, David had been getting a bit heavy. Wine them, jump them and dump them. That was his motto. Jamie was having none of it.

As she stepped out of the lift, past the main on-air studio, she picked up David's post. Don, the breakfast show deejay, waved to her as he delivered the traffic news. She had a soft spot for Don. But he was bonking Mr Pickering's daughter. She had to be one of the ugliest woman that Jamie had ever laid eyes on. But, at least, it guaranteed Don a job as long as the relationship lasted. Clever ploy, she thought.

The highlight of her time so far at City Radio was meeting George Michael.

Listeners had unanimously voted George "Rear of the Year" in a telepoll organised by a men's underwear manufacturer. He pole-vaulted into the lead well ahead of other famous contenders, such as Kevin Costner and Cliff Richard, who seemed to feature in every single phone poll the station undertook. The staff were flabbergasted when a fax arrived from George's management company to say that he would be arriving at the radio station to receive the award personally the following Tuesday. It was left to Jamie to organise the ceremony and some refreshments afterwards. The morning of the presentation, she tried to give the impression that she couldn't understand all the fuss and hyper-hysterics. But her legs turned to jelly every time someone mentioned his name. Looks, money and a slinky voice. Take me anywhere, George, she thought.

The ceremony was a complete disaster. No sooner had his entourage arrived at the main entrance, than the big bearded man, whom everyone assumed was George's bodyguard, caught his wide tie in the revolving door and almost suffocated. It took five minutes to extricate him. Jamie forgot the mixers. So, when the angry bouncer downed a large gin, the reaction was hilarious. The man raced for the toilet like a Formula One car off the starting grid. His face turned crimson, his eyes bulged as he held his throat with both hands.

"Jesus, are you trying to kill me? Out of my fucking way!" he shouted as he ran for the men's room.

Things were on a downward spiral. Matters got worse when David Darling introduced George Michael as Boy George, and then tried to cover this up by saying, "Well, we're all boys in this game, aren't we?"

To add insult to injury, following all the thanks and congratulations, Mr Pickering wrapped up the presentation by wishing George well and, slapping him hard on the back, asked him jokingly which Oxfam shop he bought his clothes from.

It was just before nine. Jamie bent over the side of the photocopier to plug it in. She felt a warm hand on her bottom. She swung around.

"Hey, babe, I didn't mean to scare you." David Darling pushed his dark glasses on to his forehead. He took a piece of gum out of his mouth. Then he closed his eyes and puckered his lips in the expectation of a kiss. He leaned forward. "Missed you."

Jamie quickly picked up a small flowerpot and shoved it into his face. "Missed you too, David!"

"Uurgh, Jesus!" David spat out a mouthful of soil and fertiliser. "What the fuck was that in aid of?" He pointed to his shirt. "Do you know that this was given to me by Elton John?" He ran the sleeve of his dayglo yellow jacket across his mucky face.

"Sexual harassment, that's what!" she screamed. His huge lips disgusted her. They looked great on black men, she thought. But not on this creep. His mouth reminded her of a bulldog chewing a nettle.

"Sexual harassment, my arse!" he retorted in his posh deejay London accent. "My women love it when I flirt with them."

She held the prongs of the photocopier plug up to his face. "Yeah, well, I'm not one of your bimbo women, am I? So, save the maulers for them. I'm going to have to chain your fucking hands to those record decks downstairs if they don't stop wandering. Jesus, they're worse than the Navy's."

"All you women are the same. High morals and cocky attitudes. It's all right for you to pinch our arses or grab our dicks. But as soon as one of us lays a hand on, it's 'call the cops' time." David had lost his smile. Now he was serious. "This women's lib stuff makes me sick." He moved nearer. She could feel his breath warm against her cold face. She was trapped in the corner. "You all try to give the impression that you're independent. That you're better than we are." He had switched to the voice he used while talking to callers on his radio show. His deejay voice. "And you know something? Maybe you're better than we are. But when it boils down to it, you still need us when it comes to one thing. Isn't that right, Jamie?" He smiled and ran his fingernail down the front of her neck and on to her chest.

She pushed the hand away. "You know that I could have you out of your job and on to the street quicker than you could say a prayer." Jamie tried to hide her fear. It was generally known that David Darling didn't like taking *no* for an answer.

"Oh yeah? You and whose army, darlin?" he sneered as he looked down at her breasts.

She hated being called *darling*.

"I am the biggest asset this poxy little radio station has. If it wasn't for my ratings and the advertising I pull in every week, everyone else's arse would be out on the high street. The only reason that I'm not working for Radio 1 is that they're too scared to put me on air. It doesn't matter a fiddler's what you think, darling. When all's said and done, David Darling *is*

City Radio." He grinned and chewed hard on his bubble-gum. "So I think it's only fair that people round here started showing their appreciation. What do you think, darling?" He ran his hand under her hair and around the back of her neck. Then he leaned over and whispered into her ear. "How would you fancy coming round to my place tonight? A nice curry and a bottle of baby oil, perhaps?"

Jamie pushed him away from her. "Don't you ever ask me to make you a cup of coffee again. Do you hear me?"

"Why's that, then?"

"Because next time, it won't be sugar I'll put in it!" She pushed her way out of the corner. "Stick to your dozy blondes and your dumbstruck dullards, David. A woman with brains would only make your life miserable." She held out the photocopier plug she'd been holding. "Here. How about sticking something useful into the right hole!" Jamie walked into the office and placed her bag on the desk.

"Don't you worry, darling. Some night, you and me are going to end up in the same bed. 'Cos you know something, I think that's what you're badly in need of right now. A couple of hours with an experienced man! You know what they say. A good ride relaxes the mind."

She took one final look at the radio station's hero fumbling with the photocopier plug and laughed. God, if only his listeners could see him now, she thought. "That probably explains why you're so screwed up. And, as for experience. Bart Simpson has more experience than you'll ever have. I've had just about *enough* of *men* for today." She walked slowly to the door. "Did it ever occur to you that maybe Elton John was trying to get rid of that jacket? You look like my mother's pet canary." The door slammed.

* * *

Her boss was in Leeds today at a conference. More like a freebie in a five-star hotel, Jamie thought. She didn't mind. It gave her a chance to catch up on the latest gossip. And who better to update her than her best friend, Nikki. Jamie and Nikki had worked together in the Northside Shopping Centre. When Jamie quit her supermarket job, so did Nikki. That fateful afternoon in Dublin, over a bottle of Ritz and a Pernod and Black, they made a pact with each other to check out the job scene in London.

She sat down at her desk and grabbed the phone. Come on, Nikki, answer, she urged. Jamie was dying to find out if Nikki had got back with Peter. He was a copper and a good friend of Tommy's. It was through Nikki that she'd met Tommy. Nikki had found out that Peter had been quietly bedding one of his female colleagues from the force in their bed. One evening, six weeks ago, she had no sooner got in and closed the door of her flat behind her when she sussed there was something going on. Peter's trousers and shoes were lying on the floor in the kitchen, and a half-empty bottle of wine stood open on the table. She threw open the bedroom door. Peter jumped off his friend so quickly that he fell out of the bed, pulling the quilt with him. Your woman was left sitting there, trying to cover up what she could with two arms. Nikki looked down at the naked offender crouching on the floor.

"You bastard!" Tears welled up in her eyes.

"Nikki, I have to talk to you," Peter stammered.

"I *bet* you do!" Nikki quickly interrupted. She looked at the woman on the bed. "And who the fuck is she?" She turned on the light for a better look. "I suppose this is what they mean by sticking close to your partner! Pathetic. I thought you liked a bit of breast, Peter. Jesus, you could play a game of snooker on her chest." She grabbed the woman by the hair. "Out, you bitch!" She pulled her off the bed and dragged her towards the door of the flat.

"Stop! You're hurting me," the naked policewoman cried.

Nikki ignored her. "Out, before I kill you!" Nikki didn't know where the power was coming from. All she knew was that she had it. She slammed the front door, leaving the woman in the small porch.

"What about my clothes?" the woman whimpered in a posh tone from the garden.

Within seconds, the door flew open again.

"Here's your fucking clothes. Not that you've much to cover. It's just that I'd hate you to catch pneumonia!"

The door slammed shut with the crack of an automatic rifle.

Nikki thundered back into the bedroom. Keeping her watery eyes fixed firmly on the small chest of drawers, she started to fire things into a suitcase. She picked up the framed photograph of Peter and herself, on holiday in Majorca, turned and threw it with all her might. It hit him straight on the forehead and broke into tiny pieces.

"Fuck you!" she shouted. She spent the next two weeks on Jamie's couch until she found a new flat.

* * *

The receptionist asked Jamie to hold while she transferred her call. She sat back in the chair and surveyed her smart office. It carried all the trappings of a woman who was proud of her position. Commemorative Gold Discs sent to her by record companies as a token of their appreciation for all her hard work. Autographed pictures that had been taken of her with some of her idols. Christy Moore. Lenny Henry. A colour photograph of Bruce Springsteen, signed with the message, *Jamie, where were you all those years ago? Love, Bruce*. A framed letter, signed and sent to her by three of the Birmingham Six. Each time she looked around this room, she saw the culmination of four year's hard work.

Jamie and Nikki were on the phone for close to half an hour.

"And you know what's worse?" Nikki continued.

"What?" Jamie dipped the back of her swivel chair to get more comfortable.

"Since I told him to get stuffed, the phone hasn't stopped ringing." Nikki giggled.

"Peter?" Jamie asked in disbelief.

"No! Fellas asking me out! If this is heaven, I don't want to die!" The two girls roared laughing. "I'm knackered. I'll tell you, Jamie, if you had any sense, you'd tell that Tommy character where to get off. You and me could have a ball together. There wouldn't be a man in London safe."

Silence.

"Yeah, I know." Jamie sighed. "I just did about two hours ago." She sat forward in her chair.

"What?" Nikki screamed and then laughed. "What did you tell him?"

"I told him it was something I should've done a long time ago." Jamie tried to pretend that the morning's episode hadn't affected her. Deep down, though, she was devastated. She thought she should change the subject. "Look, I can't really talk on the phone," she hinted. "I'll tell you later. That just reminds me. Wait till I tell you about the fella I met on the train when I was coming back!"

Nikki's voice twittered away on the other end of the phone. "You, Jamie Carroll, got chatting with a strange man! Jesus. Is this the new you? It's about time. I can see the headline. 'Jamie Carroll doesn't let the grass grow. Lock up your sons.' *This* I have to hear."

"Now listen, Nikki. Before you go spreading rumours, there's nothing in it! He was just nice." Jamie paused.

"*Nice!*" Nikki shouted. "*Nice.* Jesus, coming from you, he must have been gorgeous."

Jamie could see where this was leading. "Listen

Nikki, I'm going to have to go. I'll give you a shout later on. OK?"

"Wait! Don't go. Tell me more about him. Did he ask you out? Did he kiss you?"

"Nikki, will you shut up!" Jamie covered the receiver with her hand as if everyone in the building was listening. "Listen to me. You won't believe who's coming here to the station this Friday."

"Who?"

"Liam Neeson."

There was a moment's silence at Nikki's end. "Jamie Carroll! I'm sweating! I don't believe you. Jesus, let me sit down before I faint."

"Now listen, I must be mad to do this. But if you promise not to do what you did last time, I'll get you in to the building."

"What d'you mean, *last time*?"

"Nick Berry. D'you not remember?"

"No!"

"The knickers that got twisted round his neck and nearly choked him?"

Silence. "No!"

"They were yours."

"How do you know?"

"'Cos you borrowed them off me the week before. I was the one who had to help him get them off. That's how I know."

"Oh, you dirty bitch, Jamie Carroll. If there's any *getting off* to be done with Liam Neeson, I want to be in there."

Jamie ignored her. "Nikki, I'm warning you!"

"Liam Neeson!" There was a loud scream on the other end of the phone. "I don't believe you! Oh Jesus, Jamie! I swear I'll do whatever you say. He can park his bicycle on me arse if that's what it takes! Listen. What time will I meet you on Friday?" Nikki was on the boil, she was talking so fast.

"Right. Half eight outside the Tottenham Court underground."

"Great. D'you think we'll get to meet him?"

"All depends on what his other plans are. But come here to me, Nikki Coffey. Don't do anything stupid. Do you hear me?"

"I won't. I swear. Listen, tell us what happened between you and loverboy?" Nikki asked impatiently.

Jamie thought for a moment before answering. How much was she going to tell? Nikki had a habit of talking too much. It wasn't spiteful. It was more a case of "Don't repeat this but wait until I tell you . . . " Still, Jamie needed to talk to someone and Nikki *was* a good listener.

"Well, are you going to tell me or will I just have to guess?"

"I found a bag of stuff in the wardrobe last night. I didn't think it was important so I threw it out."

"What *stuff*?"

"I don't know. White stuff in tobacco. And a big black plastic bag. It just seemed like rubbish to me. Full of old rolled-up balls of newspaper. So I put it in the bin." Her heart was beginning to pound.

"So? Why did you throw him out?"

"'Cos he went mad when he came in from work this

morning. You'd swear I'd burnt his winning Lotto numbers. Jesus, it wasn't as if it was worth anything."

"How do you know?"

"For fuck's sake, Nikki, you're always taking his side aren't you? You had to be there to see him. I thought he was going to murder me. I've never been so scared in all my life. His eyes were just full of poison, I swear."

"Why did you throw him out?"

"Jesus, Nikki, are you not listening to what I'm saying? He was like a psychopath. I thought he was going to *kill* me, for God's sake."

"Tommy wouldn't lay a finger on you, Jamie. You know that. Maybe he was just tired after night shift. Maybe the stuff you threw out was important. Don't worry. He'll be back with open arms."

"That's the problem, Nikki. It was important. But for all the wrong reasons. *Bad* reasons."

"What do you mean?"

"I don't know. Well, I do kinda know. Like as if I have a bad feeling. A hunch. And I've never been wrong before when it comes to hunches."

"Like what?"

"Like . . . " She hesitated. "Nikki, I have this awful feeling that he's mixed up in drugs."

"Well, he would be, wouldn't he. He *is* in the drugs squad, isn't he?"

"I don't mean *that*! I mean . . . dealing, or something. I don't know."

"Don't be stupid, Jamie Carroll. He's a *cop*!" she shrieked.

"Keep your voice down. Look, I have to go. You open your mouth to anyone an' I'll burst you, do you hear me?"

"Why do you say that every time you tell me something juicy? You know I won't."

"This is not *juicy*, Nikki. This is scary."

"Listen, Jamie, give it a couple of days, and he'll be back with open arms. I promise."

"But I don't want him back, Nikki. After this morning, I don't care if I never see him again."

"Ah, you're just saying that in the heat of the moment, Jamie. Come on."

"Nikki, sometimes I think you'd like to get into Tommy's knickers."

"No, I would not!"

"Well you could've fooled me. You've made a beeline for every other pair you've come across. And none of them has ever stayed on for long. Why should Tommy Barrett be any different?"

"How fucking dare you, Jamie Carroll, you bitch. I don't give a shit if your boyfriend never comes back. You don't deserve him." Click. The phone line went dead.

Oh shit, Jamie thought, you've really done it now. She sat back in her chair. Let's be realistic here, she reasoned. It's not my fault that Tommy's such a bastard. Having said that, how's Nikki to know? She's never seen his darker side. She waited for a moment and picked up the phone. She'd barely had a chance to dial the number.

"I'm sorry," said the voice on the other end.

"So am I," said Jamie.

"Let's just forget it. We can talk about it when you feel better."

"Nikki, there's nothing to talk about. He deserved what he got. He had it coming to him. At least you're all right. You've got a nice cosy little place of your own. You're not living with some hotheaded bear with a permanent thorn stuck up his arse."

"Oh lovely. Tell him I'll remove it." Nikki laughed.

"Tell him yourself."

"So, what are you doing on Friday night?"

"Well, I was meant to be going out for a romantic meal. Past tense. Why?"

"Cos I got a few invitations to the reopening of the Clover Tap. We can all head up to the Gresham afterwards, chat up a couple of toyboys and then get a taxi back to my place. Make a night of it."

"Sounds brilliant. But I'll wait an' see."

"Jamie," Nikki shouted.

"What now?" Jamie asked impatiently.

"Is he Irish?"

"Who? Liam Neeson?"

"No! The hunk on the train!"

Jamie paused and looked out the window. "Yes," she answered quietly.

"Is he a ride?"

Jamie blushed. "Yes." She was dying to tell Nikki all about the night journey back from home but she knew it'd be all over London by lunchtime.

"Does he have any nice friends?" Nikki shouted on the other end of the phone.

"Goodbye." Jamie put the phone down. She smiled.

Jamie hadn't been to the Clover Tap since she met Tommy. She knew it had all the makings of a great girls' night out. And she hadn't seen a couple of the girls for quite a while. Tommy had never been into the idea. He made no secret of the fact that he felt very uneasy about having a drink in an Irish pub. English policemen and Irish drinkers didn't make a great partnership. Jamie had tried to convince him that not all Irish people were terrorists. But it always drew a big blank with him.

She sat there at her desk arguing with herself. Was he gone for good? He'd have to come back to the house for his belongings. Could she accept an apology, let alone listen to one? Definitely not. The idea made her feel sick. Deep down, she knew it was over. This time for good.

The possibility of a part on *Coronation Street* was more likely than a successful relationship with Tommy Barrett. That's it then, she thought to herself. Right. She straightened up her chair and went back to the computer.

Chapter Seven

Frank hated alarm clocks. And this one was ringing particularly loudly. He took one quick glimpse at it as he switched it off. Oh God, he muttered. Anything for four more hours. It was quarter to seven on the morning of the big day. As he lay in the small single bed, he was torn between the daunting tasks which lay ahead of him. He thought about how easy it used to be. He used to be able to knock off home when the whistle sounded at half four, or when the glasses were shelved and the pub was ready for next-day business. Occasionally, he would lock up at night. Or return overnight if there was a break-in. That was about as serious as it got. But Frank was never happy with playing second fiddle. He'd always wanted to be the boss. Now he was. From today, the buck stopped with him. He'd never been so nervous in all his life.

In less than twelve hours, the pub would be stuffed with invited guests and celebrities, all fighting to get to the bar for the free drink. The list of guests had been sitting beside the bed from the previous Wednesday night, still waiting to be examined. He thought he would work on it over breakfast before heading for the Clover Tap. It would be the only chance he'd get all day.

The flat was freezing. It didn't stop Ray from snoring like a bull in the next room. Dressed only in a pair of briefs, Frank grabbed a sweater from the end of the bed. He shivered as he pulled it over his head.

Frank had shared a small flat with big Ray Flynn for almost three years. Ray had lived in London for as long as he could remember. He was a rugged, well-worn-looking bloke. Traits that came from years of hard work on more building sights than he could count. No one would deny that Ray had a heart of gold and would go to the ends of the earth to do a favour for a blank stranger. He was a true gentleman when he was sober, but a different animal after a night on the beer. Frank McCabe had met Ray when they both worked for Conlon Bros. Construction. The company received the contract for major renovations to Terminal 1 at Heathrow airport. Frank always maintained that there was no one with a neck as hard as Ray's. He was great to have around. When he was sober.

Frank remembered the nights he had to go out searching for Ray long after closing time. Sometimes, he searched as many as ten Irish pubs. Places where Ray was likely to get a late jar. He would find him fast asleep down at the old Broadway, where all the old homeless down-and-outs would seek refuge for a few hours around a rubbish-tip fire. Or find him helping the Salvation Army to dish up soup and biscuits to the same miserable bunch. Ray hadn't been home to Ardee for years. He regularly got letters from his mother and sister. He always meant to reply but never got around to it. He drank most of his money and gambled what was left. He was known to the local police as a bit of a troublemaker. He preferred not to pay for his weekly groceries. He managed to get away with it. but there was always the next time.

He had a generous heart. Frank remembered the time when Ray saved a young child from being abducted from a shopping mall. He noticed a young man who clumsily grabbed the child under both arms and made a run for the mall exit. The child's mother screamed at Ray for help. Ray was standing between the kidnapper and the door. He squeezed through the crowd and, bending his leg, put his knee up into the path of the oncoming abductor. The effects of a knee in the groin could be heard all over the second level of the mall. Ray's picture was on the front of the London *Evening Echo* that evening, and was also one of the main headlines on RTE's news that night.

Frank was looking forward to getting out of Ray's flat. The place was a dump. Not that Frank was such a good housekeeper himself. However, the effects of finding the leftovers of a four-day-old curry under his bed kept him awake for the remainder of the night. There was never anything in the kitchen, never mind the fridge.

Ray's idea of breakfast was a large bottle of stout from the cooler, while he dabbed a wet handcloth under his huge armpits. A shite, a shave and a shower, as they'd say at home. He entertained the crowd in the local by telling them how he would slap a raw sixteen-ounce steak on to a shovel at midday each day. He made sure to sterilise the shovel first by leaving it stuck in the foreman's charcoal fire for ten minutes. The small bits of wet clay left on the surface of the shovel would ensure that all the goodness of the meat was sealed in. Then, after a good roar of flame for another ten minutes, he'd devour the steak and head for the nearest pub to wash it down with five or six pints of stout.

Ray put his name down, whenever possible, for charity drinking matches. He had helped to raise thousands of pounds for charity down through the years. He had even made the local freesheet on one occasion when, after consuming eighteen pints, he was still capable of helping the paramedics to carry three of his opponents into a waiting ambulance. Frank never doubted Ray's heart of gold, which was almost as big as his famous appetite. However, he felt that now was not the right time to tell Ray about his new job. He wanted to impress his customers, not frighten them.

"Jesus, Jesus," Frank chanted as he breathed deeply and flexed his shoulder muscles in an effort to generate heat. His jeans felt damp. He danced around the end of the bed trying to push each foot further down each leg. A shower was out of the question. He went into the kitchen and turned on the light. Frank couldn't function without a cup of coffee first thing in the morning. As the kettle whirred slowly into action, he looked around the dingy flat. It wasn't a typical bachelor pad, because Ray was not your typical bachelor. More like a bunker to crawl into for a while and let your wounds heal. Occasionally, the rent would run into arrears. This was due to the landlord's reluctance to collect it. One evening, Ray told the landlord that if he continued to annoy him over the rent, he'd take him down to the local boy's boxing club and use him as a punch-bag.

Blankets hung over the window instead of curtains. By day, they were thrown on the ends of beds, or used as tablecloths, if Ray was having his mates around for the monthly poker classic. Dirty dishes were everywhere. Ray would wash them when his collection ran out and there was nothing left to eat off. Frank examined the Indian takeaway cartons on the drainer. The rotten smell suggested Chicken Tikka Masala which was gross at five to seven in the morning. The kettle boiled. Frank searched for a clean mug. It was then that he noticed that Ray had spilled curry sauce over his new answering machine.

"Flynn, you dirty bastard!" he roared at the top of his voice. "Look what you did to me answering machine."

The snoring stopped. Some minutes later, the bedroom door opened and the bear emerged. He wore a cotton vest revealing his huge arms and a potbelly which must have cost a fortune.

"What time is it?" Ray blinked in the bright kitchen light.

"Fuck the time. Look what you did to the answering machine!"

Ray walked slowly into the kitchen.

"Jesus, is that what it is?" he muttered under his breath. "When d'you get it?"

"Brendan's kids got it for me for Christmas." Frank followed the trail of the curry sauce down the back of the machine. "You may throw it in the bin now along with the rest of yesterday's dinner."

"I'll get you a new one on Saturday." Ray about-turned and disappeared into the bathroom. There was a loud roar. "What has you up so early, Frank? I've a couple of Solpadeine in the press there if you need them."

"I've a few things on today. I'll tell you later. Where's the milk and sugar?"

"The milk's in the fridge and the Hermasetas is in the press there somewhere."

"Hermasetas?"

"Yeah." Ray re-emerged. "I stopped taking sugar in me tea and coffee for Lent. It's far too fattening."

"Too fattening? *You?*" Frank looked down at Ray's bulging gut. A piece of string held up his pyjama bottoms.

"Yep! Something like fifty calories for every spoon." Ray rinsed out a mug and took a herbal teabag from a box on the worktop.

"Where did you find that out?" Frank was astonished.

"On the telly. You know that pair in the mornings. They're married. Jesus, what's their names? Punch and Judy Finnegan, or something."

Frank watched in wonder as Ray lowered the

teabag, covered with floral drawings, into his mug. "What's that?"

"What?"

"That teabag?"

"What d'you mean?" Ray looked up at Frank. "It's a herbal teabag. Have you never seen them?"

"'Course I have. I'm just surprised you have." Frank watched as Ray carefully squeezed the flavour out of the bag. "Where did *you* hear about them?"

"Your woman, Judy, on the telly again. She says they're very good for stress. Helps you sleep at night."

Frank roared laughing. "Jesus, when did *you* ever have a problem getting to sleep at night?"

Ray flicked the teabag towards the sink. It splattered all over the kitchen wall. "Ha, ha." He took a mouthful of tea and swallowed it. "You see, budso, Ray Flynn is a changed man since you last saw him."

Frank threw his eyes up to heaven. "I think you're just losing the few mouldy marbles you've got left." He opened the fridge and took out a small carton of milk. As he poured it, a large blob of sour, curdy milk fell into the mug. He jumped back as the coffee splashed everywhere. "Jesus, it's turned to butter. How long is that in the fridge?"

"I couldn't tell you, Frank. I don't take milk any more. Bad for the heart!" Ray turned and walked back to the bathroom.

Frank was about to let out another roar when he heard a hollow thud coming from Ray's room. It sounded as if something had fallen off the wardrobe. The bedroom door swung open and a naked woman staggered out. She was blinded by the bright kitchen light. As she put her hand up to shield her eyes, she noticed Frank sitting at the kitchen table. His mouth dropped open.

"Hi," she mumbled quietly.

Frank coughed uneasily. "Hi," he muttered. Maybe he was imagining it. He'd heard that the mind can play games with your eyes when under severe pressure. He blinked. She was still there.

"It's very cold this morning, isn't it?" She looked around.

"It's the fourteenth of January," Frank replied. "What did you expect?" It was beginning to dawn on Frank what was going on. Something he'd never dreamed of in all the years he'd known Ray.

"Where's the bathroom?" she muttered. She moved her hands and arms nervously from left to right, up and down.

"In front of you!" Frank was trying hard not to smile.

The nude figure pushed her way in and slammed the door. There was a muffled conversation for a few minutes and then silence.

Frank sat there gobsmacked. He had known Ray for seven years, on and off. He'd never seen him in conversation with a woman. And here he was in bed with one! Frank decided to stir it a bit.

"Anyone for coffee?" he enquired. "Or maybe a herbal teabag." No answer. "Very good for relaxing the oul' muscles." Still no reply. He sat down in the chair like a child waiting for the main feature to begin. The silence was killing him. There was so much to do for the opening that night, he knew he would be pushing it if he hung around much longer. Ray shuffled into the kitchen and headed straight for the kettle again.

"Who's your friend?" Frank enquired.

"I was in the Clover Tap yesterday morning. Couldn't get a drink!" Ray replied. "Big night down there tonight. Will we try and gatecrash?"

"No point," Frank replied stubbornly. "Invitations only, I hear. Answer the question!"

"Invitations my arse!" Ray said gruffly. "When have we ever needed invitations? You and me? The Butch Cassidys of the London pub scene? If I want to get in, I'll get in!"

The last thing Frank needed was his best friend getting him fired on the first day. The door opened again. She was dressed now and strolled shyly into the kitchen.

"Where is this place, Carlos?"

Frank choked on his coffee. He was about to ask "who's Carlos?" when he felt the full brunt of Ray's big calf under the table.

"Eh, we're just off the Kilburn Road, love," came the loving reply. It was as if they'd been together for years.

"I better get home or I'll be late," she said quietly in a half-cockney, half-Irish accent. She took out a hairbrush and glanced over at Frank as she quickly ran it through her tattered hair.

"Hi, you." She smiled. "Are you into property too?"

Frank looked over at Ray who was fidgeting with

135

the handle on his cup. Ray glared at him and nodded his head.

"Eh, well . . . you know yourself. I dabble a bit. Frank McCabe. Pleased to meet you." Frank held out his hand.

She stopped brushing for a moment. "Davina Cripp."

"What'll you be late for?" Frank was curious to find out more.

"The kids. They have to be in school by nine." She picked up Ray's mug and took a mouthful. "Jesus, what's that?"

"Herbal tea. It helps you sleep." Ray took another sip.

"You *certainly* don't have a problem if last night was anything to go by." Davina put her small delicate arm around Ray's massive neck and gave him a kiss.

Frank's mind was doing overtime. She'd spent the night here with Ray. Where in God's name were her kids? It occurred to him that they might be in the bedroom as well. "Have you got them with you, like?"

"Who?"

"Your kids?"

She gave a peculiar little laugh. "No! The baby-sitter's got them!"

"Jesus, she's earning her money tonight."

"What do you mean?" She was serious again.

"I mean, like, it's quarter past seven in the morning. Some baby-sitter. I'm impressed."

"Oh, don't worry. She's used to it."

"Do you work late hours?"

"Eh yes." She paused and held the handle of the hairbrush up to her mouth. "I suppose you could say that I'm in the business of making people happy." She picked up her mug and drank it. "I'm a part-time kissogram."

Frank smiled. "Very nice," he replied. "You get a lot of free time during the day then?"

"It has its advantages."

Frank was on a roll. "So then, where did the two of you lovebirds meet?"

"In the gym." Ray stared into his mug.

Frank spluttered. "At the gym? Pumping iron, are we? Another thing I suppose you saw on your telly show."

"No. I was laying a new ramp at the door for wheelchairs. Davina came out and stood in the wet cement. Her footprints are still there, if you don't believe me. And so are mine!" Ray hugged Davina and gave her a gentle puck on the shoulder. She almost disappeared beneath his huge arm.

Frank turned back to Davina. "So you must spend a fierce amount of the nights running from pub to pub?"

"If only." Davina closed her carry-all. "I spent most of my time on my back during the night!"

"Did you hurt it? Frank enquired as she looked around for the front door.

"No!" She looked at Ray with a big grin. "But if I let that big devil lie on me for much longer, I'll probably break it. I'm what you might call a hooker! See you, Carlos. Try and lose a few pounds for the next time."

She winked at Frank, now sitting bolt upright in a state of shock. "See you round, love."

Frank looked at Ray.

"What the fuck are you looking at?" Ray stood up and headed for the bedroom. "By the way. Something else I saw on telly."

"What?" Frank sat motionless.

"Too much coffee is bad for you." He closed the door.

* * *

Jamie loved Fridays. It was a real doss-day. Her boss was usually away entertaining business associates at morning meetings and long lunches. Sometimes he wouldn't bother to return to the office in the afternoon. This left her in peace to make her weekly string of phone calls and plan the weekend.

On this particular Friday, the station was rolling out the red carpet for Liam Neeson, who was being interviewed by David Darling about his new film. Most of it had been shot on location in West Cork. Liam Neeson was due at City Radio at half eleven that morning.

Nikki met Jamie, as arranged, at the Tottenham Court tube exit.

Nikki had told her boss that that she had got an unusually heavy period and would have to go to the doctor the next day for a check-up! The poor man, not familiar with the modern woman, simply nodded and told her to take the day off. The two arrived at City

Radio on time, as agreed. Nikki grabbed Jamie in the lift and made her swear that she would get her inside the security cordon. Close enough to smell his aftershave.

It was decided that Nikki would be a sandwich girl from a local delicatessen.

"Nikki, listen to me. This is important." Jamie pointed her finger at her best friend.

"What? Jesus, Jamie, I'd give anything to work here. Where's David Darling?"

"To hell with David Darling! Now listen. Don't get in the way this morning. If you do, I'll be the one who'll get grief, OK?"

"Ah Jamie, will you not be worrying, for God's sake. I only want to look at him. Not ride him!"

"And if they find out who y'are, leave straight away. D'you hear?"

"I hear!"

Nikki wandered around the third floor of the radio station like a psychiatric patient on sedation. Her mouth hung open as she moved from picture to picture, oohing and aahing. I'm in heaven, she thought.

This gave Jamie a chance to check if Tommy had come back to the house. He definitely wasn't there. His mother hadn't heard from him. She'd called more times during the past twenty-four hours than she had in fifteen months. Maybe she shouldn't have thrown him out so abruptly. After all, she still hadn't heard his side of the story. On the other hand, she was glad that she had. Maybe now, he'd cop on to his selfish ways and his self-centred attitude. But she didn't think so. At least, when she could see him and knew where he was, he seemed manageable. Now, he was gone. Uncontactable. She didn't like that. He was a manipulative man. Capable of bending even his bosses around his little finger. I have them where I want them, he'd often said.

"Hello, Inspector Reidy's office. Can I help you?"

"Oh hello, this is Jamie Carroll."

"Hello, Jamie. Are you looking for Tommy?"

"Yes," Jamie said anxiously.

"So are we! He hasn't shown up for work for two days. And we haven't heard from him at all. Have you?"

"Eh, no, actually. I haven't. I was hoping that you might have." Jamie bit her bottom lip.

"Well, if you do, get him to give us a ring, will you? Thanks."

Jamie replaced the receiver and sat back in the chair. Where was he? Maybe he'd gone on a mad bender with a few of his mates. He'd done it before. Ended up in Amsterdam for two days. That had caused some argument. She looked down at the photograph of the two of them on her desk. It had been taken during a slow set at the disco one night.

She rang the nightclub to check if he'd picked up his wages. No luck. They hadn't seen him for almost three weeks. He hadn't as much as called them. As far as they were concerned, he was fired. What the hell is going on? she asked herself.

The office door opened. It was one of the

managers. "Jamie, can we have a quick run through the plans for Liam Neeson's visit?"

"Yeah, no problem." Time to forget this mess and do my job, she thought.

* * *

Their plan went into action when Nikki arrived in the main office, overlooking the high street, to take orders for sandwiches from the staff. Most of them preferred to work through lunch on Friday. That way, they could leave the office at half four. Nikki was going to be on work experience for the day. At least, that was the plan. She was taking an order for a fresh tuna roll when she heard car horns and a flurry of excitement on the street below.

"Jesus, that's him." She dropped her notepad and ran over to the window. She pushed through the staff who had been waiting at the window. "Here, out of my way, fatso. Pregnant woman coming through!" She pushed her face hard against the window. Liam stepped from the stretch limousine wearing a tasty emerald green casual jacket and plain white shirt. He waved to the hundred or so fans who had queued since early morning to catch a glimpse of him. Nikki squeezed her way in between the two women in front of her and stuck her head out.

"Yoo hoo, Liam! Up here."

The actor heard the shouts and looked around. Just at that moment, Jamie held her hand out to welcome Liam on behalf of City Radio.

"Here, you with the gorgeous eyes and arse! I'm up here." By now, Nikki was hanging out of the window. Two male members of the station's staff held her legs to stop her from falling out. "Michael Collins! I loved your last film."

The actor winked up at the crowd in the window..

"Oh Jesus, he winked at me," Nikki screamed. "I think I'm going to be sick. Here, will you pull me back in, quick! Ah, mind me fucking tits! Who's grabbin' my arse? Ooooh!" she shrieked at the top of her voice.

Jamie didn't need to look up. She tried to ignore the noise at the third floor window as she escorted Liam into reception. Unfortunately, as the lift arrived to take the entourage to the third floor, security guards were forcibly escorting Nikki to the ground floor and, more importantly, the exit. Nikki screamed as the lift door slid back. She was face to face with Liam Neeson.

"Oh, my God, you're a ride!" She leaped forward and threw her arms around his neck. The three security guards found it difficult to separate her lips from his. Eventually, one of them had to hold Nikki's shoulders while the other two extracted Mr Neeson from her clutch. She left the building in tears.

Jamie found it tough getting through the rest of the day. And that wasn't just because of Liam Neeson's conversation with her. A conversation which turned her legs to jelly every time she thought about it. But she had to fork out twenty-five quid to eight of the staff for sandwiches they'd ordered and never received.

Chapter Eight

It was almost half five. Frank was worn out. He ran his
hand across his forehead and tried to figure out how he
was going to stay awake until two the following
morning. Probably later. Still, he thought proudly, the
place looks great. He was standing on a bar stool after
putting up the last set of balloons. All we have to do
now is make money, he thought. His eyes were level
with those of the Cork GAA All-Ireland Football
Champions of 1989. They took pride of place above
the main cash register. It would have been the icing on
the cake if the lads from Glandore could have made it
tonight. They'd have been so proud of Frank. He
looked down at the young man checking the cash float.

"Philip, can you hang on till I nip over to the flat
and get me shirt and suit?"

"No problem, Mr McCabe. Take as long as you
like." the smart young man replied.

"By the way, Philip."

Philip stopped counting. "Yes, Mr McCabe?"

"Don't call me Mr McCabe. It makes me feel as old
as my da!" Frank smiled. "Call me Frank."

"OK, Mr McCabe. I mean Frank!" Philip grinned and went back to his float.

Frank walked slowly across the lounge checking the small but important things. Things like clean ashtrays, toilet paper in the ladies' and gents', condoms in the dispensing machines. He wondered what his mother would think of condom machines.

There was a time when he would have been joining Ray and the lads in their very own corner of the pub for their usual end-of-week session. He walked over to the small snug where they all used to congregate religiously. A framed black-and-white photograph hung on the wall overhead. It had nearly been thrown into a rubbish skip during the renovations. Luckily, Frank had spotted it. He moved closer to the picture and examined it. "Winners in the Clover Tap's Darts League." Mossy. Paddy. Bilbo. Colin. Decco. Joe. Ray. And Frank.

"Sorry, Frank." Philip, his senior barman, stood a small distance behind him. "Are you all right?"

Frank felt a shiver run down his spine. He looked around at Philip.

"Yeah. Just thinking about old times."

"Did you know them?" Philip nodded towards the photograph.

"Know them?" Frank shook his head and smiled. "I suppose you could say that all right." He threw his jacket over his shoulders. "Any calls for me, I'll be back in an hour."

The brewery had decided on black tie for the evening so Frank had hired one for the weekend. Rain was pouring down as he pulled up his collar. Typical Friday evening. Traffic was at a standstill. As he stopped to cross the busy street, he noticed a red Golf GTI pull away from the front of the pub. He reckoned that he'd seen it somewhere before but didn't give it another thought. He made a mental note of what still had to be done before the guests arrived.

Two stops on the tube got him to the front door of Ray's flat. As he turned the key, he couldn't help thinking how nice it would be to have a big place of his own. The builders had finished the renovations in the pub, so they could start on the upstairs quarters within the next few days. Two bedrooms, a bathroom, kitchen and a giant living-room. It sounded like heaven. The brewery guaranteed that it would be ready within a few weeks. Frank despised the word *few*. Typical vague expression used by management when they'd more important things to be thinking about. He knew it wasn't a priority. In the meantime, he would have to go on counting to ten and biting his lip.

"Ray, I'm home," Frank shouted as he banged the door behind him. No answer. He could hear the radio in the bathroom. Ray had obviously brought his copy of *The Irish Field* into the men's room for a quiet read! Best not disturb him.

Frank looked at the kitchen clock. Quarter past six. He'd barely three-quarters of an hour to get ready.

He set up the ironing-board and dragged the iron out from under the sink. No plug!

"Fuck it, that's all I need. Ray. Have you got a plug somewhere?"

Silence.

"For the bath?"

"No! For the iron!" Frank looked around the room uneasily. "Hang on. Where's my white shirt?" His face stiffened as he looked at the spin-dryer. "Ah, Ray. You promised to dry the clothes." He threw open the door and dragged everything out. All wet. All dark blue! He found his shirt. It was like something that a navy cadet would wear. "Raaaayyy!" Johnny Weismuller would have been proud of a roar like that.

"What?" came the tired response.

"Get your arse out here now!" Frank screamed.

"What?" The bathroom door creaked open. Ray toddled out in his bare feet, holding his trousers around his thighs.

"Jesus, a man could do serious damage to himself being interrupted like that." He pulled up his zip and buckled the belt. "Those iron vitamin tablets have brought my otherwise healthy temple of fitness to a grinding halt, Frank."

"What are you talking about?" Frank held the blue dyed shirt up to the light.

"Those vitamin things. The iron capsules. I can't go to the jacks with them. The place is on strike down there!"

"Good! I'm glad! Now what did you do to my good white shirt?" Frank roared.

Ray studied the shirt Frank was holding from a distance. "It must have got mixed up with me building overalls."

Frank focused his stare on Ray. "Get that shirt you're wearing off!"

"And what am I going to wear?" Ray looked as if someone had just run off with his pint.

"How about this!" Frank threw the patchy dark blue shirt at him.

"Ah come on Frank!" he moaned. "I'm going on a big date. I'm trying to make an impression."

"Well, if she's as short-sighted as I think she is, she probably won't even notice!"

Frank ran for the bathroom. "By the way, speaking of dates, there's a letter from *Blind Date* on the hall table for you." He brushed his teeth in a mad frenzy.

There was silence in the hall.

"Well?" Frank shouted. "What do they want?"

"Nothing. It must've been the wrong address." Ray pushed the envelope into his working boots which were sitting beside the door. "By the way, I fixed your answering machine," Ray shouted. "I got all the gunge off it."

"With what." Frank kept brushing.

"A toothbrush I found in there beside the sink. The green one. It did a grand job!"

There was a loud curse and a cough from the bathroom followed by string of foul language. Ray took the white shirt off and disappeared into his room.

Within five minutes, Frank was a transformed man. He struggled with the gold cuff-links while he listened to the messages on the machine.

. . . *Beep* . . . "Hi Carlos. It's Davina. I hope we're still on for tonight. Remember? Half eight at the Clover Tap. Bring loads of that property money of yours. Byeeeee . . . "

"Oh Jesus, no," he muttered out loud. Not the Clover Tap. Ray and Davina. That's all I need."

. . . *Beep* . . . "Hello Frank. It's your mother. I hate speaking into these machines. Good luck tonight. I hope you're getting plenty of sleep and eating well. Brian got a new car. There y'are, I always told you to apply for that job in the bank, but o'course you wouldn't listen to me." A short silence. "Hello, hello. I don't think this yoke is working at all. Frank, ring me if you can hear me. I hope you're getting Mass of a Sunday. Hello . . . " *Beep* . . .

. . . *Beep* . . . "Hello Frank, it's Nigel Bumpster from the brewery. It's ten past five on Friday evening. Just confirming that the Minister for Tourism will be able to make it tonight. Keep an eye out for him. Make sure he gets well looked after, will you? He's a very influential character when it comes to promoting the Irish side of the business. And I want to make sure that we get into the Bord Fáilte Pub Guide next year. See you later." Beep . . .

Frank fought with his bow tie while the messages were running. Then it dawned on him. *The Minister for Tourism!* Frank hadn't a clue what he looked like, never mind what his name was. He ran across the bedroom and went through the pockets of his jeans. He pulled out the list of invited guests and feverishly started studying it. Something he should have done earlier in the day.

"Oh, my God!" he muttered. It read like a *Who's Who* from that year's Academy Awards ceremony. The local President of the GAA . . . The Minister for

Tourism. The list went on and on. Keith Floyd . . .
Jimmy Saville . . . Ray Flynn!

"Ray Flynn!" Frank screamed at the top of his
voice.

"What now?" came the muffled reply from the
bedroom.

"How did *your* name get on to this invitation list?"

"What invitation list?"

Frank knew that he shouldn't have said anything.

"What are you talking about?" Ray stepped into the
landing in his underpants and socks. "What invitation
is this?" He smiled.

"Nothing, OK?"

Frank was in a heap. He grabbed his dinner jacket,
shoved the bow tie into a pocket and ran for the door.

"Frank?"

Frank spun around on his heels. "What?" he roared
exasperatedly.

"Where are you going dressed like that?" Ray
enquired.

"Where am *I* going? You've the cheek to ask me
where *I'm* going?"

"Well?" Ray waited for a reasonable answer.

"On a date," came the reply. "I'm *trying* to
impress!"

"We could make it a double date," Ray suggested.
"I have four tickets for that Irish fella, Brendan
O'Carroll. He's playing in the Town and Country."

"That scruffy bastard? You wouldn't get me within
an ass's roar of one of his gigs. Two chances!"

Frank opened the front door. He was about to step

out into the dark corridor when he noticed the envelope with the *Blind Date* logo on it sticking out of Ray's dirty boot. He turned to check that the bedroom door was closed and pulled out the letter.

Dear Ray,

Thank you for your enquiry about joining one of our male panels on next season's Blind Date. *Unfortunately, it appears from your application form, that you are too tall for the show's requirements. Nonetheless, you still sound like a smashing guy. One, I'm sure, who'd make lots of women's knees just turn to jelly. Good luck in future romantic endeavours and thanks for writing to* Blind Date. *A lorra lorra luv, Cilla.*

P.S. I hope you find that special woman who can beat you when it comes to drinking a pint in under three seconds!

Frank held his breath until he had stuffed the letter back into the boot. He jumped over the step and slammed the front door behind him. Half the street must have wondered what he was laughing at.

* * *

Jamie was late getting home. She had gone for a drink with the girls after work to celebrate her birthday. All they could talk about was Nikki and Liam Neeson, and their passionate embrace at the radio station that morning.

The house was cold and dark. She looked around at the uninviting spaces before turning on the lights. She'd half expected to find Tommy there. Maybe that's why she hadn't phoned the house. She'd hoped he was going to be standing there with a big bunch of flowers when she walked in. Maybe champagne. Even an apology would have been a good start. She just wanted to believe that it was all a bad dream. He annoyed her so much that, at times, she felt like killing him. Well, maybe not literally. But close enough. Then again, there was always something – that indescribable *thing* – that always made her end up loving him again. Even after the worst arguments. Explanations could have waited for another time. She wanted tonight to be special. God knows, she thought, it's been so long since we've had a nice night just to ourselves. And she was still mad about him. In a mad sort of way. But what was he ranting and raving about the other morning? Drugs. No, never. He might be crazy but he wasn't that stupid. Nikki was right. Perhaps he was tired. Long shifts at work mixed with late nights on the door at the club. A holiday would be nice. He probably wouldn't think so. Sure what would he do all day? Just the two of them. He'd miss the lads. Yeah, the lads. Tonight, though, Jamie was worried. Worried sick. Not so much for Tommy as for herself. That morning's argument had been different. There were things he wasn't saying. Explanations he wasn't giving. He was colder than usual. Even menacing. She shivered. Leave me alone, she thought to herself. Just leave me alone forever.

As she struggled to get her wet coat off, she studied the photograph of Nikki locked in a bear hug with Liam Neeson. She smiled and shook her head.

She was sorry she hadn't stayed with the girls. The evening was just beginning to get going when she'd had to leave. Leave for what? she asked herself as she looked around the dull room. She was a worse fool.

She lit the gas fire and switched on the television. She felt the radiator by the window. Cold. There wouldn't even be enough hot water for a bath. She placed the giant birthday card from the girls beside the telly and kicked off her high heels. She stretched out on the couch. The room heated up quickly. She lay back and propped up her head against two cushions. I'll have a rest here for twenty minutes, she thought. Then the water should be warm. Quarter to ten should be time enough for hitting the Clover Tap. Nikki would keep her a seat. Frances Black was on the television. She was playing live from the Ulster Hall in Belfast. Her voice was magic, every song a gem. Jamie closed her eyes. Why is life such a mess? she asked herself. It can't be all my fault.

Before she knew it, she was fast asleep.

Chapter Nine

Half-eight on the button. The juke-box had been stacked with most of the Elvis Presley catalogue. People milled up and down carrying things. Boxes. Stools. Balloons. Hats. Bottles. Coats.

Frank stood at the end of the bar. He washed pint glasses after he removed them from cardboard boxes and speedily stacked them upside down close to the beer taps. Tonight was a night for celebrating. Here he was, Frank McCabe from west Cork, running the trendiest Irish pub in one of the biggest cities in the world. He stuck out his chest. This was all his. You've done it, Frank, he thought to himself. You've arrived!

Just at that moment, so did a group of well-dressed strangers, each carrying an invitation card. Frank didn't recognise any of them. He had asked the lads behind the bar to tip him off when the English celebrities arrived. But what about the Minister for Tourism? That couldn't be him with the flashing tricolour dickie bow, could it?

No one had the remotest idea what he looked like and Frank had long departed the old sod when the new government was sworn in.

"Philip," he shouted to the barmen, "get those folks a drink over there."

"Right, Mr McCabe."

"And, Philip, collect their invitations so that I'll know who they are."

Philip gave Frank an odd look. "Right, Mr McCabe."

"And, Philip, call me Frank, for God's sake."

As Philip picked up a tray of champagne glasses, Frank could hear him mumbling. "Right so, 'Frank for God's sake'."

Five to nine. There was a nice crowd gathering by now, generating a warm friendly atmosphere. Like all landlords, he hated an empty pub. An old expression he'd once heard came to mind. It was like the Jumbo sitting idly on the ground at Dublin Airport, making no money.

He mingled with the crowd hoping to hear a few names.

"Frank," a familiar voice called from behind.

When he spun around, he was relieved to see a smiling Nigel Bumpster.

"Good evening, Mr Bumpster. Glad you could make it." They shook hands.

"Call me Nigel, please." He swiped a glass from a passing tray. "Oh, Frank, I'd like you to meet my partner at the brewery, Martin Tipple." Martin Tipple had a huge wart on his nose. Frank held out one hand while he put the other up to his own nose and squeezed it. Tipple automatically did the same.

"Nice of you to stick your nose in, Martin."

154

Realising what he'd just said, Frank backed away towards the bar. "Pleasure to meet you."

"Likewise, Frank."

All of a sudden, Frank's face froze in horror. "Oh God, he's here!" And it wasn't the Minister for Tourism.

"Your eyes are like spanners. When I look into them, my nuts tighten!" There was a huge roar of hysterical laughter from the end of the bar where a small group was rapidly growing into an unpredictable thirsty mob. Ray Flynn! Frank pretended he didn't hear. He shook hands and mumbled half names.

"Sorry for interrupting, Frank," Mr Bumpster muttered quietly. "Who is that fat, red-haired man at the end of the counter?"

Frank pretended not to see him. "Who?"

"The shaggy man with the funny tie and jacket?" he continued.

Frank had to think fast. "Oh, him!" he shouted. "He's one of the top up-and-coming comedians on the pub circuit. I'm telling you, in huge demand."

"Well, I sincerely hope you're not thinking of employing him?" Mr Bumpster stared at Frank.

"Ha ha, not at all," Frank laughed nervously. "Sure we couldn't afford him! Could you both excuse me for a minute? Just a quick check to make sure everything's OK." Frank manoeuvred his way through the crowd, smiling and gesturing. He had an embarrassing problem on his hands, if it wasn't nipped in the bud quickly. Had Ray found out that he was the new boss, he wondered. He called Philip over.

"Everything OK, Frank?"

"A slight problem, Philip." Frank tried to give the impression that everything was under control. "Don't look around just yet. But do you see the big bloke in the corner with the red hair?" Frank chanced a quick glance over his shoulder. "The fat bloke with the rake of pints in front of him?"

Philip took a peep over Frank's left shoulder.

"The bloke with the sick-looking tie?" he asked in his strong Dublin accent.

"That's him," Frank replied as if taking part in an identity parade. "He's not to get any more drink unless I say so. Is that clear?" He looked sternly at Philip.

"But he told me that he was your adopted brother and that you said it was all right for him to run a slate!"

"Did he now." Frank looked over at Ray. "You just do as I say."

"No problem, Frank. Everything else OK?"

"Brilliant by the looks of things. I'll be up with the band if you need me." Frank headed off in the direction of the stage. He couldn't figure out what was delaying the music.

"Excuse me, I'm Ivan Y . . . "

Frank interrupted a smart, young-looking blond-haired man who was trying to introduce himself. "Sorry sham, I'm in a bit of a rush," Frank replied rather abruptly. "Problem with the fucking music," he muttered to the stranger who seemed astonished by Frank's choice of words. "These bands are all the same. Think they're U2. Half of them can't sing to save their lives." He left the man standing with his hand outstretched and kept walking.

"Jesus, who's your man in the monkey suit?" came a frothy roar from the corner. Frank knew the voice. He was determined that Ray wasn't going to wind him up. "Hey, Frank, I hear you're the new manager." Ray finished off his pint and belched loudly. "What happened? No one else turn up for the interview?" He picked up another waiting pint and demolished half of it. "The Guinness is a bit flat, but the barmaids make up for it!" There was a huge burst of laughter. Frank tried to ignore it.

"What's the problem, lads?" Frank asked, addressing the worried singer who was sitting idly on a stack of equipment.

"We can't find the transformer," one of the others replied as he scurried around on his hands and knees looking for the missing component.

"And what does that do?" Frank asked.

"It equates the power of the amplification system with the power supply that the pub works off," the hairy musician replied in a pseudo-yuppie accent.

"Jesus, I'll take your word for it. Would I have one behind the bar"?

"I doubt it," replied the singer.

Frank was worried. "What would it look like?"

"It's a small black box . . . like a mobile phone," the drummer said.

"And what if you can't find it?" Frank was getting irritated.

"Well, we could take a chance and plug in to the power. But if it's the wrong current, we'll all end up in the dark for the night!" The singer lit the cigarette which dangled from his mouth and inhaled deeply. Frank watched him as he closed his eyes and threw his head back. He held his breath for what seemed like forever. Then out came the smoke accompanied by a loud groan. The singer squatted down on the stage. He started to hum to himself.

"Jesus, you should give up smoking," Frank remarked as he watched the singer take another drag of the cigarette.

"Look man, this isn't just smoking. This is inner peace. The correlation of common sense and absurdity. The harmony of one's chakras. A surrender to one's ultimate energy source. The great being that all of us strive to be like."

Frank looked at the other members of the band. "What's wrong with him?"

"He's just after getting through a fairly bad nervous breakdown, mate. Doctors told him to avoid stress. I don't think he's fully recovered." The drummer put his hands into his pockets and sighed. "I don't think he's going to sing much tonight."

"What's with that cigarette?" Frank argued.

"Cigarette?" the drummer sniggered. "Pure Morocco cannabis, more like it!"

"I don't believe this," Frank grunted as he pulled at his hair.

The singer eased himself on to his feet and held out his hand to Frank. "Hi," he gestured in a funny voice. "I'm Bob Dylan and you are . . . ?"

"Get him out of here," Frank shouted to the drummer. He walked off in the direction of the bar and looked at his watch. Almost ten to eleven and still no music. Just as well they had an extension till one . . . or was it half twelve?

"What's the problem, Frank?" It was one of the brewery heads.

"Well, Mr Tipple," Frank replied cautiously, "there seems to be a problem with the band's gear. Nothing to worry about, though. We should be up and running shortly." Mr Tipple returned to his colleagues. Frank headed for the bar.

"Oh, Frank." It was Philip. "We've run out of Smithwicks!" He waited for an answer.

"Jesus, don't do this to me! How could we have run out? Sure, I got an extra three kegs on Wednesday." Frank said.

"Pint of Smithwicks, Mr Manager!" came the order loudly.

"Sorry, we're out of Smithwicks." Frank spun around to see a well-oiled Ray Flynn leaning against the bar with the smile that always gave it away.

"Actually, sir," Frank continued sarcastically, "there probably would have been enough for everyone in the audience if you hadn't drunk it all yourself."

Ray roared laughing. "Actually, *sir*, I'm on the Guinness. The ould ale keeps me up all night pissing like a leaky tap. Like a well-watered flowerpot sitting in the sink. Sure, you'd need a garden hose and a jubilee clip to drink that stuff safely."

"How did you manage to get an invitation?" Frank asked, his nose only inches from Ray's.

"Ah now, Frank ol' pal, there's no need for that

tone of voice, *please*." Ray leaned over and held Frank's shoulder. "More to the point, budso, how the fuck did you convince them to give *you* the job?"

"Excuse me?" blurted Frank. "I'll have you know I've work in some top-class pubs. Pubs that you'd *never* see the insides of in a lifetime!"

"Excuse me?"

Frank and Ray stopped arguing and stared at the blond-haired man who had approached Frank earlier. "Sorry to interrupt but I'm Ivan Young, Min . . . "

"Excuse me, but I've already told you," Frank replied, cutting the small man short, "I'm busy at the moment!"

"Yeah, pal, don't interrupt my partner when he's talking business." Ray stared at the man. "Look at the state of him. I hope you've ID on you if you're looking for a drink. Does your mammy know where y'are this hour of the night?"

"I beg your pardon?" the man enquired.

"Here, hold this." Ray handed him an empty glass. He turned his back to the man and looked at Frank who gave him the killer stare that Ray had always taken to mean serious business. Out of the corner of his eye, Frank could see his brewery bosses approaching the bar.

"Ray, if I'm left looking like a bloody eejit tonight, I'm going to drag you down with me. And so help me God, there won't be a safe place on this earth for you to hide if this night is not the success I want it to be! Am I making myself clear?" Frank grasped the end of Ray's rainbow-coloured tie.

"Jesus, Frank," Ray pleaded. "Easy boy, just tell me what's to be done and we'll get on with it."

Frank let go of the tie. "I need two kegs of Smithwicks, *now*!" he said.

"Where am I going to get two kegs of Smithwicks at eleven o'clock of a Friday night?" implored Ray.

"That's your problem!" Frank cut him short. "I also need a transformer for the band's gear. Preferably before they all get stoned. We don't have much time, Ray."

"What's a transphoner, Frank?" Ray asked.

"A *transformer*," Frank shouted.

"Well, what's a transformer? And more to the point, where am I going to get one this late?" Ray asked.

"I don't know, Ray. Just get one."

"Right, I'll try that twenty-four-hour chemist up the street."

Frank strolled back over to the brewery heads and their distinguished guests and turned back around. "And, for God's sake, tell your girlfriend to cover up a bit. I'd hate to hear that she caught pneumonia in my pub."

Ray was left staring up at the Cork team adorning the space over the cash register. He glanced over at Davina. She was drinking her seventh yard-glass of lager, dressed in a tiny basque and hot pants, her left boob precariously hanging out. Those outfits were not meant for figures like Davina's, Ray thought. Still, she seemed to be enjoying herself this evening. Ray looked at his watch. It was five past eleven.

He left the pub by the side door. Two strangers in a red Golf GTi called him over to the car.

"Any chance of getting in, mate?" one of them enquired.

"Not a hope, lads," Ray replied. "Invitation only. Anyway, it's so stuffed, there'd be more room in a pair of nun's knickers." He continued to walk briskly. The car started to move alongside.

"New management, is it?" the man in the passenger seat asked.

"Yeah," shouted Ray. "Best Irish pub in London. Youse should drop in some night. Great crack." Ray's pace quickened. He had no time for the yob type. Anyway, he was on a mission.

"Who should we ask for?" the driver enquired as Ray turned and walked up Bromley Road.

"Ask for me, Ray Flynn!" Ray laughed. "I'm the new manager. I'm always there!" Ray smiled to himself. *The new manager.* Sounded good. He didn't notice the two men make a note of his name. He had too much on his mind to be worrying about trivialities tonight. Time was money. And this was a waste of valuable drinking time. He was one of the team now, and he felt important. Suddenly, he stopped.

"Here, you lads wouldn't have such a thing as a transphoner, would youse?"

They looked at each other. "Yeah, we might have. But we need it for the car engine," replied the small man in the passenger seat.

"Not if you're both inside drinking pints, youse don't!" Ray winked at the men and climbed into the back seat.

Jamie fell off the couch and immediately woke up. She didn't know where she was. She looked at her watch. Twenty past eleven.

"Shit!" she shouted. "Tommy, it's half eleven! Why didn't you wake me?" She waited for an answer. The house was empty. She ran upstairs into the bedroom to see if he had fallen asleep. No one there. She had slept through her twenty-seventh birthday. Where the hell was he? Then she remembered she'd thrown him out. She sat down for a moment. She picked up the phone and rang Nikki. No answer. Jamie was sure that she had gone down to the Clover Tap for the opening night. She glanced at her watch again and ran into the bathroom. Within seconds she was out of her clothes and into the shower. Nikki had told her that there was a bar extension until one. She could be there by twelve. Then they could go on to a club afterwards. That's what she'd do.

* * *

Frank looked up at the clock. Ten to twelve. What the hell is keeping him? he kept asking himself.

He stayed on the move, making sure everyone had enough to eat and, more importantly, drink. No one seemed to notice that the juke-box had dried up. Just as well, he thought. Then he had an idea. He pushed his way through the crowd. He put in a fiver's worth of fifty-pence pieces and pressed a few keys. If one man could save the night, it was Elvis Presley! Hey presto, "Jailhouse Rock". "Well, since my baby left me . . . " There was a loud cheer. Couples and small groups here and there started to dance and sing. Frank sang along as he scoured the pub for Ray.

Nikki Coffey was coming back from the ladies' room when she noticed Tommy Barrett standing near the door with another bloke. She headed in their direction.

"Is Jamie here, Tommy?" she shouted over all the noise. Tommy looked around.

"I don't know," he replied casually before resuming his conversation with his colleague.

"Jesus, I would've thought the least you could do would be to apologise to her. You treat her like shit. Maybe now, she's giving you a taste of your own medicine."

"What do you mean by that?" Tommy asked.

"Well, she threw you out, didn't she? About fucking time, if you want my opinion."

"Yeah, well, I don't want your opinion, do I?"

"Oh yeah? That's wasn't the way it seemed when you gave me a lift home a couple of weeks ago, was it?" Nikki moved closer to Tommy. He avoided her stare. "You couldn't keep your hands off me in the car that night. What was it you wanted? To strip off and and do it on Hampstead Heath?"

"Well, you didn't seemed to object to going down on me, did you?"

Some of Nikki's friends were standing close by. Their conversation had stopped now and they listened to the heated arguement, visibly shocked.

"You pulled me down on top of you, you dirty bastard! You nearly suffocated me." Nikki was on the verge of tears.

"I bet you'd never seen anything like it in your life," Tommy bragged.

"Don't kid yourself. I was afraid I might choke on a chicken bone."

"Well, that's our little secret, isn't it, Nikki? No need for Jamie to know if you just behave yourself and be a good girl." Tommy smiled and took a sip from his drink.

"You wouldn't dare, Tommy Barrett."

"Want to bet? How would she react if she heard that you took advantage of her drunk boyfriend when he asked you to help him get home to the woman he loved?"

Nikki took a deep breath to hold back the tears. He was winning. Just like he always did.

"You're just a horny little bitch who likes using people, Nikki. At least we've got something nice in common. Now would you like a lift home or are you waiting for your best friend to arrive?"

"Jesus, you're some bastard!" Nikki backed into a table, toppling a glass as she walked away. "Jamie's better off without you."

"That sounds choice coming from you. How many more of her boyfriends have you screwed?"

Frank heard a woman's voice shouting, followed by the sound of a glass breaking. He looked across the pub and noticed two casually-dressed blokes standing near the main door which was locked, now that all the invited guests had arrived. He thought he recognised one of them, a tall, dark, good-looking guy. He beckoned to one of the bouncers.

"Everything all right, Mr McCabe?" the doorman asked.

"The two lads beside the door, Jack." Frank pointed discreetly. "Did you see their invitations?"

"One of them showed me a police badge, Mr McCabe, so I thought I should let them in," the bouncer replied.

"No problem, Jack, that's grand. See if they'd like a drink, will you?"

"Sure, Mr McCabe." Jack strolled to the door. "Would you like a drink, lads?" he asked in an intimidating sort of way. The two men looked too scared to say yes.

"Eh, no thanks, mate," they replied.

Jack looked the two men up and down. They were dwarfed by Jack's huge build. He sneered at them. Big was the only way to be, he'd always thought. They spoke quietly to each other and sipped their half-pints of shandy. One of them wore a pink shirt and had a pullover draped around his shoulders. Definitely not *real* men. "Chasing a bit of skirt?" he asked abruptly.

"Not at all," Tommy replied.

Jack looked at them suspiciously. "Been working late, lads?"

"I suppose you could say that," replied Tommy.

"Helping a few old ladies across the road?" he jibed.

"Sorry?"

Frank walked over to the door. "Evening, lads, can I help you?" he enquired politely.

"Just in for a late drink, mate," the small man replied casually.

"Jack tells me you're police officers." Frank waited for an answer. The two men looked at each other and quickly finished their drinks.

"Not at all!" the more familiar tall guy replied. Frank tried to get a good look at his face. He was convinced now that he'd seen him before.

"Ali was just showing one of the doormen his ID card. No one believes he's twenty-four. Isn't that right, Ali?"

"That's right, Tommy." The two men laughed unconvincingly.

Tommy! That's his name, Frank thought as he tightened his big eyebrows. He couldn't figure out why the name kept ringing a bell. "Well, it's invitation only tonight, lads, so I'll have to ask you both to leave," Frank cautioned.

"Don't worry, mate. We were just leaving," Tommy snapped.

"But you'll be very welcome to drop in any other night," Frank added. He certainly didn't want to get on the wrong side of the law. That's if they *were* policemen.

"Oh, you can be sure we will," replied the small man. "Nice place." They put their empty glasses down and left.

Frank still couldn't get a handle on the tall bloke's face. He knew it would come to him eventually. "Good night, lads."

The two men nodded at Frank and squeezed their way cautiously past big Jack.

"Goodnight, Penelope," Jack said jokingly as he opened the door.

As Jack closed the door behind them, Frank heard the sound of backfiring. He stepped out into the cold night air and saw a well-worn Transit, its back doors swinging open, pull into the lane at the side entrance to the pub. He asked one of the bouncers to close the door behind him and ran towards the van.

Ray had already disappeared in the side door. Frank recognised two of Ray's mates from Conlon Construction struggling with a full keg.

"How are you, Frank?" they grunted simultaneously.

Frank waved. "How are you, Dimmy? How are you, Bob? You've saved the night!" He glanced into the back of the van. Five kegs, an accordion and a keyboard. "Jesus Christ, where did you get this stuff?"

"Let's just say, we borrowed it!" one of the men whispered. They thumped each other hard and started to giggle like children. Frank knew better than to ask. He would leave that until tomorrow.

Ray had already set up one of the kegs behind the bar by the time Frank got back inside. From behind the bar, he took a quick scout around. Plenty of loud laughter. The juke-box was still blasting out Elvis. But where were Bumpster and Tipple?

Just then, Frank's eyes nearly popped out. For a moment, he thought he was having a horrible dream. Davina was sitting bolt upright on Mr Tipple's knee, urging him to down a yard of ale in one go. His tie was knotted around her forehead and his shirt was open down to his navel. The crowd stood around him and cheered him on wildly.

"Go on, you good thing," they roared. "You make enough of the piss. You should be used to drinking it!"

Mr Bumpster was deep in conversation with a couple of Davina's friends. He turned to Philip the barman and, in a slightly slurred tone, ordered a bottle of the best champagne.

"Dom Perignon, please, young man," he shouted as the barman walked back behind the counter. There was another cheer.

Frank took a deep breath and smiled. Maybe it wasn't such a disaster after all.

Just as Ray was about to head back to the gang, Frank put his hand on his shoulder.

"Where did you get the kegs?"

"I borrowed them from a pub down the road." Ray smiled. "You know the one where all the United supporters hang out?"

"The one you're barred from?" Frank continued.

"Just temporarily, Frank!" said Ray. "I happened to find a key for the back yard. But don't you worry, I'll leave them back tomorrow before he opens up . . . empty!"

Ray laughed heartily as if he had just repaid an old debt.

Chapter Ten

Jamie was at the entrance, pleading with one of the doormen. She stood on her toes and looked over the bouncer's shoulders.

"It's my birthday. I swear, my friend has my invitation," she argued. "She's inside. Nikki Coffey is her name. She's got long, brown curly hair. Get someone to call her and she'll show you!"

"Sorry, love." The burly doorman was adamant. "Strict instructions. No one gets in without an invite!"

"But *she* has my invitation with her!" Jamie shouted. The door slammed shut.

"Fuck you! It's true what they say. You are as thick as shite!" she shouted. "Nearly took my fucking fingers off." She rapped her knuckles on the door again.

She heard a muffled voice from inside. "Happy Birthday. Now, fuck off!"

The door stayed closed. She ran into the side lane and saw two men take an accordion and keyboard from the back of a van.

"Can I get in this way?" she pleaded.

"Sorry, love, we're just delivering," one of the lads replied. "Knock on the front door."

"But I'm having an asthma attack and my friend has my medicine!"

They closed the side door behind them.

"Jesus, what if I suffocate?" Jamie waited, clutching her bag. *"Bastards,"* she screamed at the top of her voice. *"It's my birthday,"* she roared. Her voice echoed across the quiet late-night sky.

The silence in the street was more deafening than the noise from the pub. Tears welled up in Jamie's eyes as she searched in her small bag for her cigarette lighter. She couldn't find it. Why hadn't she just stayed with the girls after work? she wondered. Some birthday. She headed into Bromley Road for the short walk home.

"Jamie," a voice called from behind. As she turned around, David Darling was running across the road.

"Bit late to be walking home on your own?" he gasped, out of breath.

"Yeah, well. If it wasn't for those dullards on the door, I could be inside enjoying meself!" She started to walk again. David walked alongside.

"Were you at the Clover Tap party?" he asked politely.

"No, I wasn't. Wait till I get Nikki Coffey. The bitch was supposed to leave my invitation at the door for me. She probably got pissed and forgot!"

"I was in there for a while. I left though. You can't move, it's so packed."

Jamie was curious. "How come you were in there?"

"You know me. I got an invite through the job."

"Oh yeah, how could I forget?"

"Listen, Jamie," David gently took her arm and they both stopped, "about the other morning."

"What about the other morning?" Jamie strode on. "You're just a rude bastard, David. A typical male chauvinist pig. Go on. Admit it. Your smug sense of superiority makes me puke."

David caught up with her. "No, listen. I just wanted to apologise for the things I said. I was under pressure."

Jamie sneered at him. "You know what your problem is, David. You have this hang-up about women. You're afraid that we might outsmart you, aren't you? You're hung up on this macho trip. Put them down and keep them down. Tie them to the washing machine. That's where they belong. Rearing babies and pushing supermarket trollies. Let them out to the hairdresser's once a week. That'll keep them happy. Ride them whenever you like and that'll keep you happy. A woman should be seen and not heard. Isn't that what you think, David? Well, let me tell you, David Darling. I've had all I can take from you." Jamie gestured at her chest. "Up to my tits. Maybe that's the life that your mother and my mother had. But it's certainly not my idea of a good time."

"I know, but I just wanted to say . . . "

"Just let me finish. You always have your say. And, if you don't mind my saying it, you do an awful lot of talking through your arse. What you said and did to me won't just go away with the word 'sorry'. And do you know why, David?" Jamie stopped.

"Why," David asked, sounding quite genuine.

"Because you don't mean it. That's why. You won't do it to me again. That's for sure. But I'll put money on it that you'll do it to some other poor unsuspecting woman who's taken in by all your name-dropping bullshit, when all you want to do is get into her knickers. Sure, people think I'm a bit bolshie. But, believe me, sometimes it pays off. And I meant what I said today, David. If you ever put your hands anywhere on me again, you'll be able to sing in the local boys' choir for the rest of your pathetic little life."

David swallowed loudly.

Silence.

Jamie started to walk on. "Goodnight," she muttered.

"Hang on, Jamie." David ran after her. "Do you mind if I walk you home? I'm heading this way anyway."

"I don't seem to have much choice, do I?" Jamie walked faster.

"Do you live near here?"

"Yeah. Down here on the left."

"I still think that you're crazy to be walking alone at this hour of the night."

"Really? Sure, they can't come any worse than you, David."

They both laughed.

"I never told you. My mother comes from Leitrim."

"Is that supposed to make me like you?" She smiled.

"Ah, come on, Jamie. There must be something

you like about me. Some teeny weeny little thing?" He danced around her playfully.

"Is that your brain that you're talking about?"

"Ha, ha. Good one. I must remember that line." He was serious again. "Well, then, you tell me. What *would* make you like me?"

Jamie thought mischievously. "A personality transplant?" She paused. "Or maybe if you emigrated to Australia."

He laughed like an alarm hooter. "Heh, heh, heh, heh. Oh, you're funny. Well, now that the ice is broken and we're friends again, would you like to have dinner with me some evening?"

"What?" Jamie shrieked.

"Eh, nothing serious. Maybe just a movie and a takeaway."

Jamie laughed more out of disbelief than anything else. "Are you for real? Have you been listening to what I just said? After what you did, you really think my heart misses a beat for you? Jesus, gimme a break!"

"Jamie, please. Listen to me." He linked her arm again. She didn't like that. "Maybe I've gone about this the wrong way."

"The wrong way? Jesus, this is like a bad dream. I'm going to wake up any second."

"Right, just allow me to explain quickly."

"It'd better be very quickly. This is my house and my boyfriend's asleep upstairs.

"Your boyfriend? You never told me about your boyfriend."

Jamie knew that nothing could be further from the

truth. The house looked exactly as it was. Empty.

"Well, boyfriend's a bit choice after the way's he's been carrying on. Bastard would be more suitable. He was meant to take me out for my birthday but he never bothered to come home. So maybe ex-boyfriend would be better." She had no intention of telling him the real reason behind the split. Fuel for his morning radio show, she thought.

"Your birthday? Why didn't you tell me?"

"Why should I tell you? Sure, you'd probably have told half of bloody London this morning. Leave them thinking that I'm just another one of the notches on your bedpost. And I can do without that stigma, thank you very fucking much!" She realised then that she should have kept her mouth shut.

"Listen, it's still not too late to catch a club in the West End. Come on, I'll take you to Tramps. We'll have a bottle of wine and a dance. What would you say?"

She looked at him. David Darling and Tramps. They go together, she thought.

"No, thanks." How was she going to get rid of this prat? "I'm tired and I've got to be up early. Thanks anyway." She smiled.

As she turned to walk away, David took a single red rose out of his waistcoat pocket. "This is for you. I think it says all I'd like to say but can't at the moment. Please accept it from my heart."

Jamie looked at the rose. And then at David. She didn't know whether to collapse or vomit. Or both. "Jesus, I'm weak," she whispered.

"Sorry?" David's eyes opened wide.

"Eh, I just said it's been some week with all that's happened, like." She took the rose.

"Jamie, I'm crazy about you."

"What?"

"Yes. I know it's difficult for you to take it all in after the way I've carried on."

"Jeesus!" What was that she just said, she wondered. "Eh, I mean, yeah. It's lovely. I have to go."

"Don't go just yet. Maybe you could make us a quick cup of coffee."

"No way," she shouted. "I mean, I can't."

He stepped forward to kiss her. She could see by the way he was swaying on the footpath that he was very drunk. In fact, transmogrified would be more like it!

"Here, give us a little kiss." He was beginning to slur his speech. "Just a peck on the cheek."

She leaned over and kissed him on the cheek. It was a mistake. He swung around and planted a big slobbery kiss on her lips. She tried to pull away but found herself pinned against the wall. He put his arms around her shoulders and pulled her tighter.

"Jamie, I love you," he stuttered. "Come on, let's make a night of it."

She gathered up all her strength and pushed him away. "Go home, David. You're pissed."

Jamie quickly walked up the garden path. She stood at the door and searched for her keys. It was a good thing Tommy wasn't home. He'd probably have ended up bursting David. He hated him on the radio. He always thought he was a prize prat.

176

David went on shouting from the garden gate.

"Make us a coffee, Jamie. Please. I love you. Will you let me stay with you tonight? Even just on the couch."

She tried to ignore the noise as she searched for the right key.

"I'll stay here all night till you tell me you love me."

Oh Jesus, no, she thought. She turned the key in the door and stepped inside quickly. *Bang*. Shit, she thought. She switched on a light. This'll wake the neighbours. She peeped out from behind the sitting-room curtain. David was singing like a banshee. His version of *Crazy* would have made poor Patsy Cline turn in her grave. Jamie went into the bedroom and switched on the bedside lamp. The racket on the street was getting louder. She could hear dogs barking up the road. She opened the small bedroom window and stuck her head out.

"David. Fuck off or I'll call the cops. Do you hear me?"

The swaying figure in the middle of the road tried to focus on the upstairs window.

"Jamie, will you let me in? I'm not leaving till you let me in for the night. Let's make love beneath the stars. I don't want to leave you. Please." Next thing she knew, he was pretending to play requests on the radio for her.

"Yes indeed, this next one goes out for the gorgeous Jamie Carroll. From the love of your life, David Darling."

"David," Jamie shouted in a whispering voice,

"people know who you are. Will you shut up before they see you?"

"I don't care who knows me, Jamie. I only want you to know me. To love me. Please."

Best thing to do is turn out the light and see if he gets fed up and goes away, Jamie thought. She undressed and got into her baggy baseball shirt. She switched out the light and climbed into bed. David was now waltzing on the street below. His shadow danced on the ceiling above her. He'd started into a medley of songs by The Carpenters.

"Jamie, *We've only just beguuun to live,*" he sang from the street.

She pulled the duvet over her head and fell into an exhausted sleep.

* * *

The party was still in full swing at twenty to three.

Frank had to call a taxi for Mr Tipple who wasn't feeling too well. Davina offered to take him home but Ray objected. He needed her by his side, he said, while he entertained his guests. Right now, he was standing in the corner with an inflated condom over his head, drinking a pint. The crowd was chanting, "5, 4, 3, 2, 1." There was a huge roar as Ray put down his empty glass.

Dimmy played the accordion in the background tapping his feet and shaking his head while his body weaved and swayed like a sick man having a convulsion. There was a huge sigh of relief from the crowd when he finally finished the eighth verse of "My

178

Beautiful Ballinalee" and announced that he was too tired to go on. He pulled the microphone over to him for an announcement.

"One, two . . . ladies and gentlemen," he paused, "and Davina!" There was a big cheer. "On behalf of Frank McCabe and all his wonderful staff here at the Clover Tap, we hope you're all enjoying the hospitality tonight." Everyone roared encouragement at Dimmy's professor-like grasp of the English language. "I'd like to call on a good friend now for a few numbers. That's if we can tear him away from the love of his life!" Another big roar. "Will youse welcome please, Mr Ray Flynn!" Thunderous applause.

Ray got stuck into the old reliable favourites. "The Fields of Athenry", "The Oul' Triangle", "The Town I Loved So Well". He brought the house down.

The evening came to a close with a request for Frank to sing "Danny Boy", as only Elvis could have sung it. He took his guitar and shyly headed back up to the side of the stage amid loud applause and whistling.

"Excuse me, Mr McCabe," came a voice from behind.

Frank swung around.

"I'm Ivor Young, the Min . . . "

Frank interrupted. "Sorry budso, can you not just enjoy yourself like everyone else? I'm just going to do a couple of numbers. I'll talk to you in a moment."

There wasn't a dry eye in the house when he had finished. What could follow that? He thanked them for coming and invited them all back the following night. Everyone cheered as he lauched into the Irish national anthem. That was the only time he'd ever seen Ray Flynn in tears.

The crowd dispersed quickly. Frank looked around and decided to leave the cleaning up until later that morning.

"Frank, give us a pint!" He'd recognise Ray's voice anywhere. "I'm dying o' the thirst!"

Mr Bumpster came over to Frank. He adjusted his overcoat and held out his hand.

"Well done, Frank. A brilliant night. Say thank you to everyone for me, will you?" He buttoned up the coat. "Pass on my special thanks to your comedian friend. What's his name?"

"Ray," Frank replied as he looked around for the character. There he was in the corner with Davina, having his photograph taken for *The Leinster Leader*. Frank smiled.

"Oh, by the way, before I go," Mr Bumpster continued. "I take it you've met Ivan Young?" The small, blond man who had tried to introduce himself to Frank all night was standing there. "Ivan, this is Frank McCabe."

Frank laughed. "Sure, Jesus, aren't you the man who followed me around all night. How are you? What can I do for you?"

Smiling hesitantly, the blond-haired man stretched out his hand. "At long last we meet. I'm Ivan Young, Minister for Tourism!"

Frank felt weak.

Chapter Eleven

Jamie woke up with an awful shudder.

Her mother used to say that that was someone walking across your grave. Jamie had never understood what she was talking about. Her head twitched. She leaned over and grabbed the small alarm clock on the bedside table. Ten past five. She lay back and stared at the ceiling. It was still dark. Her mind raced over all that had happened that night. The Clover Tap. David Darling losing his marbles. Did he get home safely or was he arrested? She shook her head and closed her eyes. Getting back to sleep wasn't going to be easy. She'd had a tough week. She tried to relax, to forget.

She remembered what a health expert, who came to the radio station, had told her. Lie on the flat of your back, hands by your side and feet barely apart. Then tense each limb and each set of muscles starting with your toes and moving up. Each time, release the tension and move on to another limb.

Just as she began to tense her hands and wrists, she heard a sound outside. She popped her head forward just in time to hear the garden gate open and close. For a split second, she wondered if David had come back. No. He would have lost it hours ago at the rate he was going, she thought.

Tommy! Could he have come back? There was a quiet rap on the front door.

"Coming," she shouted. She didn't want him to start shouting out her name at that hour. There'd been quite enough of that. Her mind was racing again. What excuse was he going to try this time? She decided that the best course of action was to say absolutely nothing. Let him stew on it! Another louder rap on the front door. Something hard on the window. He'd better not break it, she thought.

"*I'm coming!*" she shouted anxiously. She eased her way down the dark stairs.

Another loud bang on the front door.

"Jesus, are you deaf as well as drunk?" She pulled back the door chain and turned the lock, ready to let him have an earful. "Do you know what time of . . . " Her eyes opened wide.

A black figure lunged forward at her. A hand grabbed her by the cheeks and painfully forced them together. An arm pushed her backwards. Almost off her feet. Her eyes bulged. Then the head came through the door. It was hooded – a balaclava. All she could see were two huge eyes. They stared at her. They wanted to kill her. She tried to breathe, but couldn't. Steam came off his hot breath through a small slanted hole in his black hood. His breathing was deep and unsteady. He trembled all over. A huge knife shone in the light from the street as he placed it perilously close to her throat.

"Don't!" was all he said. She could feel the power in his grip. He kicked the front door closed with a flick of his foot. He held her head in such a way that she could only see the tip of the knife and the top of his balaclava.

"You're going to do exactly as I tell you. Is that clear?" He jolted her jaw. She could smell the leather glove which covered the lower part of her face. Jamie nodded. She was finding it harder and harder to breathe through her mouth. Tears began to stream down her face. She shivered.

They stood there. Motionless. Her legs had given way. His evil grip was what was keeping her up now. Could it be David? Maybe someone who'd followed her home from the pub that night? Maybe one of these weirdos who hung around the radio station.

"Anyone else in the house?" he grunted in a whisper. It couldn't be his real voice. It was too harsh and strained.

Jamie shook her head.

"Good!" He moved the knife up to her eyebrows. She could clearly see the serrated edge. It was as sharp as a saw. Jamie swallowed hard.

"You do exactly what you're told and you stay alive. Clear?"

Jamie nodded again.

"Turn around." He released his hold on her jaw and replaced it with the edge of the knife. He quickly spun her around. Jamie lost her balance and fell against the knife. He grabbed her hard by the back of her hair. Jamie squealed with the pain.

"What did I say?" He put his hand around her mouth from behind. "Another move like that and I'll kill you!"

Her heart was beating like a kettledrum. She sobbed silently to herself as she stared at the ceiling.

"Now, upstairs." The two of them staggered awkwardly up the fifteen steps to the small landing. He kept a tight grip on her face. The knife was never more than an inch from her throat. Into the dark bedroom.

"Lie on the bed. I'll kill you if you try to scream."

She moved away from his grip, not daring to look around. She passed the ghettoblaster on the dresser. Her mind raced. She could throw it through the window. It might alert the neighbours. On the other hand, she could be dead by the time it smashed into the driveway.

"Take off your clothes."

"Please don't," she stuttered. She put out her hand to feel the side of the bed. She was still afraid to look around.

"Take off your clothes," he repeated. Sternly this time.

Jamie could hear him fumbling with his own clothes. Maybe he'd left the knife down. Would he take the hood off? What if she screamed?

She sat on the side of the bed. Her hands were shaking violently as she opened the knot at the front of her dressing-gown. She bowed her head. She felt the shoulders of the gown slip slowly down her back. Her teeth chattered as she waited for his next command.

He dropped his heavy leather jacket on the ground and walked over to the window. He opened the curtains and looked up and down the street. He closed them quickly.

Jamie thought she would throw up.

The hooded man quickly walked over to the bed and grabbed Jamie by the jaw again. He placed the knife on the bedside table.

"You're sure there's no one else here?" he grunted. His breathing was deeper now. His eyes pierced her skin. They were like something out of a horror film. Dark and dead. They had no life. Yet they wanted to eat her.

Jamie tried to nod her head. "My boyfriend is coming now," she stuttered.

"Is he?" the monster casually replied. He grabbed the top of her baseball shirt and picked up the knife again. She felt its sharp teeth flick through the neckline of the garment. With one horrible yank, he tore it to shreds revealing her bare breasts and pants.

Jamie closed her eyes and held her head back. She was crying and shaking.

"Shut up, I said." A jangling noise. He grabbed her wrists forcefully with one hand and pushed them back, hard, over her head. She gasped and squealed as handcuffs cut into her flesh. He secured them to the top of the metal bed frame. She was helpless now.

She felt his freezing cold hand on her breasts. It felt as if he was wearing some sort of nylon glove. Then it moved down her body. He pulled at her pants. She felt the cold tip of the knife. She heard them tearing. Then they were gone.

"Please. No," she was begging him each time she could catch her breath and hold back her tears.

185

He wasn't listening.

She felt his hand between her legs. Instinctively, she squeezed her knees and thighs together.

"Relax!" came the order.

But she couldn't relax. She wanted her mother. Her sister. Nikki. Her father would murder him.

He forced her legs apart. She could feel his fingers feeling her. Her sobbing breath almost made her choke. She could hear him pulling his trousers down. He was flustering. He pushed them down to his ankles. Then he pulled her knees apart and moved in between her legs.

"Easy now," he urged, almost sympathetically. He entered her.

Her face contorted with the sudden, horrible pain. She wanted to put her hand up to her mouth. Not me, she thought.

He rocked up and down as he held her shoulders hard. He never once made a sound. Just stared at her all the time.

She tried to remove her mind from what was happening. It'll be over in a minute, she kept telling herself. She looked up at his dark outline above her. It was too dark to see anything clearly. Too dark to see anything but his bulging eyes. Those mean eyes. Those evil eyes. They were saying something to her. *I hate you.* She stared closely into them. She knew them! She looked away quickly and bit hard on her lip. It started to bleed.

Seconds later, he arched his back and gave one last push. He groaned through his clenched teeth. Jamie cried out loud from the agonising pain. Her attacker stood up from the bed. He wiped himself with her baseball shirt and pulled up his trousers.

Jamie lay on the bed. The duvet was on the ground. She needed to keep her eyes open. He might still kill her. After all, he'd just raped her. Raped. Her. She never thought it could happen. *Not* to her.

She found it difficult to keep her eyes open. Her eyelids were heavy and swollen from crying. But they were getting used to the dark. She could see a lot more now. Suddenly, she was cold. Naked.

He uncuffed her hands.

She covered her genitals with her hand. She held her left arm across her breasts. She could feel a large bruise where he'd bitten her. Tears began to stream down into her ears. Down on to the pillow.

Her rapist yawned as he pulled on his leather jacket. He looked at her and picked up the knife. She froze. He tucked the knife inside the jacket. She watched him through squinted watery eyes. He was about to leave when he turned. He walked back over to the bed.

"No, *please*," she begged. She pulled her knees up closer to her head.

"Happy Birthday!" He pulled a clenched fist out of his leather pocket. She noticed his watch. The blow caught her below the left eye. Then there was no pain.

* * *

She didn't leave the house that day. She had to get out

of bed as soon as she woke. The rotten smell of her intruder seemed to be everywhere. On the pillows. The duvet. As she eased herself gently on to her feet, she glimpsed at the clock. It was only then that she realised how sore her left eye was. She could barely see.

It was five to ten. She could hear the bell of the local church ringing for ten Mass. Every muscle and bone in her body ached. She ran her hand through her matted hair. He had pulled it so hard, some of it had almost come away at the roots. She turned towards her reflection in the full length mirror. Tears appeared from nowhere. Lots of them. Jamie put her hands up under her throbbing chin. Around her swollen neck. She was able to feel the marks of his coarse leather gloves. It was as if she'd had a large rope tied around her neck. She trembled as she cried out loud. Then, after a minute, maybe five minutes, she took a deep breath and forced herself to stop. She opened her eyes as wide as she could and slowly looked at her naked body in the mirror. It was marked and scratched. Her lip and wrists were badly cut and bloody. Bruised where he had held her so forcefully. The blood had dried on the inside of her legs. She looked over at the bedclothes. Small patches of blood here and there. He must have cut her with the knife when he grabbed her pants.

She staggered into the bathroom and, lunging across the bath, turned the taps quickly until there was a thunderous flow of water. Steam quickly filled the room. She picked up the hard nailbrush and started to scrub her body. Her arms. Her neck. Her legs. Anywhere that he might have touched her. Scratched her. Bitten her. She took long gasping breaths in between the cries. The brush fell out of her hand. She grabbed the bottle of bath salts and threw a handful into the hot water. Then she threw the lot in and turned off the water. Stepping into the bath slowly, she could tell the water was too hot. Yet, there was no real burning pain. She sat down and slowly lay back until her head was resting on a sponge. Jamie closed her eyes. She didn't want to think about it for a while. She flinched as a quick muscular spasm ran through her body. Then another one. All she'd seen was the black hood. It was too dark to see anything else. She could still smell the stale alcohol from his heavy breath. She never felt him ejaculate. But she knew that he had. The smell was terrible. Questions flooded her mind.

Why did he rape her?

Who was he?

Did she know him?

Was she just a random victim or had he stalked her for a while?

Was it something she had done to cause the attack?

Did men find her cheap and easy?

Was she a slut?

There was a noise at the front door. Jamie opened her eyes quickly and leapt up. Water sloshed out over the side of the bath. Was he coming back? No! He wouldn't. Would he? Where's the towel? The water felt a lot colder. She waited and listened for a moment. Silence again.

She stood up and eased her legs over the side of the tub. She listened at the door and opened it just enough to peep out on to the small landing and down the stairs to the door. The local freesheet was sticking through the letterbox. She breathed a sigh of relief. Then she noticed it. Lying on the carpet, halfway down the stairs. The knife.

Jamie crept slowly down the steps to where the weapon lay. She looked at it, almost afraid to touch it. One of the things she'd often heard Tommy say after incidents involving knives and guns was never to touch items of evidence with your bare hands. She ran back to the hot press and found a small soft handtowel. Back at the spot, she covered her hand with the towel and carefully picked up the knife by the blade. She wrapped it gently and carried it at arm's length back to her room. She placed it in the drawer of the small dresser on her side of the bed. Her hands shook as she closed the drawer. It was a cold morning. Yet, she didn't feel cold despite the shivering attacks she'd been getting. As she put on her dressing-gown, she glanced at the clock. It was quarter past twelve. She'd been asleep in the bath for over two hours. So what. She sat into her favourite wicker chair and curled up.

Suddenly, the bedside radio alarm clock went off. Music filled the room. Jamie sat motionless. Then the voice of David Darling.

"Yes, there you go, that's the highest climber on the City Radio top forty chart this weekend jumping sixteen places from 29 to 13 for Irish hearthrobs, Boyzone."

Jamie's hand came down hard on the *off* switch. She started to cry quietly. She could feel the pain and anger well up inside her, as she placed her hand hard against her mouth and cried. She cried for over an hour. Then she slept.

During the afternoon, Jamie drifted in and out of an uneasy sleep. Her mind bombarded with the weirdest dreams and memories.

She dreamt that she'd married Derek Jones and they left the church in his vegetable van. As she looked back at the crowd standing outside the church, her mother and father and sister and brothers were waving at her. She could see a tall stranger standing at the back of the small crowd. He wore a balaclava and a leather jacket. He was waving a knife at her.

She lurched forward with the fright and almost felt off the wicker chair. The phone was ringing. Jamie sat still for a moment and found her bearings.

She'd been raped. That's right, she thought as she gently ran her hand around the front of her neck. The feeling of revulsion was nauseating. She felt she'd nothing special left. No more dignity. Her privateness had been stripped away like an unhealed scab. No one could have prepared her for anything like this. She'd heard about other women being raped. But never, in her worst fears, could she have imagined it would be like this. She ached. The pain was like severe hunger. But worse. How long more? Why did she let him do it? She should have put up a struggle. Maybe he would have stabbed her. Then he wouldn't have raped her. She wished he *had* knifed her now. At least she'd be dead. She wouldn't be left with this nauseating, stifling isolation. And anger. More anger than she'd ever felt in her life. She wanted to find a knife like *his*. And then find *him*. Then she'd cut him up into tiny pieces and flush them down the toilet. She felt dirty. Filthy. She shuddered. Had she taken a bath? Why couldn't she remember? Yes. She could smell the bath salts. But she still felt unclean. Maybe that was her mother on the phone. She needed her mother. She didn't want to talk to her. She just wanted to hear her voice. Then everything would be all right for a while.

She moved towards the bedroom door. The phone stopped. She sat back into the chair again and looked at the clock. She was barely able to focus her eyes. Her throat felt red raw.

The phone started to ring again. She stood up and straightened her dressing-gown. Holding on to the bannisters tightly, she edged her way down the stairs. It dawned on her that *he* might be phoning her. She'd often heard it said that rapists pursue their victims afterwards. No one knew why. They just did. She looked at the phone before touching it. It kept ringing. She lifted the receiver slowly.

"Hello," she said warily. A familiar voice twittered away on the other end of the phone.

"Could I speak to Jamie, please?"

"This is Jamie speaking."

"Jesus, I didn't recognise your voice." There was an uncertain pause on the other end. "Jamie, it's Nikki. Is that *you*? Listen, where were you last night? It was brilliant." Another pause. *"Jamie?"*

"Yeah?" She sniffed and put her hand up to touch her swollen eye.

"Jesus, are you sick? You sound awful. No, let me guess. You're still in bed with a hangover. 'Cos Tommy went home last night and took you somewhere posh for a nice meal and loads of drink. An' he apologised. An' the two of youse have been bonking all night!" Nikki gave her smutty laugh. "Go on, you bitch. I know what you're like."

"Nikki," Jamie said slowly.

"Listen, you missed a great night in the Clover Tap. We got chatting to these blokes from Belfast. And one of them asked me out."

"Nikki," Jamie repeated.

"He's gorgeous. And runs his own business. He drove me home in his Merc. Wait till I tell you . . . "

"Nikki! I've been raped!" Tears began to stream down her face again. There was silence.

"What?"

"Someone broke into my house last night and raped me!" Jamie held the phone with both hands. Her legs were trembling as she dug her toes into the carpet.

"Did you call the police?"

"No."

"Jesus Christ, Jamie."

The two girls said nothing for a moment. Then, "I'll be round to you in ten minutes."

"Thanks," Jamie replied quietly. She'd hoped that that was what Nikki was going to say. She cut the connection and left the receiver off the hook. She was terrified that *he* might call. She shuffled over to the door. The chain went on the lock.

She edged her way back to the couch and sat down. The grey box was exactly where she had left it earlier during the week. She lifted the lid and ran her fingers around the edges of all the sentimental photos and documents that had been gathering dust for years. There was a photograph of Jamie with her mother, taken when she visited Jamie in London two years before. She let out a few big unguarded sniffs.

"Mammy, I'm coming home," she said quietly to the picture. "I miss you." She touched her mother's face with her thumb. She had decided earlier that morning that she was quitting and getting out. The sight of her mother made her decision all the more definite.

There was a loud succession of knocks on the door. Jamie put the photos back in the folder and waited for a voice. Silence. Then more knocks.

"Jamie, it's Nikki. Are you there?"

The chain went back and the door opened slowly. Nikki's eyes opened wide as she lifted both hands to her face in horror.

"Oh Jesus, Jamie . . . are you all right?"

"No." Jamie burst into tears. Then an loud uncontrollable cry.

Nikki rushed into the hall and threw her arms around the injured girl as she tried to struggle with the front door and close it without releasing her grip.

"Ssshh. It's all right. He's gone. No one's going to touch you now, Jamie." Nikki stared at the walls as she hugged Jamie tightly and gently ran her hand over her head. "Come on now, sit down and I'll stick on the kettle." Nikki eased her backwards on to the sitting-room couch and then ran up to the bedroom for a blanket. As she pushed back the bedroom door, she put her hand up to her mouth.

"Oh, Jesus." The master bed was in bits and there were bloodstains on the sheet and duvet. She pulled the door closed and ran into the spare room. She pulled the quilt off the bed with a flicking motion and thundered back down the stairs, three steps at a time.

"Now," she gasped, "put this over you. You'll freeze without knowing it because of the shock."

"Some shock," Jamie muttered as she pulled the quilt up over her legs.

"Now, just relax for a minute. I'll make a big pot of tea and then we'll talk." Nikki realised just then what she was saying. This wasn't just another of their gossipy chats. "Well, I mean, *only* if you feel like it, OK?"

She hurried into the kitchen and filled the kettle. then she took down the familiar small tray which had become the trademark of long conversations for the two of them. Two mugs. Sugar and milk, Nikki muttered to herself while she waited for the kettle to boil. She wasn't quite sure what she was doing.

"I think the two of us should go on a holiday together. What d'you think?" she called from the kitchen. She stepped into the sitting-room and looked at Jamie. Her head was bowed. She'd curled up into a ball. "How about a week at home? We'd have some *craic*."

"Sure, you're broke and anyway, I'm just back from holidays," Jamie whispered.

The kettle boiled. Nikki opened a press under the sink and took out a bottle of Irish whiskey. Jamie kept it there for when the girls might come back to the house after a night out. As soon as the tea was made and in the mugs, Nikki poured a generous measure and a half into Jamie's. She arrived out with the tray and put it on the small coffee table.

"Now, get all this into you. You'll feel much better." She lifted the mug with Jamie's name on the side and turned around to give it to her. She was fast asleep. Nikki put it back on the tray and pulled the quilt up around Jamie's shoulders. "Jesus Christ, God love you." She picked up her own mug and then put it down again. "Jesus, I need something stronger meself after that!" She picked up Jamie's mug and took two good gulps out of it.

Nikki sat in the fading light listening to Jamie's breathing. She tried to imagine what she'd been through. It must have been terrifying. She looked at her mug. It was still half full, but cold now. She must have been sitting there for an hour.

A door creaked. Nikki leapt out of the chair. Jesus, she muttered, don't do that to me. She walked out into the hall and looked up the staircase. She could see the window in the bathroom was open. She ran up the stairs and into the bathroom. As she closed the window, she noticed the bath was full. At least she's had a bath, she thought.

She walked slowly into the master bedroom. A

large empty pillowcase lay in the corner on top of some dirty washing. Right, she thought. I'll do her a favour. Nikki picked up the pillowcase. She pulled the bloodstained sheet off the bed. She bundled it up into a ball and forced it into the end of the cloth bag. Then she did the same with the cover of the duvet and Jamie's torn clothes. She looked around to check if there were any more offending items to be binned, and stuff the bag into a plastic sack.

The door of the wardrobe was ajar. A quick check, thought Nikki. She opened the door fully. She lifted some of the clothes strewn around inside. Jesus, what a mess! she muttered. Then she noticed it, jammed between a jacket and the back of the wardrobe. It looked like a foreign banknote. One she'd never seen before. She reached in and pulled it out. Her eyes bulged. One hundred pounds. She gulped. This single piece of paper was really one *hundred* pounds! *One hundred pounds!* A bundle of newspapers lay on top of some clothes inside. Nikki picked up the bundle. Being more interested in the hundred pound note, she was about to discard the twisted rubbish when she detected something more solid inside. Curiously, she unravelled the pages and out fell two loose blocks. More money. Lots of it!

She tiptoed over to the door and listened to hear if Jamie was still sleeping. She pushed the door closed. As she sat down on the bed, she began to examine the two bundles more closely. One hundred pound bills, every single one of them. She fingered the corners carefully, counting as quickly as she could. As she placed the two bundles neatly side by side, she gazed out the window. She felt weak.

"Five thousand pounds!" she squeaked.

She looked back down at the two tightly-packed wads. She looked at the door again. She grabbed the two bundles and the single note and wrapped them up in the newspaper again. She tiptoed across the room and put them on top of the wardrobe.

She came thundering down the stairs like a small child on Christmas morning. So noisily that she woke Jamie. Jamie looked up uneasily as Nikki stumbled into the sitting-room.

"What's wrong?" Jamie asked as she sat up.

"Nothing!" Nikki shouted.

"You look like you've seen a ghost."

"No!" she shouted. She felt like a competitor warming up for the London City Marathon. "Eh, more tea?"

"Yeah, please." Jamie tried a small stretch. "What time is it?"

"Quarter to six."

Nikki went into the kitchen and lashed the rest of the bottle of Paddy into the two cups as she waited for the kettle to boil. Five thousand pounds, she thought. But whose?

Moments later, she arrived back in with the tray. Nikki had calmed down considerably now. Get a grip, she thought. She was here to help her best friend, not lose the head over something that was none of Nikki's business. She handed Jamie a mug and sat down opposite her with her own.

Jamie glanced over at her and then looked back down at her mug. "Sit over here, will you?"

Nikki sat down beside her best friend and waited for a couple of minutes.

"What happened?"

Jamie took a deep breath. Then, in as much detail as was possible, she relived the nightmare all over again. Jamie talked quietly for over an hour. Occasionally, she paused as tears ran down her face. Then she would shout and curse. Nikki sat there with her arm around her and listened.

"You'll have to go to the police, Jamie?"

"*No!*" she answered adamantly.

"But *why*?" Nikki implored. "They can catch him and lock him up. If you don't, say he comes back again?"

"He won't come back again." Jamie took a sip out of her mug.

"Where's Tommy?"

"I don't know."

"What d'you mean you don't know? Where was he last night when all this was happening?"

"He never came back after I threw him out. I called work and *they* don't even know where he's gone." Jamie wiped her eyes slowly. "*He* won't come back."

"Who? Tommy?"

"No. *Him*."

"Jamie, I don't want to scare you, but how can you be so sure?"

"'Cos I'm going home tomorrow, that's why."

"To *Dublin*?" Nikki took her arm away.

"Yeah. To Dublin." There was a long silence.

"Why?"

"*Why?*" Jamie's face twisted with anger. "Because I've been *raped*! That's why. I want to go home. That's where I want to be right now."

"Sorry, I didn't mean to sound like . . . "

"I know."

Nikki took a hold of Jamie's hand. "It's just that I'll miss you."

"Yeah, I know."

"I still think you should get the police."

"Why? Sure, what can I tell them? I couldn't even get a good look at him. The bastard almost broke my neck trying to keep my eyes turned away from him!"

"But at least it'll be on record. And you never know what they might be able to turn up."

"Big fucking deal, Nikki. And if they do catch him, I'll be the one dragged through the fucking courts. My face in all the papers. He'll get five years if I'm lucky. And then he gets out. Then what? My life's ruined enough as it is, for Christ's sake!" Jamie stood up and put her empty mug on the tray. "I'm getting dressed. I've got a lot to do." She headed for the stairs. "Do me a favour." She turned around to Nikki. "Ring and see what times flights are tomorrow evening, will you?"

"Yeah, right." Nikki followed Jamie out to the hall and picked up the telephone directory. Then it dawned on her. "Who will I ring?"

"Anyone. I just want a flight out of here."

"OK." She thumbed through the pages as Jamie climbed the stairs. As soon as she heard the bedroom door closing, Nikki picked up the phone. She dialled 999.

"Hello. Emergency. Which service do you require, please?"

"Police!"

Within a couple of seconds, she could hear the dialling tone. Then a man's voice.

"Hello, Metropolitan Police, can I help you?"

Nikki took a sharp intake of breath. "Yes. I'd like to report a rape!"

* * *

Jamie arrived downstairs looking fresher and slightly more relaxed. She'd thrown on a baggy sweatshirt and a pair of jeans.

"Nikki," she called, sounding a bit worried.

"I'm in the kitchen. Be out now."

"What are you doing?" asked Jamie.

"Just putting away these things."

"Ah, leave them." Jamie looked for her bag. "Come on, I feel like a drink."

Nikki emerged from the kitchen. "We'll go later. I'll ring us a Chinese first."

Jamie looked surprised. "*You* saying no to a drink? I can't believe it!" She put on her denim jacket slowly. "Jesus, my shoulders." She pulled the jacket together at the front. "Anyway, I'm not hungry."

"Jamie, you really *should* eat something. Will I make you a sandwich?"

"There's no bread."

"I'll run around and get some. It'll only take me five minutes. Then we'll go an' have a few drinks."

Jamie stared at Nikki. "What are you talking about? I just told you, Nikki. I'm not hungry. And if *you* don't feel like a drink, I'll go on my own. Did you ring City Jet?"

"Eh, yeah. They're full up. But I got you a flight with Aer Lingus from Heathrow. Ten past eight."

"How much?"

"Eighty-nine pounds."

"Jesus, daylight robbery." Jamie checked to make sure she had her purse.

"Do you have much money saved?" Nikki asked quietly.

"Why?" Jamie didn't bother to look up.

"Nothing. Just wondering," Nikki replied. She took a deep breath and stuck both hands firmly into her jeans pockets. Just then, there was a loud knock on the door. The two girls stood and looked at each other.

"Who's that?" asked Jamie.

"I don't know." Nikki walked back into the kitchen. "You better open it."

Jamie walked slowly to the door. She turned the handle and opened it. An elegantly dressed blonde-haired woman with a leather bag over her shoulder stood there.

"Yes," Jamie enquired.

"Jamie Carroll?"

"Yes?"

"I'm Detective Sergeant Anne O'Brien from the Special Crime Squad, Metropolitan police." She produced a badge and handed it to Jamie. "I was hoping maybe I could have a talk with you."

Jamie looked up at the woman and handed back the badge. "About what?"

The woman smiled sympathetically. "About last night?"

Jamie swung around and looked at Nikki. "You *bitch*!" Tears began to roll down her cheeks again. She closed the door out and took the chain off. She opened it again.

The woman stood into the hallway and put her arm around Jamie.

The three women sat down in the front room.

"I'll make some tea." Nikki jumped up and rushed to the kitchen.

"I don't think that's necessary," the police officer replied.

Nikki stopped in her tracks. "Maybe later." She sat down in the armchair. The policewoman continued to stare at her. Nikki looked at Jamie who was gazing at the floor, squeezing her lips. Then she looked at her watch. "Right then, I'm heading home." No reply. She stood up and put on her jacket. "I'll see you later, all right?" she said to Jamie.

"Yeah," Jamie answered quietly.

Nikki left.

The police lady stayed for almost two hours. She wasn't like what Jamie had imagined. She was an attracive brunette, soft-spoken, with shoulder-length hair, tied up at the back. No more than thirty-one, maybe thirty-two. After a short while, Jamie began to feel comfortable with her. It wasn't like an interrogation.

More like a chat with a friend she hadn't seen for years. Someone she didn't realise she had so much in common with. After describing the terrifying ordeal that she'd been through, she fell back into the chair and cried.

"I can't stop crying," she shouted in frustration.

"I know. But I'm glad you *are* crying. It's a way of getting rid of all the anger. It will make what happened a little easier to deal with."

"Why do I feel like it was *my* fault?"

"Most rape victims *do*!" The woman took Jamie's hand. "They seem to feel that they could have prevented it. But we both know that's not true. I felt the very same way when it happened to me."

Jamie stared across at the woman, her eyes wide open.

"You were *raped*?"

The Detective Sergeant nodded her head. Her face was serious but compassionate. "Three years ago. I was on my way home from evening shift. I got dragged down an alley by two hooded blokes. After they'd both raped me, they put me out." She paused and looked down. Jamie squeezed her hand. The policewoman looked up and smiled.

"Where are you from?" Jamie asked, curious about the woman's accent.

"I'm from Swords. Why?"

"Oh, Swords," Jamie replied with a wry smile. "The posh part of the northside."

The policewoman laughed. "Where are you from?"

"Artane." Jamie went quiet for a second.

"Go on, ask," the woman prompted.

"Ask what?" Jamie enquired.

"How did a girl from Dublin become a WPC in London?" the officer asked.

"WPC?" Jamie looked intrigued.

"Woman Police Constable. Actually, I'm a DS. Detective Sergeant."

"How did you get that job?" Jamie relaxed in the chair.

"Well, I came over to London to work as a nurse in Great Ormond Street Hospital. And I saw an ad in the paper one day looking for police recruits of different nationalities and cultures. I liked the idea of working as a copper, so I gave it a shot and here I am." Then she was serious again. "Do you know who did it?"

Jamie was dreading the question. Here it was.

"It was too dark, I think."

"What do you mean, you *think*?"

"Well, all I could see were his eyes. And his watch." Or was it *his* watch? She couldn't remember. Why not? She was good at remembering details like that. Jamie looked across at the woman again. It didn't seem like a real police interview. She wasn't taking any notes.

"It's not a lot to go on. We have an alert out. So we'll wait and see what that brings in."

Jamie paused and sniffed loudly. "I think I know who owns the watch." She put her hand up to her mouth. She knew she had to say the name out loud. But it was so hard.

"Who?" The woman sat forward on to the edge of the couch. There was no answer. "Jamie, you've got to tell me who it was, if you think you know."

Jamie took a deep breath and blurted it out. "His name is David Darling."

The woman looked at her for a moment. "The deejay?"

Jamie nodded. "Yeah," she whispered. A great sense of relief ran through her.

"Do you know him well?"

"Sort of. I work with him at City Radio. He walked me home last night."

"Had you been out together?"

Jamie laughed sarcastically. "With *him*? You must be joking. I couldn't get into the Clover Tap and, when I turned to go home, he just appeared out of nowhere. He was drunk an' asked me if he could stay the night. I said no and that I'd call the cops if he didn't go home."

"Did he hang around for long?"

"Long enough, I suppose. I fell asleep after a while. And then *that*."

"Where was Tommy when all this was going on?"

Jamie sat upright in the chair. "How do you know about Tommy?"

"Oh, just that I've heard him talking about you. We used to be on the same shift together when I was in uniform." She smiled. "It always struck me that he was crazy about you. He never stopped talking about you."

"Obviously a long time ago," Jamie sneered. "Anyway, we're not seeing each other any more. We split up a few days ago."

"Why?"

"Domestic dispute. Isn't that what you people call it?" There was no way that she was going to tell her the reasons for their split.

206

"Anything to do with his former partner being shot dead in the drugs bust?"

"How do you mean?"

"Well, sometimes this work can get to you. The pressure, the long hours, the money. And sometimes, particularly when you're a witness to something awful like *that*, you can just . . . snap. Did you two have an argument?"

"Yeah. But it wasn't over that."

"How do you know?"

"Because I *do*!" snapped Jamie.

"Where is he now?"

"I don't know," Jamie replied in a subdued way. "I rang his boss. *They* don't even know where he is." There was a moment's silence.

"Is there any reason why *he* might have done this to you?"

Jamie looked up, disbelief written all over her face. "Of course not!"

"Fine, fine. I was just wondering." She paused. "It's just that, you know."

"You know what?" Jamie asked, on the defensive.

"They have been known to lash out like that."

"*Who?*"

"Partners."

"Well, it couldn't have been him."

"Why?"

She felt embarrassed even saying it. "We haven't been sleeping together for almost a year!"

"More's the reason for such an attack. Sexual frustration."

207

Jamie looked up. "What do you mean?"

"Some men feel that, unless they are sexually fulfilled, they're not in control. He may feel that because you're possibly reluctant to have sex with him, for whatever reason, that you are controlling him. Many blokes like to have it the other way round. Best policy is for you to *be* in control, but let him think he's the boss."

Jamie smiled. Then her face turned serious. She shook her head. "It wasn't Tommy."

"I hope you're not just trying to shield him because he's your partner. Women have been known to do that."

Jamie refused to be drawn.

After a minute or so, the policewoman stood up and put on her coat. "I'd like you to come down to the station with me. The doctor will need to examine you just to check that you're OK, which I've no reason to doubt that you are. And I'd like to take the clothes that you were wearing at the time."

Jamie sat there and looked up at the woman. This was like a scene out of *The Bill*.

"When?" she asked.

"Now."

Jamie switched off the gas fire and turned out the light. She put on her denim jacket and threw her red scarf around her neck to hide the marks.

"I've got some mascara in my bag if you want it," the policewoman said as she looked at Jamie's eye.

"No thanks," Jamie said. She thought long and hard for a moment.

"What's wrong?" the sergeant asked.

"Wait here for a minute," Jamie said. She was back within a minute. "Here," she said, holding out a towel.

The policewoman looked curiously at the towel. "What is it?"

"It's his knife."

The police officer carefully unfolded the towel and examined the knife without touching it. "How did you get this?" she asked Jamie seriously.

"I found it halfway down the stairs this morning."

"He must have dropped it." She carefully dropped it into a transparent plastic bag and put it in her handbag. "Well done. This should prove to be very useful."

The two women walked slowly into the hall.

"Thanks for coming, Sergeant."

"Oh, don't thank me. Thank your friend. What's her name again?"

"Nikki," Jamie replied.

"And by the way, call me Anne. The only person who calls me Sergeant is my boss. And that's usually when I'm in trouble."

Jamie smiled. "I don't suppose you fancy a drink?"

"Funny you should say that. I was just about to ask you the same question. But let's get the doctor over with first, OK?"

Jamie nodded. "Nikki said she'd put the clothes and stuff in there," she said, pointing to the black refuse sack which stood on the floor.

"Right," the policewoman replied. She picked up the sack and the two women left, the younger of the two pulling the door shut behind them. They might have been two mates heading out for a Saturday night on the town. No one paid any attention to the small police car as it turned out of the sleepy side street.

Chapter Twelve

Sunday had always been a day for lazing about. Read the papers. Couple of drinks at lunch-time. then sleep off the roast for the afternoon.

Jamie packed as much as she could fit into the two bags. She held up one of them and looked at it. Frank McCabe had carried that for her down the platform after they'd got off the train. Wonder what's he doing now? she thought. The words were from a song on the radio downstairs. She rushed down the stairs and turned it off. Now wasn't the time.

The doorbell rang. Jamie could see Nikki's outline through the red- and green-coloured opaque glass. At least she wouldn't have to look at that horrible glass any more, she thought. She opened the door. Nikki stood there like a drowned rat.

"Well, are you still talking to me?"

Jamie nodded.

"And are you going to invite me in?"

Jamie stood back from the door and let Nikki step into the hall. They looked at each other for a brief moment and threw their arms around each other.

"Are you all right?" Nikki asked cautiously.

"Yeah, I suppose so." Jamie let her go. "Thanks for ringing your woman yesterday."

Nikki smiled. "I had to. I knew *you* wouldn't."

"Yeah," Jamie whispered.

"Was she all right?"

"Yeah, she was great. Well, as good as she could be. She's Irish. From Swords."

" Oh good," Nikki replied nervously. "Jamie, there's something I have to tell you."

"What?" Jamie asked ominously.

"I was going to tell you yesterday but then *she* arrived."

"Go on," Jamie urged.

"Well, when you fell asleep, after I made you the tea, I went upstairs to clean the room and put the clothes in the plastic sack like I told you. 'Cos I knew you wouldn't feel like doing it yourself. Well, when I was checkin' the wardrobe for anything else, I found this bundle of old newspapers, all wrapped up. I didn't think it'd be anything but when I opened them, I found, well, money."

"How much money?"

"Wait here." Nikki shot up the stairs. Less than a minute later, she was back in the sitting-room. "Here, have a look."

Jamie cautiously took the clumpy bundle. "How much money?"

Nikki breathed in and then out. "Three grand!"

Jamie's eyes opened wide. "Three thousand pounds?"

"Yeah!"

"I knew it," muttered Jamie.

"Knew what?" asked Nikki.

She hesitated. "Nothing."

The bank notes were oozing out through the torn paper. She poured the money out on to her lap. She swallowed as she stared at the small fortune in front of her. Then she smiled. She bundled it back into the newspaper.

"Well, aren't you going to count it?" Nikki asked in a state of shock.

"No, why should I? It's not mine?" She leaned across and stuffed it into the back of her carrier bag. "But it is now."

* * *

Nikki offered to go to Heathrow with her that evening. Jamie had called her sister to tell her that she was coming home. She wouldn't tell her why. Eventually, Lisa managed to get the story out of her bit by bit. After Jamie told her what had happened, she made her promise not to tell her mother.

She travelled light. Nikki offered to look after anything that was left behind. They walked up Bromley Road without as much as a word to each other.

"You missed a great night on Friday," Nikki said as they passed the Clover Tap on the way to the underground. Then she realised what a stupid thing that was to say.

"Yeah," Jamie muttered. "I don't give a shite! All right?"

"Sorry." Change the subject. "What time's your flight?"

"You booked it. You should know. Ten past eight." Jamie kept the hood of her jacket up so as not to draw attention to her black eye.

"It'll only take an hour to get to Heathrow. So that gives us time for a drink." Nikki pointed to the pub.

"I don't mind." Jamie shrugged her shoulders.

* * *

The Clover Tap was quiet. The calm after the storm of the two previous nights. A few lads huddled at one end of the long bar watching a Gaelic football match. Now and again, they would give a wild roar of encouragement, sometimes followed by a disgruntled moan. Ray stood at the other end of the bar reading a copy of the *Sunday World* that one of the punters had left behind. He didn't care much for the Gaelic matches. Not since he'd suffered a groin injury back in 1984. He told everyone it was caused by a nasty tackle during a inter-county hurling match. He was far too embarrassed to explain that he'd tried to enter the grounds the wrong way, and a pay-booth turnstile had spun backwards and hit him hard where it hurt most. He tried to sue but was told in no uncertain terms where to get off.

He'd convinced Frank that he could look after the business while he took a well-deserved rest for a few hours.

He noticed the two girls make themselves comfortable in a corner of the pub. He closed the paper and strolled over.

"What can I get for the ladies?" he enquired, thoroughly enjoying his new status. Nikki looked up.

"I'll have a bottle of Ritz," she said, searching for her purse. "What do you want, Jamie?"

Jamie looked up to reveal the cut below her left eye. "A bottle of Heineken, please," she replied in a subdued voice.

Ray couldn't help but notice her black eye.

"Jesus, that's a bad one," he remarked. "How did you come by that?" It quickly dawned on him that maybe he shouldn't ask. But it was too late.

"I fell getting off the train," she stammered.

"Don't mind her!" interrupted Nikki. "Some bastard beat the shite out of her. On her birthday . . . can you believe that?"

"Shut up, Nikki!" Jamie urged. "Anyway, I told you not to talk about it."

"Jesus. The bastard!" Ray pulled up a stool and sat down beside them. "Did you report it?"

"Yes and no," Nikki replied quickly. "She didn't tell them that she had to throw her boyfriend out of the house."

"Nikki Coffey, *shut up*, or you'll have two to match this one," Jamie spluttered. "I just want to forget about it, OK? Anyway, in a few hours I'll be home and I'll never have to face this kip again!" She sniffed loudly.

"I'll tell youse here and now," Ray said, sounding authoritative, "I've a young sister at home, same age as yourself. If any fella laid a hand on her, I'd be on the next plane home to tear his fucking head off . . . excuse the French!" He stood up.

"Ritz and a Heineken?" He paused.

"Thanks," Nikki replied. Ray headed back to the bar. "Anyway, why didn't you tell the policewoman that Tommy was treating you like shit?" she demanded.

"'Cos he didn't do this the other night. That's why!"

"How are you so sure? You said it was too dark to see anything." Nikki studied Jamie for a moment. Her eyes opened. "You know who it was, don't you?"

"No."

"Yes, you do. It's written all over your face." Nikki looked around to see if anyone was within hearing distance. "Who was it?"

"I don't know," Jamie replied. "Well, not for sure."

"*Tell me.*" Nikki gritted her teeth.

"I can't. The police told me not to."

"Are they going to question him?" Nikki persisted.

"Yes. Now, can we leave it at that?"

* * *

Just then, Ray arrived back with the drinks and the Sunday World he'd been reading.

"There youse are, on the house! And the *World*, so you can catch up on all the scandal back home." He shook his head disapprovingly at Jamie's eye. "Give us a shout if you need anything."

The two girls were chuffed and said thanks.

215

Nikki suggested they read *Dear Cathy's* agony column. Nikki found the page. "Right, here's the first letter. Let's see now. She coughed and cleared her throat. *Dear Cathy, Three weeks ago I was . . .* " Nikki just managed to stop before saying the word 'raped'. She froze. "Nothing much in here this week," she calmly remarked as she quickly closed the paper. "Here, you have a gander." She threw the paper at Jamie.

Jamie just sat there slumped over her drink doodling with the pen on the page. She wrote her name four or five times while sipping her drink and then put down the pen. "Let's go, come on." They gathered their belongings and walked towards the door. The TV news theme caught Jamie's attention as she passed the bar. She stopped, almost instinctively, and looked up at the screen. She could feel her body stiffen as she listened in total dismay.

"The main story this afternoon . . . a refuse disposal worker today discovered what is believed to be the money connected to the north London drugs bust last week in which a 43-year-old detective was brutally murdered. The black plastic bag, found at a disposal tiphead in south-east London this morning, is understood to have been collected in the Highbury area of north London, not far from the murder scene. It's estimated that over a hundred and fifty thousand pounds was recovered. Rubbish bags, such as the one retrieved, would normally be crushed by the truck's disposal mechanism. A police spokesman said that the discovery of the sack, intact, was due to a malfunction in the disposal mechanism. Otherwise the money would almost definitely have been destroyed. Police are carrying out door-to-door enquiries."

It was all coming back to her now. Too abruptly to take in, all at once. The plastic binbag peppered with small holes. The same musty smell you sometimes get from old bank notes.

The mucky bootmarks on the stairs when she arived in from the boat trip that morning. No wonder Tommy was livid. A hundred and fifty thousand pounds. And she'd thrown it all in the bin. A shiver ran up her spine. The money Nikki'd found must have fallen out of the sack. The TV screen seemed to be getting further and further away. The announcer's voice seemed all disjointed now. She didn't feel well. "Quick, Nikki, I'm going to faint . . . "

Nikki grabbed her and eased her into a chair. "Jesus, Jamie, are you all right?"

Jamie's head slumped forward on to the table.

"Here, help . . . quick!" Nikki shouted.

Ray climbed up over the counter and grabbed her shoulders. He then sat her back up into the chair to prevent her from sliding under the table. "Is she all right?"

"I don't know. One minute, she was watching the news, the next, she was gone," replied Nikki.

"Will I call an ambulance?" he asked.

"*No!* She's just fainted. She'll be grand in a minute."

"Here, hold her till I get some water." Ray hurried back inside the bar and filled a small glass with brandy.

"See if she'll drink a drop of that. It'll perk her up. Put the colour back in her cheeks."

Nikki took the glass and sniffed it. "Jaysus, they'll be putting her on to the plane in a wheelchair!"

Jamie pulled back from the rim of the glass. The smell of its contents was repugnant. "I'm all right," she whispered. She made a feeble attempt to stand up. "I'll miss me flight. I have to go."

"Sit down for a few minutes, love," Ray urged. "Get the blood flowing again."

Jamie shook her head. All the time, she was thinking of the money. Of Jimmy Grant. Of the grisly notion that this whole nightmare was a lot deeper and sickeningly more sinister than she could imagine or prepare herself for. Now she knew, beyond a shadow of a doubt, that she was in terrible trouble. Unknown to herself, she'd become part of a gruesome plan which had obviously gone horribly wrong.

They said goodbye to Ray as they disappeared into the quiet city evening.

Ray cleared off the table and walked back to the bar. He put the paper behind the cash register and the double measure of brandy, untouched, on top of the bar. He licked his lips and raised it to his mouth.

"I don't know what made him throw it away."

Ray's head swung left. He peeped over the rim of the glass just as his lips were about to make contact. He straightened up. At the end of the bar sat an unusual-looking character. He looked well-weathered. His face showed signs of years of hardship. Notched and dented, it was a real stony, outdoor face. Ray guessed he looked a lot older than he really was. Yet he wore a stylish, full-length coat. Brand new by the look of it. His hair was neatly groomed. Beneath the coat, an elegant shirt and matching tie. "What was that you said?" asked Ray.

"I said I don't know why he threw the bag away. He must have got cold feet."

"Which bag?"

"The bag full of money . . . on the telly . . . from the drugs bust. He took it with him that night after he shot his mate . . . in the back. Most awful thing I've ever witnessed. I'm still having nightmares about it. I reported it to a mate of mine. He's a cop. One of the good ones. Still didn't do much about it."

"Hang on, hang on," urged Ray. He put the glass down. "Who shot who?"

"The cop who shot his partner. Maida Vale. Only last week. I'd had too much of that cheap piss and I went down the alleyway to get out of the rain until the hostel opened up. I must have fell asleep. And then this unmerciful bang woke me up. It was like a fuckin' explosion. I thought it was a bomb out on the street. I was about to run away when I heard the talking. Two cops. I'm certain of that. On the Duchess's life, I swear."

"*Duchess?*"

"Me mother, God rest her. I still miss her. One of them wanted to take the money and keep it. The other wouldn't let him. So the young lad shot his older fella . . . in the *back*, God help the poor bastard!"

Ray was astounded. "What would you like to

drink?" he asked, pushing the large glass of brandy underneath the stranger's nose.

"God bless you, young fella." He held the glass under his nose. "Jaysus, this is gorgeous." He lowered it in one go.

Ray's eyes popped out as he watched the man's head go back. "What do you do?"

"Not a lot," he wheezed. "I suppose you could say that I've been a swagman for years but now I'm going to be a swanky man for a change." He tapped his nose with his finger and leaned closer to Ray. "I've won a few quid on a scratch card. So now I'm going to treat myself and the few people who've been good to me. And then . . . I'm goin' home for good. Back to beautiful Skibbereen." He gave Ray a discreet flash of his plane ticket. "Non-stop to Dublin. Then a coach to west Cork. First time in my life I've ever held one of these. Is Frank here?"

Ray smiled. "No, it's his afternoon off."

"When's he due back?"

"About six."

"I'll hang on and have another one. Will you join me?"

"Might as well!"

"I'm Paddy . . . Paddy Last." He held out his hand.

Ray smiled. "Ray . . . Ray Flynn." The two men shook hands.

* * *

Frank found it difficult coming back to work on

Sunday evenings. Everywhere he looked, people were taking it easy. Enjoying each other's company. The light was fading as he stepped on to the street from Coburn Road tube station. He walked slowly through the crowds of people at the entrance. A couple of buskers cut through the cold evening air with their version of "Dirty Ol' Town". A small crowd gathered to listen. He rooted in his pocket for a few coins and threw them into the guitar case lying open on the pavement.

"Thanks, Frank!" an Irish accent echoed.

Frank turned around. The man playing the guitar and harmonica winked at him. Frank recognised them as two of his regulars.

"All right, lads," he shouted and waved. No doubt the money will make its way back over my counter tonight, he thought. Mind you, come to think of it, a ballad night would probably go down well mid-week! He thought about work as he waited to cross the street.

As he looked left before stepping out, he noticed her. His heart began to race. It was the girl he'd met on the train. Jamie. He quickly looked up and down for a break in the traffic. Come on, he thought as he gritted his teeth.

"Jamie," he shouted. *"Jamie!"* Louder this time. *"Jamie!"* He was shouting at the top of his voice. *"It's Frank. Remember? On the boat."* Still no reaction. People were beginning to look at him.

"Excuse me, love." He pushed through the small group waiting to cross the street. He made a run for the other side. Cars and buses honked their horns.

"Are you trying to kill yourself?" he heard one bus driver call as he narrowly missed the front of his double-decker.

"Ah, get a life," he shouted as he dodged and weaved through the traffic. He kept his eyes on the two girls. He was right. It was definitely Jamie. She was wearing the same coat that she'd had on that night.

"*Jamie!*" He was running and roaring and quite out of breath. "*Hang on. Wait!*"

Jamie looked back curiously. She kept walking. She was heading for the tube. Frank paused on the traffic island.

As he waited for another break in the flow, he watched her pass under the entrance and disappear down the long flight of steps. Shit, he thought. Here goes. He crossed the traffic lanes like an athlete running the hundred-metre hurdles sprint. As he arrived at the station entrance a crowd emerged, blocking his way completely. He squeezed through them.

"Here, steady on, mate," one angry man shouted. Another pushed against him as Frank tried to move towards the stairs. The only thing he could do was to keep moving towards the platform. Maybe it wouldn't be so busy there. Shit, I don't have a ticket. Forget it. I'll think of something if I'm stopped. He pushed his way through the ticket toll gate on the heels of a small Chinese man just after he had inserted his ticket.

"Jamie, wait!" He was shouting into an abyss. Strangers coming and going. He jumped off the end of the escalator and ran on to the Northern Line platform. Twenty people. Maybe twenty-five. No sign of Jamie. About turn. He jumped into the lift which would take him down to the Piccadilly Line. When the lift doors finally opened, Frank rudely squeezed past the other travellers.

This platform was for those going east to Elephant and Castle. Only a few here. He backtracked on to the other platform. This line went all the way to Heathrow. It was jammed with passengers waiting for the next train. Frank jumped up and down in an attempt to see to the other end of the platform.

"Jamie," he shouted. No answer. "*Jamie*," he shouted louder. A silence fell over the crowd. "*Jamie, it's Frank!*"

A falsetto voice replied from the other end of the platform. "Where are you, Frank? I love you." Everybody laughed. Frank could see that this wasn't going to work. He heard the train approaching. He could feel the gush of hot air as it got nearer. It thundered out of the black hole and came to a standstill. The doors opened. People pushed to get off as those waiting to get on squeezed through. He watched as many doors as he could and scoured the carriages as they filled up. It was all happening too quickly. Before he knew it, a voice on the intercom warned passengers to stand clear of the doors. Then he spotted her. She was sitting in the middle of a carriage towards the front of the train. He ran towards the door. Too late. It closed and almost caught his fingers. He ran to the window and banged loudly. "*Jamie!*" he called repeatedly. She didn't see him. He noticed that one of her eyes was blackened and swollen. The train moved forward and gathered speed. Within a few seconds, it had disappeared back into the black hole. Frank turned and looked for the exit sign as the platform began to fill up again for the next train.

Two uniformed transport policemen stood close to him, blocking his path.

"Could we see your ticket please, sir?" the smaller one enquired. The tall one was holding a truncheon in one hand, tapping it against his leg. "The ticket inspector upstairs seems to think you didn't bother buying one!"

Frank had to think fast. "Eh, yes, that's right. My girlfriend left without her medicine." He quickly pulled his inhaler out of his trouser pocket. "She's an asthmatic. She needs this with her all the time. I just thought I might've been able to catch her. But naturally, I didn't want to chance getting on the train after her without a ticket."

One of the officers inspected the inhaler closely.

"I see, sir. Do you think, she'll be all right without it? 'Cos we could get it to her if it's an emergency." The two officers gazed sympathetically at Frank and the inhaler.

"Ah no, sure, that's not necessary. She'll be fine. Sure, she can take it later. Thanks, anyway."

"Pleasure, sir." The officers watched as Frank climbed on to the UP escalator. He waved to them. They stared at each other and then back at Frank.

It was dark and rainy as he stepped back out on to the street. He was mad with himself, even though he knew that there was absolutely nothing that he could've done. He looked at his watch and quickened his step. He was late.

* * *

Tommy tore the house apart looking for the money. How was he going to explain that five thousand pounds had just vanished into thin air? He needed the cash to buy a consignment of heroin he had been offered that night. The rest of the money was already two days overdue to his contact who wasn't a very pleasant person. He thought he'd left the money securely hidden in his locker at work. No one would ever think of looking for it there. Unfortunately, he had to stay away from all his usual haunts now that the money had gone missing. Work was under surveillance. So was the house, he was sure. They wanted their money and they'd been known to kill quite unpleasantly if they didn't get it on time. Shit, why couldn't he remember? He pulled Jamie's wardrobe apart. Then he started on the dressing-table drawers.

He knew what would happen if he didn't come up with the money. Even a deposit would tide him over for a couple of days. This was the second disaster in a fortnight. Apart from the hiding he was sure to get, he wouldn't be able to feed his own habit. He shouldn't have got so drunk last night. It'll come to me eventually, he thought.

He slumped into an armchair. He was sweating profusely and beginning to shiver violently. Everything was getting blurred. He tried to remember if he'd searched upstairs. He couldn't remember where he'd been that afternoon. How did the money go missing in the first place? Where was that bitch of a girlfriend of his, anyway? Time was running out. Shortly, he knew, the whole world would come tumbling in around him. He leapt forward in the chair and placed his hands over his face. And screamed.

* * *

Heathrow is a bleak place, especially if you're the one being left behind.

The girls checked in Jamie's baggage at the departure desk in Terminal 1 and decided to have another drink until it was time to go. They had loads to say to each other, but neither wanted to be the first to get upset.

Nikki tried to break the ice by reminding Jamie of the night their flight home was cancelled due to snow. Even though the airline laid on hotel accommodation for them, they preferred to spend the night in the airport bar with a gang of rugby supporters travelling back from Twickenham. They sang all night and couldn't talk for two days. Jamie smiled and shrugged her shoulders. Silence.

"*Passengers for Aer Lingus flight EI154 to Dublin should proceed immediately to Boarding Area B6. This is the final call.*" instructed the high-pitched voice.

Nikki picked up Jamie's carry-all and they headed for the departure gate. Neither spoke. They were both fighting hard to keep back the tears. It was no use. Almost simultaneously, they threw their arms around each other and cried their eyes out.

"I wish I was going too," Nikki bawled.

"So do I," Jamie whispered.

"I'll ring you tomorrow from work," Nikki said as she wiped her eyes.

"All right." Jamie squeezed Nikki's hand and was gone. The airport was unusually quiet. Almost like a ghost town. Nikki wandered around the shops for a while. She decided to get the bus back into London. Down the back of the coach, where no one would disturb her, she pulled a small plastic shopping bag out of her inside pocket. She opened it just enough to see the folded bundle of bank notes. Two thousand pounds. She'd never seen so much money. But who's was it? It wasn't Jamie's. What if it was Tommy's? She felt nervous for a moment. It couldn't be his. If it was, surely he'd have taken it with him before he left the house. She folded the bag again and put it safely back in her pocket. She'd felt bad about what she'd done today, but not any more. Jamie would never find out that she'd taken the money. For all she knew, there was only three grand in the wardrobe when Nikki found it. How could she ever find out that Nikki had taken two thousand? Anyway, Jamie had gone back to Dublin. She smiled and thought of all the things she could afford to buy with her new-found fortune.

Twenty minutes later, as the bus climbed up the slipway on to the M4 eastbound for the city, Nikki watched from the back window as the big green 737 jet climbed into the air on its way home. A shiver ran down her spine. She pulled her jacket tightly around her as the lights of the plane disappeared into the darkness.

Chapter Thirteen

Jamie's head slipped off her hand where it had rested for most of the flight. Her fingers had gone numb. She opened her eyes and looked around. The woman beside her was finishing her coffee. For a moment, she forgot where she was.

"Cabin crew, ten minutes to landing," the pilot's voice reminded the busy flight attendants. There was the usual flurry of activity up and down the aisle as the staff prepared for the descent into Dublin airport.

Jamie peered out into the darkness. She could see lights down below. Lots of them. But not enough for them to be Dublin. It was rare for her to fly home. The boat was her usual choice. But now that fares were cheaper, it was definitely more convenient and she enjoyed pampering herself.

Lisa had told her that she'd be at the airport to meet her. Jamie hoped Lisa would be on her own. Deep down though, she knew they'd all be there. She just hoped that Lisa hadn't told her mother. She swore she wouldn't. But she knew Lisa. She meant well but everything was an open secret with her. Still, Jamie thought, she was on her way home for good. Well, for now, anyway. She always remembered the expression, the great thing about being away is coming home. She couldn't remember who'd said it to her, but they were right. What would she say to them all? Oh God, what'll I say? she wondered.

She'd told her mother that she had some annual leave that she had to take before the end of March. Otherwise, she'd lose it. She almost got caught out when her mother suggested that St Patrick's weekend would be a better time. Jamie told her that she was looking at a couple of job opportunities at home and the holiday coincided nicely with an interview. Needless to say, her mother was delighted at the prospect of having her daughter back home for good. Maybe she'd never need to tell her the real story. That was, provided she didn't know it already.

Suddenly, the lights in the cabin went out. Total darkness with the exception of a few overhead reading lights. The darkness made Jamie uneasy and slightly nauseous. Her forehead felt clammy.

Crunch. The plane was on the ground. She listened as the brakes pulled back the huge jet. It was a windy night and the plane swayed slightly. Jamie gripped the sides of her seat. It seemed as if the huge jet didn't want to stop. The lights in the cabin returned as quickly as they'd vanished. The plane's speed dropped to a gentle roll. She could see the familiar terminal building now through the small window.

People around her were already beginning to put

on coats and collect their belongings. Jamie remained in her seat. She'd have loved another hour in the air. Just to postpone the inevitable. Here goes, she thought. She stood into the aisle and put on her jacket. Then she pulled her carrier and a small bag of duty-free she'd bought for her dad from the overhead compartment. She knew that he'd drink the lot in an hour if the real reason for coming home ever got out. But it won't, she thought. Surely it won't?

She followed the crowd off the plane, through the winding tunnel and into the baggage reclaim area. The place was jammed. Everyone was dark brown with the most enviable suntans she'd seen in years. Jammy bastards.

She looked for the sign, *EI154 London Heathrow*. There it was at the other end of the arrivals hall. She moved through the crowd as quickly as she could, careful to keep her head slightly at an angle to avoid drawing attention to her eye.

"*Jamie!*" called a familiar voice from one of the revolving carousels. This was the last thing she needed. She pretended not to hear it.

"*Jaaamie!*" It was louder this time.

Jamie took a quick peep across at the carousel. A girl was waving to her as she pushed her way through the crowd. It was Sheila Hoey. A girl she'd been at school with and hadn't seen for nearly ten years. She'd been a slut for as long as Jamie had known her. "Martini", the girls use to call her, after the ad on telly. "Any time, any place, anywhere", they'd all sing behind her back. It wasn't Sheila's fault that she was ugly or that she had a hen's brain, so everyone accepted that she couldn't be choosy when it came to fellas. Strange thing about it was that the fellas didn't seem too choosy when it came to Sheila. Being with Sheila was like collecting Batman cards. Every boy in the nearby college did it. Most of the girls at Loreto reckoned that she'd be more at home chained to the railings outside with the rest of the bicycles than sitting in a classroom. Rumour had it that more men passed through Sheila Hoey's hands than through the stiles at Croke Park on All-Ireland Sunday.

The girl broke into a dash. "How are you?" she asked as she grabbed Jamie's hand. As she studied Jamie more closely, she spotted the black eye but didn't make any reference to it.

"How are you, Sheila? long time no see." Jamie tried to look happy. "Where are you coming from?"

"My honeymoon," Sheila replied. She blushed slightly and adopted a snobby accent. "I suppose you could say that it all happened very quickly. Love at first sight!" She giggled again with a high-pitched shrill. A bit like a dog yelping.

Jamie smiled. "You look terrific. Where did you go?"

"Oh, you know me. Only the best will do." She opened her eyes wide. "Jersey." She tapped the back of her head with her finger. "Well, Simpson had some people to meet on the island. So we stayed at the Gouchon Hotel overlooking the bay. Beautiful." She leaned forward. "Never got out of bed any day before three!" she whispered.

The notion of a man in bed with Sheila until three in the afternoon! Either he was some sort of scientific researcher carrying out a gruesome experiment, or she had his knickers wired with explosives and she carried the detonator.

"Simpson?" Jamie tried to look impressed. "Jersey? That's fabulous. Sounds gorgeous.

"What does he do?" she asked curiously.

"Sperm bank," Sheila replied at the top of her voice. People looked across at the two girls. Jamie didn't notice them. She was too busy trying to keep herself from laughing.

"A sperm bank? Like what does he do?" She was dying to hear.

"He owns a chain of Artificial Insemination clinics. Two here in Ireland. Eight in Britain," Sheila replied proudly.

"For men and women," Jamie asked with open eyes.

"*No. For cattle!*" Sheila leaned across Jamie's trolley. "You wouldn't believe the *size* of their you-know-whats." Her eyes were out on stalks.

"Really," Jamie replied. She decided it was time to change the subject. "And come here to me, are you gonna keep your own name?"

"Well, yes and no. When you marry an important man, you want people to recognise you." She slipped back into her posh accent. "I'm going to keep my own name but from now on, I'm calling myself Sheila Hoey Langer."

Jamie couldn't help it. She started to laugh.

"Is there something wrong?" the new bride enquired.

"No," Jamie sputtered. "Great name!" She couldn't restrain herself. "I'm sorry. I'm gonna have to go." Jamie walked quickly towards her baggage carousel.

"But wait, you haven't met Simpson," the woman called.

Jamie hurried away laughing. A sperm salesman with a name like Langer, she thought. Leave it to Sheila.

Baggage was pouring out on to the moving carousel faster than she could focus. Meeting Sheila was a tonic. She grabbed her bag and heaved it on to a trolley. She noticed a few people looking at her swollen jaw but she paid no attention. Right, she thought. Here we go. This is it! She gave the trolley an almighty push so that it dragged her along behind it into the Blue channel. She could hear the swelling crowd outside the Arrivals doors. Past the security guard and through the sliding windows. Wall-to-wall people as far as she could see. Some of them held up signs with strange foreign names. A huge sign was being waved over a large group of people. LANGER. She looked in the other direction. All around her, people were being met. Passengers were being called. Exchanging handshakes and hugs. She stood there in the hope that someone might find her. Quickly, she hoped.

"Jamie. Over here!"

Lisa was waving to her. Oh God, she thought. The whole family's here. She pushed the trolley in their direction, weaving in and out of the crowd.

Lisa ran towards her and threw her arms around her.

"How are you?" she asked quietly as she squeezed her big sister.

"I'm all right. Glad to be home," Jamie replied. "You didn't say anything, did you?"

"No, I swear. Nothing."

"To Ma, I mean?"

"I told you, no, I didn't."

Jamie gave her another squeeze.

Her mother was within hugging distance by now. "Welcome home, love. How are you?" She threw her arms around Jamie.

"Oh, Mammy, I missed you," she whispered.

"I missed you too, love." She stood back at arms length. Suddenly her smile disappeared. "Jesus, Mary and Holy Saint Joseph, what happened your eye?"

There was dead silence. It felt as if the entire airport had stopped talking to hear Jamie's explanation.

"Ah, nothing." She tried to sound casual. " I was making some popcorn in the microwave the other night. And the bowl shattered as I was taking it out. A bit hit me in the eye. That's all. It's grand." She needed to change the topic quickly.

"That's *all*!" her mother shouted. "Jesus, you could've lost your eye. And look at the colour of your jaw. That could be dislocated. Did you get it seen to?" Her mother put her hand up to her face.

"Yeah, Ma, I did." She noticed her father studying the wound from a distance. She'd never really hugged him before. Why not now, she thought. She threw her arms around his neck and kissed him on the cheek. "Hi ya, Da."

"Hello, love," he whispered. He was delighted with her greeting.

"This is Jabs," Lisa announced proudly, pointing to a skinny young man with an earring and a crew cut. His red football stripe left no mistake as to who his life was devoted to.

"Nice to meet you, Jabs." Jamie shook his hand. He said nothing. So much for taste, Lisa, Jamie thought as she gave Jabs a closer look. "Are you two madly in love?" she joked.

"Don't start," Lisa warned.

* * *

The journey home was a silent one. Jamie couldn't understand why her mother hadn't said a word since she'd arrived. She looked across the back of the van at Lisa.

Lisa shook her head. "Are you all right?"

"Quiet!" Jamie growled. She looked back to see if Lisa's fella had heard her. "Does me ma know?"

Lisa nodded. "No."

Jamie looked at her again.

"I swear!" Lisa pleaded.

It was nearly ten when the van pulled into the driveway at the end of Church Avenue. Sunday evening was different to any other day. It reminded Jamie of the Sundays when they'd all go to the People's Gardens in the Phoenix Park. Lisa would insist on throwing bread to the ducks. She remembered the day when Lisa grabbed another kid's bread because hers had run out. Her father never noticed what happened and both he and the other child's father almost came to blows when the question of whose bread it was had to be sorted out. It seemed like a lifetime ago. She looked over at Lisa. All grown up. Although, looking at Jabs, she wasn't so sure.

She cherished the atmosphere of her mother's house. She felt safe. The smell was lovely. It was the same smell for as long as she could remember. Her mother loved gaudy colours and the floweriest wallpaper Jamie had ever seen anywhere hung on every wall in the house. Except for Lisa's room. Her mother could have saved on that wallpaper bill if she'd been able to predict how popular *Oasis* were going to be. It wasn't Jamie's idea of stylish decor but it was home. Her home.

"I made you those nice scones you like," her mother said quietly as she opened the press beside the fridge, "without the currants."

My God, Jamie thought to herself. She's talking at long last.

"Would you like a cup of tea, love?" she asked.

"Yeah, please," Jamie replied as she sat down into the big old grandfather chair in the corner of the kitchen.

"I'm nipping down to Madigan's for a pint," her father said, apologetically.

"Yeah," Lisa continued. "I'm just going round to Jabs's, Ma."

"Well, be home before eleven. Do you hear me?" her mother warned.

"Sure, I wouldn't even be halfway through me first pint by eleven," her father moaned.

"Not *you*!" her mother shouted. "Sure you always suit yourself and come home when you want, no matter what I say. It's Lisa I'm talking to. Where is she? Lisa," she shouted at the top of her voice as she went out into the hall. "She's gone. I can't turn me back on that child. She has me heart broken. Ever since that evening at the tea table when she was ten. 'Mam,' she says, 'what's an orgasm?' Your poor grandmother nearly choked on her Complan."

"Ah, Ma. That was eleven years ago. She's twenty-one for God's sake," Jamie argued.

"It's not her I'm worried about. It's that yoke of a thing she's seeing. I'll tell you, the night your father took me to see that film, *Forrest Gump*, all I could think of was *him*. He has a brain the size of one of me rosary beads."

Jamie laughed.

"God forgive me. I shouldn't be saying that. But I don't know what your sister sees in him."

"It mightn't be his brain that she's after, Ma," Jamie said in a naughty sort of way.

"Well, I can't imagine it's anything else," her mother articulated. "Anyway, I think your sister is saving herself for what's-his-name, the film star, Brad Spit!"

Jamie roared laughing. "His name is Brad *Pitt*, Ma. And I don't think our Lisa has much of a chance of getting his number."

"I'm serious. I can't get that Jabs boy out of the house. I'm sure his own mother and father are thanking God that he met our Lisa. He's here when I come down in the morning and I refuse to go asleep till he's gone home at night. The other night he didn't leave until three in the morning. The heels of me shoes are worn out from banging the ceiling, I swear. I'm gonna have to get rid of that television. They seem to spend half the bloody night glued to it. And yet there's not a sound down here after I go up. I can't figure out what they do be watching."

Jamie tried to hide the amused look on her face.

Her mother smiled and brought two mugs of tea over to the table.

"Here, I'll get the scones and the butter," Jamie walked to the worktop and brought back the plates. Silence. Her mother took a sip from her cup and put it on the table.

"This is just like old times. You and me having a cup of tea when you'd come in from *Jets*. It was the only time I'd be able to get a word in edgeways. It wasn't you that would be talking, it would be Nikki. Tell us, how is she? Is she still wearing those ridiculous hot-pants?"

"Not in the middle of winter, Ma."

"That girl's going to get herself into trouble one of these days."

Jamie didn't like the direction the conversation was taking.

"Are you pregnant?" she asked abruptly.

"Not *again!*" Jamie groaned.

"Well, I presume that's why you came home? Well?"

"Of course not!" Jamie spluttered. "Why do ask that every time I come home? Jesus, Ma, you asked me that before Christmas?"

Her mother swung around in the chair. "Did he do that to your eye?"

"No." Jamie looked down at the scone.

Her mother walked over to her. "You'd tell me if something bad was after happening to you, Jamie, wouldn't you, love?"

"Yeah, of course I would."

"Well then, if nothing's happened, why are you upset?"

Jamie knew she was getting too close. "I'm not upset."

"You don't have to tell me now. Whenever you're ready." She stood there almost defiantly.

Jamie mumbled something.

"What, love?" Her mother placed her hand on her shoulder.

"I was raped," she whispered. This time she didn't cry.

Her mother put both arms around her neck gently and gave her a tight squeeze.

Jamie could smell her jumper. It was a comforting smell. It reminded her of the times she fell off her bicycle or hurt herself as a child and her mother would hug it better.

Jamie drew back. "You knew, didn't you?" She could see the tears in her mother's eyes. She nodded.

"Lisa told you, didn't she? She swore she wasn't going to tell anybody."

"Lisa didn't tell me. Well, not directly. I walked into her room the other night. I thought that Jabs fella was upstairs with her. She was talking in her sleep. She seemed upset and was repeating your name. 'Poor Jamie,' was what she was saying over and over. She was crying in her sleep. I thought I heard her mention that word."

"What word?" Jamie asked.

"Rape."

Jamie looked down.

"I turned her over on her side and she stopped." Her mother lifted her chin. "Why didn't you tell me?"

"Why d'you think, Ma? I didn't want to upset you. That's why."

"But you have to tell someone who can help you."

"I did. The police."

"Will they catch him?"

"They don't know, but they're gonna try. That's all."

"Did you talk to them?"

"Yeah."

"No, I mean, did they examine you?"

"Yes. A policewoman called to the flat. We got talking. She seemed real nice. She stayed all afternoon." Jamie felt very uneasy. She didn't want to talk about what had happened. But right now, there didn't seem to be anything else to talk about. There was a long pause before the next question.

240

"Are you pregnant?"

"*No!* Mammy, don't be stupid."

"How do you know?" There were tears in her mother's eyes.

"Because they gave me the morning-after pill."

"And weren't you on the pill with that bloke of yours? What's his name?"

"Tommy," Jamie replied in a subdued tone. She paused. "No."

"*No?*" her mother shouted. "And what if he'd made you pregnant?"

"You have to sleep with someone to get pregnant, Ma. You should know that."

"Don't be cheeky, Jamie Carroll." Her mother took another sip from her cup.

Jamie sighed. "Well, it's true. We haven't slept together for nearly a year. So what's the point of poisoning me system with a drug that I don't need?"

"What sort of a relationship is that?" Her mother banged her mug down on to the table.

"*I don't know,*" Jamie roared.

"Anyway, where was he when this happened to you? I presume it was in the middle of the night."

"We've split up. He wasn't there."

"Well, he should have been there. I don't know what it is about men today. Your father couldn't wait to meet my mother. He nearly broke down the front door to shake her hand and make an impression. Mind you, I'm not saying that your father is perfect. But that fellow of yours reminds me of Dracula when he comes on the phone. He gives me the creeps. And as for getting to meet him! It'd be easier to get an audience with the Pope. I always told you he was just using you. I always knew you were mad moving in with him. You could have got yourself a nice Irish fella. One of your own sort from home," her mother preached.

"An *Irish* fella. Like who? Jabs? Oh yeah. Someone like him would really make me happy. Sure, look at me. I'm beside myself with excitement thinking of a man like him. What a man. Do me a favour, Ma, shut up." Jamie put on her coat. "I'm sorry I ever said a word."

"Where are you going? It's five to eleven."

"I'm going down to Madigan's for a drink with me da," Jamie shouted.

"Sure, he'll be there with all the other men talking."

"Well, at least the conversation will be a bit more interesting and I won't have to listen to any more of this crap!" Jamie opened the hall door.

"Jamie, wait, love. I'm sorry. It's just that I'm upset." She began to cry. "Come back and finish your tea."

* * *

Madigan's was black when she arrived. God, she thought. It was still the same old grotty kip she remembered from the times she used to skip down for cigarettes for her father. Dirty cracked ashtrays on wobbly, smoke-charred tabletops. A stale smoggy film hovered above the small clusters of hardened drinkers, mixed with that classic Madigan's whiff of booze. *"Same again!"* was all they'd shout. It was always difficult to see properly, no matter what time of the day or night it was. She'd dreaded that job more than any other. The place always seemed to be full of old, gummy men with bad coughs using bad language, always sitting in the same places. They'd stare at her through squinting bloodshot eyes. They almost seemed homeless. Now she knew why. Ten past eleven on a Sunday night. What could you expect? Some things never change, she thought. She looked around the smoky bar for her father.

"Jamie," he shouted.

She made her way over to the counter. She looked around at the faces. Patsy Nolan. Jimmy Quinn. A few of the other men from the road. All drinking pints of stout to beat the band and slowly but surely deciding what was best for the world and mankind.

"How are you, love? Strange to see you in here," her father said. The men shuffled their stools around to make room for the lady.

"Well I'm not normally here, am I? I'm in London," she replied smartly. She noticed a couple of the men leering at her.

"What happened your eye?" Patsy Nolan asked, exposing the couple of rotten teeth he'd left in his mouth.

"I was picking me nose and my finger slipped, Mr

Nolan," she replied brusquely. "What do *you* think happened my eye?"

"What'll you have, love?" her father asked.

She thought for a moment. "A glass of wine, Da," she replied. "Thanks."

"Come on in to the lounge and we'll relax." Her father stood up.

"No, I'm grand here." Jamie noticed the men were uneasy. "What's up?" She looked at her father.

"Well, see, it's like this," her father answered uneasily.

"What?" Jamie demanded.

"It's sort of been a tradition that the women drink next door in the lounge. Leave the men to chat, like."

Jamie's mouth dropped open. She looked around. Sure enough, she was the only woman in the entire room. To add insult to injury, every man in the bar was staring at her, mouths hanging open. Jesus, she thought, I feel like a kissogram.

"Here, Da," she said, "forget the drink. I'll see you at home." The crowd in the bar remained motionless although last drinks had been called. Jamie walked quickly to the door. She felt as if she'd just stepped back fifty years in time. A pub with no women. More important, a pub that encouraged couples to drink separately? Jesus wept, she muttered. She pulled up her hood and walked up Collins Avenue in the misty rain towards home. She couldn't help worrying that she might be pregnant. She felt her hair. It was soaked. Yet she couldn't feel heavy rain. Just a light mist. It was a depressing night. She was pissed off. That was for sure.

Everyone had their routine which they loved and lived for. Her father went drinking with his friends in a place that was more like a *Ballroom of Romance* than a public house. The women in one room, the men in the other. Her mother made her scones and then sat down to watch the repeat of Daniel O'Donnell's New Year's Eve concert. Lisa was up snogging with the moon man. Both of her brothers were away working, in the States. Seán had carved a nice niche for himself renovating old dilapidated houses for the rich folk of Boston, and Barry was working for a coast-to-coast haulage company in San Francisco driving an articulated forty-foot. That left Jamie.

She thought coming home would make her feel good. But it hadn't. She was numb. Nothing seemed right any more. She should've been at work by nine tomorrow morning. How would she explain that? Where would she start to look for a job now that she was home? She didn't even *want* a job. It would be weeks before she could claim the dole. At least she had the three grand. But what if *he* came after her? No. He wouldn't. Sure, he couldn't. She was far away from all that now. Time to let the wounds heal. Try to forget. Can't forget. The pain. The police doctor's plastic gloves. The forceps. That horrible feeling. She looked up at the street light shining against the rain, which had become heavier now. He was out there. She knew that. She just wanted him to stay out there.

She turned the key quietly in the front door. All the

lights were off except for the small one in the kitchen over the cooker. There was a note on the kitchen worktop. It was from her mother.

Jamie,

There was a phone call from Anne O'Brien. She said she was a friend of yours in London. She just called to say hello and will call you later during the week. Make sure Lisa is in before you lock the front door and that she's on her own.

Love,

Mam.

PS I nearly forgot. Check that your father is in too and that he doesn't go near the chip pan. I have to go to the launderette in the morning. I won't wake you.

Jamie filled a glass with water. She switched off the kitchen light and headed up the stairs. Her mother had tidied up Barry's old room for her when she heard she was coming home. She sat on the side of the bed and pulled open the top drawer of the dressing-table. Empty. Just then, she heard a rap on the window of the front door. Her heart almost stopped. For a split second, she was back in the flat and it was happening all over again. She started to shake.

"*Mammy,*" she called at the top of her voice, almost unable to get the word out. "*Mammy!*" she shouted again. She felt like a helpless child being chased by a barking dog.

Her mother rushed into the bedroom, pulling on

her dressing-gown. She grabbed Jamie and hugged her as hard as she could.

"It's all right, love. No one's going to touch you now. You're safe here. It's all right."

Jamie moaned. The rapping on the front door got louder and more insistent. Her mother ran to the bedroom window and opened it. She leaned out into the darkness.

"Who *is* it?" she roared.

"Who do you think?" Her father replied as he hiccuped and belched. "The man from the *Black Magic* ad."

"You'll feel my black magic if you break that window. Where are your bloody keys?"

"I lost them."

"Well, what were you banging on the glass with?" she continued.

He felt in his pocket with his left hand. Then, as a last resort, he opened his right hand. His keys! "Ah!" He held them up and laughed. "Here they are. Jesus, Móna, you're brilliant." He took aim for the door lock.

"Yeah," she shouted. "It's a good job someone is. And by the way, you're sleeping on the couch tonight." She shut the window and returned to the bed. "He farts likes a bear when he's had too much to drink."

Jamie had relaxed considerably.

"Are you all right, love?" her mother asked.

"Yeah." Jamie clutched her mother's hand. "It's never gonna go away. Is it, Ma?"

"Of course it will. You'll just have to give it time.

Lots of time, love." She stroked Jamie's tossed hair. "You know I'm here if you need me. Don't worry." She stood up. "Now, get into bed and have a good sleep. It'll do you the world of good."

Jamie stretched and gave her mother a hug. "Thanks. And sorry for fighting tonight."

"Lie down." Her mother went to switch off the light.

"Don't." Jamie jumped. "Leave it on."

"OK. Goodnight," her mother gestured quietly.

"'Night," Jamie whispered. After a few minutes, she closed her eyes.

Chapter Fourteen

"Jesus, what's the world coming to? Three hundred and fifty grand for a pub in Drogheda." Ray was reading the property supplement in the *Irish Independent*. "I'd give anything to own me own pub at home." He stared at the picture of the pub. "It's only two minutes' walk from me mother's. Ah yeah. Some day."

"And pigs will fly," the lush on the bar stool muttered.

Ray shook his head and sighed. "Where would anybody come up with money like that?" He folded the paper. "I can see why they're robbing banks. Here." He handed the paper to one of the drinkers. "I shouldn't be making meself homesick."

"Excuse me, mate," a small man called from the quiet end of the bar. He was so small that he could barely see over the counter.

"Who said that?" Ray asked. He could see a small head with whitish hair just above the bar top. "Jesus, a real live leprechaun." He strolled down to the man. "What can I get you, apart from a ladder?" The drinkers laughed.

"All right?" the little man asked. "Remember me? Opening night?"

"*Our* opening night. Sure that was nearly two months ago. And to be honest, after fifteen pints and four hundred guests, I can't say that I do."

"I gave you a transformer for the band. Remember?"

"Jesus, I do. You and your friend were in the small red car. Jesus, if you stuck a hat on your head with a bell on it, I'd swear you were Noddy."

The small man forced a smile. He was definitely not amused.

"You told me to drop in if I was passing. Luckily, there was a parking space right outside the door so I thought I'd avail of the chance and say hello."

"That's very kind of you. And if you don't mind me asking, where did you get your driving licence? No, let me guess. In a lucky-bag?"

"I thought you might be interested in a bit of business," said the stranger meaningfully.

"Oh yeah, and what might you be selling? Dodgy glasses? Or maybe duty-free spirits? Sorry, pal, not interested." Ray began to clean the counter.

"Actually, I thought you might be interested in some security."

Ray laughed.

"What, like?" He smiled at the man. "You, a bouncer? Ha. Did you hear that, lads? This fella wants to be a bouncer like our Jack!" The punters spluttered at the notion. "I tell you this for nothing, sham. You'd have a better chance of getting a job with Fossett's Circus as the world's tiniest man."

The man was saying something but Ray couldn't hear him above the laughter.

"Quiet, lads," he shouted. "Sorry about that. Move down here a bit. That's better. Now I can hear you. What were you saying to me?"

"Anyone serving down here?" came a drunken roar.

Ray scoured the end of the bar. "Tommy Quinn. I thought I told you you'd enough to drink. Now get out of here and go and look for a job." He turned back to the man who was growing more impatient by the minute. "His wife thinks he's down at the job centre every day. And where is he? Sorry, go on."

"Not door security. That's not what I had in mind. More like protection." The stranger waited for a reaction.

Ray stood up, revealing his awesome build.

The small man's eyes opened wide.

"What sort of *protection*?" Ray asked.

"Simple. You pay us an agreed monthly premium and we look after your premises."

"Who's *we*?" Ray asked angrily.

"My firm. We look after most of the offices and premises in this area. A lot of landlords pay a few bob for our services."

"Why?" Ray demanded.

"Because they just do. You know. Little boys do what their big brothers tell them to do. You know what I mean. You pay us and you don't have any problems."

"From who?" Ray folded his arms. "Anyway, what happened to *your* big brother?"

The little man threw his eyes up to heaven and

251

laughed. "I'm not getting the message across to you, Paddy, am I?" He reached out to pick up some peanuts from the bowl in front of him.

Ray grabbed it. "They're for people who spend their money here. Not for parasites like you. And the name's Mr Flynn, to you."

"Choice is yours, mate. Take it or leave it. I suggest you take it and avoid the hassle. Next time it won't be me who'll be talking to you." He put his hands in his pockets.

Ray looked down the end of the bar. The lads were all huddled around the newspaper. Nobody seemed to have noticed what was going on.

"What's it going to be then, mate?"

Ray leaned over the bar. "You're not my friend, so don't call me *mate*. As for your protection idea: how would you like to be six inches smaller? They'll have to bury you in a shoe box if you don't get off the premises right *now*. All right?" Ray clenched his right fist so hard that his knuckles made a cracking sound. He leaned closer. "Now fuck off!"

"Please yourself," the man replied as he turned and walked towards the door.

"Hey, sham," Ray roared. There was instant silence in the bar.

The man turned around.

"Don't bother coming back, you hear me?"

The stranger smiled at Ray and pushed open the door. It closed behind him.

Ray flicked the towel he'd been holding around his neck as if back in his boxing days.

"Everything all right, Ray?" Frank closed the door from upstairs behind him.

"Ah, yeah. Just an undesirable, that's all. He won't be back."

"I need three kegs changed."

"No problem."

"And, listen, Ray, will you drop two kegs of Guinness up to the Irish centre in Camden. They've got some big name up there tonight. It looks as if they'll get a huge crowd."

"Grand job. I might even head over there after we close tonight," Ray shouted from the cellar.

"Nice clientele you got 'ere, mate."

The strange, commanding voice made Frank look up. Two men stood on the other side of the bar. One of them showed a ID card. "Scotland Yard. Are you Frank McCabe?"

"Yes. Can I help you?"

"Anywhere we could go for a quiet chat, sir?"

Frank nodded towards the other end of the bar. The two jackets followed him. "Now, what can I do for you two gentlemen?"

One of them produced a dirty, pulverised scrap of paper. It was covered in filth. He held it out to Frank. "Does this look familiar, sir?"

Frank took the strip of paper. It had been carefully folded prior to falling into the dirt. As he unfolded it, he noticed the inside was spotless. He recognised the print. And the writing. It was the page from his diary that he'd given to the tramp outside Euston with his own name and address. "Yes, I gave it to a . . . a friend.

It has my name and address on it. Where did you get it?"

"When did you give it to this man, sir?"

"Eh, a couple of weeks ago, I suppose. Why? Has he been arrested?"

The two men looked at each other.

"Is he in some sort of trouble?"

"What's this man's name, sir?"

"Eh, I'm not sure what his real name is. But he was telling me that everyone who knows him calls him Paddy."

"Paddy?"

"Yeah, that's right. Paddy . . . Last."

"Paddy *Last*, sir?"

"That's right." Frank coughed.

"Do you recognise the man in this photograph, sir?"

Frank examined the picture. It looked like a police shot. The type taken when you've been charged with a criminal offence. "Yeah, seems to be him, all right. Where have you got him?" he asked nervously.

"He's down in the city morgue, actually. Michael Lenane, according to our records. Small-time petty theft, mainly. We've locked him up in the cells overnight, once or twice. We scraped what was left of him off the tracks at Euston underground last Sunday night, sir."

"Off the *tracks*?"

"That's right. I'm afraid your *friend* jumped under a train. This was the only identification he was carrying at the time. How did you know him?"

Frank was shellshocked. "Under a *train*?"

"Did you hear me, sir?"

"What?" Frank mumbled.

"How did you know this man?"

"Eh, we're from the same place back at home."

"Funny . . . you don't look alike, at all," sniggered the second officer.

Frank stared at him. "Why did he do it?"

"Jump under a train, sir? No one knows. We deal with at least three every week. These poor hobos eventually just can't take any more, I suppose."

"Because they're afraid," whispered Frank. Paddy Last's words were coming back to him now. Now, it was making sense.

"Sorry, sir?"

"Nothing."

"OK, sir, that'll be all. Oh, just before we go, one more thing. Mr Lenane was carrying quite a substantial sum of money on his person when we recovered his body. Nearly eight hundred pounds in cash. I don't suppose you know where . . . "

Frank was disgusted. He shook his head hard. "*No!*"

"Miserable bastard probably stole it!" muttered the accompanying detective. The two men turned to leave. Their path was blocked.

"He won it on a scratch card, *actually*!" Ray's teeth were locked together, he was so angry.

"How do *you* know?" asked Frank.

Ray never took his eyes off the detectives. "Because he came in here dressed like a gentleman last Sunday evening. He wanted to wait for you, Frank. But his flight was at twenty to eight." Ray thumped the counter so hard that three glassed jumped off and smashed. "He was *going home*! Tell me, *detective*, why would someone who was looking forward to going home after twenty years of misery and shit want to kill himself?"

The two detectives looked curiously at each other.

"Get *out* before you have to lock *me* up!" Ray thundered.

They left without another word.

Ray stared at Frank. "I'm sorry. I meant to tell you he came in to see you. I just completely forgot. He was a really nice bloke." Ray put his hand into his pocket and took out an envelope. "He asked me to give this to you."

Frank opened it reluctantly. Inside was a twenty-pound note and a picture postcard of the sun setting over Skibbereen. The message was simple.

Frank . . . you'll never know how much your kindness meant that morning.

I hope you didn't mind me buying a scratch card out of the money.

It paid off. See you back home . . . soon, I hope. God bless you . . . your friend,

Paddy L.

Frank carefully placed the card and the money on the counter. "I'll be back in a while."

Ray nodded. "Take as long as you like." He patted his friend on the back.

Frank picked up his jacket and left.

* * *

Ray walked towards the cellar door. As he turned the key in the door, he noticed a solitary figure sitting close to where the detectives had been standing a few minutes before. He was sitting behind a pillar, almost as if he was hiding. He was reading a newspaper. Ray left the keys hanging in the door and walked back to him.

"Can I get you something there?" he asked in a friendly voice.

The bearded man looked up from the paper. He seemed young. Yet his features were old and worn. No more than thirty-five, Ray thought. He studied him more closely. It wasn't a full beard. More like a week's heavy growth.

"I'll have a pint of Double Diamond, mate," the man answered in a quiet voice.

Ray could detect a Northern accent. He wasn't sure how to react. "*Double Diamond?* Are you having me on? I haven't seen Double Diamond for almost ten years!"

The stranger looked at what the others were drinking. "I'll have a pint of Guinness, then."

Ray eyed him doubtfully. "Where've you been, then, Mars?"

"I suppose you could say that."

"Are y'on holidays?" Ray asked curiously as he picked up a glass and put it under the flowing tap.

The man smiled, almost sarcastically. "I suppose you could call it a holiday. In fact, every day feels like a holiday these days." He went back to his newspaper.

Ray scratched his head as he tried to figure out what the customer was talking about. He flicked the tap handle slightly to give the pint a creamier head and put it in front of the man. "Two pounds and fivepence to your good self, please." Ray noticed four or five tattoos on each arm. Maybe he was a builder. He was certainly broad enough.

The man counted out the money carefully. "Thanks."

Ray was going out of his mind with curiosity. "I haven't seen you in here before."

"Have you not?" He continued to read his paper. "You musn't have been here eight years ago, then."

"That's true," Ray replied, hoping that the man would tell him more.

The stranger picked up his pint and stared at Ray. "That fella's more dangerous than you realise." He took a long drink.

Ray's eyes opened wide.

When the glass was put back on the counter, it was three-quarters empty.

"Which man?" Ray asked, his eyes glued to the almost empty glass.

"The little bloke you just threw out before the police arrived."

"Do you know him?" Ray moved closer to the bearded man.

"Know him?" The man smiled and finished off the drink. "Let's say I had to share digs with him for four years. Miserable little bastard. Put us on another, please."

"Where are you from?"

The man studied Ray. "All over the place. Mostly Derry."

"Are you working over here?"

The man shook his head. He seemed reluctant to talk. "I worked here for a while. A long time ago."

"What did you do?"

He smirked. "I built carparks."

Ray scratched his head. *"Carparks?"*

"Yeah."

"I was in the building game myself. But carparks. That's interesting. They're the sort of things you wouldn't have thought needed too much careful planning."

"The planning came before the carpark. No two carparks were ever the same."

"Oh, yeah. I think I know what you mean, all right. Beautifully put!" Ray watched him in disbelief.

"More like *de*construction, as distinct from *con*struction, I suppose."

"Aye. Are you a bit of a poet, maybe?" Ray felt mortified asking.

The stranger didn't seem surprised at the question. "Aye, I've written some poetry in my time. Mainly to work off frustration apart from anything else. Too much time on your hands can be dangerous, if you know what I mean."

"Oh, you don't have to tell me. I used to spend it drinking like a fish!"

"You were the lucky one. I didn't see a drop of alcohol in eight years."

Ray was shocked. Apart from not having a clue where this conversation was going, he was beginning to think that this Irishman had lost his marbles.

"Living out where the buses don't run, are we?" he asked cagily.

"Funny you should put it like that. I was . . . for years, actually. In some of those places, you'd be lucky to see a sheep, never mind a bus."

"*Sheep?* Interesting."

"No sheep. Just men in white coats? If you're lucky to spend a couple of days in the infirmary. Although some of them were butchers too."

Ray hesitated. "Loony bin?"

"Hell on earth!"

"With hell to pay?"

"There will be now." He smiled and drank from the full glass.

Ray was convinced he was talking to a lunatic. He had to find out more. "Mental asylum?"

"All those things and more. Call it what you like. I definitely won't be going back. I'll die before they drag me back there."

"And what did you do all day?"

"Studied."

"Studied what?"

"Freud, mainly."

"Fried what?"

"*Freud.*"

"Yeah, but fried what?"

"Freud, the writer. You know, the bloke who diagnosed mental illness and all that?"

"Oh, that Freud, of course I do. He hasn't had anything out lately, has he?"

"How could he? He's *dead* for fucking years!"

"Of course, sure, now that you say it, I remember . . . he used to do those dog food commercials on the telly, didn't he?"

"That's *Clement* Freud!" he shouted, throwing his eyes upwards.

Ray scratched his head. "Oh, now I got you . . . he did the food programmes from Kinsale . . . loves a drop of red wine."

"Keith *Floyd*, the fucking chef . . . that's who you're thinking of. Do you ever read anything of literary value?" he asked in amazement.

Ray thought for a moment. "*The Field?*" he said quietly.

"By John B Keane?"

"Who?"

"*The Field*. About inter-family bloodshed over the rights to inherited land?"

"About . . . horses. *The Irish Field*. It comes out every Friday. Well, actually, we don't get it here till Saturday."

The stranger nodded sadly. "Anyway," he huffed, "where was I?"

Ray decided to change the subject. "So you're cured now?"

The stranger chuckled. "I suppose you could say that."

Ray was about to add more when the stranger stopped him dead. "Listen, pal, I know what you're thinking. You're thinking, 'am I talking to some mentally deranged psychopath who's going to jump over the counter and slit my throat from ear to ear in a minute with a bread knife?' Aren't you?"

Ray gulped.

"I'm not mad. Maybe I was, then. Not any more. I'd babysit for you if you wanted me to and guarantee you that your kids would never be so happy or well looked after."

Ray was wondering if the stranger noticed a look of horror on his face. "Are you considered dangerous?" he asked clumsily.

"Deadly. *Booo!*" the man roared as he lunged towards Ray.

"*Holy fuck!*" Ray's eyes opened wide with fright as he jumped back. "Jesus, don't be doing that."

"My name's Paul." The man roared laughing and stretched out a huge hand.

"Ray."

"Pleased to meet you."

"Your friend was murdered. Very discreetly. *Very* definitely."

"*Who?*"

"Paddy? Was that his name?"

"Paddy *who?*"

"The tramp those pigs came in to question your mate about earlier on."

"*Murdered?*"

"I saw it happen on Sunday night. I was just getting my bearings again. Trying to see if a couple of mates were still living local, like . . . if they'd put me up for a couple of days. Trying to stay in the shadows. About quarter past six. Euston underground. It was fairly busy. Obviously, a lot of people making connections after the weekend. I was watching the guy who did it.

A cop. He was the bloke who robbed me of eight precious years. Deported my girlfriend back to Dublin with my daughter so that I would never see or hear from them again. I was watching him watching the tramp. I reckoned he'd hassle him. Give him gyp. 'Move along, you dirty knacker.' I was just waiting to see what was going to happen. I never thought he'd grab him by the arm and fuck him out in front of the train. No one saw him doing it, the platform was so busy. Of course, with all the screaming and fainting afterwards, the cop just disappeared. But not before I walked out in front of him. He was rushing to get to the emergency stairs. He saw me. Nearly shat himself, I reckon. Poor bastard never knew what hit him. Only a few thousand tons of train. That's all."

Ray was devastated. He didn't know where to look. He leaned against the counter and shook. "I don't believe you."

"Do you not?" Paul shrugged his shoulders. "Why should you? You'll never hear of anyone being convicted of *murdering* an homeless tramp. Certainly not a member of the London Metropolitan police force." He sipped more slowly from his drink.

"Why didn't *you* report it?"

"Long story."

"*What* story?"

"A story you *definitely* wouldn't believe!"

"Who *are* you? And why do I keep thinking that I've seen you somewhere before?"

"I'd be surprised if you hadn't."

Ray felt disturbed. Insecure. "What do you want?"

263

"I don't know any more. I suppose . . . my life back; the people I love; my identity; my dignity. That's not much to ask. Is it?"

"You were on the TV!"

"Was I? I don't have one. So I didn't see it. How did I look?"

"That's *it*! You're a wanted man. Aren't you?"

"For what?" He smiled. "Ten minutes ago, you thought I was a raving lunatic." The man stood up from the stool.

"Are we busy?" Frank banged the door behind him.

"You could say that." Ray kept his eyes fixed firmly on the Derryman's. "This man saw Paddy being *pushed* under the train at Euston last Sunday."

Frank's expression sharpened. "Who are you?"

"Just passing through, that's all. I used to drink here eight years ago. You must be the new manager?"

Frank nodded.

"He was on the news during the week, Frank. The *serious* news!" Ray scraped at the counter nervously.

"Why was that, then?" Frank asked.

"Gardener of the year, you could say. Or so *they* say. They reckon when it comes to digging big holes, I can't be beaten." He pulled his jacket up around his shoulders. "Don't underestimate him. His name is Barrett. DC Thomas Andrew Barrett. He's currently with the Drug Squad . . . now one less. R.I.P." He pulled the green check cap firmly down on to his head. "At least I used to think we had motives for doing what we did. Now I know I was wrong. But this guy is *evil*." He looked squarely at Ray. "What did you call it . . .

264

'living out where the buses don't run'?" He tipped his cap. "See you round, I hope."

"I know his girlfriend," Frank mumbled.

The tall stranger spun around. "What did you say?"

"I said I know his girlfriend."

The stranger's cold, noxious stare seemed to soften for a moment. "Tell her to get out. I did!" He pulled the door shut behind.

"What the hell was he talking about?" Ray asked discountedly. "What a load of bollock!"

"Do you think so?" Frank replied softly. He continued to stare at the door. "If only I'd got her address."

"*Whoes* address?"

"Ah . . . no one."

Ray ran for the door.

"Where are you going?" Frank roared.

"I have to find out something. I'll be back in a minute." Ray ran out on to Bromley Road. A regular Saturday afternoon. Not too busy. Just nice and easy-going. He glanced quickly in all directions. Then he spotted him. "*Paul!*"

Paul didn't look back until he dodged down an alleyway, away from the main road. Once they were out of view, he caught Ray's arm. "Jesus, man. Are you trying to put every cop in north London on to me?"

"So you are wanted!"

"In a manner of speaking, yes . . . unfortunately."

Ray scrutinised him. "You're Flaherty, aren't you?"

The man nodded. "Yes."

"You're the IRA bomber, aren't you? That was you

on the news, wasn't it?" Ray could barely finish the question.

"I am not a *bomber*. And I'm certainly *not* a member of any paramilitary organisation!" He looked as if he was about to pulverise Ray.

"Then why did they say you were?"

"Because, like your homeless friend, I happened to be in the wrong place at the wrong time eight years ago and I met the *wrong* man. Does *that* answer your question?" He turned to walk back towards the main road.

"Paul. Listen. The small man that I threw out earlier? Tell me about him."

"Who was that?" Flaherty looked edgy and scared in the open.

"Remember. You mentioned that small bloke earlier. The one I threw out. You said he was dangerous?"

"Aye, very dangerous."

"Dangerous in what way?"

"Dangerous in every way. Small jockey, big whip!"

"What d'you mean?"

"He's linked to the wrong sort of people. People you don't want to get involved with."

"Like who?" Ray asked curiously.

"Like the lowest of the low. At least, I'm sorry now for what I did and I hope that God has forgiven me."

"Did you ever murder anybody?"

"*No, no, no!*" He thumped the wall. "With my hand on my heart, I swear. These people are different. These *monsters* hurt old women. They sell drugs to kids. They're into any scam that yields a few bob. Nothing gets in their way. That particular guy is just a messenger. His name is Alistair. Ali, for short. His associate is Tommy Barrett, the cop I was telling you about. Tommy's well able to cover his arse. He was the bloke who put me away. He'd been watching me for weeks. Even tried to sell me a bit of gear. And a gun, if you don't mind. I didn't like him so I said no. Of course, you can imagine how I reacted when I discovered he was a cop. I could tell you stories about that pervert that still make my hair stand up straight."

"Go on," Ray urged.

"I don't have time, mate. Another afternoon when neither of us is rushing away."

"Do I know this copper?" Ray asked, intrigued.

"Well, if that small parasite is lurking around your pub, his police friend isn't too far away, let's just say."

"But surely he can't go too far overboard if he's a cop?"

Paul's face immediately adopted a sinister stare. "Overboard? That bastard doesn't know the meaning of the word. He asked to be allowed join the high security team that escorted me in the army helicopter to Long Lartin prison the day after I was convicted. I knew they weren't going to sing, 'For he's a jolly good fellow'. But I wasn't expecting what they had in store. As soon as they got me inside and closed the door, he stuck the snout of a .38 Special into my mouth. He started banging it around from side to side." He opened his mouth to bare his teeth. Ray could see that most of them were either cracked or chipped. "The pain was unbearable. The dentist in prison said that seventeen of them were broken. Then he pushed the barrel in further. I could see the chamber turning slowly. I knew that if he discharged the weapon, he'd probably destroy the helicopter. But then again, this bastard didn't seem to care. He laughed. The others were horrified. They begged him to ease off and stop messing. He just told them to fuck off."

"Then what?" Ray pleaded breathlessly.

"The gun clicked. I wet my pants. Everyone just laughed. It was a jittery sort of laughter. It didn't sound real."

"What did he say?"

"Not a lot. But what he did say I'll never forget for the rest of my born days. As he slowly pulled the trigger, he kept telling me to repeat three words, 'dare I die'."

"Dare I die?"

"Dare I die. For months I used to wake up in prison at night screaming those words, thinking of what he'd put me through that morning. There was worse to come. Barrett put a black sack over my head. They handcuffed my hands to the roll-bars above the sliding side door of the chopper. It was in the air for what seemed like a couple of minutes at this stage. I knew they couldn't throw me out because, after all, they'd be held accountable for my death. I reminded them of that. *He* just laughed. 'What if we were to say that you tried to escape?' He laughed again. Then I heard the door opening. He took off the handcuffs and gave me the choice of jumping on my own or being thrown out.

They told me we were five hundred feet above ground. I could feel the cold air blowing around me. I kept thinking, 'they won't do it'. Next thing, I felt a hand grab my shoulder and push me. They threw me out." He wiped the sweat back off his forehead.

"Jesus Christ, how did you survive?" Ray asked.

"Because what they didn't tell me was that we were hovering only six feet above the ground!"

"Jesus, the bastards!" Ray shouted.

"Ssshhh!" Paul looked around him nervously.

"You must have nearly died?" Ray whispered.

"From a heart attack more like it. I shat my trousers, I got such a fright. It was only half an hour later that I realised my collar bone was snapped." He pressed his shoulder with two fingers. "I couldn't even walk up the stairs for months without nearly shitting myself. I think it would have been less frightening if they'd shot me."

"My God," Ray said slowly.

Paul smiled. "It's a long time ago. I'm free now. Please God, I won't have to go back. I'm a different person."

"I'm not surprised," gasped Ray.

"I'd love to marry. Few kids. But who'd have me?" Then he turned serious again. "Different with one exception. Constable Barrett," he rattled off the words with a sarcastic, poisonous tone in his voice. "I'd love to watch him die. Maybe I'll get my chance some day. Him and his friend." He looked at the sky. "You know he used to ring up my poor mother while I was inside and threaten her. It takes some monster to do a thing like that."

"Go on, tell me," Ray blurted.

"Another time, my friend. Thanks for the drinks. I'll remember them for more than one reason." Paul gently thumped Ray's shoulder.

"Will you go back to Derry?"

Paul considered the question. "Derry's got a lot of happy memories. But it's got a lot of bad ones too. Too many painful wounds. Too much bigotry. I've seen enough of that to do me till I die. No, I'll try an' get a wee job in Dublin. Bring me mother down if she wants to come. She's on her own now. She's eighty-two. I miss her. She was too sick to visit. Me brother's a taxi-driver in Dublin. He'll let me cosy for him for a while. Anyway, I've got a couple of little things to sort out before I settle down for good. Things I've been waiting to do for a while now. You seem like a nice guy, Ray. Be careful, 'cos they're watching you right now and they always get what they want."

"I'm not afraid of anyone," Ray insisted.

"Seriously, Ray. Be careful. See you round." The stranger disappeared up the busy high street.

Ray headed back to work.

"Jesus, Ray. Your friend seems to have the knack of clearing the place. Can you arrange for him to come at closing time rather than lunchtime?" Frank joked.

Ray looked at the clock. Just after four. He had to collect Davina from Sainsbury's at five. He switched on the small radio behind the bar. The story might be on the news . . .

" . . . another woman has been attacked in the Crofton Road area of north London. Police are asking witnesses who may have seen a man acting suspiciously in the area between the hours of three and four this morning to contact them . . . Finally, anti-terrorist squad officers are still appealing for help in their efforts to track down a convicted IRA bomber. Paul Flaherty escaped from Brixton's top-security prison on Sunday last. The Derryman, serving life imprisonment for the Shaftesbury Avenue car bombing in 1989, in which eight people died, was among a small group of Republican prisoners taking early morning exercise in the main prison yard. Police are warning members of the public that Flaherty is extremely dangerous. He's described as five feet eleven in height; athletic build; dark hair and a moustache. He may be armed and should not be approached under any circumstances . . . "

Ray felt weak. His knees knocked against each other. He looked over towards the dimly-lit corner of the bar at the two empty pint glasses that sat on the counter. He quickly stuck a half-pint glass under the cider tap, filled it and drank it down. He took a deep breath and shook his head. Who'd believe me? he asked himself. Sure, they'd only think I was living out where the buses don't run.

Ray hadn't realised that Frank had been standing beside him listening to the news bulletin.

"I remember that case years ago. They reckoned he was one of the most dangerous men in Europe before they managed to catch him."

"He didn't do it," Ray remarked casually.

271

"How do you know?" Frank asked mockingly.

Ray looked up from the radio. "Frank, you're not going to believe what I'm about to tell you."

Frank's face turned serious. "Try me."

"You're going to think I've lost it completely."

"What?"

"Barrett framed him!"

"Sometimes, Ray, I just don't know about you."

* * *

The telephone seemed to be ringing for ages. Everyone's gone out, Jamie thought. Then she realised where she was. In her own bed, at home. The answering machine was off. She ran into Lisa's room and picked up the extension.

"Hello?"

It was a woman's voice.

"Hello," Jamie replied quietly.

"Could I speak to Jamie, please?"

"Speaking."

"Jamie, this Anne O'Brien in London."

"Oh, hello." Jamie tried to sound pleased to hear from her.

"How are you feeling?" She waited. "If that's not a stupid question."

"OK. So-so I suppose."

"I've had some job trying to locate your number in Dublin. You could have told me you were going home."

"I didn't know I was going home," Jamie answered defensively.

"Well, at least we've found you. We were beginning to get a bit worried about you."

"Why?"

"Well, another woman was attacked close to your flat the night before last. Seemed to have all the same hallmarks as your attacker."

"Is she all right?"

"Who?"

"The woman he attacked."

"Yes. She's badly shaken. But she was able to fight him off and raise the alarm."

There was a silence. "Jamie," the policewoman began, "we're bringing in your deejay friend for a little talk."

"It wasn't him," Jamie shouted.

"How do you know?"

"Because I just do! I've had time to think."

"Well, we'd still like to talk to him. He may have noticed someone else in the street when he was leaving."

"I doubt it. He was twisted. He wouldn't have been able to see the parked cars."

Silence again.

"It might give *you* some peace of mind."

"How? To know that he raped me?"

"We can bring him in whether you like it or not, Jamie." She was authoritative now.

"OK. But please don't tell him what happened me."

"I won't. But maybe he will. Are you going to be at home for long?"

"I don't think so. My mother's driving me mad

already. It'll only be a matter of days before she starts telling me what time to be home by."

Anne O'Brien laughed. "I know. My mother's the same. Every time I go home. She's even afraid to look in my handbag these days in case she finds a gun."

Jamie laughed.

"Have you told the people at work that you're home in Dublin?"

"No. I was going to ring them this morning."

"This *morning*? It's quarter to three, dear girl," Anne shrilled. "Still, you need the rest. If you like, I'll call and say I'm just a friend. That you had to go home at short notice, will I?"

"Oh, Anne, you're a little pet. Would you mind? Don't say anything though, please. Tell them I'll ring later in the week."

"No problem. It's City Radio, isn't it?"

"Yeah, on Marleybone High Street. 787 8787. Thanks a million." Then she turned serious. "How long will you keep him?"

"David? Only a couple of hours. If we think he's a suspect, we'll keep a constant check on him."

Jamie waited a few seconds before asking her next question. "Have you any leads to go on?"

"One or two. I can't say much more over the phone."

Jamie was about to say goodbye.

"Before you go, any word from Tommy?"

"No. Why?"

"It's just that he hasn't been seen around here for a few days. I thought maybe he'd be trying to get back in your good books again."

"No!" Jamie replied abruptly.

"All right. Well, maybe if you hear from him, you'll let me know. Will you?"

Silence. "Yeah, sure. Thanks for calling, Anne."

"No problem. Listen, Jamie. You know where I am. If I can do anything for you, call me. You have my home number, haven't you?"

"Yeah, thanks."

"'Bye."

She replaced the receiver. She was about to go downstairs when the phone rang again.

Jamie picked up the receiver thinking that Anne must have forgotten to tell her something. "Hi, again," she said cheerfully in anticipation.

The line crackled. Silence. She could hear sporadic breathing.

"Hello." She waited. "Anne?" Jamie looked down at the cable to see if it was loose. "Hello," she repeated.

Nothing.

The line went dead. She put the phone down slowly. Probably a wrong number. She hoped.

Chapter Fifteen

Tommy hadn't noticed the two men sitting in the dark blue Opel Vectra at the corner of Shepton Avenue. He rang the doorbell again. No reply. He peeped through the misted glass and could see a figure coming to the door. Slowly, it opened.

"What do you want?" Nikki Coffey asked as she dried her hair with a towel. She held the door firmly with her other hand. She didn't want to let him in. Or did she?

"We need to talk." He stood there with his hands in his pockets.

"We've nothing to talk about. And if you don't leave now, I'll call your friends to have you removed." She draped the towel across the radiator and swept her long hair back over her left shoulder.

"I just need someone to talk to, that's all."

"Maybe that sort of line works on others, but not on me."

"Things aren't really going the way I wanted them to go," he pleaded.

"Well, what can you expect if you go around treating your friends like shit," Nikki retorted.

"Please Nikki, let me come in," he persisted.

"Tommy Barrett, do you really think that I can't see through you?"

He smiled and stood there looking at the clinging T-shirt she was wearing.

Nikki closed the door over slightly. "Some things never change, do they?"

"Well . . . what do you expect if you're going to walk around the house dressed like that?"

She opened the door and quickly walked into the sitting-room. "I don't know why I'm letting you in. I should really be calling the police."

"Why?" he asked as he made himself at home in the small armchair.

"Because of what happened to my best friend. Remember? Jamie? Your girlfriend?" She disappeared back into the small bathroom.

"I don't know what you're talking about." He stared around the room.

Nikki stuck her head around the corner of the bathroom. "Jamie was raped on Saturday night. Don't tell me you didn't hear?"

"Yeah, I know."

"Is that all you can say?"

"Well, it depends on what you're implying, Nikki." He was defensive. "Are you saying that I raped her?"

"No, I'm saying nothing of the sort. Do you think I'd let you in here if I thought you'd raped Jamie?"

"Probably not," said Tommy nervously.

"It's just that I'm not in the habit of letting male strangers into my house," she said. "So how did you come to hear?"

"Down the station. She reported it. I read it in the incident files."

Nikki emerged from the bathroom in the T-shirt and a pair of denim shorts. "And where the hell have you been for the last few days?" She waited for the crucial answer.

"Undercover."

"Ha! Underground more like it. Why didn't you call her and tell her where you were?"

"Because she threw me out. Because she didn't want to hear from me. That's why?"

Nikki stared at him in disbelief. "You don't give a shit about what's after happening to her, do you?"

"Of course I do. I tried to ring her."

"You don't even know where she is."

"She's gone home to Dublin," he shouted.

"And how did you find that out?"

"Nikki, will you stop shouting, for Christ's sake. Because I tried to ring. There was something wrong with the phone line. I could hear her. She couldn't hear me," he pleaded.

Silence.

"Look, Nikki," Tommy said softly, "why are we arguing like this? I'm as upset as you are about what's happened. I like Jamie as much as you do. I just think that maybe we're better off as friends."

Tommy watched Nikki as she fidgeted with the leaf of a plant. He could see that she wasn't wearing anything under the T-shirt. Her nipples were hard and stood out through the thin fabric. Her legs were tanned, gorgeous. Then he realised that she was looking at him. "Would you like to go for a drink?" he asked playfully.

"Why?" she asked curiously.

"Does there have to be a reason?" He smiled.

"For you to ask me out for a drink, I would have said yes," Nikki replied quickly.

"Well?" He wasn't taking no for an answer.

"Well, I should really take that stuff to the launderette." Nikki pointed to a large pillowcase in the corner.

"What's that?" Tommy asked curiously.

"Some of Jamie's things that the police dropped back. There's not much. They kept most of her gear. That stuff needs to be washed."

"I think you need a drink." Tommy tried to sound sympathetic.

"I think I need my head examined," Nikki muttered under her breath.

"Sorry?" Tommy asked.

"Ah, some things they examined . . . in the pillowcase."

"You didn't come across any money when you were cleaning the flat, did you?"

Nikki froze. How did he find out? she asked herself. Sweet Jesus, what now? "No!" She gulped.

"I'll ask you one more time." Tommy stood up. "Did you find any money?"

She felt crushed. Best say something, she thought. Anything. "Yes," she whispered.

"What did you do with it?"

"I gave it to Jamie."

"And what did she do with it?" he asked, drawing out each word.

"I don't know." Nikki tried to sound relaxed. It wasn't working. "What about that drink you promised me?" She forced a smile. Maybe it was the wrong thing to suggest, but she knew she had to get out of here. He couldn't lay a finger on her in the pub.

"Yeah, that'd be nice." Tommy stepped closer to her.

She stepped backwards towards the bathroom door. "Let me get my coat," she said.

"It's OK. I've got money," Tommy shouted after her.

"So have I." She regretted saying that.

* * *

They stepped out on to the front porch. It was quarter past five and getting dark. Nikki threw her coat around her shoulders and pulled the door behind her. She noticed Tommy staring at the car outside the garden gate.

"Yours?" he asked.

"Sort of," she replied nervously. "More like the bank's."

"I don't get you," Tommy said. "Did you buy it?"

"Yes. Over three years. Sorry . . . *five*, I mean. Works out quite reasonable. Thirty-four fifty a week."

Tommy ran his fingers across the roof of the brand

new Ford Escort. "Very nice." He looked at her and sneered. "Thirty-four fifty a week would be *three* years . . . actually. That still leaves you a couple of grand short, doesn't it?"

Nikki didn't like the sound of that. "What do you mean?" she asked nervously.

"Well, if you're paying thirty-five fifty a week over *three* years, you're still going to owe them a couple of grand." He smiled. "Surely you had to pay a fairly hefty deposit on top, Nikki?"

She looked at the car. "I meant *five* years." She walked up the road ahead of him.

"Are we going in your new car?" he shouted after her.

"Not when I'm having a few drinks."

"But, you're with a member of the police," he continued.

She threw her eyes up to heaven. As she rounded the corner of Shepton Avenue, she looked back. "Come on, hurry up, will you? I'm freezing." As she waited for a chance to cross the street, a blue Opel Vectra moved slowly up the road on the other side.

"Kilo seven to control, over . . . "

"Go ahead Kilo seven, over . . . "

"We've got our man in view, Sarge. He's heading out of Shepton Avenue with a woman, over . . . "

"OK. Keep him in your sights, Kilo seven. We don't want to be rumbled, over . . . "

"Where are we going, Nikki?" Tommy asked when he managed to catch up with her.

281

"The Clover Tap."

"I don't like the Clover Tap."

"Well, I do. And since you asked me out, I'll decide where we go."

"You're the boss," he muttered.

* * *

The pub was busy. Garryvoe Wanderers had just won their match against Brimston Athletic.

Nikki took off her saturated coat and pulled up a couple of stools close to the fire. Tommy threw his jacket on the floor beside the fireplace. He sat down.

Nikki waved to a couple of the lads from the football team who stood in a cluster at the end of the bar. She looked back at Tommy. "Well," She smiled. "Are you going to get the drinks?"

Tommy stood up and took some change out of his pocket. "What would you like?"

"Bottle of Ritz, plenty of ice in the glass. Thanks."

Tommy approached the bar.

* * *

Frank McCabe was on his own and run off his feet. Normally, Garryvoe lost their matches. Usually, two or three of them would come in for a quiet drink and head for home after an hour or so. However, this evening had become a turning point in history. Their first win in over two years. And to add to the post-match fever, one of their supporters had got most of the winning action on video. Frank was worried that someone was going to break the *pause* button on the video remote control as they watched the winning goal over and over again.

"What can I get you?" he shouted at the tall, dark man who stood at the counter.

"Bottle of Ritz, ice in the glass and a pint of Tennant's, please," he shouted. The noise of the crowd was deafening.

Frank looked at the man. He'd seen him at the opening night. Then, out of the blue, it dawned on him. Jamie's boyfriend. His mouth fell open. It was as if a huge pressure had been lifted from his shoulders. He'd made contact at long last, albeit with her other half. It was better than nothing. A wave of resentment washed over him as he remembered all he'd been told about this character. It was as if he'd known him for years. He despised him. But he couldn't let it slip.

"How's the girlfriend?" he asked cheekily.

Tommy looked back at Nikki who was sitting near the fire. "Fine, thanks," he replied.

"Jamie," Frank shouted.

"Who?" Tommy asked.

"*Jamie*," Frank shouted louder as he reached for a bottle of Ritz in the cooler.

"She's gone back home," Tommy replied casually.

"Why?" Frank asked.

Tommy shrugged his shoulders. "Got fed up, I suppose." He put a ten-pound note on the bar and picked up the drinks. "Drop the change over, mate. Cheers." He walked back to Nikki.

Frank watched him as he carried his drinks. Gone home, he thought. Obviously got sense and got out.

* * *

"There you go." Tommy put the drinks carefully on the table.

"Thanks. This is nice, isn't it," Nikki said as she looked around.

"Yeah." Tommy watched the mayhem at the bar. "Real nice."

"I love a few jars on a rainy evening."

"Why aren't you working?" Tommy asked curiously.

"Two-day week. No work." She sipped her drink.

"So how did you manage to buy a new Ford Escort, if you're only being paid two days a week?"

"'Cos I won some money."

"Where?"

"On the Lotto, that's where!"

"How much?" he persisted.

"Enough," she replied abruptly. "And that's enough about my car." She had to change the subject. "So tell us about this undercover operation that they put on. Checking out the sewers, were you?"

"Top secret."

"Oh, excuse me." Nikki clinked her empty glass against the bottle. "Ahem, you wouldn't like me to die of thirst, would you?"

Tommy smiled. Maybe his plan would work. A few more of them and he might introduce her to the

Snakebite. Then he'd have her singing. If he had an objective in life right now, it was to get his money back. His life depended on it.

* * *

By ten past seven, Nikki Coffey, well-pickled, was the life and soul of the football celebrations at the Clover Tap. While she sang a few songs with the winners, Frank carefully watched the character sitting close to the roaring fire. He seemed to enjoy the way she flirted with the footballers. Hugging them and kissing them. He liked it, even when applause erupted at the end of each song. There was something not right about him. Something evil, thought Frank.

As soon as Nikki returned to her seat, Frank brought over a couple of complimentary drinks for the two of them. Perhaps, if he mentioned Jamie to him again, he might pick up some more valuable information.

"Fair play to you, my dear. Ten out of ten. It's Ritz and ice and a pint of Tennant's, isn't it?" He put the drinks on the table.

"Ah, that's very good of you," Nikki slurred.

Tommy nodded. "Yeah, thanks."

Frank saw his chance. "I hope I didn't upset you when I mentioned Jamie a while back?"

Tommy froze. He was about to say something when Nikki burst in, "Ah, do you know Jamie? Wait till I tell you, she's my best friend."

"No, mate," interrupted Tommy.

Frank ignored him. "Do you know her?" he asked Nikki excitedly.

"Do I know her? She's my best friend for as long as I can remember. She's gone back to Dublin." Nikki bowed her head.

"To work?" Frank asked, interested.

"She got raped last weekend. She's devastated."

Frank froze. *Raped?* he thought. Maybe he hadn't heard her right. "What?" he shouted.

"Yeah, last weekend. In her flat."

"She's all right," Tommy muttered.

"All right?" Nikki shouted. "How do you know? Oh yes, she'll be all right when they catch the bastard who raped her, and cut his fucking balls off."

Frank was shocked. He'd only known Jamie for a few hours. But he suddenly realised he cared about her. More than he'd ever cared about a girl before.

"Can I have another bottle of Ritz, please? Nikki pointed to her near-empty glass.

"Sure, no problem. I'll get you one now." After delivering another round, Frank decided to leave the couple alone. He watched them from a distance. He wasn't quite sure what was going on between them, but it was clear to him that they were more than just good friends. He watched as the man put his arm around Nikki. After a short while, she was in good form again. Frank saw the man mix Nikki's drink with his own, aconcoction known in the business as Snakebite, a lethal mixture of lager and cider. It seemed to have its desired effect. By half eight, Tommy Barrett was helping Nikki Coffey into a waiting taxi.

Frank would have asked Nikki for Jamie's address, but not *him*. Tommy nodded to Frank as they walked slowly towards the door.

"Thanks," Frank muttered. He walked over to the table and started to clear away the empty glasses. He was livid at what he'd just been told. But powerless as to how he might help. Just then, he noticed it. Her handbag. He ran to the door. The taxi had gone.

* * *

The fresh air seemed to breathe a bit of life back into Nikki. The driver kept all the windows open, ready in the event of an accident. Tommy paid him as Nikki rooted in her pockets for the keys of the flat.

"My handbag," she shouted. "I left my bag in the pub."

"With the keys?" Tommy asked in a concerned voice.

Nikki pulled a bundle of keys out of her pocket and jangled them in front of Tommy's face. She smiled and ran her tongue sexily over her dry lips. "It's a good job I'm pissed."

"Why?" Tommy put his arm around her waist and kissed her on the forehead.

"Because I'd have to send you home." She giggled.

"And why don't you?" Tommy kissed her nose.

"Because . . . "

He cut her short by kissing her on the lips. His tongue searched for hers. She could feel his hands pull up the back of her T-shirt. His cold, wet hands stroked her bare back. His fingers played with her ribs. His hand moved around and cupped one of her bare breasts. He playfully squeezed her hard nipple.

287

She groaned as her hand felt his stiff member through his tight jeans. "Bastard," she heaved. Suddenly she stopped. She moved away and pulled her T-shirt tightly around her well-toned waist.

"What's wrong?" Tommy asked.

"Not in the middle of the garden. Come on, quick." She turned the key in the door.

The blue Opel Vectra was parked discreetly behind a tall hedge three doors further up the street. The radio crackled to life again.

"Kilo seven to base, over . . . "

"Go ahead, seven, over . . . "

"Our man looks as if he's grounded for the night." The two men smiled at each other. "Request to return to base, over . . . "

"Roger, seven. Request granted. Over and out."

"Have I shown you my holiday snaps?" Nikki shouted from the kitchen.

"Don't think so." Tommy threw his jacket over the back of the armchair.

Nikki uncorked a bottle of wine. She opened a drawer below the television and took out a photograph album. "Only certain people get to see these," she whispered. She leaned across and bit his earlobe.

Tommy smirked. He opened the album. More boring holiday snaps, he thought as he leafed through the first three pages. As he moved further into the album, however, he realised that Nikki and her friends were quickly losing their clothes. By page seven, everyone was naked.

"They were taken last November. Santa Ponsa," she said seductively.

"That explains the suntan, then." Tommy was stunned by one particular photo.

"Which one is that?" Nikki gloated, noticing the shocked look.

Tommy was speechless. He lifted up the album and pointed to a particular shot.

Nikki looked quite surprised. "Oh, Jesus, I didn't realise that one was in there."

Oh yeah, Tommy thought to himself.

"The owner of the club offered the first girl who'd strip off completely and pour two pints down her bare front a hundred quid." Nikki laughed.

"So, let me guess who won?" Tommy teased. He was becoming quite aroused. He leafed through the photos. He didn't notice Nikki beginning to strip off in the kitchen doorway.

"Hey, Mr Policeman, can you help me over here?" She beckoned seductively.

Tommy looked up. His heart began to beat faster.

She had unzipped her denim shorts. She had no pants on underneath. Her tight black bush pressed against the zip. She ran the palms of her hands slowly down inside the shorts, pushing them down her legs, inch by inch. Down over her knees. As they dropped to her bare feet, she stepped out of them and kicked them to one side. She ran her middle finger seductively over her black crop and then down between her creases of flesh. She lifted her head slightly and sighed.

Tommy squeezed his knees together and stood up

slowly. He put the photo album down on the floor and moved towards her.

She nodded her head towards the stereo. "Put on some music," she whispered.

Tommy fidgeted with the tuning switch on the radio until he found something slow and moody.

Nikki turned off the main light, allowing just a small streak from the bathroom to gently caress the room. She slowly lifted her T-shirt above her head, revealing her enormous breasts, firm and beautifully tanned. She breathed in. "Am I all right?" she asked playfully.

Tommy ran his fingernails down her ribs. Her breasts looked majestic. The most desirable he'd ever seen. "Yes," he whispered as he ran his fingertip across one of her hard nipples. He squeezed it firmly with his finger and thumb.

She pulled his head closer and shoved her nipple into his mouth. "Go on," she urged. She moaned as he sucked her breast. "Harder," she cried. "Bite it . . . harder."

He bit hard and grabbed her back. He ran his fingernails up and down her backbone. She moaned louder and threw her head back, pulling Tommy's shirt up his back in the process. She pulled his broad chest against her breasts, moving her cold, erect nipples roughly from side to side against his torso. She groaned again as she unbuttoned his trousers and ran her hand down inside. She felt something hard in his pocket. She pulled out a pair of black handcuffs and smiled. "Wanna have some fun?" She dangled them in front of him.

Tommy Barrett was *not* amused. He grabbed them forcefully. "*Don't* mess with things you don't know anything about!"

For a moment, Nikki felt frightened. Forget it, she thought. She grinned as she pulled his jeans down, his giant, erect manhood throbbing to attention. She stood back to examine it. "Oh yes!" she cried. She ripped open his denim shirt with her other hand and kept pulling at his clothes until he finally stood there in front of her, naked. She swallowed hard as she slowly ran her eyes over his firm, well-built body. His broad chest. His tight stomach. His strong, muscular arms and solid butt. His dark, hairy legs. She pulled him towards her, his stiff cock pressing against her navel. A small dribble of jism kept its magnificent helmet moist and playful.

Tommy stared down at her magnificent body. He ran his hands over her nakedness.

She shivered and closed her eyes. She knew this was wrong, but right now she didn't care. She'd yearned for him ever since she met him, through her ex-boyfriend, Peter. She'd always fancied him particularly when he displayed that naughty bulge in the front of his jeans. Nikki used to wonder if it was as big as it looked. Now she knew for sure. It was even bigger that she could have imagined and now she was going to have him. She'd worry about the consequences later. She could feel his tongue running up and down her stomach. He was squatting between her arched legs now. She held on to his shoulders to prevent herself from flaking out. Each breath became a hungry moan as her intense desire took over. He licked and sucked. Gently. Then a little harder. Then slowly down over her navel. On down, nibbling and gently tugging at her hair with his lips, up the insides of her legs with his darting tongue, gently flicking it in and out of her sex, teasingly poking her clitoris.

Nikki arched her back, the armchair catching her fall. She let out a loud groan of pleasure. Her entire body was trembling. Every limb and muscle reacting to the indescribable sensations that she was experiencing. Just as she was about to orgasm, he would stop short and run his tongue back up across her flat stomach to her breasts. Now and again, his mouth would close over her nipple. Gently. One. And then the other. As he slowly kissed her neck and hugged her tighter, she could feel his huge erection between her legs. God, she wanted him now. She looked at their reflection in the bathroom mirror, through the half-open door. He had a terrific body. But then, come to think of it, so had she. She stood up and leaned out towards the couch without moving away from his grip. She pulled the blanket off the back of the chair and threw it on the carpet. Then she pushed him slowly backwards, easing him on to the floor in front of the gas fire.

He watched the mirror. The reflection of her body made him more excited than he'd ever been. "I want you," he whispered.

She leaned over him and pressed a finger against his lips. "Don't be so impatient," she said. Now it was her turn to explore. To satisfy. She swept hair back over her ears. Then she moved Tommy around so that he was facing the mirror each time he sat up.

"What are you doing?" he asked curiously.

"Quiet," she whispered. "You'll see in a minute." Nikki bent over him and kissed his neck. "Nice aftershave," she said. She ran her tongue across his shoulders and up to his ear. Then she carefully took his earlobe in between her lips and nibbled it gently. She could hear him moaning, his mouth close to her ear.

He tickled her earlobe with the tip of his tongue for a couple of seconds. Then he plunged it deep into her ear.

"Yes!" she moaned.

Her huge, bountiful breasts heaved against his chest, her hips gyrated against his. He looked up at the mirror. Its reflection almost made him shoot his load. Nikki was bent over him resting on her elbows. Her legs were spread out across his and her gorgeous rocking natch was the first thing he could see. Her wet vagina in full view, aching to be filled with his throbbing stiff.

"I thought you might like that," Nikki purred. She ran her tongue down across his stomach, exploring his navel as she darted further down through his thick sex hair. His cock looked even bigger in the flickering light. She moaned as she touched it with her tongue, exploring its thick base with her fingers. Playfully, she pulled it with an upward motion.

Tommy moaned as he stared at the mirror behind her. "Yes, please," he begged.

Nikki ran her tongue up the back of its huge shaft. She kissed its helmet softly with her lips, tasting the bitter sweet trickle which splashed against her mouth as she began to pull harder.

"Not too hard or I'll come," he whispered.

"I'm ready for it," she groaned. She moved forward, placing the palms of her hands on Tommy's chest as she lifted her leg to straddle him again. As she sat down on to his swollen shaft, she took a deep breath and moaned loudly. She ran her fingers across her nipples, playing with them, as she manouevred his cock in between the warm, inviting lips of her wet crotch. "Oh yes!" she gasped. "It's huge. More. I love it." She began to rock backwards and forwards slowly. "Harder," she groaned. The rythym quickened. Drops of sweat ran down Nikki's breasts and body.

Tommy slipped his fingers around the base of his soaking, buried cock, heightening the already burning sensation for both of them. "Oh, I love you, Nikki," he whispered.

"Shut up and fuck me!" she shouted.

* * *

Midnight. Tommy lay across Nikki. Both exhausted. Neither had said a word for what seemed like hours. Nikki lay there staring at the ceiling. She felt awful. "All right?" she whispered.

Tommy moved off Nikki and slumped on the floor beside her. He slowly climbed on to his elbow and stared at her body.

She felt exposed. She didn't like him staring at her like that. Earlier on, yes. But not now. "*Stop!*" She sat up and looked around for her clothes.

"What are you doing?" Tommy asked.

"Going to bed," she muttered.

"I'd say yes to that invitation."

"I don't remember inviting you," she snapped.

"Well, go on then. Invite me."

"No. You're going home."

Silence.

Nikki stood up and covered herself.

"Not before we have a little talk," Tommy said slowly.

"Ah, for God's sake, Tommy. Why did I know this was going to happen? You've got what you wanted tonight. So did I. Why can't we just leave it at that?"

"Because there's more." He followed her into the bedroom and caught her roughly by the wrist.

"Let me go," she shouted as she pulled away from him. She could see that he was getting hard again.

He smiled.

She was crazy about him. But she knew he couldn't give a shit. "I'm tired, Tommy. What do you want to talk about?"

"You getting a job."

"I have a job."

"I mean a *real* job."

"Oh yeah. Where?"

"In the Clover Tap."

Nikki stared at him as he pulled on his jeans. "Why?"

"Because I need you to, that's why." He pulled on his socks and then his boots.

"For what reason? Tell me," she pleaded.

"Because I might be doing a bit of business with

those people shortly and it would help to have you on the inside."

"No way."

Tommy grinned at her. "I don't think you've any choice in the matter, Nikki. Remember, this is our secret. And I wouldn't like to have to go and ruin your new car on you, now would I?" He closed his shirt. "Let's just say I mightn't ask for the money that you stole from me if you just do as I say."

"You bastard," she shouted, "you just used me."

"Oh, give yourself a bit of credit, Nikki. Life's all about using people." He sat down on the side of the bed.

Nikki had both hands up to her face to stop the tears.

He took one of her hands. "Now listen to me. I'm going to make it very easy for you to get a job down there within the next couple of days. I'll be in touch. You'll know when the time is right. All you'll have to do is be in the right place at the right time." Tommy walked out of the bedroom. "Talk to you later, *love*," he shouted. She heard the hall-door bang. She burst into tears. Just then, the phone beside the bed rang. She grabbed the receiver.

"What do you want?" she roared into the mouthpiece.

"Nikki, it's Jamie. Were you trying to call me last night?"

Nikki froze.

"Nikki, can you hear me? Are you all right?"

"Jamie, I'm busy. I can't talk right now." She felt sick.

"Nikki, is everything all right?"

Nikki slammed down the phone.

Chapter Sixteen

Frank opened his eyes. He could hear the phone ringing in the kitchen. The luminous hands on the bedside clock showed quarter past four. He leapt out of the bed. It could only be an emergency at this hour, he thought. He grabbed the phone. "Hello," he said anxiously.

There seemed to be plenty of activity at the other end.

"Hello, I'm looking for Mr Francis McCabe," a voice requested.

"This is Frank McCabe. Who's this?" He waited hesitantly.

"This is Duty Sergeant Jim Burrell, London Metropolitan police, Mr McCabe. We've had a break-in reported by one of our patrol units at the Clover Tap. I believe you're the landlord."

Frank rubbed his eyes. "Is there much damage?"

Ray hurried into the kitchen. He looked at Frank.

"Well, our patrol unit is still at the location but won't enter until a keyholder is present." There was a short pause.

"Would you like us to collect you, sir?"

"No thanks, I'll be fine. Give me twenty minutes. I'll be there as quickly as I can."

"What's the problem?" Ray asked, wide awake and very worried.

"Pub's been broken into. They need me to go down."

"I'll come with you," Ray shouted as he hurried towards his bedroom, pulling off his pyjama top.

Within seconds, all the lights at number 34 were on. The flat was ablaze with activity.

Before Frank had time to throw on a pullover, Ray had fired up the power in his Transit. Frank wasn't sure which was worse, the sound of the broken exhaust or the choir of dogs barking all over the neighbourhood. He could hear a loud conversation going on outside. He peeped out through the ragged curtains. It was the milkman. "How's it going, Ray?" he shouted in his familiar Iraqi accent from his float. "You're up early."

"All right, Salman?" Ray replied. "Some proper little fuckers have broken into the fucking pub. The barracks called and told us we have to go down there."

"Sorry to hear about that, man. Does that mean you won't be showing the match this evening?" The milkman waited for the reply with a worried look on his face.

"We'll have to see how bad the damage is, budso. There mightn't even be a telly left when we get down there."

"All right, man. Give me a ring if they stole the

milk. I left the crate around by the side door." He waved his portable phone at Ray and smiled.

"Jesus! A milkman with a mobile phone. The wonders of modern technology." Ray looked at the dilapidated delivery van. "Did you get the float free with the phone?"

The two men laughed.

Frank climbed into the passenger seat of the Transit. He wasn't amused.

Ray reached for the gear-stick. "See you, Salman. I'll ring you if I need you." Ray moved off towards the main road junction.

"Why do you call him Salman?" Frank asked curiously.

Ray seemed surprised by the question. "Because he looks like that writer fellow. You know the one they have the reward on for writing that book?"

"Rushdie?" Frank muttered.

"That's him. Fucking madman, if you ask me."

"For writing the book?"

"*No!* For following Leeds United. They haven't won a match in over two months."

Frank stared at Ray in disbelief as they moved out on to the main A1 towards the city.

"And how Salman puts up with that milk round every morning in this weather is beyond me. He must eat plenty of curries the night before. Can you imagine the state of his bedroom?"

"*Ray,*" Frank shouted.

"What, Frank?" Ray realised he was ranting. Something which annoyed Frank greatly.

"Just drive and shut up!"

"Yes, Frank."

* * *

The scene that greeted the two Irishmen was beyond their worst fears. Two police cars and a fire tender were outside the Clover Tap. The street entrance leading to the cellars had been forced open. The intruders had broken open the cellar doors at the end of the bar. Beer taps had been left running and the entire floor space was flooded. Most of the furniture was broken. Frank's treasured juke-box had been badly vandalised.

Ray ran his huge hands up his arms and hugged his broad shoulders. "What's that awful smell?"

Frank raised his head as he tried to figure out what the rotten odour was.

"Jesus Christ," Ray muttered as he glanced around.

"What?" Frank said anxiously.

"They've pissed all over the walls!" Ray stood, horrified.

Frank put his hand over his mouth. He suddenly felt sick. "Why?" he whispered.

No one answered.

"*Why* is right," Ray replied. "But what I'd like to know is *who*?"

A policeman walked across to Frank.

"Mr McCabe?"

Frank nodded.

"I'm Inspector Carbury. I believe you're the landlord?"

Frank nodded again. "That's right," he mumbled.

"Nasty bastards, whoever they were." The senior police officer paused. "I don't suppose you'd have any idea who might be responsible?"

Frank looked at him as if to say, you can't be serious. "*What?*"

"Well, usually in situations like this, the perpetrators have a specific reason for carrying out this type of revenge."

"*Revenge?*" Frank stood motionless.

"Well, normally it's revenge. Born out of an event or incident they were party to."

"I'm not too sure I understand you, Inspector," Frank said.

"I think what the inspector is saying, Frank," Ray interrupted, "is that whoever did this might be a regular here. Is that right, Inspector?"

"Well, regular might be too strong a word. But someone you *crossed* recently, most likely."

Frank stared at Ray. "Who did you cross lately?"

"Hang on a minute, Frank. I didn't cross anyone!" Ray shouted defensively.

"Gentlemen, please," the inspector said calmly. "We're not going to get anywhere with this sort of attitude." He looked around. "Now there's not a great deal we can do here, tonight. Forensics will be here first thing in the morning. Hopefully we'll know more then. Maybe get a lead on the culprits."

"*A lead?*" Frank snorted. "This sounds like something I read in higher infants, for God's sake! Anyone could've been responsible for this," he roared, pointing at the damage.

"Not just *anyone*, Mr McCabe," the inspector replied. He looked around the pub. "I think you'll find that whoever did this knew what they were doing and, if I may be bold enough to say so, had a perfectly legitimate reason in their own sick minds for so doing." He looked at Frank. "I think you'll find they'll be back. And that's where you can help us. A number of areas in north London have been affected lately by protection rackets. I'm sure you've come across them."

"Only on television, to be honest with you," Frank replied.

Ray coughed. "Beg your pardon."

"Well, some large stores and supermarkets, one or two well-known pubs . . . even a school . . . they've all been targeted. Now, it's up to the people in charge of these establishments whether they want to play ball with these gurriers. If you pay them, that's your business. But I'll have to stress that you'll get little or no co-operation from the police if you go ahead and do business with these law-breakers."

"What's the alternative?" asked Ray.

"Give us as much information as you can about these people and we'll try to protect you from any further infringements on your business or premises. Simple as that." The inspector put his hat back on. He took out a handkerchief and blew his nose. "Sick bastards," he muttered.

"Do you think," Frank asked calmly, "it could have been an anti-Irish attack?"

The inspector paused briefly and took a deep breath. "It's hard to know in the present climate.

Twenty years ago, I'd have told you to get the next boat home. But today, I doubt it." He moved slowly towards the door. "OK, men," he told his colleagues, "that's it for the moment." He looked back at Frank and Ray. "The forensics people will be here at some stage during the morning. Try not to touch anything." He said goodnight. The other men filed out behind him.

Ray found two unbroken chairs. "Here, sit down. Do you want a drink?"

Frank nodded. "Whatever's there."

Ray walked up and down the bar. "Not much. Most of the spirits are gone. Taps are dry. They even managed to take the eight kegs from the cellar. Bastards."

"Could it have been that crowd from the pub in Cricklewood? You know, where you swiped the kegs the night of the reception?"

"No. Sure, I had a game of cards up there on Wednesday," Ray replied confidently as he pulled two pints. He brought them over to the table and sat down. "I'd say they were familiar with this place."

"Why do you say that?"

"Jesus, they obviously knew what to leave behind," he said as he nodded at the two pint glasses full of ale. "They left behind the piss no one ever buys." He held the full glass up to his lips and contorted his face as if about to undergo a dental filling. "This stuff's as bad as what's up on the walls!"

* * *

The pub didn't open that day. Word quickly got

303

around about what had happened. Many of the regulars arrived to give a hand with the repairs and the general clean-up operation.

"How are you, Mick?" Ray shouted at one local as he walked through the door and hung up his coat. "Nice of you to take a day off from looking for a job. I'd say the wife'll be pleased!"

The mood was cheerful as temporary, makeshift furniture arrived and damaged articles were removed in a giant skip.

"Help yourselves to a pint of Plancton's Mild," Ray shouted encouragingly. "It's all we've got till the brewery arrives."

Everyone declined.

Despite the shock of the previous night, and the disruption to his business, Frank enjoyed Ray's kidding. It helped them through the long day and the difficult task of getting the pub back together. Shortly after twelve noon, Frank noticed an attractive brunette who was straightening the photographs on the wall opposite the bar. She stood on a chair with her back to him. As she stretched up to take down another photograph, Frank couldn't help but notice her figure. She wore a pair of tight, figure-hugging jeans. Each time she raised her arms, her sweatshirt climbed higher, revealing a gorgeously tanned back. An introduction was definitely in order. No time to waste. He walked over to her, keeping his eyes on the lower part of her back. He coughed.

She looked down.

"Hi, how are you?" he asked pleasantly.

She seemed surprised. "Fine." She swept her long hair back out of her face and climbed down off the chair.

"I'm Frank." He held out his hand. "Don't I know you?"

"Oh, hi. You're the owner," she said with an enthusiastic grin. "I've heard a lot about you."

"Well, landlord more than owner, actually," Frank replied shyly as they shook hands. "I hope all you heard was good. Was it?"

"Well, actually, I haven't heard that much but it sounds good. Nikki Coffey. Pleased to meet you . . . again."

"What has you here today?" he asked.

"Well, I heard you were looking for some help, so, since I wasn't working, I thought I'd come down and lend a hand."

"Great. We can certainly do with all the help we can get. I'm hoping to be open again tonight. Are you a regular here?"

"Now and again. Mainly after work. But since I lost my job, I haven't been in that much. You know yourself, money and all that." She looked disheartened.

"You were here a couple of evenings back . . . with that policeman."

"Oh yeah, that's right. *That* evening? I hope I didn't make a show of myself?"

"Not at all. In fact, you were great fun. You left your bag behind you. Don't ask me where it is today. I'd say those scumbags took it with them."

"There was nothing valuable to take."

"What did you do?"

"Where?" she asked.

"At work."

"Oh, at work. Eh, I was a physiotherapist. But I hurt my back on holidays a few months back and I haven't been able to work since."

"A physiotherapist?" Frank looked really interested. "Nice job."

"If you can get the work. They're ten a penny these days. So a *physiotherapist* with a bad back isn't really at the races, is she?" She smiled. Why did she pick physiotherapist? she asked herself. She could barely pronounce the word. And what if he knew more about the job than she did? She would've liked to have been a physiotherapist. She had to settle for sowing zips into men's trousers.

"Where were you on holidays?" Frank asked.

Thank God, she thought. "Cyprus. With a gang of friends. It was great."

"Nice tan," Frank remarked.

"Thanks," Nikki replied coyly.

Frank couldn't help noticing that she wasn't wearing a bra under the thin sweatshirt. By the looks of things, this was no restricted suntan. He tried to keep his eyes above the shoulder line.

"Yeah, I was in Majorca last year with a bunch of friends. You can't beat getting away from it all."

"Now you said it."

"You're Jamie's best friend, aren't you?" Frank asked tentatively.

"Am I?" Nikki waited for a second before

answering. "Sort of," she answered awkwardly. "I know her through Tommy, her boyfriend." She felt that she'd handled the question well without giving too much away.

"It's just I couldn't forget what you said when you were in for a drink with *him* that evening."

Nikki was getting nervous. "Really. What was that?"

"That she'd been . . . raped."

Nikki didn't feel comfortable with the conversation. "Yeah? Well, she's a lot better now. She's better off at home."

"Why do you say that?"

Nikki was clutching for answers. "She never really liked London."

"She liked her job, didn't she?"

"Look, I was very drunk that night. I'm sorry if I upset you." She looked at Frank and smiled.

"Have you got a number for her?" Frank continued.

"She said she'd ring. But she never did." Nikki was sick. The last thing she needed was Frank telling Jamie that *she'd* been out drinking with Tommy.

"Who've we got here?" Frank turned around to see Ray giving Nikki the eyes-over treatment. "Well? An introduction might be in order, Frank."

"Oh, right. Nikki Coffey, Ray Flynn. Ray, Nikki."

They shook hands.

Ray looked closely at her.

Nikki tried to avoid his gaze.

"We met before," Ray remarked as he studied her.

"That Sunday a couple of weeks ago when you were in here with your friend. Remember the girl with the black . . . "

Nikki tried to cut across him. "Oh yeah." Considering she'd just slept with her boyfriend, albeit *ex*-boyfriend, she didn't feel much like talking about Jamie right now. "What's to be done?"

"Are you here for the clean-up?"

Nikki smiled and nodded. "Wherever I can lend a hand," she said politely.

"I'll talk to you later." Ray shook her hand again. "The brewery's just arrived. Time to get some decent juice back in the taps. We can have a drink later."

Suddenly, there was a loud roar from the bar. "*Ray Flynn!*" Ray looked around. Davina was watching the handshaking ritual. "Could I see you for a minute, *darling?*" she shouted sarcastically.

"Of course, my sweetness." Ray walked to the bar.

"He's a good lad," Frank assured Nikki.

"He seems nice," Nikki replied.

"Well, look, thanks for coming over to help. I really appreciate it. If you need anything, give us a call. There'll be a few drinks and a bit of food later on if you feel like staying."

"That'd be great." Nikki climbed back up on to the chair and went on cleaning and replacing the framed pictures.

Frank headed back to the bar. That's certainly very nice, he thought.

Nikki glanced around. Jesus, he's gorgeous, she thought. She looked around the pub at the damage and the dirt. She couldn't believe that Tommy was responsible for this. Yet, deep down, she knew he was capable of organising something this rotten and evil. But why? And what was her role? She was afraid to think about that. All she knew was that she had to get a job in this pub. She wouldn't mind. But why the urgency? She was afraid of Tommy. Scared to death of him. She was in the middle of some sort of conspiracy and she felt uneasy. Almost sick. How it was all going to end, she didn't want to know.

* * *

Frank decided to sleep in the pub. The alarm company were due to install a new security system the following day and he didn't want to take any chances. Davina provided a camp-bed which she told Frank she used when she ran her mobile escort agency. He was sure she was only joking.

It was a freezing cold night. Frank bedded down close to the fireplace. The heat was grand for a few hours. By three in the morning, he was awake and shivering. No matter which way he turned, there was no getting comfortable. Steel bars stuck into his back and the musty smell was giving him violent sneezing attacks. By half three, he was watching television, wrapped in a sleeping bag. He looked at the bottle of whiskey sitting on the bar top. I've already had two large ones, he thought. Shag it, I'll have another. It'll help me to sleep. He moved off the stool and stood still. No, I won't. Three of those things will give me a blinding headache. He looked at his watch again. Jesus, what'll I do for the next few hours?

He wandered aimlessly around the cold, dimly-lit lounge. Glancing at the furniture oddities, he scratched his head. Kitchen chairs. Hall tables. Anything he could get his hands on. They don't look so bad, he thought. They'll do for now. He straightened the All-Ireland photo above the cash register. Standing back, he admired the winning heroes. He noticed a pile of old papers and pages perched precariously on top of the full bin. He lifted off the top few and looked through them. Obviously stuff that had been lying in nooks and crannies around the pub. There was an invitation to the opening night. An invoice from the brewery and a few old Irish newspapers. One of them had names scribbled above the crossword. Frank held the paper close to the light to examine the writing. He froze. *Jamie Carroll.* No, it was definitely a mistake. He switched on the spotlight above the cash till and studied the writing. No mistake. It *was* Jamie Carroll. Frank felt a rush of excitement. He looked around for the date on the top of the page. *Sunday, January 8th.* Where did this come from? he thought. Maybe she'd been in for a drink. Maybe she'd been looking for him? Then a creeping feeling of disappointment. Maybe it wasn't the same woman at all. Even if it was, the paper had been lying gathering dust in the pub for a while.

Frank gripped the paper tightly and ran into the kitchen behind the bar. He grabbed the phone and dialled his flat number. Come on, he snapped, answer!

Ray looked at the clock as he fumbled with the phone beside the bed. "I'm on my way. Eh, is it all right?"

"Ray," Frank shouted down the phone with a real rush of excitement. "Jamie Carroll!"

"Eh, hello, Jamie . . . eh, do I know you?" Ray rubbed his eyes. "It's a bit on the late side. Where are you calling from?"

"No, Ray, it's Frank." His voice was urgent.

Suddenly, Ray found his bearings and threw his legs out on to the floor. "Jesus, Frank. Are you all right?" He grabbed the T-shirt which lay on the floor. "I'm on my way. Ten minutes. Have you rung the guards? Jesus, I knew I shouldn't have left you there on your own."

"No, Ray," the excited voice crackled at the other end, "nothing's wrong. Listen to me. Jamie Carroll. Where is she?" he asked hurriedly.

"Who?" Ray rubbed his eyes again and looked at the clock.

"*Jamie Carroll* . . . the name written on the newspaper. Over the crossword." Frank was beginning to speak faster. "January 8th. It was a Sunday, remember?"

"Frank, it's ten to four in the morning. Have you been drinking that whiskey? I warned you to take only two. That's jungle juice," Ray roared. "Can you hear the crying in the background? Well, in case that doesn't ring a bell in your strange love-filled brain, you've just woken the baby. So much for a handy night's baby-sitting. Davina's gone to a friend's party in Coventry. She's not due back till morning. Thanks a lot. Now will you go back to your shagging bed!"

The phone went dead.

Frank dialled the number again. The phone was engaged. Frank turned off the kitchen light and went back to his squeaky camper bed. He stared at the name. It was all coming back to him. The car ferry. The train journey. The red Golf GTi. But what were the chances of meeting her again? God knows where she was now. His mind did somersaults and backflips. His mother always told him that he thought far too much for his own good. Always thinking, always dreaming, she would say to the neighbours. But this was different. He'd never felt like this before. Probably a waste of time, but it felt good. On the other hand, if she was going out with that copper, what was he doing in here with her friend that evening? And how come she ended up in the pub the previous day, so willing to help with the repairs? He always remembered what Mr Brady, his English teacher, told him many years before. If you really want something badly enough and you're prepared to go to the ends of the earth to get it, you'll always succeed. Anything is possible.

Frank was stared at the ceiling, clutching the paper and reciting words over and over: *anything is possible* . . . Within a few short minutes, he was sleeping like a baby.

Chapter Seventeen

Saint Patrick's Day was going to be a gold mine for the Clover Tap. Frank could feel it in his bones. It was all his regulars could talk about. He meticulously planned the day from early morning to early the following morning. All hands on deck from breakfast-time through to lunch. Spend the afternoon at the Irish music festival in St Alban's, then back for the hectic night's business that he hoped lay ahead.

Ray drafted in Davina to help behind the bar. Frank recruited Nikki to help out with the small buffet he was throwing for the regulars. By midday, everything was ready. The lounge was decked out in as much green as possible. Frank objected to the green leprechaun balloons which Ray mysteriously found, but now that they were hanging up beside the tricolour balloons, they did look well. For the day that was in it.

Frank couldn't figure out where the rapping and tapping noises were coming from. He checked the beer lines. Then it struck him that the noise was coming from the street. He peeped out through the curtains and gasped. The queue stretched as far as he could see down Bromley Road. More shamrock than Sherkin Island, he thought.

Suddenly, one of the regulars spotted him peeping out the window.

"There's Frank," he shouted, alerting the others.

They all started to shout.

"How are you, Frank? Any chance of a drink?"

"Let us in, Frank."

"It's the one day in Lent that she'll let me drink, Frank, and it's nearly half over."

"I think there's a bunch of Pioneers running this place!"

Each comment that was passed brought with it a burst of laughter.

"OK, Ray," Frank shouted, with a broad grin on his face, "it's show time." He clapped his hands and pulled back the huge bolt on the main door.

The rush to get in reminded Frank of the first day of the January sales at Roches Stores. His mother would queue for a whole night. By the following afternoon, they'd each have a new school uniform.

Within seconds, the regulars were five deep at the bar, waving their money in the air.

Ray's idea of live entertainment, needless to say, was almost as painful as electric shock treatment. A young, greasy-haired lad belted out the old reliables. Occasionally, they sounded familiar.

"Who's next?" Frank roared above the din, as the singer murdered a classic.

"Jesus Christ, Frank, where did you find your man?" a punter nodded at the guitarist on the stool.

Frank shook his head. "Ask Flynn. He's entertainment manager. Next!"

"He's like a cat in a mangle!" The man closed his eyes, lifted his pint and disappeared into the huge crowd.

Frank tried to add up a round on the cash register, but couldn't concentrate with the racket in the background.

"Everything I dooo, I dooo iiit faaar youuu . . . Zank you very much, ladies and gentlemen."

Everyone burst into a huge round of applause. The young singer was delighted. The crowd was ecstatic.

"Jesus, a bit of peace at last," one of them shouted.

"Put a muzzle on him, quick. Before he starts again."

"There's a woman crying over here."

"Is she homesick?" Ray asked.

"No, she's a music teacher!"

"Where the hell did you find him?" Frank asked Ray.

"Frank, please. A bit of recognition for young talent," said Ray. "He's going to be huge. His girlfriend is Rod Stewart's hairstylist." Ray nodded his head proudly.

"Really? Well, I hope she has a better effect on heads than he does." Frank rooted in his pocket and pulled out a twenty-pound note. "Here," he said to Ray, "give him this and tell him to take a break. A long one, preferably."

Suddenly, the pub went quiet.

"God save all here," a husky voice muttered as the main door banged.

315

A clear aisle was made quickly as a small man in clerical clothes made his way triumphantly to the bar counter. An empty stool appeared out of nowhere. It was Father Duffy, the local parish priest. He was affectionately known as Dickie Duffy. "Dickie", because there seemed to be a light on but no one home, as Ray put it.

Frank moved down the bar to welcome the distinguished guest.

"Good afternoon, Father. Happy Saint Paddy's day to you." He stretched out to shake hands with the priest.

"And to you and yours, Frank. You weren't in the congregation this morning."

"No, unfortunately. We were up to our eyes. Last-minute preparations for the day that's in it," Frank reassured the priest. "I'll be there eh, this evening, Father."

"Make sure, Frank. You cannot serve God and mammon." The priest meant business. He stood and stuck out his chest. "In life, there are many temptations to neglect the soul for material things like money and thoughts of the flesh. But in death and judgement, the Lord will expect to see your soul as he loaned it to you at the point of conception, as pure and white as the driven snow." Father Duffy winked and shook his finger at Frank. "Today, let us celebrate the brave young man who took it upon himself to drive all the poisonous snakes from our beautiful country."

A stifled snigger could be heard from the other end of the bar.

The priest turned his attention in its direction. "Obviously he missed a couple."

"I know what you're saying, Father. Don't worry. I'll be there this evening," Frank said humbly.

"Good man." The priest leaned over the counter, within whispering distance of Frank. "Give us a double whiskey, water, no ice. Thanks very much!"

As Frank held the small glass up to the whiskey bottle, the elderly priest turned and eyed the gathered flock warily.

"Ah," he scoffed, on spotting one individual. "Mickey Dunne from Durrow. I met your lovely wife at Mass this morning. I didn't notice you, though. Does she get to see much of you nowadays?" The priest waited for an answer.

The entire pub waited for Mickey Dunne's answer.

The weedy man gulped and fiddled with the shamrock that trailed from his jacket. "I had to mind the kids, Father," he whispered.

"What?" the priest roared.

"The kids were sick. I had to mind them," Mickey Dunne replied, on the verge of tears.

"Make sure you see me at the five-thirty, then. Do you hear me?" the priest snapped.

"Yes," Mickey replied.

"Yes, *what*?"

"Yes, *Father*."

"That's better."

More gentle sniggering around the lounge.

"I don't know what youse have to laugh at. Look at the state of youse all." He pointed to a tall, lanky individual who had four pints stacked in front of him and one in his hand. "You there, Jack McCaffrey. A good Catholic father of eleven fine children." Jack McCaffrey looked as if he was waiting to be sentenced. "Well, Jacko. Will you make it to twelve or has she tied a knot in it?"

There was a loud burst of laughter.

"You should be at home rearing your family, but no. You too have given in to Satan's selfish ways. Pints before penance, isn't that right?" He shrugged his shoulders and turned back to the bar.

"There you go, Father. It's on me." Frank gestured to the whiskey and the water.

"Thanks," the priest said softly. He muttered a quick prayer and downed the double spirit in one swallow. Just like his routine on the altar at Mass. He shrugged his shoulders again, as if in the middle of some sort of fit, and let out a deep rumbling sigh. Those who knew him said it was like a dying man's last breath. It was a ritual which put the fear of God into the hardest of non-believers. He slammed the empty glass down on the counter and picked up his coat.

A sigh of relief ran through the bar.

It was to be short-lived.

He pulled out his wallet and produced a dirty ten-pound note. "Same again, Frank," he rasped. He looked around and carefully studied the terrified faces at the bar. Then he studied the number of fresh pints lined up on the counter. "I count eight men at the bar. Mind you, *men* might be a bit of an exaggeration." He paused. "And forty-five pints on the bar top." He glared at the eight men. "Greed. One of the seven deadly sins." There wasn't a sound. He downed the drink again and followed it with a quick prayer. He winked at Frank who promptly lined up another double. While Frank filled the glass, the parish priest put the tenner back in his pocket.

"Feel free to buy a drink for your pastor," he urged the crowd, "and we might discuss dispensations for those of you who can see the error of your ways."

Immediately, the pub was filled with the sound of jangling coins as the regulars searched for change. It was like a bank robbery where intruders forced everyone to hand over their valuables. Punters close to the door picked up their jackets and slipped out unnoticed. Within minutes, the bar in front of Father Duffy was stacked with drinks.

"Do you ever see old Mr Mulligan these days, Frank?" he enquired.

Frank looked amazed. "Mr Mulligan died three years ago, Father. Do you not remember burying him?"

"Did I? Well, Lord God, doesn't the time fly." He knocked back a glass full without the slightest hint of a swallow. "I was only wondering last week why I hadn't seen him around." He was beginning to spit and slur now as four doubles took their effect.

"Who's your man, Frank?" Nikki quietly asked.

"Father Duffy. Local parish priest. Member of the gestapo, if you ask me. He's been doing this twice a year for as long as I can remember. Paddy's Day and Christmas Day. I used to see him at it when I'd be in here having a drink. Not nice. Thank God I'm on this side of the bar this year." Frank smiled. "You haven't seen the half of it yet. Here comes Ray."

There was a loud bang as the side door slammed shut. A passage was made for Ray as he squeezed his way through the crowd to the bar.

"Who have we here?" Father Duffy shouted incoherently. "Ah, sure, if it's not Ray Flynn."

"How are you, Father? Can I get you a drink?"

"Well, that'd be just grand. Thanks." Holding out his free hand to greet Ray, he lost his balance and fell into the arms of Davina who was standing behind him. There was a big cheer.

"Oh, falling for the girls, are we, Father?"

The priest tried to focus on Ray while waving his empty glass at Nikki. "Not at all."

Ray didn't look at the drunken priest who now had most of the bar counter to himself. "How's old Mr Mulligan, Father?"

"Well, Frank says he's dead these last three years. But sure, I was talking to him only yesterday."

"Were you, and where was that?" Ray chuckled.

"Above in the cemetery."

A punter came up behind Ray. "Jesus, Ray, where do you get them? I mean, between that singing, hairy git and the holy soldier of destiny, a man can't have a quiet drink in his local any more."

"Let me tell you something, Mick Flanagan," Ray said, giving him a real frosty look, "we don't settle for anything less than the best here. Do you know who that, as you put it, hairy git is? Well, do you?"

The man shook his head.

"That hairy git happens to be a cousin of Daniel O'Donnell's sister-in-law. So there!"

The man's eyes opened wide. "You're not serious, are you?"

"Are you calling me a liar?" Ray snapped.

"No, Ray. I'm just amazed." The man put his coat back on the stool and picked up his drink. "Actually, now that I think of it, he's pretty good."

"*Pretty* good?"

"Brilliant, actually."

Ray smiled. "Now buy me a pint."

"Hey, Ray." The slurred shout came from Father Duffy's direction.

Ray picked up another pint and sat down beside him. "What can I do for you, Father?" He placed his drink on the table beside the priest's seven empty whiskey glasses.

"Your friend Frank says I can't have any more drink."

"Well, Father, he's the boss."

"Well, I'm going to have a bet with you." The priest leaned forward.

Ray caught his arm before he fell off the chair. "What's that then?"

"I'll have an arm wrestle with you. Best of three wins a bottle."

A small crowd gathered around the table.

"Ah, come on now, Father. You remember what happened when Mrs Fitzsimons sat on your knee at the Christmas sale of work last year?" Ray grinned.

"Well, the truth is that I only got hurt because she had such a big arse." Father Duffy rolled up his sleeves and sat back in the chair." So, what do you say?"

Without as much as a word, Ray unbuttoned his check shirt and rolled up his sleeve to reveal an arm that looked more like the hind leg of a bull.

"Mother of Jesus," muttered one onlooker.

Ray flexed his arm while Father Duffy struggled to get his jacket off and, at the same time, stay upright on the chair.

Frank was getting more nervous by the minute. "Ray," he called above the mounting excitement, "get up here."

Ray winked at Frank. "Not now. Just give us a loan of your watch for a minute."

Frank unbuckled his gold watch and tossed it over to Ray who put it on the table in front of him. He gripped Father Duffy's small fist. The priest's hand disappeared completely inside Ray's giant, grasping fist. There was silence around the table as everyone's attention focused firmly on the big fight.

"Here, Mick Dooley."

"Yes, Ray?"

"You'll act as referee. Make sure the good Father isn't gripping the side of the table with his other hand."

"May God forgive you for even thinking that, Ray Flynn."

"OK, Mick. On the count of three," Ray ordered.

"Ready. Three, two, one and away youse go."

The two men were immediately locked in vicious

combat. It was as if they'd both received the same electric shock. Grunting and gasping. Clenching their teeth and staring into each other's protruding eyeballs.

The crowd loved it. Each time an arm would sway in one direction or the other, there would be a huge cheer.

"A fiver on Ray," one spectator cheered.

Everyone dived into their pockets.

"No gambling!" Father Duffy grunted.

The two hands swayed violently for almost five minutes. Almost completely to the right and then a sudden jolt back to the left. Then, without anyone noticing, Ray kicked the leg of the table so hard that it snapped with an enormous cracking sound. At the same time, he conceded victory to Father Duffy by letting his own arm fall limply on the table.

Ray jumped to his feet, gripping his fighting wrist with his other hand. "Ah, Jesus," he roared in pain, "it's broken. My fucking arm is broken! Call yourself a man of God, and you go and break my fucking arm." Ray howled in agony. The crowd were horrified. Father Duffy sat rigidly in his chair.

"But I didn't try *that* hard," he said reproachfully.

"You didn't try that hard? You should be in the SAS, not the priesthood."

"Here, show me your arm." The priest stood up to get a closer look.

"Ah, don't let him near me. He's dangerous. He must have some sort of supernatural powers."

Father Duffy searched for his coat. As the priest made a quick getaway through the side door, people gathered round to comfort Ray. As soon as the door closed behind him, Ray pulled down his shirt-sleeve and walked over to the bar. "Right then, it's time for a nice, quiet pint."

There was a huge cheer.

Frank grinned at him. "You know what, Ray Flynn?"

"What's that, boss?"

"You're a bad bastard!"

The two men laughed.

* * *

It was nearly half two by the time the last few stragglers went home. Ray had left a few minutes earlier to collect the van. Frank reckoned it would take them the best part of an hour to get to St Alban's. He was hoping to be there before Christy Moore took to the stage. He locked the cellar door while Nikki set the house alarm.

Just as she activated it, Frank heard the chimes of an ice cream van. It seemed to be getting nearer. Frank peeped out on to the main road from behind the closed curtains. It was slowing down. It came to a screeching halt outside the pub.

Frank stared. A bright green *Mr Whippy* van covered in dark-green shamrocks. Luminous dayglo writing said *Mind the Children*. Then he felt his heart stop. Ray was sitting behind the front wheel. Davina was sitting beside him, a child on each knee, each licking a 99. He didn't know whether to laugh or to leg it out the side door and down the back lane. Too late. He was caught peeping.

"Frank, will you hurry up? You're the one who wants to see Christy Moore," Ray roared.

Frank walked slowly out the main door into the bright afternoon sunshine. He was almost afraid to go too close to this spectacle.

"Ray, explain *this*," he shouted angrily, pointing to the van.

"I thought since we're going to be at this thing for a few hours that we might as well make a few bob, like. Make ourselves useful, like," he explained.

"Turn off that fucking racket, *please*!" Frank roared over the sound of the chimes. The music died.

"Frank, there's going to be twenty thousand kids at this thing today. Now see, I knew that Benny Cafolla wouldn't be taking his ice cream van out until the weather got finer, so . . . I asked him for a loan of it."

"*So I asked him for a loan of it*," Frank mimicked. "Well, you can take it straight back to Benny Cafolla. I wouldn't be seen dead in that thing. Davina, can you not talk sense into him for once?"

Davina shook her head, as she searched for one of the children's ice creams which had fallen out of its cone and down between her legs. Suddenly, she screamed. "Jesus, Ray! Take that out of there . . . it's freezing."

Ray roared laughing at the commotion.

Frank began to smile.

Nikki moved in on the argument. "Makes sense, Frank. If you were to sell a couple of hundred cones at a pound a go, that's a nice day's work, isn't it?"

Frank pulled his jacket tightly around him and looked up at the sky. "Suppose so. But who in his right mind is going to buy ice cream on a freezing cold afternoon like this?"

"Ha, ha," Ray shouted. "Never fear, Flynn is here. Now are you getting in or what? I'm afraid if the engine cuts out on this thing, we'll never get it started again."

"All right then, but let's get one thing clear from the start. I'm not having anything to do with this, OK? It's my afternoon off, and I'm going out there to enjoy a bit of music."

Frank helped Nikki climb into the cab. He followed carefully, avoiding the gallons of liquid ice cream stacked precariously around the back of the van.

"Off we go, so," Ray sang. He stuck his right hand out the window and moved into the flow of traffic, heading for the A5 to St Alban's.

"This is taxed and insured, isn't it?" Frank asked anxiously.

"Don't worry, we'll be all right," Ray replied.

"*Ray?*" Frank called from the back.

Ray looked around and winked.

Frank looked over at Nikki who was squatting on the floor. She was wiping one of the children's mouths with a tissue. She was beautiful, no doubt about that. Never bothered with much clothes, Frank thought to himself. Bit flirty. Still, it worked with the customers. Particularly when she'd lean across the counter with their change. He'd never seen so many twenty-pound notes going into the cash register before. Come to think of it, he'd never seen his regulars looking for change for the public telephone as much as they had been. Not since Nikki started part-time.

"Ah, shag that for a game of cowboys," Ray roared.

Everyone looked out the front window. There was a slow-moving funeral procession right in front of them, and the traffic was moving from a dual-carriageway system into a normal single flow, with heavy traffic in both directions.

Frank took a deep breath. "For God's sake, I knew something like this was going to happen. We might as well turn around and go home."

"*Go home?*" Ray shouted. "After paying five hundred quid for this thing for the afternoon? You have to be joking."

"*Five hundred quid?*" Frank burst out laughing. "Jesus, Ray, Benny Cafolla must have seen you coming."

Davina thumped Ray's shoulder. "You never told me you spent five hundred quid on this heap of rubbish. *Five hundred quid?*"

"No problem to Ray Flynn," he quipped proudly. "I've done me sums on this one, baby." He pulled out and passed the funeral cars, one by one. He had just about managed to do it, when a large lorry approached from the opposite direction. Ray had no choice but to pull back, right behind the hearse. Suddenly he realised that the hearse was travelling a lot more slowly than he was. He slammed on the brakes.

Davina shot foward, hitting her head against the button which started the chimes.

Frank and Nikki looked at each other in horror.

Davina lay crumpled on the seat, unconscious, and here they were in a *Mr Whippy* van tucked in between a hearse and the chief mourning car with the chimes playing "Always look on the bright side of life"!

Ray lurched forward so that he could switch off the awful din. He didn't realise that the hearse had stopped to see what all the commotion behind was about.

Crummmpp . . . !

The *Whippy* van ran straight into the back of the hearse. The button controlling the chimes broke clean off in Ray's hand. There was no way of switching off the music.

All hell broke loose.

Mourners poured out of nowhere, queuing up to lynch Ray.

"I only bent the fender, for God's sake," he shouted. "I mean it's not as if someone's dead!" He ran frantically between the two vehicles. A large crowd of people, all dressed in black, followed him. "Is there a doctor about?" he shouted. "My girlfriend is unconscious."

An elderly lady, resting against the black taxi, sobbed even louder. "My husband, the finest doctor in Hertfordshire," she wept.

"Where is he?" Ray asked, a look of relief breaking out across his face. "Tell him we need him urgently. I'll pay whatever it costs."

The woman sobbed even louder.

"I think he's in the box," Frank whispered as he grabbed Ray's arm.

Frank went around to the front of the ice cream van to inspect the damage. The *Whippy* van's front bumper was firmly lodged under the back of the hearse.

"Well, at least there's no fear of *him* getting whiplash!" Ray pointed to the coffin. Another woman began to cry unconsolably.

"Is anyone in the AA?" Frank asked.

Unfortunately, it turned out that there was only one person in the AA. He was in the box. Leaving Ray and the two girls behind to sort out the mess, Frank walked back along the road to an emergency phone to call the AA. He tried to explain that, while the AA member hadn't been killed in the crash, he *was* dead. No luck there. The girl hung up.

He couldn't believe his eyes when he arrived back at the scene of the accident.

Not a man to miss a chance, in Frank's absence, Ray had sold each of the mourners a cornet with a Cadbury's flake stuck in it. Meanwhile, Ray himself was talking to the chief undertaker about the art of embalming.

The mourners grew worried that the cemetery would be closing shortly. There was nothing left to do but for the ice cream van to push the hearse all the way to the cemetery and wait for the police there.

It was a day Frank and Ray would never forget. Neither would the priest and police who witnessed the funeral procession arriving at the cemetery chapel.

As the cortège pulled into the small forecourt, the waiting officials gasped in horror. The hearse looked as if it was being humped by a *Mr Whippy* van playing music from *The Life of Brian*. Mourners staggered out of their taxis and cars crying into their 99s and, because the ice cream van was jammed against the back door of the hearse, the coffin had to be manoeuvred out through the sun-roof!

* * *

By the time police statements were taken, mourners interviewed, apologies offered and the radiator in the ice cream van repaired, it was half six. The concert was over. Frank was going to be late getting back to open the pub and Ray was down almost a thousand pounds. Five hundred for Benny Cafolla and another five hundred for repairs to the hearse. Not to mention an imminent summons for no tax or insurance and a second for dangerous driving *with* two minors on board.

The two men sat silently in the back of the police car and watched the ice cream van being towed away. The battery was almost dead now and the chimes sounded as if they were playing "The Dead March".

Ray looked at Frank.

"*Don't* . . . say a word!" Frank fixed him with a look that said, "*Kill!*"

Ray hesitated for a moment. "I was just going to say that I think I left your watch in the ice cream van. That's all."

Chapter Eighteen

"Hello, Glandore gardaí," the voice stated. "Can I help you?"

The garda's voice was just like his, Jamie thought. She asked herself yet again what she was doing. What if the police thought she was one of those nuisance callers?

"Hello," the garda shouted into the phone.

"Hello." Jamie tried to disguise her voice. "I'm wondering if you can help me. I'm trying to locate a person from Glandore." That was enough, she thought.

"Are they missing?" the garda asked in a concerned voice.

"Em, no. They're working in London." She didn't want to sound as if she knew too much about Frank.

"How many is *they*?"

"He . . . just one."

"What's *his* name?"

"Frank."

"Frank *who*?" the garda asked, trying to speed up the conversation. "This sounds a bit like *Where in the World*, if you ask me."

Jamie cringed with embarrassment. "Frank McCabe."

"Aye, young Frank. He hasn't been around here for a while. He's gone back to London, I think."

"Yes, I know. But I was just wondering if you knew *where* in London?" Jamie felt herself blush.

"In *London?*" the garda snapped. He laughed heartily. "Jesus, love, we've enough trouble trying to keep an eye on the people who still live here. Never mind the rest of them who've packed up and left. Are you serious?"

Jamie knew she wasn't getting anywhere. She was about to hang up when she heard the garda ask someone else if they knew where Frank had got to.

"Hello," the voice shouted.

"Hello, yes," Jamie replied eagerly.

"One of the lads here says that if you ring Molloy's up the street, someone there's bound to know what he's up to. All right? And tell him Sergeant McLoughlin was asking for him."

"Thanks." Jamie felt pleased with her investigative work.

"Here, hang on. Hello?"

Jamie quickly put the receiver back up to her ear. "Sorry, yes?"

"Do you want the number?" the sergeant shouted.

"Oh yes," replied Jamie.

"Right. Let's see." The garda thumbed through some pages, muttering to himself. "Now, Molloys . . . Molloys," he repeated. "Here it is. 21774."

Jamie scribbled it down on the cover of the well-worn telephone directory. "Thanks a million," she said gratefully.

"No problem. Jesus, lads, that's an odd one!" The phone went silent at the far end.

Jamie looked at her watch. It was nearly quarter to twelve. She dialled the number. Same prefix as the garda station, she thought. She listened for a dialling tone and closed her eyes. No one answered. Perhaps it was just as well. She'd ring tomorrow. In any case, it would give her a bit more time to ask herself if she was stone mad.

* * *

It was still dark when the phone rang. Frank lunged out of his bed and fell on to the floor. Was it his mobile? No, too loud. It was the kitchen phone. He felt his way through the dark pub, stumbling across small stools and chairs. It couldn't be the police. A phone call at this hour could mean only one thing, trouble. He picked up the receiver and listened for a moment to the static. He rubbed the sleep out of his eyes and took a deep breath.

"Hello," he said quietly.

There didn't seem to be anyone at the other end.

"Hello," he said again, this time more firmly.

"Frank, is that you?" a frantic voice asked.

Frank immediately recognised the voice. It was his brother, Brendan. "Brendan? Is everything OK?" He looked at the time. Five to six. The news couldn't be good.

"Frank, it's Mammy . . . " There was a very long pause.

"What's wrong with Mammy?" Frank shouted.

"She's . . . not well, Frank."

Frank was becoming exasperated. He needed to know what was going on. "What happened her, for God's sake?"

"Frank, calm down," Brendan said.

"Where is she?"

"She was taken into hospital below in Skibereen tonight." Another long pause. "She came over about five for her tea. She was playing with the children when she . . . collapsed. I helped her upstairs and rang Dr Whelan. Fair play to him, he was there in minutes. Mind you, it felt like hours . . . "

Frank cut across him. "Brendan, stop rambling, will you. Is she going to be all right?" There was an eerie silence. A pause that Frank didn't want. *"Brendan!"*

"No," came the tearful reply. "She's had a massive stroke."

Brendan's voice broke and gave way to tears. "The doctors below in the hospital said it was a very serious one and that it's only a matter of . . . " He couldn't say the word.

Time, thought Frank. Time is all she needs. She'll be grand. He'd bring her to London for a holiday when she was up and about again. Frank could feel the tears welling up in both eyes. No way, he thought. This is not the time. Anyway, sure, she's going to be all right. Not *his* mother, God. He needed time himself. "I'll ring you back in a while," he said softly.

"Are you coming home?" Brendan asked.

"*Of course* I'm coming home!" Frank shouted. He slammed down the receiver. He was furious and sick with worry. Why do I always have to be so far away? he asked himself. He sat on a chair beside the giant stove and pulled his wallet out of his jeans pocket. On the inside was a plastic frame. In the frame was a photograph of Ray, Frank and his mother, taken on her last visit to London, outside Buckingham Palace. He studied the beautiful smile on her face. She was enjoying herself tremendously. Please, God, don't take her. Not yet, he whispered as he squeezed the photo. He sat there in the darkness. In the horrible silence. He could hear Salman's milk-float on the street outside. Half six, he thought. It reminded him of the morning he ran into the kitchen and proudly told his mother that Jack Cleary, the local milkman, had taken him on as his helper for the summer holidays. It seemed as if he was on his way to his first million. All the kids wanted to work for Jack Cleary. Frank got the job because he was able to carry the most empty bottles without letting a single one fall. He remembered how embarrassed he was when his mother hugged him tightly and kissed him on the forehead. She was so proud. He was nine.

He swallowed hard and picked up the phone. A gravelly, sleepy voice answered at the far end.

"Ray, it's Frank."

"Ah, for God's sake, Frank. You're not still thinking about her, are you? What time is it?"

Frank knew he had no time to lose. "Mammy's been

rushed to hospital in Skibereen, Ray. She's had a stroke. I'm going to have to go home for a while to see her."

"And how is she now?" Ray asked sympathetically.

"Not too good."

"Will she be . . . " Ray cut his question short. Not a good idea, he thought. "I'll be there in ten minutes."

It was getting bright now. A silhouetted brightness. The darkest hour of the soul, as his mother would say, is the hour between the dark and the light. If God wants you, that's when he takes you. A cold shiver ran up his spine. He looked at the phone and thought about ringing Brendan again. Just to make sure she was OK. No point. He'd be home later in the day anyway.

* * *

By early afternoon, he was miles above the Irish sea, on his way home. It was the first time he'd had a chance to relax in weeks. He didn't really care about the possibility of things going wrong in the pub. That side of his life had simply paled into insignificance a few hours earlier. As he sipped a beer and looked out at the cloudy sky, he tried not to think about how life would be if his mother . . . he couldn't even bring himself to say the word. That was for later. Much later. He looked into the plastic carrier bag between his knees. A couple of toys he'd picked up for Brendan's kids in the duty-free. They were mad about this film he kept hearing about every time he rang home. He'd bought them some books and a couple of small clay models. It would be great to be that young.

* * *

Dublin Airport was a mad frenzy. People heading out after Saint Patrick's Day. He walked out into a swarming multitude in the arrivals hall. Brendan waved from the back.

Frank watched his gloomy face as he pushed his way through the waiting crowd. They shook hands but said nothing.

Mary, Brendan's wife, threw her arms around Frank and gave him a kiss. "She died in her sleep this morning. Quarter to eleven." She smiled.

Frank took a deep breath and rubbed his eye. He looked down at the two small boys. He could see that they weren't too sure what was happening. "How are youse, lads?" He patted them both on the head.

"Hello, Uncle Frank," they both said in unison.

"My nana's in heaven," one of the small boys said assuredly.

Frank smiled down at him. "I know she is." He looked down at the bag he was carrying. "I've got a surprise for the two of you." He pulled out the books to a chorus of *oohs* and *wows*. Soon they were busy colouring in the pictures as they sat silently in the back of the car on the long journey home.

It was a beautiful spring afternoon. Cold and fresh but with brilliant sunshine. It was a quiet journey with little conversation. Frank looked at the fields and the small towns as the time ticked by. He thought of his mother lying on a mortuary slab. What a miserable end. All on her own. He had to talk.

"Who was there?" he asked.

"Her friend, Bridie. Brendan and myself. And Father Conlan," Mary replied quietly from the back seat.

"That's nice." Frank hoped that she hadn't missed him. He looked out the window again at the bright blue sky. Not a cloud. He couldn't believe that she was gone. All the times that he was going to call her and didn't. Later on, he would say to himself. Not any more. He wished that he'd told her how much he loved her. He wished he'd been there just for the last couple of minutes. He clutched a dark shawl in his hands. He'd bought it at Heathrow before he boarded. She would have liked it.

As the car swept in around the cove, the sun was setting over the bay. The water was calm. The sun threw a giant, shimmering reflection across the ebbing tide. It seemed to stretch all the way out to the horizon. As far as the eye could see. This had always been his mother's favourite time of the day.

Chapter Nineteen

Wedding and funerals. Great to see you. A firm handshake. Sorry to hear about your mother. By half eight that evening, it was a well-worn greeting, said hundreds of times by the people who'd loved her.

It was nice to see all the old, familiar faces in Molloy's later that evening. Frank didn't want to go back to the house after the church service. The thought of facing the memories of thirty-eight years was too much for him. The old reliable was in order. His mother had been one of Glandore's most loved and cherished residents. It was as if she'd always been there.

Her bright, breezy character and her sound advice would be greatly missed. A saint if ever there was one, Frank was told throughout the evening. He nodded and said thanks.

He noticed his father sitting in the corner. His dark suit and black tie blending in with the gallons of black stout that sat on the table in front of him. Frank winked and nodded to him. The old man smiled and waved back. He was going to miss her. The old man was a self-righteous old fool. For years, he'd worked hard on their small farm, often into the early hours of the morning. Old-fashioned. He had traditional beliefs and old-world values. Frank had often despised him for that and for the way he treated his mother. He never seemed to be there to help when she needed him. He could see how tired his mother would be at the end of the day. Yet his father would expect his dinner and his pipe to be ready. After dinner, he would sit by the fire and watch television.

Now he was left to carry on alone. Frank looked closely at him. He was somewhere else tonight. His big red eyes gave it all away.

"Frank," a deep, gruff voice called from behind.

Frank turned around. It was Sergeant McLoughlin, a great friend of his mother's.

"Sorry to hear about poor Dottie," he said respectfully as he shook Frank's hand. There were only two people in the town who addressed his mother by her pet name, Dottie. One was Father Conlan. The other was Sergeant McLoughlin.

Frank used to wonder if he was secretly in love with her. "Thanks very much, Sergeant."

"Aye, she'll be missed." McLoughlin was getting sentimental in his old age. It was a far cry from the days when he would wait outside the chip van until the crowds of young people would clear after the disco. No one dared to make a sound or step out of line. McLoughlin's reputation was feared the length and breath of west Cork. He was just about to go back to his whiskey when he turned. "By the way, there was an anonymous phone call to the station for you the other night." He stared at Frank.

"To the garda station . . . for me?" Frank looked at the sergeant in disbelief. "About my mother?"

"No. Someone looking for you. Wanted to know your whereabouts in London." McLoughlin took a gulp from his drink. "Female." He winked at Frank. "She sounded impressed. But then why wouldn't she be?"

"Did she leave a number?"

The sergeant shook his head. "Afraid not. I'll talk to you later. Come here, Terry Boyd, did you get your car tax sorted out yet?"

Just as Frank was about to head back to his stool, the phone near him rang. He looked at it for a moment and picked it up. "Hello, Molloy's."

It was a female voice on the far end.

"Hello, I'm trying to trace a Frank McCabe. Can anyone there help me?"

Frank looked astonished. "You're speaking to him. This is Frank."

The phone went dead.

Frank stared at the receiver and hung up.

* * *

Jamie sat in the darkness wondering if someone was playing a joke on her. It had certainly sounded like him. She didn't want to talk to him, though. Well, not yet, anyway. She hadn't planned on hearing his voice at the other end of the phone. It couldn't be him. Sure, he was in London, wasn't he? Was he? Maybe she should try one more time. She picked up the receiver. Then she put it down. She stood up and paced the floor for a few minutes. She decided to go through what she'd say to him. Just so she wouldn't sound like a complete neurotic.

Hi, Frank. This is Jamie. Remember me? No! That sounded pathetic.

Hello, is that Frank? Hi, it's Jamie.

Nope. Definitely not.

Then she had an idea. What if she'd found something that he'd left behind on the train? She stared at the phone. Why, in God's name, was she doing this? She'd hate him to think she was stalking him. Anyway, what if his girlfriend was there with him? She grabbed the phone.

The noise at the far end made it almost impossible for anyone to hear what she was saying.

"*Frank McCabe. Mc . . . Cabe . . . !*" She shouted.

"*This is Frank,*" the voice at the other end shouted back. "*Give me your number and I'll call you back in ten minutes,*" he roared.

Her heart almost burst with excitement as she rattled off her number to him. "*And make sure to put 01 in front of it.*" She hung up and waited. And waited. She was still waiting forty minutes later. Shag this, she thought. As she turned out the light on the landing, the phone rang. She ran back down the stairs in the darkness, taking three steps at a time.

"Hello," she shouted impatiently.

"Jamie?"

"Frank?"

"Yes. How are you?" He was dying to ask her about her attack. But he was afraid of upsetting her.

"I'm not too bad . . . now." Jamie curled a strand of hair around two fingers and smiled. "How are you?"

"I'm not bad . . . well, I suppose that's not true. I came home because my mother died suddenly."

"Oh no, Frank, I'm really sorry. I can call back?"

"*No,*" he replied quickly. "No, it's grand. Just nice to get out of that mad place for a while. Are you home for long?"

"I don't know," Jamie replied cautiously. "I had, well, sort of an accident. I got attacked."

Frank didn't know what to say. "I heard."

Silence. "How?"

"From Nikki." Frank got the feeling he was treading on dangerous ground.

"*Nikki?*"

"Yeah."

"When were you talking to Nikki?"

Frank had to think quickly. He wasn't sure if Jamie knew that Nikki had been out with Tommy and he didn't want to tell her that he'd met them together, that Saturday evening, in the pub. "She came in to help with the clean-up. Eh, the pub was broken into. The one I run, the Clover Tap. Whoever did it wrecked the place. I put the word out for a few volunteers to help get the place back together. Nikki showed up to give a hand. We got chatting and your name came up in conversation." Frank knew he was clutching at straws. How could it make any sense?

343

Change direction, he thought. "I was really worried about you."

Jamie looked shocked. She was speechless for a moment. "The Clover Tap," she whispered. "The night I was . . . " She stopped. "You were inside. I was outside."

"Are you all right?"

She waited before answering. "As all right as I can be, I suppose. I reported it to the police, so they're looking after it."

"Jesus, why didn't you get in touch?"

Jamie laughed gently. "Sure, how could I? I didn't have your number."

Frank knew it was a stupid question. "Can I meet you?" he asked. "I mean, before I go back, like."

It felt good to hear his sexy voice again. But she was still afraid. "When are you going back?" Jamie didn't want to think about him going back to London, and she didn't want to end this conversation either.

"Probably in a few days. But I can head up to Dublin a day early. What are your plans?"

"You tell me when. You're the one who's travelling."

"Eh, Wednesday next. How's that?"

"Sounds great. Where do you want to meet?"

Frank scratched his head. He hadn't a clue where the trendy spots were, he'd been away for so long. "You name the place, I'll see you there."

Jamie smiled. At long last she was going to see him again. "Bewley's in Grafton Street?"

"Great," said Frank.

"On the mezzanine level," she added.

"On the *what*?" Frank asked politely.

Jamie laughed. "Bewley's in Grafton Street at two."

"This coming Wednesday?" he repeated.

"This coming Wednesday. See you then. Frank?" She paused.

"Yes?" He held his breath and waited for her question.

"Are you OK?"

There was a short silence. "Yeah, I'm OK. Now that I've talked to you, I'm very OK."

She thought for a moment as she fidgeted with her hair. "It's lovely to hear you again."

"It's lovely to hear you too."

"See you Wednesday," she whispered the words into the phone.

"Goodbye."

Jamie put the phone down. She closed her eyes. Everything was all right again.

Chapter Twenty

Tuesday night was spent twisting and turning. Hours of sleepless questions, predictions and hallucinations. She hadn't had such a bad night in weeks.

Wednesday, on the other hand, was a day Jamie had been looking forward to all week.

She'd got a part-time job in a local crèche from half nine till twelve. The money was a joke but she enjoyed working with the children. By a quarter past twelve, she was back in front of the bathroom mirror putting on her face, as she called it. By one, Lisa was giving her the final going-over. She debated which would be better, a bus or a taxi. She decided on the taxi. No point in being late. She'd imagined this rendezvous for a long, long time. She didn't want to blow it.

She walked to the end of Church Avenue on to the busy Whitehall Road. Taxis went up and down all the time. There'd be no problem getting one. She was right. Almost as soon as she'd stepped off the kerb, there was a taxi sitting in front of her. She climbed into the back and closed the door. The driver smiled.

"Hiya, that was quick," Jamie said.

"How are things?" the driver replied in a rich northern accent.

"Grand."

"Where are you going?" he asked as he looked for an opening into the busy traffic.

"Stephen's Green, top of Grafton Street, please." She took out her small make-up mirror and touched up her lipstick.

"Great weather," said the driver.

"Yeah, not bad for this time of the year, I suppose," Jamie replied. She hated having banal conversations in taxis. She just wished they'd shut up and get her there.

"When did you get home?" he asked.

"A while back." The words came out without as much as a thought for the question. She looked at the rear-view mirror, suddenly shocked.

His eyes watched her.

"How did you know I was away?"

"I was away myself."

Jamie felt nervous. "No, not that. Your last question."

"I just guessed you were away, that's all. I'm a taxi driver. It gets easy to tell after a while. Dublin people aren't quite sure where they're going. That kind of thing. That's all." He signalled and turned right on to the Malahide Road.

"But you're not from Dublin, are you?" She wasn't sure where this was all leading. She also noticed that he was driving slowly. Slower than the other traffic.

"That's right. Derry, actually. Still, Derry, Dublin,

there's not much difference when you're driving all the time. London?"

Jamie's heart beat faster. She couldn't keep up with the conversation. "Sorry?"

"I said London. I bet you were in London."

She looked out the window. "Yeah, good guess," she said nervously.

"Ah, it wasn't a guess." He laughed. Suddenly, his expression changed. It was almost as if he'd seen her somewhere before. "You took a bit of a beating."

Jamie looked at his eyes in the mirror. They weren't *the* eyes. She felt a great sense of relief. But where had he got all this information? Was he a detective? Hardly. She'd never met a northern detective working in Dublin. Certainly not driving a taxi. "How did you know?" she asked calmly.

"That mark under your eye. I'm a karate instructor. That's like the scar left by a sharp karate chop." He looked over his shoulder at her. "Am I making you nervous?"

Jamie nodded. "Yes." Relax, she thought. Nothing can happen in a public taxi in the middle of busy traffic. "Why do you ask?"

"Because the last thing I want to do is to make you nervous. Do you want to get another taxi? I'll call one for you if you want?"

Jamie could see the identification on the dashboard. She tried to read the driver's name. She nodded. "No, it's all right." Then she wondered if she should ask more. Why not? she thought. I'm in the thick of it as it is. "Who are you?"

"Paul." He smiled. "Me brother owns the cab. I'm just giving him a dig out."

"How do you know all those things about me?"

"What things?" he asked.

"London. The attack."

"Tommy?"

She froze.

The eyes were watching her again.

Her stomach was a knot. Her forehead was on fire. "Tommy . . . who?" She could barely get the words out.

"Tommy Barrett." He waited and watched.

Jamie picked up her bag. "I think I *will* get another taxi. Stop the car and let me out, please." She eased her way across the leather upholstery towards the door. "*Stop the car . . . now!*" she demanded.

"*Here?*" he asked in dismay. He shook his head. "I'd lose my job if I let you out here." He nodded at the flats on his right-hand side. "One of the roughest kips in the city here. A guy murdered over there on Friday night. Knifed eight times." He drove faster. He looked around at Jamie. "You won't get a taxi around here, love."

Jamie clenched her jaws hard.

"They rob your hub-caps if you stop at a red light around here. There's not a man in the city who feels comfortable driving around here, never mind a woman. I've only been here on the job less than a fortnight. It was the first thing they told me." He looked around at Jamie. "Don't worry, Jamie, you'll be OK."

Her head flew back with the shock. "What did you say?" She looked petrified.

He watched her in the mirror. "I just said you'll be OK."

"How do you know my name?" she asked slowly.

He smiled and flicked his head. "Through our mutual friend."

Jamie fiddled with the catch on her bag. "Listen, just who are you and what do you want?" she demanded.

"My turn to ask you a question. That's if you let me?"

Jamie looked at the mirror. The eyes were different. They were telling her much more now than before. They didn't want to hurt her. Quite the opposite, she thought. Maybe, though, she was imagining all this. The police doctor had told that, as a direct result of the attack, she'd suffer from a condition called Post-traumatic Syndrome Disorder. Paranoia was one of the chief side effects of this disorder. She nodded. "OK," she whispered.

"Do you really think that this taxi pick-up was a coincidence?"

It dawned on her that it couldn't have been.

"I've been wanting to meet you and to talk to you for some time now. We've got a lot in common, Jamie. I want what you want. Vengeance. That man ruined my life. Eight years lost. I want to make sure that he never makes another person's life miserable again."

Jamie was getting more nervous by the minute. Eight years gone. What did he mean? "I don't know what you're talking about. I've got to get where I'm going for quarter to two. It's twenty to two now, and I don't want to be late . . . "

"Listen!" He pulled into the side of the road. "You obviously don't understand what I'm trying to tell you." He turned around in his seat until he was face to face with Jamie.

Jamie studied his features. His moustache failed to hide a long, deep scar to the right of his mouth, above his lip. As he put his elbow across the back of his seat, she noticed two tattoos above his left wrist. *Paul loves Maggie* and a more recent one, *Peace*. They seemed quite fresh. For some strange reason, she didn't feel nervous any more.

"I don't want to scare you but *your* life is in danger," he stated calmly. "Serious danger. The man who attacked you is coming looking for you." His eyes stared into hers.

"But why?" she whispered. "He was the one who hurt me. I didn't do anything to hurt *him*."

"Why? Because you know something about him that could destroy him for ever. Maybe even get him killed."

"But I'm not going to tell anyone about the attack," she insisted.

"You told the police, didn't you?"

"Yes." Her mind was a complete muddle now. Here she was on her way to meet a man she was crazy about. And she was reliving the worst moments of her life with a man she'd never met, a man who was telling her that her life was threatened. "But I didn't tell them it was *Tommy*!" she yelled back.

"So, you're telling me that it was that bastard who raped you?"

"*Yes . . . I think,*" she shouted. "I don't know. Now, are you happy?" Jamie rubbed her eyes. "Maybe I should have told them. Maybe I was hoping all along that it wasn't him. That it was somebody who looked just like him."

"Did he put a gun in your mouth?"

"No."

"A knife?"

"Yes," she whispered.

"Did he handcuff you?"

She nodded. "Yes."

"And the money?"

"What money?"

"The black sack of money . . . that ended up on a rubbish tip. You knew about that as well, didn't you?"

"Yes."

"And you knew where it came from, didn't you, Jamie?"

She raised her hands to her face. They were shaking. "Please don't hurt me. *Please!*"

He reached out and took a gentle hold of her hand. "I'm not going to hurt you. I just want you to realise fully what's happening here. You're at the centre of one of the most explosive situations that even *I've* ever come across. His plan has gone catastrophically wrong on him. It has backfired, *bigtime!* You obviously don't really know what this monster is capable of doing."

"But he loved me!"

"What are you trying to say?"

"Maybe I was just hoping that he wasn't that evil.

Sure, I knew he was bad. But he wasn't all bad. At least, not until he . . . "

"That's irrelevant. Anyway, you don't seriously think that his colleagues in the force are going to believe your word against his. Even if you *do* spill the beans on him. You've heard of corruption, haven't you? Well, believe me, the people you're dealing with are the worst bunch of corrupt bastards you're likely to meet in this life. Excuse the French. An Irishwoman's accusations against a fine, commendable, hard-working police officer? A judge looks at you and then at him? You've got to be joking!"

"But it was an Irishwoman who took the statement."

"Of course it was. Makes it all look very believable and above-board, doesn't it?" He laughed and threw his head back. "Listen, Jamie, with due respect, I'm sure what you've been through is worse than most people could ever imagine. But let me tell you, the situation that you're facing right now is more horrible than your worst nightmares."

Jamie started to cry. "I'm sorry," she whispered, as she brushed away the tears. "Why is this all happening to me? What have I done to deserve this?"

"I asked myself that question for eight years. Finally I decided to do something about it. Listen to me, please," he whispered insistently. "I don't know why all this is happening to you, but all I know is that it *is*. I'm only trying to help you. You knew about the drugs. Now you know about the money and how he came to have it. That could destroy him. He's got to silence you."

Jamie stared at him.

"Someone stole five grand from him. He's in trouble if he can't repay the money. No one's been able to locate him for weeks." He looked out the window and stared at the graffiti on the walls of the flats. *Up the IRA. No surrender to the British.* He smiled. "Anyway, where was I?"

"He's been missing for weeks," Jamie repeated.

"Oh yeah? I think he may turn up here shortly." He looked sadly at Jamie. "Is there anywhere you can go?"

She sniffed and shook her head. "Not really. Are you a cop?"

He snorted. "Me? A *cop*? No, I'm not a cop."

She thought carefully for a moment. "But it was only three grand."

He smiled. "So you *do* have it. Fair play. I'm glad to see someone's making him feel the pinch." He looked out the window as a police car slowed down. The driver signalled him to move on. "Up yours," he muttered. He looked back at Jamie. "Well, someone else must have the other two grand." He waited for an answer. "Any ideas who that might be? Because they're in the soup as well."

"Nikki," Jamie whispered.

"A friend of yours?"

Jamie nodded. "Best friend."

"Does she know this bloke?"

"Yeah."

"Have you talked to her in the last few days?"

"No. Should I have?"

"No. Don't talk to anyone for a while. See if things settle down. Although I doubt if they will."

"You never answered my first question. Who are you?"

He thought for a minute. "Who am I? Now that's a good question. You know, years ago I thought I knew who I was. But then I realised that that wasn't really me at all. So, I've spent all the years in between then and now trying to face up to the real me."

"Can *you* help me?" Jamie asked. "I can pay you."

He smiled. "I don't want your money. Although I'd like to think I was taking that bastard's money. In fact, it wouldn't be a good idea if I was to get involved. Tommy and me have our own bit of sorting out to do."

"But what *did* he do to you?" she asked.

He shrugged his shoulders. "Maybe you'll just have to wait and read the book. I'm not all bad. I have a little girl. I hope she gets the chance to grow up to be as beautiful as you."

"Spare me," Jamie muttered. "Are you some sort of celebrity?"

The taxi-driver burst into a fit of uncontrollable laughter. "A *celebrity*? Brilliant. I've been called a lot of things down the years, but never a celebrity. Thank you, I'll take that as a compliment. Paul Flaherty, reformed terrorist, recently turned celebrity." He clapped his hands. "Ah, that's brilliant." He turned serious again. "We'd better get a move on. You're late." He signalled and moved out into the traffic. "I'd like to meet you."

"Why?"

"To talk to you. To fill you in more on what's been happening. I think you should know."

Jamie was reluctant. "I suppose so. When?"

"As soon as possible. I think things are about to happen around here pretty quickly."

"Now?" She needed to know. More about Tommy. *More* about this stranger.

The taxi driver seemed surprised. "I can't. I've got a fare at two. I'm not finished till three. Then I have to drop the wagon back to my brother in Killiney."

"I'll meet you in Killiney. Half three?"

"Whereabouts?"

"That big hotel on the hill. The Castle. Do you know it?"

"I'll find it. I thought you said you were meeting someone."

"I never said I was meeting anyone. Who's getting paranoid now?" She picked up her bag again. "Let me out."

He pulled in to the kerb.

Jamie moved to the door. Before she opened it, she searched in her bag. "How much do I owe you?" she asked.

"Nothing. Or maybe your life." He turned around again. "Did you believe me when I told you that you were at risk?"

"I don't know what to think any more." She got out of the car and banged the door.

"I've got a friend you can stay with in Killiney for a while. You'd never be found out there." He waited for a reaction. "Do you want his number?" He held a card out to her.

Reluctantly, she took the card. "Does he know anything about what you've told me?" she asked.

Paul shook his head. "Nothing. He knows about me. But only because I chose to tell him. I've stayed there recently. It's a beautiful spot and his wife makes gorgeous brown bread." He smiled.

Jamie was bewildered. "And what is it about *you* that you're afraid to tell me? After all, you seem to know enough about me."

He leant out the window. "Now's not the time. It might only complicate things."

Jamie stood rooted to the spot. She felt cold inside. Cold. This was going on and on.

The taxi edged slowly back into the moving traffic.

Jamie looked around. She was outside Tara Street DART station, in a right bind. She'd waited for this day for months. At last, she was going to see Frank again. But now, her happiness had been overshadowed. She noticed a telephone kiosk on the corner. She could leave a message in Bewley's explaining to Frank that she got waylaid. There were things she had to find out *now* rather than later. Questions had to be answered and her nagging fears eliminated. Frank would have to wait. She prayed that he'd understand. She took some change out of her bag and picked up the receiver. No such luck. The phone had been vandalised. She turned half-heartedly and began the long climb towards the ticket office. She was relying on her instinct. It had never let her down before. She would explain to Frank later. If there *would* be a later.

"Return to Killiney," she said to the cashier.

"Three pounds fifty, please."

She pushed a note under the window and picked up the ticket.

"Excuse me, miss," the cashier called from behind the glass. "Excuse me. Your change. You gave me a twenty-pound note. Excuse me . . . "

Jamie didn't hear him. She just kept on walking.

* * *

Frank looked at his watch. Quarter past four. He looked down at the four drained coffee cups in front of him. He decided to walk around the restaurant again just to be sure that she wasn't sitting somewhere else.

His mother always went to Bewley's when she came up to town each year. December 8th. It was an annual pilgrimage. He could see why she liked this place. It had an atmosphere all of its own. Students over there. A couple holding hands across the table in the corner. Two elderly women having a cosy gossip in another corner.

He'd asked the girl who was cleaning the tables to watch out for Jamie and to tell her that he'd be back in a moment.

She asked Frank what Jamie looked like.

He tried to describe her, but found he couldn't. All he could remember was the colour of her hair and eyes. Her lips and smile. And the unmistakable bond they'd formed that night on the train which wasn't really any help to this busy waitress.

She looked at him as if to say "Are you for real?"

Why didn't I ask her what she'd be wearing? he asked himself. He'd only seen her once. Maybe she'd dyed her hair. Maybe she was decked out in a completely new style and he wouldn't know her. Why didn't I ask?

There was no sign of her when he got back to his table.

"Been stood up?" the waitress asked cheekily as she ran a cloth across the tabletop. She looked Frank up and down and winked. "She must be mad."

"*He*, actually," Frank wasn't amused at her joke.

The young girl froze, almost dropping the heavy tray she was carrying. "Oh I'm terribly sorry."

Frank laughed. He picked up his jacket and slung it over his shoulder. As he walked by the girl who'd just passed the remark, he noticed that she was being reprimanded by her supervisor. "Here," he said, holding out a bunch of flowers, "thanks for making me laugh. I needed that."

* * *

Grafton Street looked beautiful in the late afternoon. A bitter wind blew down the street as the setting March sun stretched shoppers' shadows into great lanky black giants. Frank looked up the street towards Stephen's Green and then down towards Trinity College. Which way? he wondered. He'd plenty of time to spare now that his plans had taken a dive. It was half four. His flight wasn't until twenty to eight.

He couldn't understand why she'd stood him up. It couldn't have been anything he'd said. Sure, they'd spoken for barely five minutes. Something must have happened. She'd sounded quite keen to meet up when he spoke to her on the phone. Then he thought of the other Bewley's in Westmoreland Street. No, she'd definitely said Grafton Street.

He wandered slowly down Grafton Street looking in the occasional window at nothing in particular. Then it struck him that he had her number in one of his pockets. Luckily he'd remembered to stick it in his bag just in case. After a thorough search, he managed to find a telephone kiosk that was still in working order. He dialled her number and waited. It seemed to ring for ages. A woman's voice answered.

"Hello, is Jamie there?" Frank shouted, trying to block out the busy street sounds behind him.

"No, she's gone out for the evening. Who's calling?

Frank hesitated. "Em, just a friend. Is she due back shortly, can you tell me?"

"I wouldn't think so. She was meeting a friend and she told me not to expect her back till late."

Frank's heart sank. She was meeting someone else. Maybe another man. "Thanks," he said politely.

"Can I tell her who called?"

He hung up without answering. He flagged down a passing taxi. "Dublin airport, please."

* * *

The salty sea breeze felt like small hailstones blowing hard against her face. Jamie squinted as she stared out at the choppy sea. Killiney beach still held that childhood magic for her. It must have been almost twenty years since she'd last set foot on this spot. Maybe more. She looked around her as the sun made its slow descent down the back of the hill behind the busy railway line. Holding a hand up to her eyes to shield them from the glare, she watched the green DART commuter train pull away from the station and head slowly for Dalkey tunnel.

Jamie smiled as she spotted the narrow, grassy path up to the railway track. It was still there. She walked slowly up the beach to the granite wall and touched the sandy trail with her hand. She looked at the wall. Back then, it was a major achievement to climb up over it and on to the path above. Now, the top of the wall was level with her knees. She looked around quickly. The small tea-shacks that had lined the back of the beach below the steep hill were gone.

Her mother would bring the teapot over to the red one beside the lifeguard's hut for boiling water.

Jamie used to go with her, wearing the teacosy so as not to lose it. The lifeguard would wink at her.

Her brothers teased her. "*Jamie's got a boyfriend . . . Jamie's got a boyfriend . . .* " they chanted when they caught her looking up at him.

"*He is not!*" she protested every time. Jamie thought he was gorgeous. She could never figure out why he had a hairy chest and her father didn't.

She shivered violently. She hadn't realised how cold it was. She looked up and down the long, stony beach. She had it all to herself. Well, almost. A man was walking with his dog close to the water's edge. Another man was trying to get to grips with his windsurfing equipment. He wasn't having too much luck. She smiled as he drifted further and further away from the shore.

A man sitting on a stool behind a huge fishing-rod

at the water's edge laughed as he watched the surfer's desperate attempts. "What a plonker," he roared at the top of his voice. "Probably watches *Baywatch*."

Jamie walked on up the beach. She checked her watch. Quarter past three. She debated whether or not to meet this *Paul*. He seemed to know a lot. Too much, in fact. She was intrigued. And frightened. Another train was pulling out of the station. It was difficult to understand how, less than two hours before, she had listened to a mad taxi-driver tell her that her life was in danger. Here she was on Killiney beach where time seemed to stand still. She didn't feel threatened here. She didn't want to leave. As she looked back at the darkening sea and the clear horizon between Ireland and Britain, she wanted to be back there sitting beside her mother on the big blanket in the sunshine humming along with her to the songs on *Hospitals' Requests*.

"Hello," the familiar voice said.

Jamie spun around. It was Paul. "What are you doing here?"

"I got here sooner than I thought. Me brother doesn't need the taxi till five. So I was sitting in the carpark up there passing the time, having a cup of coffee, when I saw you."

Jamie looked back out at the sea. "It's gorgeous here."

"Yeah. It reminds me of Carlingford Lough in the summer when I was a kid."

"Who are you and *what* do you want?"

He thought for a moment. "Probably the same as

you: happiness and revenge. Apart from other things. I want all the wasted time back. I know I can't have that. But I want the next best thing."

"What's that?"

"Maybe you wouldn't believe me."

They started to walk along the beach close to the water's edge, moving in and out to avoid the gentle, lapping waves.

"Who am I?" he said, repeating her question. "My name's Paul Flaherty. I'm thirty-three and I come from Coleraine."

"Were you in prison?" Jamie asked unsympathetically.

"Does it show?"

"I'm not being funny."

"I did eight years. It felt like eighty."

"You're a terrorist."

He stopped walking, visibly shirty. "I am *not*!"

"You said you were, in the taxi."

"I *was* what you might call in active service for a few years. But that was a long time ago. I'm a very different person now."

"The army?"

"No."

"The *provos*?"

He said nothing.

"Bastard!"

"It wasn't like that."

"What do you mean *it wasn't like that*?" Jamie aped. "Killing and slaughtering innocent people. Get a life, for God's sake!" She about-turned and started to walk briskly back towards the station.

"Jamie, wait!" he called.

"They *should* have given you eighty years. Even that wouldn't have been good enough! I can't believe I was so stupid as to come out here in the first place."

Paul scampered after her. "Listen to me, *please*. I have some important news for you, if you'll only listen to me." He grabbed her arm. "You *know* why you came out here."

She pulled it away. "*Don't you dare* lay a finger on me." She stood facing him, silently watching him. "Tell me the truth. Have you ever killed a person?"

He shook his head violently. "*No!*"

Jamie seemed to relax slightly.

"I am *not* a member of the provisional IRA," he pleaded. "Believe me, please."

"You said you were."

"I *was*, past tense."

Jamie was confused. "I always thought once a member, *always* a member."

"It doesn't work like that. At least, it didn't then. I told them I wanted out. They said OK, I'm only a liability to their operation if they feel I'm weak and can't be trusted. That makes sense, doesn't it?"

"I suppose so. Why did you leave?" she asked softly.

"Because I stopped believing."

"You mean you got sense?"

"Maybe. I have a ten-year-old daughter I haven't seen for nearly six years. I just wanted to stop all this mindless stupidity and be . . . " He thought for a minute and smiled. "Liked? Yeah, a good old-fashioned daddy. Bringing my kids to the pictures.

Telling them bedtime stories. Helping them with their homework. Hugging them and telling them I loved them." His face dropped. "But that never happened."

"Why?" She sat up on the small granite wall.

Paul sighed. "I handed in my notice nine years ago. I told the man from the Army Council that I'd had all I could take. I was starting a new life and I just wanted to be left alone. I got a call to say that that was fine. They warned me not to divulge any trade secrets. Needless to say, I'd no intentions of talking to anyone. It would've been a bit like signing my own death certificate." He sat alongside Jamie and took a long deep breath of sea air.

Jamie looked at him. It was almost as if he was hesitating. "So what happened?"

"It was a Thursday afternoon. I'd just started a new job as a motorbike courier. I had to do something to make a few bob. I'd been up around Kilburn looking at a small flat for the girlfriend and Noni . . . that's our wee girl. You see, you have to remember, *they* were looking after me while I was in London. Sleepers, that's what we were called. Lying low, making bombs until we got a tip-off for the next *job*." He cleared his throat. "Now, I had to get a job and support myself and the girls. I even remember the time. Ten past five. I'd just finished my last run for the afternoon. I was going to get rid of the bike and go for a couple of pints before going home. It was Maggie's twenty-first and we were having a wee party in me mate's house for her." He sniggered. "A *surprise* party, or so I thought. I'd just turned off Charing Cross Road on to

Shaftesbury Avenue. The traffic was bumper-to-bumper. It was handy on the bike. You could weave your way through all the traffic." He delayed. "Then I spotted him."

"Who?" asked Jamie.

"He was stuck in the traffic. Stuck solid. I knew the car had been stolen. False plates. Something instinctively told me that the bag on the back seat wasn't your average Thursday late-night shopping. I reached out and tapped on the window. He looked up at me. He was planking himself. I'd shared a house with this guy for six months. That evening, it was like as if he'd never seen me before. He ignored me. I started to bang on the window and call his name . . . "

"Fergus!"

"He still ignored me and gripped the wheel tighter. I could hear the radio. It was blaring. He kept checking his watch and banging the dashboard. I knew he was in big trouble. We were all in big trouble. That bomb was due to blow at any minute."

"Open the door, son. Let me help. I can defuse the detonator if you let me in."

"I clawed at the window, trying to get it down a couple of inches. It wasn't working. I parked the bike in front of the car. When I looked back, Fergus had already started to run away from his delivery."

"Fergus, come back!"

He turned around for a split second. *"Get the fuck out of there, Paul. That's gonna lift any second."*

"That was the last time I saw Fergus Gilmore."

Jamie shivered. "What happened?"

Paul's hand shook as he ran it through his hair. "I couldn't think. I didn't know what to do. I was looking around. A few people were watching the commotion, too far away to hear what was going on. I roared at them 'get outta here, *now!*' I looked across at the other side of the street. There was a crowd of school kids queueing for a pantomime at one of the theatres . . . or something. I could see a couple of women pushing buggies, little innocent kids licking ice creams, holding their hands . . . queueing patiently, laughing and talking." His voice was quivering. "I knew I had a choice. I could get back on my bike and disappear, or . . . " He stopped.

"Or what?" whispered Jamie.

He gulped. Then he jumped down from the granite wall and seemed to go into a dazed, ecstatic trance. *"Get out of here, everybody, get out of this street. There's a bomb in this car. It's going to explode in a few minutes. Get out of your cars."* His hands waved about wildly. *"You . . . get out of your car. Fast. Get those small kids inside. Get them further back down the street, please. Help me. Move them away. It's a fucking bomb!"* He went quiet. Then he started to cry.

"What happened?"

He sniffed. "Two policemen standing on the corner of the crossroads and the avenue obviously saw what was going on. They were running towards me, calling me, telling me to freeze. One of them was on his radio, shouting for back-up. I started up my bike and took off. I'd managed to reach the top of Shaftesbury Avenue when the explosion rocked the West End." He wuthered. "It killed eight people . . . wounded forty-three, sixteen of them were kids."

Silence.

"It wasn't your fault," whispered Jamie.

"*What?*" Paul cried in disbelief. "It still doesn't matter. It shouldn't have happened in the first place."

"But look at all the people whose lives you *did* save."

"That's not the point. Look at all the people who *were* killed and brutally maimed for life. That should never have happened," he ranted angrily.

Jamie waited a while. "What happened then?"

"That was when the nightmare got into full swing. A couple of the girls had got Maggie out of the house around eight for a while. The plan was that she'd come back and we'd all be there to surprise her. It was just as well she'd gone out, 'cos I spent the two hours locked in the jacks drinking brandy and throwing my guts up. Shock, I suppose. Believe it or not, I'd never seen anything like that before. I'd helped at different stages of the procedure but, may Jesus Christ forgive me, I never realised that it could be so bloody monstrous. So futile. All that carnage . . . for what? So worthless and so sick."

"Did you tell your girlfriend?"

"I didn't get a chance to wish her a happy birthday, never mind tell her what had happened. Sure, she'd heard it in the news. But she knew I was out of it. Or so we both thought until twenty-five past five that evening. That was when my whole world fell apart forever."

"What happened?"

"I began to feel a wee bit better about eleven. Probably just the bottle of brandy taking effect. A few friends had got some grub together downstairs for the gang coming back from the pub. One of the lads had nipped out to the off-licence for extra beer and stuff. About half eleven there was a knock on the door. I thought it was Larry back with the booze. I should have known from the sound of the knock that it wasn't a hand doing the knocking. I opened the door and what seemed like twenty huge bastards trampled me to death. I was lying on the floor looking up at these guys running over me, jumping up and down on me, screaming and shouting, kicking and digging. I knew what was going on. But it still scared the shite out of me, even to this day. I'll never forget it. One of them grabbed me by the hair and dragged me into the kitchen. He pinned me head-on against the fridge door. 'One move and I'll break every bone in your body, you fenian bastard!' he shouted. I felt handcuffs going on. They took chunks out of my wrists. Then I felt a hard boot bludgeon the side of my head. I could feel my ear filling up with blood. Then everything went dark and quiet. I don't really remember anything else."

"What happened to Maggie?"

"I don't know. We were all arrested and taken to Paddington Green. That's a high-security police prison where they hold you and question you. I knew we were all there but we were all separated. Then I heard two weeks later that she'd been deported back to

Dublin. Because she'd never be allowed back on to British soil, that was the last I saw of her."

"And your daughter?"

"Noni? A photograph." He pulled a dog-eared picture from a small wallet and handed it to Jamie.

Jamie studied the shot. "Is that your girlfriend?"

"Ex-girlfriend."

"Your daughter's beautiful. How old is she now?"

"Nearly ten."

"Have you seen her since . . . "

"Yesterday. She hasn't a clue who I am. All she knows is that I'm her daddy and I've worked in England for eight years. All the other kids in her class have real daddies. Respectable family men. I've a bit of making up to do there. But don't worry. It's just nice to be home."

"Do they know who *you* are?"

"Who, the *real* daddies?"

"Yeah."

"Don't think so."

"And Jacqui?"

He sighed. "She wrote for a while. Then the letters got further and further apart. Then they stopped. Then, out of the blue one morning, I got a letter from her to tell me she was getting married. I couldn't blame her, really. I still love her though. It's difficult to fall in love with other women when you're locked away in a high-security cell twenty-four hours a day. The only woman I got to see for years was Julia Somerville reading the news on telly. I have to admit I came pretty close to falling in love with her."

Jamie laughed.

"I'm glad you laughed. The last thing I want to do is terrify you."

Jamie stood up. "Let's walk. I'm getting cold."

"Here, I'll drop you back to the station."

"And miss this? This is better than any book I've ever read." They started to walk. "So how did you break out?"

"A mate of mine smuggled in a gun. I reckoned they owed me one big favour after what had happened. They said no way. Not if I was going to turn my back on the movement. I thought then that that was it until, one day, this bloke arrived in with a small piece buried inside one of his trainers."

"*Piece?*"

"Gun."

"Did you use it?"

"Only to let them know I was armed. I let off two shots in the air. That kept them at bay."

"So how did you get out?"

"During exercise. They let us out into the main yard every morning before breakfast – they'd never let us exercise with the other prisoners in case they'd attack us. I mentioned to two others that I was going out. They couldn't believe it. But they were willing to help and cause a diversion. I knew that the laundry van would be leaving the prison around nine and that it had to drive along the narrow perimeter road that runs around the exercise yard. Most of the screws were inside, while the bulk of the prisoners were eating their breakfast."

"Were you not afraid?" asked Jamie.

"If anyone else had asked me that question, I'd have said no. But . . . yes, I was planking myself. There were two watchtowers with armed guards in each. Their shift changed at nine. There were two guards, one with a hungry-looking German police dog, in the prison yard. They were chatting to each other, not really paying any attention, from what I could gather. I had the gun hidden in my Y-fronts with a big hole in my trouser pocket for rapid access. That was a delicate moment." He laughed out loud. "You can be sure that I wasn't thinking about the nuts in the gun at that particular moment! Anyway, to cut a long story short, I could hear the laundry van. I knew it would be no more than thirty seconds before it appeared around the corner. I had to think fast. There'd been no time to rehearse so it either worked or it didn't. As soon as I said 'good luck' to the two boys I was walking with, they started a fight. One of them knocked the other to the ground and dived on him. I took a quick look back. It looked like the real thing. Change of shift was taking place in the tower so they were disarmed and confused. The two guards in the yard saw me running towards them and thought I was bringing the scrape to their attention. So when I grabbed the bloke with the machinegun and held my weapon to his belly, he nearly shat himself. No one could see me doing it. The other copper kept running in the direction of the fight. His dog was dragging him even faster. Reinforcements were on hand in seconds. But the lad kept on fighting."

"What did you do?"

"I told the guard that if he as much as squeaked I'd put a hole in his back the size of a golf ball."

"And then?"

"I told him to walk calmly towards the gate that the reinforcements had just come through. I held the gun in my pocket against his back. It was still hidden so no one could suspect anything. We walked into the driveway leading down to the main gatehouse. I told him to flag down the laundry van. We both climbed in beside the driver and I told him to keep on driving. As we drove up to the main security checkpoint, I jumped into the back and held the gun to the back of yer man's neck. Next time I looked up, we were out in the country."

"And what did you do with the copper and the laundry-man?"

"Well the laundry-man was Irish. He didn't seem too pushed about telling anyone that I was gone. As for the copper, he tried to go for his gun so I had to get rid of him."

"You *shot* him?" Jamie asked alarmedly.

"He shot himself, actually. In the foot, if you don't mind! There was nothing I could have done. Of course, they'll say *I* shot him. I didn't. I just kicked him out the back door."

"And the laundry-man?"

"He just asked to be tied up. That way, no questions." He looked sideways at Jamie. She was looking out to sea. "I suppose you think I'm a real monster now."

She shook her head. "No. It just seems awful that

373

you had to wait eight years to start living again. Has it affected you?"

"In ways. I'll get over it. Soon."

"How did you meet Tommy?"

"Tommy was the one that pinned it all on me. That night, when we were all arrested at the party, I reckoned they'd probably question us for seventy-two hours and hopefully let us go then . . . the usual. I was wrong. Tommy filled up the boot of some stolen car that had never been claimed with Semtex, a couple of kalashnikovs, a few hundred rounds of assorted ammunition; you know, the sort of story the tabloids love; the sort of headline that guarantees you'll never get a fair trial. He pinned it on me. Said it was my car. There was absolutely nothing I could do."

"But surely the car wasn't registered in your name?"

"Correct. That's because I was meant to have stolen it for car-bombing purposes."

"But your fingerprints would have to be somewhere."

"Well, that's the problem. They were. They were all over the handlebars of my motor-bike. *They* matched with the prints they found on the driver's door of the car in Shaftesbury Avenue. The door was blown clean off by the power of the explosion. They found it later, still intact. My prints were all over the window that I'd been trying to open with my bare fingers."

"But they were on the outside of the window."

"Outside, inside, they didn't care. They had their man. I was a sitting duck." He shivered. "God, it's cold."

Jamie linked his arm. "Are you OK?"

Paul smiled. "Yeah. Thanks."

"I'm sorry for being such a bitch earlier on. It's just that everything is so screwed up now. It's . . . "

"Scary?" mumbled Paul.

"To put it mildly . . . yeah. Did you hear about Jimmy Grant's murder?"

He seemed cautiously wary again. "Through my sources. The cops went in there thinking it was an IRA house. Tommy was obviously assigned to the anti-terrorist squad that night, for some reason."

"They sometimes call up reinforcements from different divisions if they need back-up. Especially with firearms."

"Well, that's what happened. Tommy was more familiar with the drugs bust procedure. The story going around is that Tommy was due to be moved to the ATS full-time shortly, anyway."

"ATS?"

"Anti-terrorist Squad. They're known as SO13 in the business."

"Go on."

"They wouldn't necessarily have been looking for money because they thought this was a terrorist hoist. Arms and bomb-making materials. That sort of thing. As it turns out, Tommy found the money and thought he could keep it; the same bag of money that ended up on the rubbish heap."

"The bag I threw out." Jamie was numb. Not from the biting wind. She unlinked Paul's arm and stared at the choppy sea.

"You see, Jamie, you're the missing piece in the jigsaw. And until Tommy finds you, he won't feel safe. He won't feel safe until his horrible past has been totally wiped out forever."

* * *

Day slowly turned to night. The journey home on the train was making her feel slightly edgy. Nervous. People sat silently side by side. She tried to avoid the stares and glances of the men sitting opposite. They propably didn't mean her any harm. She knew that. She just didn't like it. She wished she had a book. Or better still, a newspaper. She couldn't get comfortable. The seat was too hard. She pressed her head into her hand against the window and shut her eyes. The train left her in Tara Street. A short walk to the bus for Whitehall and home, she thought.

* * *

It was raining when she got off the bus. She was exhausted and slightly flustered. It was a bit late to take the short cut down Lover's Lane. A dark lane used normally by under-aged courting couples who fancied a quick grope before going home with phoney excuses. It was a dark, sinister lane when the romance was taken away, only one way in and one way out. The rain was getting heavier. Jamie knew she'd get soaked if she walked down the full length of Church Avenue. The short cut would leave her thirty seconds from her hall-door. Anyway, on a night like tonight, who'd be hanging around Lover's Lane? She walked quickly towards the dark, slightly obscured entrance. She never noticed the car driving slowly behind her. The engine was difficult to hear, the dimmed lights impossible to see through the spitting rain.

She turned left into Lover's Lane, pulling the collar of her light jacket up around the back of her head. Might as well be wearing a paper bag, she thought.

The car engine died. Silence for a moment.

All that Jamie could hear was the sound of her own footsteps sloshing in puddles she couldn't see. She looked to her left and then to her right, keeping her head bowed as she walked quickly. The lane got darker the further down she went. She looked around to see how far she'd gone. Her mouth dropped open. "Jesus Christ, no," she muttered. A tall figure stood at the entrance to the lane. She walked faster, trying to avoid the deeper water. Without any hint or warning, she walked straight into a tall, hard, immovable object. She screamed at the top of her voice. She looked again. It was a tree. She looked behind. The shadowy figure was nowhere to be seen.

As she turned full circle to reassure herself, a hand grabbed her arm and swung her around. It was a policeman. Not an Irish one, but a British one. He held up a pair of handcuffs and smiled. "Hello, Jamie. Where's my money?"

She froze and stared into the dark eyes. *His* eyes. She wanted to scream but couldn't.

He grabbed her hands and forced a cuff painfully on to each wrist. "Now the time has come for *you* to pay. Dare I die," he whispered. He started to laugh.

Her hands were tied. Locked together. "No! Please. *No!*" she pleaded. She tried to swing out and hit him.

* * *

"*Excuse me, young lady!*" a voice beside her urged angrily.

Jamie opened her eyes. A woman beside her held a hand up to her nose.

"What do think you're doing?" the stranger growled as she picked up her small suitcase.

"Oh Jesus, excuse me. I'm terribly sorry. I must have been dreaming." Jamie looked around and tried to figure out where she was. She was still on the bus. She must have been on it for ages. The bus conductor and two male passengers were standing in front of her.

"This woman's after assaulting me," the female passenger said to the official. "I'd like you to call the police."

The bus conductor looked at Jamie. He could see she was upset. "Are you all right, love?"

"Where are we, if that's not a stupid question?"

"Departures . . . Dublin Airport." He stared curiously at her.

"Shit. I missed my stop." Jamie looked at the woman she'd accidentally clobbered. "It might sound stupid, but I dreamt I was being attacked. I'm really sorry."

"*You* were being attacked? *I* was the one who was attacked!" She moved up the narrow aisle towards the front of the bus. "Out of my way," she snapped to the onlookers.

The conductor followed her. "Are you all right, love?"

"Don't you *love* me, young man! If you'd been doing your job properly, that wouldn't have happened. This *Ecstasy* thingy is ruining the modern generation." She pushed her way towards the door and got off.

Jamie watched her through the window. *"Ecstasy?"* she laughed to herself. That was something she hadn't felt for a long time.

* * *

She thought about staying on the bus and going back to Whitehall Road. The conductor even offered to let her stay on for nothing. Big deal, she thought. But why go home? The dream had upset her. Maybe a stroll around the airport would take her mind off things. Anyway, she needed to stretch her legs and she could always get a later bus.

As she stepped down from the bus, she noticed the fog. The airport buildings must be well lit up as usual. Yet tonight she could barely make out the lights through the thick, murky haze. Where had it come from? It had seemed all right a couple of hours before. There wasn't a puff of wind, either. Weird. She was cold and hungry. Grab a burger and a drink, she thought. Why not?

She was fascinated by airports. Powerhouses of emotion. People crying their eyes out saying goodbye to each other. Other people bawling as they were welcomed back home. Strange, really.

She walked towards the escalator. Head for the viewing lounge and have a drink. She felt her shoulders. "My bag," she shouted. "I left my bag on the bus." She ran back down the *up* escalator. It took ages to get to the bottom and back to the main door. Just as it slid open for her, the bus sped away from the kerb and disappeared into the dense fog.

"Hold on," she shouted and waved with both hands.

She could just about make out the red lights as the bus sped down the giant ramp and out on to the main road.

"Shit," she shouted as she kicked the sliding door which kept opening and closing beside her. Her bag was gone. No house keys. No money. She put her hand up to her face. People pushed their way past her. In and out of the busy terminal. It felt as if life was just passing her by. She turned around and headed back to the escalator.

Chapter Twenty-One

The lounge was hopping. Small groups of people crowded together. Waiting to be told what to do and where to go next. One man shouted at a small bunch of tired children to sit down and stop fighting with each other. Elevator music, as Jamie called it, played in the background above the din. Constant *bing bongs* over the busy public address system. A stream of messages for individuals to "pick up the red courtesy telephone". What was all the fuss about? Then it became obvious.

A large group of people huddled under two television screens in a corner of the lounge. Jamie moved in behind them to get a closer look. One screen was for *Arrivals*, the other for *Departures*. Due to the atrocious weather conditions, each flight's arrival or departure was either *delayed* or *cancelled*. Tempers frayed. The mood of the exhausted travellers was brittle, bordering on ballistic. One man was even arguing with a member of the bar staff.

"I didn't pay one and a half grand to sit in the fucking airport with my family," he roared.

"I'm sorry, sir. But one thing we've got no control over is the weather."

"But I thought you'd managed to build planes that can fly in the fog these days," he shouted. He looked around for support from the swelling crowd.

"We have, sir. They've no problem *flying* in the fog, but sooner or later they're going to have to land. And *they* can run out of *fuel* just like *I'm* running out of *patience*!" He plonked a full pint down in front of the man and held his hand out for money.

"This should be free because of what you shower are putting us through." The man shook his fist at the barman.

"Two pounds and ten pence, please!" The barman said through gritted teeth.

"Right." The man counted out small change on the counter and swayed from side to side. "Let's establish one thing . . . you're telling me that they can fly in the fog but they can't take off or land in the fog?"

"Bravo!" the barman shouted. "Which university did you graduate from, then?" The crowd laughed.

"Well, that's the most stupid fucking thing I've heard in years. Have they ever *tried* to take off in the fog? Whoever designed those things should be made fly them. And youse expect us to pay good money to travel in them?" He grabbed his pint and edged his way back from the bar.

"Excuse me, sir?" the barman called to the customer. He waved a packet of peanuts over his head. "These are on the house." He handed the man the peanuts.

The man examined the packet suspiciously. "Is this your way of apologising?"

The barman shook his head. "No. It's just that we don't normally serve monkeys but you're the first talking one I've ever seen, so I think we'll make an exception." The crowd roared laughing. The man skulked away with his pint and peanuts.

Jamie smiled as she walked to an empty table and sat down. Right, she thought. I can get a taxi home. Someone would give her the money when she got there. What if there was no one in? She looked at the two half-finished glasses of orange sitting on the table in front of her. She placed one in front of her and the other opposite the empty chair beside her. That way, people would think she was waiting for someone to return from the loo.

She moved her chair closer to the window. She could barely make out the orange lights around the apron area.

Every now and then, an announcement would be made over the loudspeakers . . . "*bing bong* . . . ladies and gentleman, we would like to apologise for the long delays in our schedules this evening. Adverse weather conditions both here, in Dublin, and at a number of major airports abroad have made it impossible for many scheduled flights to depart and land at their scheduled destinations this evening. As soon as the situation changes, we will let you know. Once again, we apologise for these unfortunate but unforeseen delays. Thank you . . . "

One angry man started to shout at the speaker.

"Thank you, my arse. She's been reading out that same fucking message for the last three bleedin' hours. At least she can go home to her nice warm, little bed tonight. We'll probably be stuck here till breakfast time."

His wife pleaded with him to sit down. "Please, Charlie, will you relax? She's only doing her job. Anyway, I'd say she's long gone home. That's a recording."

"A *recording* she says. How the fuck would you know?" He stood up. "They should have you up there talking through the speakers. That way, we'd all be asleep in minutes. I'm going to the bar."

Jamie turned her attention back to the empty runway. She remembered how she loved to go out to the back road of the airport with her father early every Saturday morning and watch the planes landing and taking off. He had this special radio so they were able to listen to the pilots talking to the control tower as they taxied and landed. Jamie was fascinated by the coded language they used to each other.

"What does that mean?" she'd ask her father.

"Ssshhh!" he used to say.

She remembered the story he told her about the pilot who lived on Howth Head. When he prepared to land the plane, he'd contact Dublin Airport's control tower and ask permission to divert his approach and fly in over his house on Howth Head.

The air-traffic controllers used to laugh and grant him permission.

They joked with him that she must be some woman

if he was that keen to go home so quickly.

His wife would hear the low-flying aircraft while she was out gardening and would take this as a signal that he needed a lift home after he landed. She'd get into the car and drive to the airport to collect him.

Jamie was always fascinated that a man flying such a huge machine could be concerned with something so trivial as a lift home.

"Is anyone sitting there?" said a voice from behind.

"Yes!" she replied without any hesitation. The last thing Jamie wanted was to sit opposite a stranger. Least of all a man. "There is!" she emphasised. She looked up to see who was asking. Her eyes opened wide.

"Hello," Frank said quietly. He smiled. "I'd a funny feeling it was you."

She watched him say the words. But she couldn't hear anything. Her heart was doing somersaults. "What?" she whispered.

"I said *hello*," he mimicked.

"Hello," she answered quietly. She looked at him. Here he was. The same as he was that night. Gorgeous. Tall. Nice. Attractive. Everything.

"Do you mind if I join you?"

She nodded. "No." She couldn't think of anything to say. How had he found her? What was he doing here? God, he was gorgeous. Again.

Frank put his bag down and sat on the chair opposite her. "Seeing someone off?"

She realised she was staring. "What?"

He nodded at the second glass sitting beside hers.

She looked at the two glasses. "Oh, no," she smiled. "I left my bag on the bus."

"*Sorry?*"

That must have sounded stupid, she thought. "No, I'm sorry . . . I mean I fell asleep on the bus on the way home. When I woke up, I accidentally hit a woman sitting beside me and when I tried to get off the bus quickly, I forgot my bag. Then I realised I was here . . . with no money, like." She looked at him with a pathetic smile. Garbled bullshit.

Frank nodded. "I see." He waited for a moment and kept nodding his head. "Who did you hit on the bus?"

"An old woman. I mean, no . . . it wasn't deliberate. You see, I was having a nightmare and I lashed out with my hands. I accidentally hit her at the same time as I was hitting someone in the . . . night . . . mare, like." She put her hands up to her face and laughed hysterically.

Frank started to grin. Until he noticed a tear rolling down her cheek. "Are you all right?" he asked gently.

"No!" she whispered.

"Would you like a drink?"

She nodded again. "Yes, please."

Frank signalled to the glass in front of her. "What's that?"

"Somebody else's. It was a way of keeping other people away from my table. It was there when I arrived. I didn't have any money so I couldn't buy anything else."

"What would you like?"

"Bottle of Heineken, please."

He walked away through the crowd towards the bar.

Jamie wouldn't let him out of her sight for a second. Even when he'd disappeared into the mass of people fighting to get to the bar, she stood up to check where he'd gone. She was so delighted he was here. It wasn't going to be so bad now. Even if he was only going to be here for a short while.

It seemed like ages before he returned to the table. He placed the bottle and glass carefully down on the table in front of her and sat down opposite. He put the pint of lager on the beer-mat and moved the two decoy glasses to a different table.

Jamie smiled. "You don't know how pleased I am to see the back of them." Frank looked a bit annoyed, she thought. "Are you OK?"

"Yeah, why?" He took a long drink from the glass.

"Nothing, only asking." She poured most of the contents into the glass. "It's nice to see you at long last." She smiled.

Frank twitched his nose as he fidgeted with a spare beer-mat. "It would have been nice to have seen you this afternoon as well." He didn't look at her.

"So that's why you're shirty," she said.

"It's just that I came all the way from west Cork to see you. That's all." He waited.

"Well, you would have been going back anyway, wouldn't you?"

"Not for another two days, actually."

"Well, what are you doing here, then?" she asked smartly.

"You never answered my question. Why didn't you show up today?"

"You never *asked* that question. Anyway, I got side-tracked. I hadn't any way of getting in touch with you and . . . I'm sorry. So there." She slammed her glass down on the table.

"I'm sorry. I didn't mean to make it sound like that. It's just that I was looking forward so much to seeing you again . . . what with my ma's death and that. You know . . . meeting people you don't want to meet . . . "

"Tell me about it," Jamie whispered.

"Sorry?"

"Nothing. I'm sorry about your mother." She glanced across at Frank. He looked the way she was feeling.

"Thanks."

She scanned the lounge for a moment. Why did she feel threatened? After all, he was a sight for sore eyes. "So why are you here?"

"What does it look like? I was meant to fly out at twenty to eight. They told me we'd have a twenty-minute delay. That was two hours ago." He nodded to the window. "If you ask me, I don't think we'll be going far in that tonight." He grinned and shook his head. "Probably just as well."

"Why?" Jamie's eyes lit up at the thought of what his answer might be.

"I lost my boarding pass," he muttered and laughed. He turned serious again. "Besides, I got to see you again . . . at long last."

Jamie's heart was skipping and missing beats. Butterflies were moving furniture around in her stomach. She smiled.

"You look lovely. Same as you were that famous night."

She shrugged. "Will you get off! I wish I did."

"So, what *are* you doing in the airport on a mad night like tonight. You never answered my question."

"I told you. I fell asleep on the bus and woke up outside the departures door. Simple as that. I'd no money so I couldn't go home."

"What happened?" Frank nodded to the mark below her eye.

"You know what happened. *Nikki* told you."

"I'm sorry. I'm not trying to be nosey. I just care. I . . . don't know what to say."

"Nothing."

"Sorry?"

"Then say nothing." Jamie stood up. "Look, can we get out of this snake-pit?" She looked down at Frank. He looked up at her. "Maybe go to a quiet pub, or something?"

"Yeah, sure." He stood up.

"Do you need to check if your flight's going to leave tonight?"

"I wouldn't say so. They've closed all the check-in desks. I'd say that's a fairly good clue as to what's happening. And I've no intention of queuing at the information desk."

"So where are they going to put all these people for the night?" Jamie nodded at three children asleep at the next table.

"In the airport hotel. Very posh, I hear," he whispered.

Jamie picked up her jacket which was bone-dry by now. "Come on, let's go?"

"Where?"

"Anywhere, I don't care . . . anywhere quiet."

They pushed through the crowd towards the main door of the lounge. The place was on the brink of war, judging by the comments that were flying about.

"If we all demand free drink, they'll have to give it to us! There's only three of them. There must be thirty of us." There was a loud roar of approval.

"I think we should elect a spokesman," one loud, fat-looking man suggested.

"And what's wrong with a spokeswoman?" came a loud shout from the corner.

"Because a woman can't carry six pints, that's why!"

"Fuck off . . . I've often carried you up to bed after *sixteen* pints!" There was a huge cheer.

Chapter Twenty-Two

Frank hailed a taxi. It almost ran him down as it drove past, showering him with water. "Jesus, did you see that? Madman!" he shouted as he waved his fist.

"Don't worry, one'll come along shortly," Jamie said quietly.

Frank looked up. "This is weird, isn't it?"

"What is?" Jamie asked as she paced up and down the footpath anxiously.

"The last night we met, you couldn't see because it was raining so hard. Tonight, you can't see because of the fog."

"Yeah, if I remember rightly, the last night we met, you were arrested by the police for trying to be a hero." She stood close beside him. "I hope we're not going to have a repeat of that tonight?" She stood inches from his face and looked at him.

No answer. Without any warning, Frank leaned over and kissed her on the lips.

She leapt back. Now why did you do that? she wondered. She moved forward again. This time, *she* kissed *him*. She closed her eyes. For a few seconds, she was able to forget about everything. This was what she'd dreamed of for months. This was what she'd regretted not happening that morning when they said goodbye outside Euston station. This was what she used to imagine when she sat at her desk telling Nikki about the gorgeous man she'd met on the boat that night after Christmas. The kiss seemed to last forever. His lips felt gorgeous.

Then it was over. She opened her eyes. She felt embarrassed. She barely knew him. They'd only met twice . . . and tonight, they'd not even spoken properly. But yet, something felt right and good about it . . . natural, even. She smiled. "That was lovely."

"I missed you," Frank whispered, close to her lips. He squeezed her hand.

"You don't even know me," she whispered back. Maybe she was going to wake up again, like she had on the bus. She thumped the side of her leg and then thumped Frank's.

He almost lost his balance. "What was that for?"

"To make sure I wasn't dreaming," she replied, grinning from ear to ear. "I missed you, too. Maybe if I'd let my heart rule my head that morning, none of this would have happened." She threw her arms around his neck and forced herself up on to her toes as Frank's arms folded around her waist. She took a deep breath as he hugged her tightly. She could feel him against her. His strong body. His firm grip. This was all she wanted right now. Don't let it end.

"I don't get you. What do you mean?" Frank asked curiously.

"I'd hoped and prayed that you'd ask me for my number before I got into the car. That morning after the train."

"How could I?"

"Suppose so."

Neither spoke. They just squeezed each other tightly. Neither wanted to be the first to let go. But one of them had to, because there were five taxis alongside the kerb by now, and all the drivers were getting a free look. They got away from each other just in time to grab the first taxi.

Frank would normally sit in beside the driver. Not tonight, though. Not on your life, he thought. This was one opportunity he wasn't going to pass up. He dived into the back seat.

As Jamie stepped down off the kerb, the taxi behind hooted its horn. She looked beyond the bright headlights to see if she recognised the driver.

The driver waved at her.

She froze. It was him. Paul Flaherty. He waved again and was gone with a fare in the back seat. She was terrified. He was following her.

"Come on, Jamie," Frank urged from the back seat. "I'm so cold, I'll end up hugging the taxi-driver."

The driver gave him a look and quickly moved his seat forward.

Jamie took a deep breath and sat in beside Frank. She slammed the door.

"You look as if you've just seen a ghost," Frank joked.

"It's just the cold. I've been wearing wet clothes all day," she replied.

Frank thought it better to let that pass. "Airport hotel, please," he said to the driver.

"Which one?" the driver asked monotonously.

"I don't know . . . whichever one that mad bunch in there is going to, I suppose."

The driver laughed. "*That* bunch? In another two hours, they won't be able to find their way to the jacks, never mind the airport hotel. No, pal, you're making a very wise decision getting out of there early. I've seen that all happening before. That'll end up in tears before the night is over." He drove out on to the main road and crawled off towards the hotel.

* * *

"Fuck me!" Frank roared as the taxi sped off. "Pardon the French. Four quid for half a mile!"

"Yeah," Jamie muttered, "welcome to Dublin."

They walked into the lobby. The peace and quiet was wonderful. A far cry from what they'd just left.

"I hope that bunch stay where they are," Frank whispered. "This is bloody marvellous. Right then . . . what'll you have?" he asked as they walked into the empty lounge.

"Oh, Frank, I feel awful," Jamie moaned.

Frank looked worried. "Why? Are you not feeling well?"

"No, that's not what I mean. It's just that I've got no money."

"Ah, for God's sake, don't be worrying about that. Let's think of tonight as special." He took a bundle of notes out of his pocket. They sat down side by side on a comfortable couch. "Ray asked me to get him two hundred cigarettes in the duty-free. I think I'll help him to live longer by spending the money on us."

"Why?" She regretted asking that question.

"*Why?*" He smiled. "Because I suppose I didn't think I was ever going to see you again." He stopped.

"Go on," Jamie urged.

"Go on what?"

"Tell me more. I like it when you talk like that."

"Like what?" he asked teasingly.

She thumped his shoulder. "When you tell me that you like me."

Frank laughed. "Ah here, I'm no good at this sort of conversation."

"Well, you're not doing too bad so far."

There was a long silence. The drinks arrived.

Frank paid the lounge boy. "So," he started again, "you're right. I hardly know you. But I wish you could be straight with me. I get the feeling there's a whole lot more going on here than meets the eye."

Jamie sat forward in the seat and looked him straight in the eyes. "I was attacked and then raped. And now I'm told my life's in danger. How's that for straight?"

Frank felt a deep rage. Some bastard *had* hurt this woman.

* * *

It never occured to Frank to check the time until he

395

realised that they were the only people left in the lounge. It was ten to one. The remaining few staff were making it quite clear that they wanted to go home. After some major negotiating, they agreed to give Frank two last drinks.

"What if this bloke *is* telling the truth?" he asked cautiously.

"I don't know. He seemed to know a lot about me. Everything he said was fairly accurate," she replied nervously.

"Where did he come from?"

"I haven't a clue," Jamie said again. "He was outside again tonight. Waving and smiling."

"Shouldn't you tell the police?"

"Well, he hasn't done anything to me, has he? I mean, all he'll say is that I waved down a taxi and he got chatting like taxi-drivers do. He could deny saying all he did. Then I'd probably never get another taxi for the rest of my life. Can you imagine what they'd be saying? 'Oh shit, it's that mad bitch from Church Avenue. Don't say a word to her, lads, or she'll have you up for rape'. She sniffed and then laughed at the notion.

Frank laughed with her, happy to see that she was relaxing a bit more.

"When you found the small bags of powder, what did you do with them?"

"I threw them in Tommy's face."

"Do you reckon there could be more where you found them?"

"I wouldn't say so. Sure, Tommy went mad when he couldn't find them."

Another long silence. "But surely if he was taking the stuff, you would have noticed him acting strange. That stuff would do your head in after a while."

"It tasted awful. I mean, I just dabbed it on my tongue. I thought I was going to throw up. What's the attraction? I'm sure I would've noticed something strange." Jamie shrugged her shoulders. "Then again, I don't know. We were just going through the motions with each other. We'd become strangers. Lodgers sharing the same flat. 'How was your day? Awful. How was yours?' I should have called it a day with him a long time ago. It just seemed a lot easier to keep putting it off." She looked at Frank, a little concerned about how he was taking all this. "Do you know what I mean?"

Frank nodded and smiled. "I think so. Do you think that Tommy did it?"

Jamie looked at Frank. "Did *what*?"

Frank hesitated. "Raped you?"

Jamie frowned. "I don't want to know."

"But surely you must have an idea if it was Tommy. Anyway, why don't you want to know?"

"Because I just want to forget it all at this stage. I want to get on with my life. Like you. Like Nikki." She blew her nose in a tissue.

"How close is Nikki to Tommy?"

"Why?" asked Jamie cagily.

"I'm just wondering. She came in for a drink with him one evening."

"Nikki knew Tommy before I did. She introduced me to him. Why?"

"Just wondering. They just seemed quite close."

Jamie sniggered. "Show me a bloke Nikki won't get close to."

"What if the bloke in the taxi was the guy who attacked you?" Frank asked.

Jamie thought for a moment. She clasped her hands together nervously. She shook her head. "He couldn't have been."

"Why not?"

"He seemed too nice. Like, why would he be so nice to me if he was the one who attacked me?"

"Because maybe he thinks you know who he is! He knows *you* can't hurt *him* if he can watch what you're up to all the time."

"It's not *him*! He was in prison the night I was raped."

"Prison?" Frank shouted.

"Keep your voice down, for God's sake!"

"Prison," he whispered. "You gave up lunch with me to spend the afternoon talking to a bloke who was in *prison*? What was he in prison for?"

"It's a long story." She took a long deep breath. "The night we were coming back on the boat, Tommy took part in a police raid in London. One of Tommy's partners was shot dead."

"I know."

"No, hang on. I'm not finished. The money from the drugs lift was found on a rubbish dump a few days later."

"I know. I saw it on the TV. What are you saying?"

"I threw it out."

"Threw *what* out?"

"The black bin-liner full of money. I threw it out. I never realised what it was. I found it in the wardrobe. I was looking for a map to see where *you* were originally from. It was squeezed into the corner. It smelt rotten. I thought it was just old, wet newspapers. So I . . . put the bag in the bin. What'll Tommy say to his bosses?"

Frank didn't seem surprised. "His bosses? He wasn't ever going to say anything to his bosses, Jamie. Think about it. Here was a handy hundred and fifty grand that nobody knew existed. He was going to keep the money."

"No, he wasn't," argued Jamie.

"Well, why was it hidden in the wardrobe?"

"I don't know. Maybe the reason he was looking for it that morning was to bring it to the incident room that had been set up the previous night to investigate the case."

"You're really giving this guy the benefit of the doubt, aren't you?"

"Innocent until proven guilty?"

"He'll never be proven guilty."

"Why not?"

"Unfortunately, Jimmy Grant arrived on the scene at the wrong moment. He asked Tommy for the money. He was told to piss off. Tommy was the one who killed Jimmy Grant, Jamie."

Jamie was dumbfounded. She stood motionless. "He couldn't have. He loved Jimmy Grant."

"He killed him. Shot him in the back."

"Who says?"

"A witness."

"Who is he?"

"*Was*. He's dead."

"How?"

"Same as Jimmy Grant. Tommy got to him first. He pushed him out in front of a train. This poor man was homeless and helpless. The sort of person Tommy preys upon. Remember what you said that night."

Jamie put her hand up to her mouth and squeezed her eyes shut. "How do you know about the tramp?"

"Some bloke told Ray. Like your friend today, this fella was just out of prison too. Brixton. Except *he* blasted his way out. Ray works with me in the pub. You met him that evening you were in."

Jamie didn't hear the last few words. "What was his name?"

"Ray Flynn."

"Not *him*! The bloke who broke out of Brixton."

"Flaherty . . . Paul Flaherty. Apparently, according to Ray, Tommy set *him* up as well."

"Jesus Christ, you met him too." She grabbed a clump of her hair and pulled it hard. "*Jesus Christ!*" she shouted. "*What's happening?*"

Frank stood up quickly and took her hand. "It's OK. It's all right," he whispered. He hugged her to comfort her. He felt her arms wrap around his back and felt himself being pulled tightly towards her.

"Oh, Frank," she shouted, "I'm scared. More scared than I've ever been." Her voice became muffled as she buried her head in his denim shirt. "What's happening? And why is it happening?"

Frank stroked her hair. "I don't know. But one thing I do know is that we're going to get you out of this before it goes any further."

Frank checked the time again. Half past one. Jaysus, he thought. Five hours sleep. I could do with fifteen, more like it. Shag the sleep, he thought. He could have as much as he wanted tomorrow night.

The night porter jangled his keys as he sat impatiently in a dark corner of the lounge.

Frank and Jamie moved slowly towards the main reception area, still holding each other.

"Here, I better get you home. Excuse me," he called to the weary porter. "Could you get me a taxi, please?"

"*No!*" Jamie protested, as if she was just after waking up from a bad dream. "No taxis!"

Then Frank remembered. "Sorry." He made a few thinking noises. "Well, how am I going to get you home?"

She looked up at him. "I don't want to go home tonight." She looked away.

Frank walked to the reception desk. Think fast, he thought.

Jamie sat on a chair in the foyer and waited.

"I want to check in, please. Frank McCabe. I was booked on a flight to London last night. City Jet at twenty to eight. It was put on hold because of the conditions."

"Just like my bedtime," the porter muttered. "Room 428." He checked a roster in front of him. "Your flight leaves at ten past eight, *this* morning.

Perhaps you should get some sleep." He threw a key down on the desk and looked beyond Frank at the woman sitting in the armchair. "Goodnight," he said.

Frank walked back to Jamie. They slowly headed for the lift. Jamie looked shattered.

He always felt uneasy in lifts. Surrounded by strangers in a deadly silence. Everyone afraid to cough. Not tonight, though. There was something unbelieveable about being in the closed lift with the woman he was crazy about. He watched the numbers over the door. *1* . . . They climbed so slowly. *2* . . . Jamie yawned. Two fillings in her back teeth, Frank counted. *3* . . . The veins on both sides of her neck pressed through her thin, white skin. He leaned across and kissed her on the lips. *4* . . . The lift stopped. The doors slid back slowly. They stepped out on to the silent landing. Left and right, rooms as far as the eye could see. They checked their number and agreed that 428 was to the right. Frank hoped and prayed that there would be two beds in the room. He didn't care how small they were. But then again, he sort of wished there would only be one. But he just couldn't imagine how he was going to try to sort out sleeping arrangements with one large bed in the room, *if* she didn't like the idea of the two of them in the one bed.

Jamie walked ahead.

Frank's feelings were mixed. Great, but slightly awkward.

She stopped outside a door. "Here we are," she whispered, nodding sleepily to the number, "428."

Frank turned the key. He let her go in first, more out of nervousness than courtesy.

Jamie pointed and laughed. "Look!" she shouted.

"Ssshhh . . . " Frank urged gently, pointing at the bedroom walls. Then he saw what she was laughing at. "Shit!" he shouted above the laughter. "A *single* bed?"

They looked at each other.

Frank began to laugh. "That miserable bastard of a porter. He gave us the smallest room in the house. Here, give me the phone and I'll get us moved."

"Ah, come on, leave it. It would be at least another hour before he'd get us another room. We'll just have to make do with it." She disappeared into the bathroom.

Frank scratched his head. Had he heard her right? Make do? Sure, he'd barely fit into that thing on his own! Then he started to reason. Maybe she's thinking that I'll sleep on the chair. Suppose so. He checked the wardrobe behind the door. Sure enough, there was a handful of blankets on the top shelf. No excuse now, he thought. He dragged them down and set about laying them out across the chair. He could hear Jamie washing her teeth. *Never,* he thought. Suspect nothing.

"*Frank,*" she called.

"Yeah?"

"Have you a spare T-shirt in your bag?"

Frank dropped the blankets. Sounds nice! he thought. "I might have. I'll check." He almost tore the bag asunder looking for his best T-shirt. He yanked one out. *San Francisco 49ers.* A good big baggy one. Great. "Here, I have it," he shouted.

"Can you just throw it in the door?"

He avoided looking and tossed it in through the small gap of light.

Seconds later, Jamie emerged. "What are you doing?"

"What does it look like?"

"Why are you sleeping there?"

He didn't want to say it, but it sounded like a stupid question. "Because why do you think?" He gestured to the size of the bed. "You can have that."

She giggled. "The chair is *smaller* than the bed, Frank. Anyway, nothing like a tight squeeze."

She looked sexy in the baggy T-shirt which barely covered her long legs. She'd rolled up the sleeves a bit too. She quickly pulled back the covers and climbed into the bed. "Come on, quick, it's *freezing*."

Frank disappeared into the bathroom to reassess the situation. He took off his trousers and socks, leaving himself in a T-shirt and underpants. Was that enough? Jesus, maybe she'd think he was being a bit presumptuous . . . stripping off to his underwear. On the other hand, he'd hate her to think that he went to bed every night with all his clothes on! But this wasn't any old night.

"Are you any good at warming up?" she shouted.

He grinned. Why not? he thought. He clicked off the main light and edged his way over to the bed. As he climbed in carefully to claim his few inches, he lost his grip on the pillow and fell right in on top of Jamie.

"Oh, Jaysus, I'm sorry . . . I didn't mean that, sorry!" he shouted as he tried to find his bearings, his head buried in the pillow.

She was laughing hysterically. "Here," she said, as she moved over a bit. "Is that better?"

"Thanks," Frank replied. "Are we mad, or what?"

"Probably *what*," she whispered.

Frank lay there trying to think of a good topical conversation. He knew if he turned in towards her, he'd roll on to her. Turning face out would mean falling out of the bed. They'd just have to keep talking, he thought.

Too late. Within a few seconds, Jamie was sound asleep.

Frank lay there. In one way, he was sorry he wasn't a bit more experienced when it came to things like women and love and . . . *bed*! Still, though, here he was. He couldn't complain. Problem was, he couldn't sleep either.

* * *

A shudder woke him. It was so strong that the entire bed rocked. Where was he? It was pitch black. He checked his watch. Quarter to three. Then his eyes adjusted to the darkness. Of couse, the airport hotel. He felt a hand on his chest. Warm flesh. A smooth leg was rubbing against his. Jamie's hand . . . and leg! His T-shirt was twisted. He didn't want to move. Her hand felt nice.

Then it moved slowly, it seemed unconsciously, down to his stomach and rested there.

He could feel himself becoming aroused very quickly. He hoped she wouldn't notice. Just then, he felt her head lift off the pillow and move closer to his. He lay perfectly still and waited. He felt her warm lips on his ear. He closed his eyes. I've died and gone to heaven, he thought. Maybe she was sleep-kissing . . . like sleep-walking, and wouldn't remember anything about it in the morning. But she had to be in control of her senses. Problem was, was he in control of *his*?

This was a situation he would have pursued slowly and intimately if it wasn't for what had happened to her. Under the circumstances, he felt it would be better to let her make all the moves.

She kissed him gently again. Her hand moved slightly lower, on to his navel and hesitated.

"I can't," she sighed. "Not yet." She kissed him again.

He knew what she meant. He turned on his side and put his right arm around the small of her back. He pulled her to him, not that it was hard to get close in that bed. "I know. Don't worry," he whispered.

She touched his face gently with her fingers. "Kiss me, please," she urged.

Frank placed his lips softly against hers. Then more firmly.

"Gently," she whispered.

"Sorry. A bit too keen." He moved his arm up and down her back slowly.

"That's nice," she muttered.

Frank tried hard to control himself. He'd have loved to take off the T-shirt he'd lent her earlier and made love to her. He knew it wasn't going to happen because . . . the time wasn't right.

"I love you, Frank," she whispered.

Frank didn't move. He had to think about what she'd just said. Words he'd hoped to hear from her but doubted if he would. Now, there was no doubt. "I love you too," he replied effortlessly, "from the moment I laid eyes on you that night."

She put her hand firmly around the back of his neck and pulled his head towards hers. She placed her lips firmly on his and almost drained off his last breath.

He drew back and gasped for air. "Jesus, ever thought of taking up deep-sea diving?"

She didn't answer. Instead, she sat up in the bed and took off her T-shirt.

Frank's eyes had adjusted to the darkness in the room. She was wearing nothing underneath. Her body was firm and well-toned. As she lifted the shirt over her head, he could just about make out her breasts in the darkness.

She turned and looked down at him. "Take off yours," she urged.

Frank hesitated. "But . . . "

"It's OK. I don't want us to do anything, because . . . " She didn't finish the sentence. "I just want you to hold me tightly. Anyway, it'd be nice to hold each other . . . like this, wouldn't it?" She lay back down on her side with her head leaning on her elbow.

Frank whipped off his T-shirt. He knew that if he spent too long perched in a sitting-up position, he'd fall off the bed. He left his pants on and lay down. He felt her warm arm cross his body and curve around his back. "I'm sorry . . . I have a hard-on," he whispered.

He could feel her smile. "I know. It's nice. But not yet," she repeated. "I just need you to hold me."

"I know." He stroked her hair. "How long have you felt like this . . . about us?"

"Since . . . the morning we said goodbye in London."

"Me too. I couldn't believe I didn't have a telephone number for you. I almost ran down the street after your fella's . . . after you."

"Same here. I tried checking out pubs. But when someone told me that there were eight thousand pubs in London, I had to consider my health."

They both laughed.

"Is this really going to happen?" Frank asked in a relaxed voice.

"What?"

"This . . . us, like?"

Silence. "Yes . . . well, I want it to. Do you?" She looked at him.

He nodded. "Yes, I do."

They lay there and held each other until the only sound that could be heard coming from room 428 was a contented snoring one.

Jamie opened her eyes. She looked at the watch on the bedside table. Her eyes opened wide. Twenty-five past nine. She sat up in the bed and looked around. Frank was gone. As she leapt out of the bed, she realised she was practically naked. She didn't care. *"Frank?"* she called towards the bathroom. Silence. Then she remembered that his flight was at ten past eight. Almost two hours ago. *"Shit!"* she shouted angrily at the top of her voice as she thumped the dressing-table. She picked up the phone and rang reception.

"Hello, reception. Can I help you?"

"Can you tell me has Mr McCabe checked out of room 428 yet?"

There was a long pause. "But that *is* room 428, isn't it?"

Jamie suddenly realised that she could be causing problems for Frank. She hung up quickly. "Fuck him, why didn't he say goodbye?"

There was a knock on the door.

"Who is it?" she shouted angrily.

"Room service," a squeaky, foreign voice answered.

She walked over to the door and, standing behind it, opened it a couple of inches.

Frank pushed a giant trolley forward, forcing the door open fully.

Jamie screamed and thumped him. "You bastard!" she shouted. "I thought you'd gone without telling me." She threw her arms around him and hugged him.

He could see her bare back in the mirror. She was naked except for her pants. "Here, wait a minute. I wasn't going anywhere."

"But what about your flight?"

He shrugged his shoulders. "I missed it. Have to wait till ten to six before there's another spare seat."

Jamie smiled eagerly. "Ten to six?"

He nodded. "Yeah. I had to ring Ray and tell him I wouldn't be back till tonight. So while I was up and dressed, I decided to get us a nice breakfast." He took a bottle out of a bucket of ice. "Champagne, madame?"

"Later," she whispered. She gave him a soft kiss. Then a stronger one. She took the bottle out of his hand and put it back in the bucket. "You're going to need those hands for something else." She drew his hands across her back and guided him backwards towards the bed. As she pushed him down on to the bed, she looked at him, carefully . . . thoughtfully. She slid his T-shirt up over his head and took a deep breath, showing off her firm milk-white breasts.

His hands were wet from the iced water. She took a sharp intake of breath and gasped. They turned her on even more.

"But . . . I thought you said . . . "

"Ssshhh!" She placed a finger to her lips as she pouted them slightly. Morning streaks of sunlight caught her trim, radiant nakedness as they made love. Something had changed inside her. She wasn't frightened any more by the thought of giving her body to Frank. She realised he was more than an ordinary man. She loved him. She knew that now. There was nothing she wouldn't do for him because she knew *he* loved her as much. She'd waited long enough. She wasn't going to wait any longer.

The curtains remained closed in room 428 until after lunch. A *Do Not Disturb* sign hung on the door, undisturbed.

* * *

The departure time came along far too quickly for both Frank and Jamie. They sat in the airport lounge trying to make conversation.

410

"So what'll you do?" Frank asked.

"Where . . . here?"

He nodded.

"Try and get a decent job. Although they're screaming out for me to come back to London. The radio station's falling apart without me," she said jokingly.

"And why don't you come back? I've loads of room in my place. You could even work in the pub if you like. I'm always looking for attractive bar staff," Frank joked.

She didn't take it as a joke. "Being chatted up by dirty old men who get off on tits and arses isn't my idea of an enjoyable job, Frank." She touched his hand just to show that this wasn't intended against him. "You should know me by now."

He slipped his fingers firmly between hers. "When will I see you again?"

She shrugged her shoulders. "Whenever you want to. You're the rich publican. I'm only an hour and twenty minutes away." Jamie moved closer to Frank. "This morning was gorgeous."

He nodded. "I know."

"Are you worried?"

"About what?"

"Us . . . this morning."

Frank shook his head. "No."

Jamie detected a note of hesitancy in his voice. "I hope you're not, Frank. All the tests proved negative. I'm fine. Really . . . I am."

Frank hugged her shoulders. "I'm *not* worried, do

you hear me? *Not!*" He kissed her on the lips. It was one of those marathon kisses.

Two small children stood looking on. Jamie noticed the small girl seemed to be in a trance watching them, rolling her lips backwards and forward as she imitated their passionate kiss.

The small boy pulled at her hand. "I have pooh in my nappy . . . *come on*!" he protested.

"Ah, Peter, you always spoil it," his sister shouted. She dragged him back to where their mother was sitting. "Mammy," she shouted, "Peter's done a shit in his nappy!"

Frank and Jamie roared laughing.

. . . *bing bong* . . . " City Jet, flight VS247 to London city airport . . . this is the final call for this flight which is now closing at Gate B24 . . . Would all remaining passengers please board immediately . . . "

Time to say goodbye.

They walked slowly to the check-in area, holding hands. There was very little left to be said.

"Ring me?" Jamie said quietly. "Tonight?"

Frank nodded. "I thought you said you were going out tonight?"

"I'll see." She didn't want to talk about tonight. Frank would be gone by then. She just wanted to talk about now . . . to hear him talking to her while he was still here. She fought back the tears.

"Who are you going out with?" he asked, trying not to sound too suspicious.

"Just an old school-friend. She's back from her honeymoon. She's after marrying some rich bloke." She started to laugh.

"What's wrong?"

"It's just his job. He's an Artificial Insemination expert." She giggled.

"On people?"

"No, on *cattle*!"

"Jesus, I don't know why you're laughing," Frank said, "that's huge business!"

"Oh, yeah," Jamie continued, "they obviously haven't seen *yours*!" She squeezed his hand.

"I'll take that as a compliment." He pulled her towards him and gave her a long, rough kiss. "I love you so much," he whispered.

Her eyes were filled with tears. "I love you too. Is it going to work . . . for *us*?"

Frank nodded. *"Yes, it is!"* He stepped back and took out his boarding pass.

"But *how*?" she asked, almost painfully. She could see that he had a million things on his mind. Or had he? "Frank?" She pulled gently on his jacket. "I want to be with you. I want us to be together. I'm sorry," she snivelled. "You probably think I'm a right baby . . . but I don't want you to go."

Frank could feel himself getting upset. He knew that would only make matters worse."I'll ring you tonight." He hesitated for a moment but then turned quickly and disappeared into the crowd of commuters.

"Frank," she called, "please don't go. Get a later flight tomorrow. I'll pay for it, I promise."

He looked back above all the rushing heads and smiled. He blew her a kiss. Then he moved further away.

"I bet you'll be too busy to call," she shouted teasingly. "I love you," she said quietly.

He didn't hear her.

She felt a bit stupid standing there alone in this swamped mêlée of people hugging and kissing and waving and shouting. She stood on her toes to get a final look.

He was gone.

She looked at the two twenty-pound notes that he'd given her, and a silver pound coin for luck. She kissed it and put it in the breast pocket of the denim jacket he'd loaned her. She turned and headed for the exit.

Chapter Twenty-Three

It was nearly midnight when Frank arrived back at the
pub. He was soaked. The last thing he needed was a
party. And he knew from a good distance that
something was up. This wasn't the normal crowd
you'd have on a Thursday. Certainly not so late. As he
walked across the road, he could hear the band. What
the *hell*? he muttered. He squeezed through the main
door, whooshing his baggage ahead of him. The place
was jammed.

"*Frank!*" a voice roared.

He looked around to see where it'd come from. It
was Father Duffy, waving with one hand and pouring
from a half-full bottle of whiskey with the other. Frank
froze. It must be something awfully important if *he* was
getting pissed publicly on a Thursday night. Maybe
he'd won the Lotto. Highly unlikely, he thought. No
one pointed the finger at Father Duffy.

"Your friend's giving us all a day out!" he shouted to
cheers of applause.

Frank looked behind the bar. Every one seemed to
be helping themselves. "What the *hell* is going on?" he
roared at the top of his voice.

Another loud cheer.

"Ray Flynn is getting . . . *married*!" trumpeted Father Duffy as he fell backwards over a large stool. There was a loud crash as his bottle hit the floor. "May God forgive you, Jimmy Morrissey," he barked angrily at the man standing next to him. "Fifteen years hard work gone into the contents of that bottle and it takes an imbecile like you a few seconds to destroy it."

"Ten quid he'll father a dozen kids," a voice shouted.

"No gambling," warned Father Duffy.

"Where's Ray?" Frank shouted.

"*Here!*" a voice answered musically.

Frank looked around.

Ray was dancing across the pub. Davina was clutching his arm. "Ballroom dancing, eat your heart out. Frank," he shouted, "she said *yes*!"

A sudden silence descended on the entire pub. Everyone waited for Frank's reaction.

He stared, stony-faced, at the couple.

Davina seemed to be looking at his navel.

He felt shattered. A lightning strike by underground staff meant he'd had to take the bus journey into London and then walk. He'd imagined a nice shower. Maybe even a warm bath if the water was on. Give someone the keys and tell them to do the rest. Afraid not. Not tonight, he thought as he looked around at the familiar faces who'd come out to wish their mate all the best. He smiled and stretched out his arms to Davina. "Ah, shag it. Let me be the first man to give you a decent kiss tonight. Congratulations." He hugged her as Ray grabbed one of his hands and squeezed it till it hurt.

A very boozy fortune-teller arrived. She told Frank he'd be rich in love and that he'd eventually return home for good. She could see a helicopter and a blonde bombshell standing beside it. "She must be going to sweep you off your feet, Frank!" Ray shouted. "Keep your head down, Frank, and the two of you will be fine forever," the clairvoyant continued. She told Davina that she'd be under a lot of pressure for a while.

Everyone laughed as Ray stuck out his huge stomach and patted it.

Finally, she told Ray that all she could see was fire.

"Between the sheets," someone shouted.

There was a huge cheer as the crowd lifted Davina up on their shoulders and sang, "For she's a jolly good pillow"!

Ray squeezed forty quid into the fortune teller's hand as she held her mouth with the other. She was led away in the direction of the taxi rank.

"What a load of old *cobblers*!" roared Ray. "Still, she was worth it."

As Frank pushed his way through to the bar, he saw Father Duffy holding court at the counter with one of Davina's friends.

"So my dear child," Father Duffy said quietly as he studied her well-defined cleavage, "what is it about the shape of the female body these days that turns a sensible man into a senseless moron?"

Frank heard a loud slap. He looked around to see

Father Duffy holding his cheek with one hand and propping his bottle up with the other.

Nikki waved to him from behind the bar.

He nodded back and cast his eyes up towards heaven. "Howya." He threw his wet jacket into the kitchen and started serving.

"Mad, isn't it?" she shouted.

"Yeah. When did all this happen?" he nodded over to Ray and Davina.

"This evening. He thinks he might be going to prison."

Frank took a deep breath. "*Prison?* For what?"

"He got a call from Scotland Yard today. A couple of detectives are calling around tomorrow to question him about some bloke who broke out of prison last weekend."

Frank looked across at Ray. He didn't seem too worried. "What time are they coming here at?"

"Half one," she replied casually. "By the way, upstairs is all done up." She smiled.

"The bedrooms?"

She nodded. "At long last. Wonders will never cease! You can have the big one," she shouted teasingly. She walked off towards the end of the bar.

Frank walked through the kitchen and up the stairs. He was stunned by what he saw. Carpets. Wallpaper. New beds in all three rooms. Nice furniture. It was like . . . home, he thought. Even the beds had fresh sheet and duvets. Everything was so clean and . . . the heating was switched on. He returned to the bar like an excited child only to find that a policeman was standing at the counter. I'll kill Flynn for serving late drinks, muttered Frank. People were running for the doors. "I'll have them all out in ten minutes, constable," Frank shouted.

"Make that *two* minutes, mate," replied the bobby.

Might just get to bed early tonight after all, thought Frank. The pub was empty in minutes. He pulled himself a pint, took it upstairs and lay across the new king-size bed. *Heaven*, he thought. A remote control beside the bed ready to operate the brand-new portable television and video opposite. He took a long, thirst-quenching drink from the glass.

* * *

He knew by the way the sun shone through the curtains that it was late. Very late. He looked at his watch. Twenty to twelve! As he threw back the duvet, he realised that he'd slept in his check shirt and knickers. He looked around the room. Everything was brand new . . . except the jeans which hung across the back of a chair. How did *they* manage to end up *there*? He would have remembered taking them off. His shoes were on the floor beside them. The television had been switched off. Maybe he'd got up in the middle of the night and done all this. Never. He was as cute as a fox. He'd have remembered it. So who the hell . . . ?

It was then that he smelt the food. *Roast beef.* And gravy. And yorkshire pudding. He pulled on his jeans and trainers and headed for the stairs to investigate. As he reached the kitchen, his eyes opened wide. Carvery equipment everywhere.

Nikki stood beside a big machine with an instruction booklet in one hand and a huge ladle in the other. As she calculated times, she turned around and noticed Frank watching her. "Ah, the dead finally arose and appeared to . . . " Realising what she'd said, she dropped the ladle and put her hand up to her mouth. "Jesus, Frank . . . I'm sorry. I didn't mean to say that. Sorry about your mother."

"I must remember that one." Frank gazed around at the new pieces of machinery which lay all over the kitchen. "Very impressive," he remarked. "When did all this arrive?"

"Eh, Saturday," blurted Nikki.

"And why?" he asked.

"Well, the brewery people were delivering the replacement parts for the bar. And they asked if there was anything that we needed and I sort told them that, well . . . *food* . . . would be a good idea."

Frank looked at her. "*We?*"

She nodded. "Yeah."

"Who's we?"

"Well, Ray and . . . me," she replied quietly, "and, of course, *you*!"

"Oh good. I'm glad I had some say in this momentous decision. After all, I'm only the boss. Or have youse something else to tell me?"

She shook her head.

"So, this is the first day?"

"Yeah."

"And what if we lose our arses on it?" He leaned back against the huge table, normally used for making toasted sandwiches. It was covered in joints of beef and lashings of other meats and vegetables. "This gear costs a fortune," he said, nodding to the raw meats.

"It doesn't," she shouted knowledgeably. "That cost fourteen forty," she pointed to the large leg of beef, "and the rest all comes to about sixty quid."

"That's eighty quid . . . my takings for a Monday night."

She smiled. "Good credit terms. And we can give the gear back after thirty days if we're not happy."

"*Thirty days?* We might as well call them now and get them to take it back, Nikki. This is not an eating establishment. It's a drinker's pub, not Garfield's."

"Ah, for God's sake, Frank. At least give it a shot. You'll never know if you don't try it. Suck it and see," she whispered seductively.

"OK, thirty days. That's it."

Nikki was so pleased that she threw her arms around Frank and gave him a big smacker on the lips.

"Jesus, steady. I haven't left you the pub! I've simply said that *you're* going to work very hard for the next month."

Nikki winked. "It'll be worth it and more."

"Where's Ray?"

"He's upstairs . . . freshening up for the police."

Frank remembered. "That's right. When are they due?"

"About half one," she said as she stirred the gravy.

Frank ran back upstairs. "*Ray*," he roared.

"In here," a voice called from the bathroom. "Jesus, I wish you wouldn't shout like that. It reminds me of you on the phone the night your mother . . . " Ray realised it wasn't the right topic of conversation. "Sorry, Frank. I didn't . . . " Change subject. "How's all the gang in west Cork?" he asked, slapping on some aftershave to soak up a dozen cuts on his face.

"Ah, same as ever." Frank sniffed deeply and coughed. Then another violent cough. "Jesus, Ray. What's that stuff called?" He put his hand to his nose.

"Actually, it's called *Sex*." Ray applied some more. "Well?"

"Well what?"

"You're meant to say: well, it doesn't smell like sex to me!" Ray roared laughing.

"Smells more like fly repellent to me. I'll tell you what . . . keep putting that stuff on and they'll bring in the forensic experts." Frank left the bathroom in a hurry.

"Good idea . . . Jesus, I never thought of that."

Frank stood outside the bathroom door. "Ray," he asked quietly.

"Hmmm?"

"Did you put me to bed last night?"

Silence. "No." He laughed. "I can't remember getting into me own bed last night!"

Frank pushed open the door. "Well, if *you* didn't . . . who *did*?"

Ray looked at him in the mirror and shrugged his shoulders.

* * *

The two people sitting at the bar would have passed for ordinary punters. They sipped their coffees.

"Lady and gentleman, can I be of any help to you both? Ray Flynn's the name." He held out his hand to the police officers.

The lady shook his hand.

The man ignored the friendly gesture. He finished his coffee and stood down from the stool. "Mr Flynn, this is Detective Inspector Anne O'Brien, and I'm Detective Sergeant George Charlton, Anti-Terrorist Squad, Scotland Yard."

Ray's face lit up. "No relation to Jack, I suppose?"

"*Jack?* Jack who?"

"Charlton . . . eh, nobody . . . it doesn't matter."

"Mr Flynn, is there somewhere quiet we could spend a few minutes with you?" the attractive young inspector asked politely. "We'd like to ask you a few questions about Paul Flaherty."

Ray coughed and looked around the pub. He pointed to the small snug in the corner of the lounge. "In there," he whispered. He felt quite important now, what with two of Britain's most distinguished police officers looking to him, an Irishman, for help. And he was shagged if they were going to get any! "Anyone like a drink?"

The man looked at his watch. "At quarter past one in the afternoon? Give us a break!"

"Actually, I'll have a pint of Guinness, please," the inspector nodded her head.

Her partner looked shocked. "You're on duty, *Inspector!*" he snapped.

"And you're a pain in the arse, *George*!"

Ray looked delighted. "I think I might just join you, Inspector. Best pint of stout in London here. And what's your fancy, Sergeant . . . a bottle of fizzy orange and a straw, maybe?"

"Coffee, black. Two sugar, *Mr Flynn*." He gritted his teeth.

Ray told Nikki that he wasn't to be disturbed for the duration of the law's visit under any circumstances.

"And if my mobile rings, answer it for me," he shouted as he returned to the table.

"What *mobile*?" Nikki asked.

Ray coughed loudly. "Now, here we are. One black coffee." He slammed it down on the table drenching the sergeant. "Ooops, sorry, Sergeant . . . hand's a bit shaky after last night. One beautifully prepared pint of Guinness for the lady." He smiled.

She nodded her head. "Mmmm."

"And a little surprise for Ray."

"Nothing like the surprise we've got for you," muttered the sergeant.

"Sorry, son . . . I mean, Sergeant?"

"Leave this to me, Sergeant," the inspector said. "Mr Flynn, we're led to believe that you had a visit from a Paul Flaherty on Saturday afternoon last. Is that right?"

Ray took a deep breath. "Before I answer any questions, I'd like to know my rights."

The sergeant sniggered.

"Mr Flynn, all we'd like you to do is answer a few questions. You're not obliged to answer if you don't want to."

"That's right, *Mister* Flynn, but we could also arrest you and take you down to the station where we might get your undivided attention."

"For *what*?"

"Aiding and assisting in the escape of a Category A provisional IRA prisoner, *Mister* Flynn!"

"*IRA?*" Ray found it difficult to keep his voice down.

"What *do* you know about the IRA, Mr Flynn?"

"Apart from what it stands for . . . *nothing*!"

"*Sergeant . . . please!*" shouted the inspector. "Mr Flynn! I'm going to have to ask you two gentlemen to treat each other with a degree of respect. Do you understand?"

The two men nodded.

"Nice bright red tie, Mr Flynn."

"Matches your eyes, Mr Charlton."

"*Gentlemen, please . . . grow up!*" Silence. "Now Mr Flynn, this man spoke with you for how long?"

"Over an hour."

"What did he tell you?"

"Jesus, how long have you got?"

"Sorry?" The sergeant stopped taking notes.

The woman cut across again. "Mr Flynn, could you identify this man if you saw him again?"

Ray nodded. "Definitely."

The inspector put her briefcase on the table and took out a number of photgraphs. She placed two different pictures, face up, in front of Ray. "Now, Mr Flynn. Take your time. Can you tell me which of these gentlemen you think you might have spoken to last Saturday?

Ray studied each of the photographs. He didn't need to. The photo on the left was the man he'd spoken to. Protect him, he thought quickly. He picked up the photo on the right. *"That's him!"* He sat back in his seat.

The sergeant smiled and bowed his head.

"That's *who?*" asked the inspector.

"Paul Flaherty," Ray said slowly and seriously.

"Are you perfectly sure?"

"Yes."

"And you've never seen the man in the other photograph before?"

Ray shook his head. "Never."

The inspector placed a third photograph in front of Ray. It was a prison photograph of a much stockier man with a row of numbers in the foreground of the shot. "Have you ever seen *this* man?" she asked sombrely.

"No," Ray replied cautiously.

The two police officers looked at each other.

"I didn't think you had." The inspector picked up the three photographs. "From the first two, this was the man you'd met, is that what you said?"

"Yes."

"The man in the second photo you'd never seen before?"

"No."

The two police officers glanced at each other rather dejectedly.

"So . . . what does that mean?" Ray asked curiously.

"It means you weren't talking to Paul Flaherty."

"I was so!"

The two officers shook their heads.

"Afraid not," she said slowly. She held up the third

photograph. "*This* is Paul Flaherty. You were talking to Lawrence Charlton, George's younger brother." She nodded to her colleague who seemed both embarassed and furious.

"What is this?" shouted Ray. "Are you trying to make me out to be some sort of wanker?" He stood up.

The two officers were visibly mortified.

"We're very sorry for taking up your time, Mr Flynn. There's clearly been some sort of a mix-up here," the inspector gushed. "George, you're going to have to have a chat with your brother about this."

"And why is he carrying round a photo of his brother if youse are looking for an IRA man?"

"Good question. George?"

George had turned a deep shade of red. "Thank you *very much*, Mister Flynn. Sorry for taking up your time."

"Well, forget about it this time. Tell your brother to stay away from here. He obviously needs psychiatric help if he's wandering around London impersonating terrorist criminals. And the brother of a good, law-abiding policeman as well. God help him, I hope he recovers."

"Well, if you hear anything, or see anyone *suspicious*," she glanced coldly at her partner, "let me know," the woman said. She handed him a card. "That's my direct line at the station. Nice to meet you." She smiled and walked towards the door.

Ray looked down at the policeman's waiting hand and put his in his pockets.

The man walked to the door. As he opened it, he turned around. "Hey, Flynn, you really did have a heart-to-heart with this big-time IRA head, didn't you?"

Ray forced a smile. "Maybe I did."

"If he had been IRA, he wouldn't have *pissed* on you, never mind *talked* to you."

"Yeah?" Ray looked him in the eyes. "*You're* the sort of guy *he'd* have pissed on . . . after he'd torched you."

The sergeant sneered. "See you round, geek."

No one noticed the two strangers leave by the side door. All eyes were focused on the new cuisine. Compliments were flying about the Irish stew and the Yorkshire puddings. The home made soup was the best they'd tasted.

"Where did you discover her, Frank?" shouted one diner as Nikki came out to check the carvery counter.

"I'm still not sure," Frank replied proudly. He looked out at the large crowd. Huge for lunch-time. "But you can keep your eyes off her. She's mine."

"Promises, promises," teased Nikki. She pinched his waist as she went back to the kitchen.

Ray put the empty glass up on the counter and sat on an empty stool. "Same again . . . please," he mumbled. He put his head down on the counter.

"That seemed to go OK," Frank remarked.

"OK?" Ray muttered. "I suppose that's what the pilot said when he dropped the bomb on Hiroshima."

"That bad?"

"Bad? Frank, I need the afternoon off."

"Why? Where are you going?"

"I'm going to get drunk and then I'm going to . . . lie down in a dark room." He picked up his jacket and walked towards the side door.

"Ray . . . your drink! Don't bang . . . "

The door slammed shut behind him.

Chapter Twenty-Four

"You're in good form this morning," her mother remarked as Jamie handed her a mug of tea.

Jamie walked back to the cooker. "Good night last night . . . that's all."

"And what about the night before?"

Jamie refused to look around. "Which night?"

"Wednesday night . . . the night you never came home?"

Jamie chanced a quick look. Her mother seemed to be giving her full attention to the *Gay Byrne Show*. Jamie was surprised that a trivial conversation could come between Gay's dulcet tones and her mother's undivided devotion. But then, maybe this wasn't just a trivial conversation. Her mother always prided herself on one thing: being well-informed, both locally, for a radius of two miles, and personally, among her treasured family.

"So, where did you end up?" she continued.

"Do you fancy going shopping today, Ma?" Jamie tried to get off the subject. "Come on, we haven't been out together for years?"

"Jamie Carroll, if you think that I'm going into town with you, and you in that 'everything's perfect' humour, you're wrong. Anyway, Gay's giving out the results of his *Know your Neighbour* competition today."

Jamie's eyes lit up. At last, she was off the hook. "Did you enter?"

"*No!*" She laughed and took a drag from her cigarette. "*You* don't enter. Your neighbour enters *you*."

"What?" asked Jamie curiously. "Ah Ma, go on, tell us. What?"

"Someone secretly entered Mrs Connolly up the road. You know her . . . number 46. Holy Mary . . . always licking the paint off the statues' feet up in the church. She spends more time in the parish priest's house than she does at home. *His* house is like a spring-cleaned mansion, while her own is like a Corporation tip." She took a fast sip from her mug. "Rumour has it that her kids are getting subsidies from the Eastern Health Board. Calling to that parochial house is a nightmare. The ould bitch asks you what you want to see him about if you call. Tell her it's a Mass card, she wants to know who's dead. Tell her it's about a wedding, she wants to know who's pregnant!" She roared laughing.

Jamie couldn't believe what she was hearing. For years her mother had been one of the parish's most conservative women and today she was ready to burn her bra. She was enjoying every minute of this new revelation. "So, go on. What happened?"

"Where?"

"With the *Gay Byrne Show* competition?"

"Oh, that!" She started to laugh again.

"Ah, Ma . . . come on!"

"See, Gay invited the listeners to write in and nominate a neighbour. Then the man with the micro . . . thingy . . . "

"Microphone!"

"Microphone . . . thingy, the reporter fella, would come around unexpected one morning and . . . SURPRISE!, catch you at what you were doing!"

"So, tell us, what was Mrs Connolly doing?"

"Mrs Connolly? She was up in the parish priest's house . . . as usual. No, yer man off the programme arrived and knocked on the doorbell and after a few minutes, this woman answered the door in a nurse's outfit!"

"Mrs Connolly?"

"No, Jamie! You're not listening. How many times have I to tell you? *She* was in the priest's house. Anyway, your man says, 'Hello, Mrs Connolly, I'm from the *Gay Byrne Show*. Your neighbours all got together to nominate you for our *Know your Neighbour* competition.' And the neighbours, dozens of them, all standing in the front garden!"

"So what happened?"

"Well, your woman started tying her hair up in a bun and buttoning up her blouse. She says to the reporter, real cheeky like, 'Your man got my number in *In Dublin*. I'm just here to give him his weekly massage. He's a bit strange, though. He likes to lie on the bed in the nude. Then he gives me a packet of onion rings and I have to throw them at his you-know-what.' She gave the reporter her card and left in her car!"

431

"Ma," Jamie gasped, "I don't believe you. Swear to God, go on."

"On the picture of the Sacred Heart hanging over my bed . . . it's true. And I'd been thinking old Mr Connolly was going a bit senile. You'd see him at the same time every morning walking that little three-legged dog he has up to the shop for the paper. What an existence, your father used to say. Little did I know that he was just loosening up for his lady friend's magic fingers every Tuesday. And his wife up running sales of work for the missions and things."

"Ma, Jesus, you're shocking me!"

Then, as quickly as the conversation started, it changed.

"Now, I'm not budging until you tell me where you were for the whole night on Wednesday!"

Jamie waited. "With a friend."

"Who?"

"Sheila Hoey."

"That's funny. Sheila rang here at half ten on Wednesday looking for you."

Jamie clenched her teeth. No use. As usual, the ould dear was far too clever to be conned. Jamie reckoned that she'd been blessed with a sixth sense . . . common enough among mothers.

"All right. I spent it with a friend that I met in London."

"Is she back home as well?"

"*He* . . . actually." She took a deep breath. It didn't come. Jamie looked around to see if her mother had passed out.

She was finishing off her tea. "Pour us a hot drop, will you?"

Jamie was rooted to the spot. "Ma, are you all right?" Maybe she hadn't heard her.

Silence. "Yeah, *I'm* all right." She looked around at her eldest daughter and smiled. "I'm only hoping *you'll* be all right."

Jamie didn't know which way to look or what way to think.

"So," her mother continued, "when do we get to meet this *friend* of yours?"

Jamie relaxed. "Soon . . . very soon."

All of a sudden, there was great excitement in the kitchen.

"Quick!" her mother shouted, "turn up the radio."

Silence fell over the kitchen, and the entire country, as Gay Byrne launched into the final minutes of *Know your Neighbour.*

"All right then, my friends, it should have been the moment we've all been looking forward to . . . the results of our *Know your Neighbour* competition, hotly contested by all the lovely, lovely folk up and down the country over the past eight weeks here on the *Gay Byrne Show*."

"But, unfortunately, as you may recall, we ran into a very serious problem a fortnight ago when we called to a house in Church Avenue in Artane here in Dublin. Well, my friends, as a result of legal problems that were caused by what happened that unfortunate morning, a case of being in the wrong place at the wrong time, I suppose, we've had to cancel our competition. I know . . . countrywide disappointment. I can hear it from here. Instead, perhaps you'll all understand the tragedy and trauma that this particular family has suffered as a result of that morning's events, if I read out a touching, tearful letter to you sent to me this morning by Ted Connolly, proprietor of 46 Church Avenue, Artane. It reads, *'Dear Gay, My wife and I have been great fans of your show for many years. Therefore it is with deep shame and regret that I write this letter. Apologies can mean nothing after what I've put my family through in the past two weeks. Sympathy shown to a man so foolish is a commodity so rare. Still, I need to say sorry, not just to my wife, a martyr if ever there was one, but to you and to your listeners. I swear to you that that morning was the first time I met Marjorie.*

'Having checked with the VHI, my wife, Dorothy, is now convinced that Marjorie was not a member of the medical profession, and that a hand-job does not mean helping a sick person out of bed to the loo. However, I must say, Gay, her behavioural pattern over the past couple of weeks is giving me grave cause for concern. She finds it hard to pass the time now that she has resigned from the the Lay Ministers of the Eucharist Group, Church Choir, Church Cleaning Corps, School Restoration Fund, Legion of Mary, Nifty Fifties Club, Bible Class, Musical & Dramatic Society, Marriage Guidance Council, Friends of Vestments for the Missions, Anti-Divorce Action Group, Medjugorjan Support Aid, Respect for Moving Statues Association and her daily presbytery housekeeping duties. She has also suspended her annual subscription to The

Irish Messenger *magazine and hasn't passed within two hundred yards of the church in a fortnight. Last night, my daughter informed me that Dorothy has also cancelled her ticket for the forthcoming parish trip to Lourdes.*

'Gay, *as only you can appreciate, I'll never be able to forgive myself for what I've done to her. But, as she says herself, I'll spend eternity shovelling coal for the devil, and even that will be too good for me. And God knows*, she should know.

'*I'm still adjusting to life here at Meadowview hostel for homeless men. At least, I still get to hear your wonderful show each morning. Perhaps, Gay, you could convince Dorothy to stay in the local* Neighbourhood Watch *scheme, now that she's alone in the house. As you can appreciate, even a mention of my existence turns her stomach. Signed, Devastated'.*"

* * *

The mood was relaxed in the rooftop restaurant in Clery's. Jamie sipped her cup of tea as she gazed across the rooftops. All the usual landmarks. Green copper domes all over the city. The Four Courts. The GPO. She hadn't a clue what half of the buildings were. But they'd always been there.

"What are you thinking?" her mother asked, as she drew hard on her cigarette.

"That this is a *No Smoking* area, Ma. Look at the signs."

"Ah, shite. They won't mind me having one. I'm gasping." She took another long pull. "Jesus, I thought

I was bad for shopping when you were kids. You've put ten years on me in the last three hours."

"Ah, still. Sure, you're enjoying it."

Her mother nodded. "It's great. I've never gone home with so many bags in all me life. Wait till your father sees all this stuff. You'll have to tell him that you bought most of it, do you hear me?"

"Don't mind him. I bet you he'll think that new nightdress is gorgeous when he sees it on you."

"Are you joking? The only thing your father takes a good look at these days is in large pint glasses." Her mother looked serious for a moment. "Where did you get all this money, Jamie?"

"*Ma!* I don't ever ask you where you get your money."

She raised her eyes to heaven. "What *money?*"

"Where's Lisa and *thing*?" asked Jamie, looking at her watch.

"*Jabs* is his name, not *thing*!"

"What's his real name?"

"Jacob."

"*Jacob?*" shrieked Jamie. "I can see why he prefers Jabs!"

"I think Jacob is a lovely name. I only wish he'd start using it."

"Why did they call him *Jacob*? Was it your man in the Bible?"

"No . . . seemingly his father worked for Jacob's Fig Rolls, you know . . . the biscuits."

Jamie started to laugh. "You're not serious."

Her mother looked at her indignantly. "I beg your pardon?"

436

Just then, a young woman sitting at the next table tapped Mona Carroll on the arm. "Excuse me," she said in a posh southside accent, "the smell of your cigarette smoke is making my son cough."

Jamie was embarrassed.

Her mother sat forward in her chair. "Is that so?" she said sympathetically in her rich northside accent. "Well, I didn't like to say it, but the smell of your son's dirty nappy is putting me off my shepherd's pie!" She nodded her head at the shocked stranger. "Quits?" She took a long drag from the cigarette and stubbed it out in her saucer. She stood up and picked up her shopping. "Come along, precious, let's get out of here," she said to Jamie, mimicking the young woman's accent, "our driver will be waiting anxiously."

* * *

Jamie linked arms with her mother as they stood waiting outside Clery's side door. An icy wind blew down the small narrow street.

"Where the *hell* are they?" begged Mona.

"What are we standing here for?" Jamie asked.

"I told Lisa we'd meet them outside the side door. They said they'd only be twenty minutes," her mother replied.

"And what if they go up to the restaurant to look for us?"

"Well, I'm not going to sit up there listening to people with golf balls in their mouths giving out about me having a perfectly civilised smoke. Anyway, Lisa's well able to find her own way home."

"Where have they gone?"

"Lisa said that Jabs needed ointment for a verucca on his free-kick foot. She was saying that there's only one chemist in town that sells it."

"His *free-kick* foot? What's that?"

"Football! He's one of the best strikers in Dublin. He was telling your father the other night that Mick McCarthy's been keeping an eye on him."

"Don't tell me that Mick McCarthy's that hard up?"

"Don't be so cynical. Mind you, after a couple of the recent games, I'm not altogether too sure any more. The Irish Squad? More like the residents of an old-folks' home."

"I suppose the chemist sells condoms as well."

"Jamie, give it up. I'm beginning to think that you've got a one-track mind."

"*Ma!*" she insisted. "*I have not.* Anyway, I thought you'd be proud if they acted so responsibly."

"*Him? Responsible?* I wouldn't let him feed your father's pigeons! Here, let's nip into the Pro-Cathedral and say a quick prayer for your grandad. It's his anniversary on Sunday." Her mother ran a tissue under her nose. "God rest him. I've never been able to go back to the dog pond since that terrible day. If the dog hadn't brought him over that huge stick and barked at him to throw it, he'd never have fallen in." Her mother got upset every year at this time.

Jamie put her arm around her mother's small frail shoulders. "I'll tell you what, Ma. Come on into that little pub over there and I'll buy you an Irish coffee. As you say, Lisa and Jabs can make their own way home. What do ya say?"

Her mother looked at her suspiciously. She smiled and linked her arm. "OK . . . but just one."

* * *

A tall, handsome man, in his mid-thirties, glanced here and there at clothes in one of the shop windows. Every couple of minutes, he moved to the kerb at the corner of the street as if waiting for a bus. He wore dark shades and kept the collar of his thick jacket well up around his face. Now and then, he chanced a quick glance over the top of his folded newspaper in the direction of the two women standing close to the shop's side door.

A red Renault 19 was parked at the back of the taxi rank on O'Connell Street, opposite the main door of Clery's. The man in the passenger seat spoke into a two-way radio.

A passing taxi slowed down alongside the passenger door of the red car. "Hey, sunshine," shouted the taxi-driver, "can't you read the fuckin' sign? This is our pick-up, so find somewhere else to park. You're obstructing my livelihood!" He pointed to the red and white sign above their car. *Taxis only.*

The driver of the Renault leaned across his partner to the open passenger window while his colleague talked into the radio. He flashed a badge. "Get fuckin' lost before yer done for obstructing gardaí!" he shouted casually at the shocked taxi-driver. The two men leaned forward to keep an eye on movements close to Clery's.

The taxi-driver muttered something under his breath and left.

On the other side of O'Connell Street, close to the turn into Henry Street, a lone biker sat on his machine close to the footpath. He clutched his helmet. He was well-built and looked stocky in his leathers. He had a thick moustache and a number of small scars on his face. He ignored people who slowed down to admire his powerful motor-bike as they passed. He seemed more interested in what was happening outside Clery's. He took a small pad and a pen from his jacket pocket and made some notes. Eventually, he turned the key and threw the power. The bike made a thundering noise as its engine came to life. He turned it around and slowly manouevred it into a small laneway just off Henry Street. He removed the key and walked slowly to a shop across the street. It was a barber shop. He disappeared inside. Two hours later, a clean-shaven man with red hair and a khaki jacket emerged from the shop. He climbed up on to the motor-bike which had been parked in the laneway and disappeared into the rush hour traffic. The barber stood at the door of the shop and nodded his head as the biker passed him. A young woman dressed in a small black negligee waved to him from a window on the second floor above the shop. A couple of minutes later, the whiskered well-built man emerged. He crossed the street and got into his taxi.

It was quarter to six.

The red Renault 19 was long gone.

So was the young, attractive man standing on the kerb near Clerys.

Jamie switched on the light in the kitchen. Her mother put on the kettle.

* * *

Frank was reading the evening paper behind the bar, enjoying a cup of tea. Ten to six. The Friday rush was about to happen. The calm before the storm. He thought about giving Jamie a quick call. In fact he thought of nothing else. No. I'll leave it till we close and I get into bed. He smiled to himself. He closed the paper and switched on *Eurosport*. Highlights of the day's action in the *Paris – Dakar Rally* were due on at six. He knew he'd forget to change channels once the rush began. As soon as he'd adjusted the sound, he hid the remote-control device in the kitchen. This was the eighteenth remote-control he'd had to buy for the pub screen and he'd sworn to himself, after the local GAA team's winning celebration night, that there wasn't going to be a nineteenth.

"Frank, have you seen Ray anywhere today?"

The voice startled him. "What?" He looked up. "Davina." She didn't look too happy. In fact, she looked rightly miffed. "Eh, Ray? No . . . I haven't." Frank was trying to think when he'd last seen him. "Lunch-time, that's right. The cops questioned him and he had to take the rest of the day off."

"*What?*" She nearly passed out.

Frank realised what he'd just said. "No . . . eh, I don't mean that. Sure he's due in here at half six. I thought he was at home with you."

"Frank McCabe, I know what the two of you are like. Now if he's put you up to something, you'd better tell me, because I have my mother's sister staying with me tonight and tomorrow and I don't want him rolling in pissed in front of her. So come on, where is he? And what did the cops want him for?"

"I don't know," Frank said again.

"Has he gone on the batter? Or gambling, maybe," Davina asked nervously. "Oh, Frank, tell me he's not, please," she begged.

"He's not," he said. "Here, sit down in the snug and I'll get you a hot whiskey."

* * *

Davina Cripp was a deserted mother of two small children, aged four and three. Her common-law husband had been charged with petty theft. It would have been his twenty-eighth conviction if he hadn't jumped bail and fled the country two days before his court appearance.

She was glad for the children's sake that he was finally gone. But the money quickly ran out. She applied for part-time jobs, mainly cleaning. She took up one and then moved on to another because of the hours involved. Most of the jobs required her to work through the night which meant paying a babysitter to stay over. One morning, she came home to find the babysitter gone. And her few precious valuables. The children had been asleep in the flat on their own all night. She got a job in an insurance company preparing snacks for coffee breaks. It still made no sense. She ended up paying out the few quid she made each week to the crèche which took her two little girls.

Within three months, she was forced to move out of her cosy Camden Town home into a small dingy bed-sit in Islington, provided by the local council. She collected a deserted mother's allowance and an unemployment remittance. It wasn't much of a life. Stuck in a one-room flat, day and night, with two screaming kids.

She thought about going to stay with her father in Dublin for a while. But she'd never really got on with him. Her mother had died from lung cancer some years before. Her death closed down all family communication. There was no help for Davina. She couldn't see things improving. In fact, the forecast seemed pretty grim. That was, at least, until she met her neighbour.

Davina became friendly with the woman who lived in the small flat above her, always delighted when she'd drop in during the long afternoons. Sometimes they chatted over a cup of tea. Now and again, she might take the kids for a few hours. This was like a holiday for Davina.

In the beginning, Davina assumed that her friend was unemployed too. Like her, she seemed to have little to do all day. She'd hear her leave the flat at the same time, quarter to ten, every night. Occasionally, if the children were restless, she'd notice the front door opening quietly around four and her friend walking slowly upstairs to her flat. Davina assumed she had a boyfriend. But she couldn't figure out why there was only one set of footsteps arriving back at precisely the same time, night after night.

Late one afternoon, Davina called to her friend's flat. She was hoping that she might mind the children while she dashed down to the chemist for a prescription for one of them.

Her friend opened the door cautiously. When she saw Davina, she looked relieved. She smiled and invited her in.

Davina was shocked at what she saw. This was like a sheik's palace compared to her own flat. Gorgeous carpet. Beautiful furniture. Television *and* video. Microwave. Dishwasher.

"Great flat," Davina remarked casually.

"Yeah, it does the job, I suppose," her friend replied.

Davina was dying to know where all the luxuries came from. "Thoughtful boyfriend?" she asked light-heartedly.

Her friend smiled. "*Loads* of thoughtful boyfriends!"

Davina couldn't sleep that night. It was almost three when the younger of her two girls got to sleep. She twisted and turned in the bed. Her mind was racing. After a while she sat out on the side of the bed. It was time to find out more. She decided to wait up and surprise her neighbour when she came home. She could say that she thought she'd heard a prowler. She sat in the armchair wrapped in a blanket, fighting to stay awake. It was a freezing cold night. She couldn't afford to switch on the heating.

She must have dozed off. She heard a key turn slowly in the big front door down the hall. She leapt out of the chair. Without as much as a second thought, she flung open her door on to the main hallway.

"Thank God it's yourself. I thought that someone was trying to break . . . " Her words slowed. Davina stood in the hall with her mouth open. She was speechless. Unable to talk.

"You're up late," her neighbour said with a tired smile. She turned and pulled the chain across the front door.

Davina didn't know which way to look.

The woman from upstairs had either been at a vicar and tarts' party or she was wearing this gear for a bet. Black fishnet tights and suspenders under a leather miniskirt that was smaller than a curtain hemline. Her low-cut top revealed her huge swaying cleavage. A small tattoo wobbled on her left boob. Her breasts looked like bald twins bobbing around in a pram.

Her neighbour looked down and hitched up the front of her leather skirt, revealing a pair of crotchless pants. "Drives the men wild," she purred.

"A . . . *prostitute*?" muttered Davina.

"In one, honey," replied her neighbour. She pulled a wad of notes out of her tacky handbag. "Three hundred and fifty smackers for one night's work. Tell me what you'd have to do to get that anywhere else?" She strode towards the stairs. "If you don't mind walking like John Wayne for a couple of hours, it's

445

money for old rope." She climbed the stairs slowly, one step at a time. "See you tomorrow. By the way," she asked anxiously, "how's your little chicken's temperature?"

"It's normal," Davina stammered. She was in a state of shock.

* * *

Davina sat at the small kitchen table with a page out of the front of the telephone directory and a biro. Three hundred and fifty pounds for one single night. That's two thousand one hundred pounds a week allowing for Sunday nights off. That's . . . eight thousand, four hundred a month. That's . . . holy Jesus . . . that's *over* a hundred grand a year! She slammed the biro down on the table and squeezed the top of her dressing-gown. A *hundred thousand pounds*! She'd be half a millionaire in five years. And all made on her back! The kettle shrilled, unnoticed in the background. Holidays . . . designer clothes for the girls and herself . . . a video . . . a nice car. She stared out the kitchen window into the pitch-dark night. No one would have to know. But how would she account for the money? Shag it, she thought. Who would she have *to* account to, anyway? She was much better-looking than her neighbour. And younger. She looked in the small mirror which hung beside the cooker. Her face was pretty. Nice hair. She opened the top of her dressing-gown revealing the top of her breasts. She quickly closed it again. The thought of a dirty old stranger feeling her breasts and . . .

fucking her for money revolted her. She sat down again and ran her fingers through her hair. What was the alternative? She looked around the kitchen. This little kip for the rest of her life? Three hundred and fifty quid. The figure bounced around her head like a squash ball. No love or affection. Just three hundred and fifty quid. Maybe it wouldn't be so bad. There must be a knack, she thought. She slapped the side of her head. Snap out of it! she thought sensibly. Get a grip. You're Davina Cripp. Mother of two small girls. A nice decent, respectable, Irish girl. She turned out the light and went back to her bed. She lay there hoping that sleep would come. It didn't.

Two nights later, she closed the front door behind her and headed out on to the streets as the city's newest hooker. She told the babysitter not to bother waiting up. Pulling the knickers out from between the cheeks of her arse, she headed for Bromlington. It was the area everyone talked about in hushed tones and dodgy conversations. To Davina, it was three hundred and fifty quid.

* * *

The area was far from salubrious. Narrow streets. Dimly-lit doorways. A noisy bar. A grotty fast-food takeaway here and there. Shifty-looking men and women of all nationalities standing around watching each other.

Davina looked around uneasily for her friend.

Karen stood at the corner of a narrow lane leading

to the sex capital of north London, The Priory. She waved to Davina and called her name.

Davina hurried across to where she was standing. "Jesus, I'm sick."

"Don't be worrying," replied Karen, her neighbour, "you'll be fine." She checked out her gear. "You look brilliant. They'll be crawling all over you."

"That's what I'm afraid of," Davina whispered anxiously.

"First stop, *Hands*!"

Davina opened her eyes wide. *"Where?"*

"Hands . . . it's a pub where all the girls meet for a drink before they start work. You kinda have to check in with your team coach."

Hands, thought Davina. What an unfortunate name for a hookers' local. Then she got to thinking about these *team coaches*! "Pimps, you mean?"

Her friend nodded. "Coach sounds nicer, doesn't it?"

A small, shiny black man, dripping with gawdy jewellery and reeking of suffocating aftershave, joined their company. He sipped a cocktail. "Good evening, ladies."

"Hi, Larry. This is Davina," Karen said politely.

"My, my, my! Da-vin-a," he intoned. "What a beautiful name. Appropriate for such a beautiful good *thang*!" He clicked his heels and kissed her hand.

"Larry is your coach. Larry the lamb."

* * *

Davina learned a different side of life that night. A side

where money can buy love, even if it does only last for one hour. At first she was shocked at the price-list. Forty quid for a hand-job. Fifty for oral. A hundred quid for the real thing. It seemed as if every part of her body had a price on it. The whole idea seemed to be to get as many parts as possible to move in harmony at the same time. Perhaps this was what John Major had in mind when he referred to economic strategy.

A quick chat and a few stiff drinks later and she was out on her own. Karen told her to stand near the taxi rank. But not too close. The police always slowed down there when they passed.

She looked at her watch. It was five past eleven. Davina was about to light up a cigarette when a huge car pulled up alongside. The electric window rolled down. She tried to look casual as she strolled over to the car. She bent down and looked in the window.

An elderly man looked cautiously back at her. "Do you fancy a drive in the car?" he asked politely.

Davina nodded. "Where?" She swallowed hard. This was it. The point of no return.

He leaned across the seat and opened the door for her.

She sat into the soft leather seat, which felt cool against her bare legs, and closed the door behind her. She noticed that her tight skirt had climbed up to her thighs. She pulled at it in an effort to cover her legs as much as possible. It didn't appear to be working. Shag it, she thought. She looked around at the furnishings of the dashboard and the car in general. It was posh. Plenty of money, she thought. Then she looked across at the man. Jesus, he's ancient, she thought. Seventy . . . minimum!

He looked at her and smiled nervously. "I'm Donald. You're . . . ?" He waited.

"Eh, Raquel, actually." She swallowed.

"You're a new girl."

Davina stared ahead out the window. "Maybe. How can you tell?"

"Your hands are shaking." He smiled.

She looked at her hands. Shaking was an understatement. They were vibrating!

"You don't mind coming back to my house for an hour, do you, Raquel?"

Davina shook her head. Raquel, she thought. Why did she pick Raquel? She hated that name. Now all she needed was this poor old pervert moaning the name Raquel in between whiffs from his inhaler for the next couple of hours. She looked at him. He was old. But attractive. Still, the thought of *it* with *him* turned her stomach. *Three hundred and fifty pounds*, she kept thinking to herself.

His house looked more like a castle. Hampstead Heath by the look of it. Electric gates. Lights all the way up the drive. Pillars in front of the hall-door. He could have any woman with money like this, she thought.

He asked her if she'd like a drink.

Davina shook her head. What was this . . . a date? she wondered. "Let's go upstairs," she said softly, trying to sound as sexy as possible.

The old man smiled and took her hand. He lead her up the giant staircase to a huge landing. There were bedroom doors everywhere.

The knot in her stomach tightened. It reminded

her of the very first time she'd done *it* with a boy from school. His parents were at the pictures and they had the house to themselves. She'd needed some Dutch courage so she asked for a drink.

Not being one to miss out on a golden opportunity, the young man grabbed a bottle from his father's drinks' cabinet without thinking and filled a large glass. Davina drank it as quickly as possible and then proceeded to eat the young man. Unfortunately, as they kissed intimately, she threw up.

The stranger led her into the master bedroom. He said nothing. She noticed a large yellow raincoat on the bed. The sort worn by fishermen in bad weather. A large yellow rain hat and a pair of galoshes lay beside it.

"Take off your clothes and put *them* on," he said softly. He started to take off his clothes.

Davina stared at him. And then at the rainwear.

One hour later, she checked before pulling the bedroom door shut behind her. The old man lay naked, exhausted across a large net curtain which was strewn across the floor. He slept like a child. She made sure the two hundred pounds were tightly bundled into the bottom of her handbag. Two hundred pounds for pretending to be a member of a lifeboat crew who saves the man from Atlantis after he becomes entangled in fishing nets. All she had to do was stand on the bed in her rain gear and throw the net curtains to him as he lay on the floor. Strange, she thought. Larry the Lamb was waiting outside for her eagerly, as arranged.

"Everything all right?" he enquired.

She nodded and sat into the car beside him.

"All the honey intact?" he asked as he handed her a piece of chewing gum.

"Honey?" she asked nervously.

"Honey, babe. Like . . . the money?"

She nodded as she took the gum. She showed him the rolled-up bundle of notes.

He grinned, showing off his snow-white teeth. "You listen to me, Davina baby. I's gonna make you a rich Irish girl. You hear me? But you can only work for Larry the Lamb . . . you hear me?"

She nodded.

"Now, let's see." He licked his finger and thumb. "Forty per cent makes little Larry eighty pounds closer to his eternal reward. All right, baby." He held out his hand.

Davina quickly counted out eighty pounds.

He spat on it. "Nice!" he muttered. He stuffed it into his pocket.

The next man Davina met took her to a cheap hotel. He lay on the bed for the hour, just holding her. He told her his wife was dying from Parkinson's disease and he was lonely. He could talk to her but no one spoke back. He needed a woman's company. Someone who would just tell him that they understood.

Davina told him that she understood.

The stranger gave her eighty quid. No sex required. He put back on his shirt and dropped her back to the park entrance and said goodnight.

Another man asked her to sit naked on the bed in front of him. He stared at her, up and down, for a whole hour. Fifty quid. No sex.

At ten past three, she headed back to Hands pub

with Larry, her faithful watchdog. It was heaving. Davina spotted Karen. She told her about the weird night she'd had. Plenty of money and no sex. She could get used to this, she said. You will, said Karen. She didn't even feel tired and it was almost time to go home.

Just then, she felt a hand on her shoulder. She turned around. A tall, black sailor stood in front of her. He wore a white cap and uniform. He smiled.

Davina smiled back. Maybe she wasn't going to get off so lightly tonight after all. He was young . . . mid-twenties, she reckoned, and pretty much all right.

"You speak Dutch?" he asked awkwardly.

Davina shook her head. "English," she replied.

"Rumpy-pumpy?" he asked. He flashed a bundle of foreign currency.

Davina and Karen tried not to laugh.

Davina looked at him again and nodded.

"What was that you said about not being tired tonight?" Karen whispered as Davina picked up her bag to leave.

They went to a small bed and breakfast two doors away. Judging by how keen this sailor was, he'd been offshore and out of bounds for months.

Davina emerged from the bathroom after a quick cigarette. She froze. Her eyes bulged. She remembered a saying they had in school: men come in three different sizes, small, medium and Oh my God! She still couldn't figure out where these guys packed away all that equipment when it came to jumping hurdles in the hundred-metres sprint at Gottenburg.

She didn't arrive back home until quarter to eight

that morning. She bribed the babysitter to stay on till lunch-time. Now she could afford it.

* * *

Her night-time rendezvouz became part of life. An average week's earnings was anything between one and a half and two grand. She'd even managed to detach herself from her conscience. The part of her that still told her she was mad.

The night she'd always feared came that Christmas. Taxis were as rare as free money and large drunken crowds of party-goers gathered at the rank close to her meeting-point at the park entrance.

It was nearly half one when he propositioned her. He was tall and unshaven. She could smell the drink as he asked her what she did. Davina tried to ignore him. Then she told him to go away. She was tired, finished for the night. As she turned her back, he grabbed her from behind. She tried to scream but his huge hand covered her mouth. He dragged her into the small park. In behind some thick bushes.

She could feel herself choke. As his other hand pulled at her coat, she noticed a large figure walking up behind her attacker. The tall man grabbed her assailant and held him against a tree. Without as much as a word, he slammed his fist into the man's jaw. Davina could hear a loud crack. She flinched. The man cried out in pain and grabbed his jaw. Blood poured from his mouth.

"Are you all right?" the red-haired man asked Davina. She nodded. "Yeah."

He turned back to the man who was on his knees. "Bastards like you make me want to kill." He turned him around and threw him head first into the tree-trunk.

The man groaned and slumped to the ground.

"How many times have you been told," her knight in shining armour shouted mockingly, "you *don't hit a woman*!" He kicked him hard in the ribs. This time, there was no sound. He looked around at Davina. "Friend of yours?"

She shook her head.

"What was going on? Sorry," he paused, "none of my business." He took off his jacket. "Here, your coat's all ripped. Put this on till I get you a taxi."

Davina had no choice. She put on his big donkey jacket and followed him as he walked to the taxi rank. He pushed his way up to the top of the queue. No one seemed inclined to argue. "The woman's not well. She's getting the next taxi. Is that clear?"

Everyone nodded.

"Come on," he said to Davina. "They don't mind if we jump the queue. Let's get out of here in case the police arrive."

"What about *him*?"

"He won't be going anywhere for a while." He nodded to the drunks at the taxi rank. "And they think *they'll* have bad headaches in the morning? Just wait till he wakes up."

"But what if he's . . . ?"

"What?" Ray asked quickly. "Dead? He's not dead." He led Davina over to the taxi. He sat into the back seat beside her. The taxi moved away. "Christmas party?" Ray asked quietly.

"What . . . eh, yeah." She didn't know what to say. What if this guy was a cop? Then she was in big trouble.

"Fucking Christmas parties. Make me sick. They all get pissed on the free gargle and then end up licking the boss's arse for the rest of the night . . . telling him how wonderful he is and how they all love working for him."

Davina watched him talking. "And did *you*?"

"What? Get pissed on the free gargle? Bloomin' sure I did!"

"No. Tell the boss how wonderful he is?"

He laughed. "I did not. I told him exactly what I thought of him. That if I'd ever got a chance to bury him in the walls of the channel tunnel, I'd have done it."

"What did he say to that?"

"He said that it was the most outrageous thing he'd ever heard from one of his employees. So I said, 'Oh yeah? Well, how about this . . . your financial controller is bonking your wife stupid!"

Davina laughed. She was enjoying the conversation. "What did he say to that?"

"Flynn, you're fired." Ray sniggered and shook his head.

"So you're out of a job the day before Christmas Eve?"

He nodded. "Yeah. Still who needs a job when you're a millionaire. Carlos is the name. I'm a property developer." Davina's eyes opened wide. "Actually, Ray's the name. Ray Flynn."

"Millionaire?"

"Actually . . . not yet." He shook her small hand and smiled. "I didn't know you girls had staff parties."

Davina could feel her face turing bright red.

"Fancy a drink?" he asked quietly.

Davina looked at her watch. "At *this* time?"

Ray winked. "Leave that one to me."

* * *

Within days, they'd become inseparable. It only took Ray a few weeks to adapt to Davina's two girls. Soon, though, he loved them and they him. It was a strange, but common, sight to see big Ray wheeling a trolley around Sainsbury's on a Saturday afternoon, the two girls in tow.

Eventually, Davina got a job in Sainsbury's. She'd managed to collect so many *Sainsbury's Supersave Coupons* that the manager told her one Saturday afternoon she could have virtually anything she wanted. She asked if she could have a job. Surprisingly, they rang her on Monday to tell her she'd start the following day. It was only a half-day, four days a week but it was better than walking around Bromlington at two in the morning with your heart in your mouth. Besides, she loved Ray. That was something she'd never had in her life before.

Ray's friends began to notice a weird change come over him. Most noticeable of all was how he stood up at twenty past eight each night. He'd finish his pint quickly and look at his watch. "That's it, lads," he'd say, "the kids have to be read their bedtime stories."

Davina waited until half eight in the hope that Ray might show up. She asked Frank to pass on word to Ray that he wouldn't be getting past the front door that night. He never showed.

Chapter Twenty-Five

Jamie was awake bright and early. Quarter past seven. Her interview for Getaway Travel was at half ten. On a morning like this, cold and wet, the thought of a job in a travel agency sounded really appealing. She'd planned to meet Sheila Hoey-Langer at twelve. They arranged to go to a fortune-teller beside Temple Street Hospital. She was meant to be really good and accurate. Sheila swore that she'd predicted her marriage to a man whose name was linked to a huge sex drive. Little did she think that this referred to the cattle he worked with. It was only a bit of skit, but Jamie was still dying to hear what she'd have to say about Frank. Her Frank.

She came downstairs to find a letter sitting on the hall table. "Ma," she called, as she looked at the writing on the envelope. English stamp and postmark. No answer. Everyone out. Then she remembered her mother telling her that she'd got her old job back in the parish priest's house, thanks to Mrs Connolly's resignation following the Gay Byrne scandal.

Jamie opened the envelope and quickly pulled out the letter. Typewritten. Official notepaper from the

London Metropolitan Police. She looked at the last line first. It was from the policewoman, Anne O'Brien.

Dear Jamie,

I hope you're well and enjoying the company of your family again. I thought I should update you on our investigations into your attack. We questioned David Darling regarding his whereabouts that night.

He claims he got a taxi home from your house at 3.45am. The taxi company were happy to verify his whereabouts, since he got sick all over the back seat of the taxi and then passed out. The driver dropped him off at Hadley Green police station where he was put in a cell for the remainder of the night. Having examined the evidence available, I feel we can rule him out of our investigation.

I will be home on holidays in a fortnight for a week. I hope we can meet for a drink and a chat. See you then,

All the best

Anne.

P.S. My promotion came through at long last. Inspector . . . at long last!

A.

* * *

Jamie felt about as enthusiastic at her interview as she would be watching cartoons on a wet afternoon. She'd heard all these stupid questions before. What can you bring to the position? Where do you see yourself in five years' time? What would you tell an angry customer who wanted a full refund and wasn't taking no for an answer? It all sounded too much like the famous overcharging incident when she worked in Quinnsworth all those years ago. No, this was definitely not the way to go. Towards the end of the interview, she stood up and excused herself. "What's this you always say, 'don't call us, we'll call you'? Well, don't call me and I won't call you."

The interviewers looked at each other with amazement.

Jamie banged the door behind her.

Sheila was waiting for her on the corner of Dorset Street and Temple Street. "Well, how did the interview go?"

Jamie knew damn well that Sheila was about as interested in *her* job interview as she was in a vow of chastity. "Ah, I told them where to get off. I mean, would you work for twenty grand a year and an Opel Astra?"

Sheila's eyes opened wide. "Twenty . . . eh, no, of course I wouldn't. Fair play to you, Jamie. You did the right thing."

"Come on, where does this woman live?"

"Who?"

"The fortune-teller!"

"Across the street in those *flats*." She pointed disdainfully to the big redbrick fortress across from the hospital.

"Oh, Jesus," said Jamie, "*those* flats. Here, quick, hide all your jewellery."

"Why?" screamed Sheila.

Jamie broke her heart laughing. "Jesus, Sheila Hoey, you're in Dublin . . . not Bosnia! Take a joke."

The two girls climbed the five flights of stairs to the landing. From where they stood, they could see most of the docks area of the northside.

"Jesus," spluttered Sheila, "you'd think they have installed a lift by now."

"Well, why don't you suggest it," Jamie joked.

Number 72.

Sheila knocked nervously.

It took ages for the door to open. A small hunched woman peeped out at them.

"Madame Huzzard?" Sheila asked.

Jamie couldn't help laughing when she heard her name.

"Jamie, shut up," urged Sheila as the old woman opened the door to let them in.

The small flat was dimly lit. A crystal ball sat in the middle of a round table.

The old woman pointed to three chairs. "Do you want to consult alone or together?"

Jamie looked at Sheila. She shrugged her shoulders. "Together, I suppose."

They sat down.

"Fifty," the old woman grunted.

"Fifty what?" Jamie looked at Sheila.

"Fifty pounds . . . for two." She held out her hand.

The girls coughed up.

She tucked the notes down her layers of shawls and sat down. There was silence for a few minutes. Then the old woman stared harder into the crystal ball. She mumbled to herself.

Jamie kicked Sheila under the table.

The old woman ignored their antics and gazed at the ball. "Money," she shouted.

"Not more," Jamie said.

Sheila nudged her. "Shut up!"

The old woman stared at Sheila and smiled. "You . . . will inherit a huge amount of money from a dear one."

Sheila's face froze.

"A distant relation you don't know exists," the old woman continued.

Sheila relaxed. "Oh, thank God," she said in her makey-uppy accent. "I thought you meant my little Simpson."

"You will have many children by your husband."

"Overtime," Jamie quipped.

Sheila kicked her again.

"And you will become famous on television."

Sheila couldn't contain her excitement. "*Me?* Famous on the small screen. I *knew* it!"

On her back again, Jamie thought.

Silence again.

The old woman studied Jamie, a worried look on her face. "I see . . . tragedy in your life. Sinister events. A troubled period. It seems confused. There is a good man who loves you. He is not here at the moment."

Jamie nodded.

"But he will be soon. You must stay close to him. He is the man who will make your life happy. Happier than you can imagine right now. I see another man . . ." The old woman tightened her grip on the crystal ball. "I see . . ."

"*What* do you see?" Jamie asked impatiently.

"Wait," urged the old woman. She didn't take her eyes off Jamie. They opened wider. "You, my dear . . . you are in grave danger. You must be careful." She stood up. "Now, if you don't mind, I'm busy."

"Busy? We've just paid fifty quid for three minutes . . . "

The old woman swung around. "Take heed," she warned angrily. "You've heard all you need to know . . . *Jamie*!"

"Jesus, I'm weak," whispered Sheila in a rare northside accent.

Jamie stood frozen to the spot. "How do you know my name?"

"Why do you think I charge fifty pounds?"

The two girls sat speechless in the small coffee shop in Phibsboro.

"She knew your name," was all that Sheila kept saying.

"Oh, shut up, Sheila." Jamie stared out the window. She could see the reflection of her shoulder bag in the window. The letters were back to front. She turned it around so that the writing was facing her. *Jamie*. "That's how she knew my name, the stupid cow!" she shouted.

Everyone in the coffee shop looked around.

"How?" asked Sheila.

"It's written on my bag."

"Oh, I see. So she's also able to see through the table at your bag lying on the floor? Yeah, that's *well* worth fifty quid!"

"No, silly," replied Jamie. "The bag might have been on the floor during her crystal ball session but it was on my shoulder when she answered the door. Any way, I don't believe any of that shite. Waste of money if you ask me."

Sheila tutted.

It was getting dark. The two girls spoke briefly on the corner of the Phibsboro Road before heading off in different directions.

"Give us a shout," Jamie said.

"I will. Tomorrow. I may travel to Newcastle with Simpson if he's going. Otherwise, we'll do lunch. OK?"

"Great," Jamie replied cynically.

As Sheila hailed a taxi, a large truck carrying cattle drove by and splashed her. "Bastard!" she shouted.

"Simpson must be bringing his work home tonight, is he?" Jamie shouted.

Sheila didn't hear her. She climbed into the taxi and was gone.

"Snob," muttered Jamie. She stood alone at the bus stop. The first thing she'd do when she got home would be to ring Frank. She couldn't get the fortune-teller out of her mind.

A man standing at the cash dispenser outside the bank across the road seemed to be watching her on and off.

Chapter Twenty-Six

Tommy Barrett sat alone in a small room on the first floor of a guest-house at the river end of Dublin's Gardiner Street. The stay-over was popular with late-night passengers arriving off the ferry at the North Wall. He was bored and agitated. He watched the main evening news on TV with contempt. He sneered and shouted abuse at the politician who vowed to wipe out the problem of drugs in the north inner city. He held his two hands out in front of him. They were shaking. You and whose army? he jibed. His breathing was wheezy. Every few minutes, he glanced at his watch. Then he went through his small telephone book, examining numbers and turning pages. He walked over to the window overlooking the road leading to Dublin's dockland. It was quiet tonight. He looked up and down the street. The rain poured down relentlessly. No one in their right mind would want to be out on a night like that. He walked back to the phone and dialled a number.

Jamie's mother answered. "Hello," she said in a strong Dublin accent. No reply. "Hello . . . hello. Is there anyone there?"

"Who is it, Ma?" a familiar voice called from behind.

"I don't know, love. Sounds like someone with asthma."

He could hear the two women laughing at the far end. Then the line went dead.

"Bitch!" he seethed as he slammed the phone down. "We'll see what you have to laugh about shortly." He sat down beside the phone and picked up the small red phone book. He searched the pages in a frenzy. Then he picked up the phone again. He dialled another number. The phone seemed to ring forever. Then a click.

"Hello," a voice said cautiously at the other end.

Tommy hesitated. "It's me. I thought you said half eight."

"Well, there's been a small problem. So you'll just have to be patient, won't you?"

"But you said . . . "

The man on the other end interrupted. "*I* said nothing. *You* made the arrangement. Now, *don't* ring me again. Do you hear me?"

The phone line went dead.

Tommy feverishly went through his contacts book again. Again, the phone seemed to ring for an eternity.

"Hello," a voice said at the far end.

"It's Tommy. Any news?"

"Eh, next Friday, I think."

"What do you mean, you *think*?" asked Tommy indignantly.

"We won't know if we have the boat until Monday.

And we don't want to be hanging round down there loaded with that cargo. Too obvious. Also, we need someone on board with the two Spaniards. They're fuckin' crazy. I don't trust them."

Tommy smiled. "Leave that to me. I think I have just the person. Call me if you hear anything." Tommy walked to the window. He didn't feel so bad now that he knew the boat was almost in place. He fidgeted with the curtains as he looked up and down the quiet street. His eyes glanced across the roof of a large van which was parked opposite. He closed the curtains and zapped through the television channels.

* * *

"Everything OK?" asked one of the men in the back of the cramped Mercedes van. He squatted behind a small video camera supporting a huge jutting lens mounted on a tripod. His neck was arched uncomfortably as he focused on the building across the street. A first-floor window was directly in his sight. The camera whirred and then clicked to a halt. The man sat back in his chair. "Did you get all that?"

His partner nodded. He removed his headphones and banged a button on the small console in front of him. The reel-to-reel tape machine paused. Silence, apart from the sporadic outbursts of two-way conversation on the radio in the front of the van. The atmosphere in the van was more akin to a darkroom than a police surveillance unit. A sinister glow from the overhead infrared lamp gave the small compartment a sinister twilight feel. Photographs were pinned to a small notice-board beside the video tripod. Discarded burger cartons and coffee cups littered the table space. The heat from the surveillance equipment made the smell of stale sweat and smoke intolerable.

"Now all we've got to do is wait for McGrath to ring him."

"Do you reckon he'll call tonight?"

"Looks like it, unless he suspects something." He checked the camera again. "Fuck!" He fell backwards. "Get your coat," he ordered. "Come on, quick, let's go!"

"What is it?"

"Barrett's on the street. Come on."

"Hang on. Easy does it." The light went out. The second man watched from the front of the van as Tommy Barrett walked down the steps of the building, pulling the front of his jacket close to his chest. He crossed the main road and walked towards the dingy hotel bar on the corner. As he climbed the steps towards the entrance, a small camera clicked in rapid rotation inside the van.

Tommy threw some change on to the counter, examining the unfamiliar currency as he waited for a pint. He picked up his glass and headed for the corner of the quiet bar. He looked at his watch as he sat down. Quarter to ten. He'd ring her when he got back.

The two men who'd been on surveillance duty in the van walked up to the bar and ordered drinks. They did a quick recce around the pub. One of them nudged the other and discreetly pointed to their man in the corner.

"Let's sit down beside him," suggested one.

His partner spluttered. "You must be joking! Wanna lose your job?"

None of them seemed to notice the big beefy individual who'd sat down opposite with *his* pint. A stoic sort of character, he just drank and gazed. Then he'd look back across to where Tommy was sitting and stare again with cold eyes.

The swinging door of the dimly-lit bar opened. A small sloppily-dressed man with a thin moustache and a huge badly healed scar between his left eye and his upper lip stepped in and looked around. He instantly made eye contact with Tommy. He scurried across to where he was sitting. "Tommy Barrett?"

Tommy nodded cautiously.

"Are y'on your own?"

He nodded again.

"Wait here till half ten. Monty will be here then." He glanced around at the rest of the spooky clientele. Everybody seemed to be minding their own business.

"Can I buy you a drink?" Tommy offered.

"*You* buy me a *drink*? Fuck off. I don't drink with pigs. Anyway, I don't drink!" He scratched the scar gently. "Half ten." He turned and left.

Tommy headed up to the bar. "Half of lager, please."

Some of the locals looked around on hearing the foreign accent.

Tommy checked his watch. Twenty minutes, he thought. "Cheers, mate."

"A pound twenty-five . . . *mate*," aped the barman.

Tommy was about to return to his chair when his name was called from behind the bar. He turned around.

"Are you Tommy?" another barman asked.

"Yeah."

"Phone."

He crossed to the end of the bar to the public telephone. "Hello."

"Turn left when you leave the pub and walk to the end of the street to the main junction. Turn left. Ye'll see the pub. Three doors up on yer right. Grady's. Be there at quarter to eleven. No later." The voice was gravelly and very Dublin.

"Who's this?" Tommy asked.

There was no reply.

Tommy drank a mouthful from the glass and put it down. As he went to push the door, a big man stood in front of him and tripped him up. He grabbed Tommy's arm, preventing him from getting clobbered by the swinging door. "Sorry about that," he said in a deep northern accent.

"No problem," replied Tommy, straightening his jacket. He looked up at the man. Jesus Christ, he thought. He felt his heart skipping beats faster than a Buddy Holly song.

A sinister smile spread across the northerner's face.

"Don't I know you?" Tommy asked nervously.

"Maybe you do," he replied coyly. "It's a small world." He laughed and pushed his way through the swing-door and out on to the street.

Tommy watched him from inside as he sat up on to

470

the huge motor-bike. With a loud roar of power, he disappeared into the wet, misty night.

* * *

Grady's was a kip. A real pigsty. Drinkers gathered in small noisy groups at the bar. They didn't come to admire Mr Grady's decor. Everytime someone stepped into the pub, a chilling hush would fall instantly on the riff-raff. The floor was covered with sawdust. A few small tables surrounded a large, empty floor space, big enough to accomodate twenty dancing couples. A television boomed above the bar. A large group, standing underneath, shouted at the screen. "You're meant to be boxin' him, not fuckin' kissin' him. Go on, *kill* him!" roared one of the crowd. The pub was so dark, it was difficult to make out its shape and size.

Tommy walked uneasily to the bar. He scouted around for his man. He'd seen a photograph of Monty McGrath. They'd spoken briefly a few times on the phone. That was about it. He couldn't see a face that matched the picture. Then again, it was difficult to see anyone's face in here.

"What can I get ya?" the stout, heavily-tattooed barman bellowed.

"I'm looking for Monty!" Tommy shouted.

The barman stared indignantly at him. He leaned across the bar. "I mean what can I get ya to fuckin' drink, son?"

Tommy wasn't sure what to say. "Lager . . . please." He waited, afraid to look around. The mention of

Monty McGrath's name had brought all conversation in the immediate corner to a grinding halt.

"Lager." The barman slapped the pint down on the bar. "Two pounds twenty." He held out his hand.

"I only wanted a half," he replied in a cockney accent he was quickly trying to disguise.

"We don't serve *halves*!"

Tommy handed over the money.

"Have you got your ticket for the fight?" He grinned.

Tommy assumed that he was referring to the boxing match on the screen. As Tommy drank, he watched over the rim of his glass. People were moving away from him. Almost making room for what was about to happen, it seemed. Within seconds, Tommy stood alone at one end of the bar. He looked to his right. Halfway down the bar, two men were embroiled in a heated argument. The barman lowered the volume on the TV. No one seemed interested in the boxing any more. All eyes focused on the two individuals facing each other. One of them, the smaller of the two, kept apologising profusely. Now and then, he'd scratch his head or wipe his forehead. He fumbled with his pockets and fidgeted with his jacket collar.

The other man, much taller and composed, played with a large fish-knife. He juggled it in the air. Suddenly he grabbed the smaller man's left hand and slapped it, palm-down, spread-eagle, on the bar top. The silence, apart from the small man's pleadings, was uncanny. He looked around. "A bit of *palm play*," he snorted.

"Please, Monty, I swear, I didn't mean to. It's just

472

that the brother got into a bit of trouble with some gear he'd stolen. I only gave it to him for a loan . . . "

The bulky man cut him short. "What have I always told you? Ask may you borrow it, before you spend it." His dispassionate voice rhymed off the words like a schoolteacher. "You could have asked me. But you didn't. You thought I wouldn't notice." He bared his ferocious looking half-brown teeth and took a deep breath.

"No, Monty . . . *please*!" The small man's knees knocked together.

Monty McGrath raised the knife to chest level directly above the man's hand. "Let this be a warning." He slammed the needle-sharp point of the weapon down between the man's index and middle fingers. It dug deep into the wooden surface, missing the man's bones by a fraction. The small man yelped. He spread his fingers wider. Monty pulled the knife back into the air. This time, the point of the blade came down twice as quickly, twice as barbarically. It slammed down between the index and middle fingers, then up again and down between the middle finger and ring finger. Then back up. The man sobbed uncontrollably, begging Monty to stop. His voice was getting harder to hear now as the knife danced up and down, in and out, between all the finger spaces, with the power of a liquidiser. Spectators watched in horror as blood began to spatter about the bar. Monty was whisking an egg and he wasn't doing a very tidy job. The victim was on his knees as Monty, with a heaving grunt, brought the knife down one last time straight through the main knuckle of the man's middle finger. He let his wrist go, leaving the man impaled on the bar counter, weeping uncontrollably.

Tommy leaned against the bar. He was sick. He had his own violent streak. He knew that. But this was taking revenge to the extreme. Two men helped the crippled individual to his feet. He let out a blood-curdling roar as one of his colleagues pulled the knife out of his hand and handed it to the barman.

"Take him up to the Mater," Monty shouted as he sipped his mineral water. "Another fuckin' cleaning bill!" he quipped, looking down at his blood-spattered shirt. He wiped his brow.

The barman wiped up the mess. "Come on now, ladies an' gents, finish up your drinks. Have youse no homes to go home to?" he called. Drinkers chatted, laughed, joked and supped. This was a regular occurrence. A form of repentance.

* * *

Monty "The Ferret" McGrath loved his home-town. He was Dublin through and through. Many of his disciples would go as far as to say that Monty had a market share in Dublin. His own market. In fact, Monty liked to think he owned it. He'd started out in the criminal profession at the age of eight, robbing the shrine money from the local church on his way home from school. Eventually, he graduated to shop-lifting; then joy-riding; then selling drugs to local schoolkids; then payroll robberies. Some even said, off the record, he was a hitman. You name it, Monty had done it, including a stretch of ten years in prison for murder. He'd earned his name, The Ferret, because of his uncanny ability to disappear underground at a moment's notice. He regularly told undercover cops that they were only paddling in the shallow end when it came to the city's underground subcultures; drugs, prostitution and protection. His scraggy black hair and unkempt moustache, not to mention his monstrous physique, nurturing a black belt in karate, 10th dan, made him a formidable threat to any other toerag in the area. McGrath was famous for his wicked sense of humour. One Christmas, he walked up behind an undercover detective in a city centre pub carrying a balloon. He held the balloon to the back of the cop's head and touched it with a lighted cigarette. The detective crapped himself from the fright. McGrath just laughed.

* * *

The barman leaned across the counter and whispered to Monty. He nodded at the corner.

Monty turned and looked across at the tall, dark stranger. "Mister Barrett," he muttered quietly. "At long last we meet. Have a seat." Monty McGrath walked over to a table. Three men sat drinking. "Fuck off home, the lot of youse. I need this table. Anyway, youse've had too fuckin' much to drink!"

The three men vacated the table instantly.

"Sit down. I don't have long." He beckoned to Tommy.

The barman approached the table. "Do you want a drink, Monty?"

"Ballymagash." He gestured to Tommy's glass. "Drink?"

"Lager, please," replied Tommy.

"Hey, Billy," Monty shouted at the barman, "check the bin-liners you're putting out for the binman. You don't want to put out the wrong black sack, do you?" He sniggered as he looked back at Tommy.

Tommy wasn't amused.

"That was a stupid fuck-up, wasn't it, son?"

Tommy nodded. He said nothing.

"I mean to say, one of your men gets whacked and your money ends up in the back of a fucking bin lorry. What the fuck happened? You called me and said you'd loads of coins. Then I hear you give it to Benny the binman."

"It's a long story."

"Too fuckin' long, if you ask me. You promised me the goods three months ago. I'm still waiting."

"It's difficult to buy *goods* if you don't have the money to spend."

"*Your* fuckin' problem, not mine! And don't get fuckin' cheeky. You wouldn't get out o' here alive if half o' these in here knew who you were. You told me *you* were looking after everything. I hope you left no smelly trails behind your little balls-up."

Tommy shook his head. "That's my problem.

You're not involved. One or two minor things to take care of. Nothing major."

"Nothing *major*?" Monty looked up at the stocky barman. "Nothing major, he says. You owe me five grand and you don't call that major? When I got involved with you, it was 'cos you guaranteed you could get me enough gear to make me rich. Seems to me you only open your mouth to change feet. Does anyone know about our little tie-up?"

"No."

"Well, then, what gooey little plan have you got in mind this time?"

Tommy leaned forward. "The consignment is still in place. We've moved it around for a while, just in case. It'll be here next week, hopefully."

"*Hopefully?* I don't know what that word means. Billy, what does *hopefully* mean?"

"Don't know, Monty. Never heard of it," replied the barman.

* * *

Paul Flaherty sat patiently at the bar close to the heated, cloaked conversation. He wasn't interested in drugs. Far from it. He despised all peddlers, dealers, trippers and junkies. They all fell into the same category: scum. He just wanted to hear the names. "Cup of coffee, please." He listened.

The undercover officer smoked his pipe as he checked the racing results in *The Star*. Suddenly, he exploded into a violent fit of coughing. "Fucking pipe!" he croaked.

"Should've stuck to fags," Paul Flaherty muttered.

"Sorry?"

"You don't smoke a pipe. If you did, you'd know how not to cough like that. You people should just stick to your twenty Major."

"Oh yeah, so you're an expert on pipe-smoking?"

"You could say that. I smoked it for eight years. I'd nothing else to do. I gave it up two weeks ago."

The detective studied the northerner. "Don't I know your face?"

Paul smiled as he got off the stool. "Don't think so. People say I look very like Noel Edmonds. Forget the coffee," he shouted to the barman.

"See you."

"Don't think so."

* * *

"You expect me to give you *how much*?" shouted Monty in disbelief.

"A ton," replied Tommy nervously.

"*One hundred grand?* You must be fuckin' joking! Haven't I already got you a boat for the job?"

"And a gun. A .38 Special. Nothing else will do."

"The gun's no problem, but the money could be. You keep throwin' your money in the bin and you could find yourself in a lot of trouble."

"No sugar . . . no smack! Simple as that." Tommy drew his breath. He leant forward. "And *always* remember one thing. If it wasn't for me, you could be doing time for drugs in the Scrubs right now. If I hadn't let you slip away from that pub after we raided it that night, you just mightn't have been so lucky."

Monty scratched his stubbly chin. He sat back in the chair and belched. Then he slapped his knees. "Why not? Nothing ventured, nothing gained." He sat forward. "But let me tell you this, Detective Constable Barrett, if anything goes wrong on this one, I'll have your two balls decorating the top of my Christmas tree for the next ten years and those two big fuckin' ugly ears for wing mirrors!" He stood up. "Fifty up front. The rest when I see the goods. You'll have it in forty-eight hours. And don't be fuckin' ringin' me. I like my friends to think that I socialise with a gracious sort of self-respecting type."

* * *

It was half eleven when Tommy picked up the phone. "Could I speak with Nikki, please?" he asked politely.

A voice twittered excitedly at the far end. "This is Nikki."

"Hi, it's Tommy, how are you?" he said calmly.

The bar was almost clear. Frank was busy telling Father Duffy how his late mother might have come into a huge fortune, since a rich aunt of hers had died in Boston.

"God rest her decent soul. You know, Frank, I'd say she didn't want any of youse to know about it until she'd got through the gates of Heaven. That way, you'd find it easier to cope with her departure from this life. She always had her family's best interests at heart, God bless her. I'd say she said to the good Lord, Jesus," he bowed his head, "that she'd no use for such huge money. 'I know,' she probably said to the good Lord, 'it would be best spent in the hands of my dear family. Let's do it!' And, of course, your dear mother not being a woman to take no for an answer, Jesus done it." The elderly priest beat his breast three times and swallowed his fourth large whiskey. He gulped. "In memory of a wonderful woman. A saint, never to have said a bad word about anyone or to have cursed anything in her precious life."

Just then, a man came in through the side door. "Excuse me, Father."

Father Duffy swung around. "What is it, Mickey Dunne?"

"Someone's just stolen the two wheels off your bicycle."

"The rotten fuckin' *bastards*!" he roared. He downed the last of his drink and grabbed his jacket.

"If I catch the culprit, he'll be singing in the schoolboy's choir for the rest of his fucking life!" He rushed past Nikki and slammed the door behind him.

She was so deep in her phone conversation that she didn't even notice the ecclesiasticial commotion. "Why didn't you tell me that you were going?" she asked painfully.

"Because I got word that I started the job the following day. You were working, so I didn't have time to tell you."

"I didn't mean to be so mad with you last week . . .

that night, like, when I told you to leave. I was kind of sorry afterwards."

"It's OK," he replied softly. "Do you remember when I told you that . . . I loved you?"

There was a long silence. "Yeah," she said quietly.

"Well, I meant it. I *do* love you."

"You're just saying that, Tommy. I don't think you know *what* love is."

"Nikki, listen to me. I've had a lot of time to think this all out since I got here. I want you to come over to me. To be here with me."

Nikki held the receiver away from her ear. She couldn't believe what she was hearing. The world's greatest bastard was pouring out feelings she never knew were in him. Not only that, but here he was, nearly five hundred miles away, screaming *I love yous* down the phone at her. Her heart beat faster and faster. She tried to weigh up the pros and cons. She was crazy about him. She was wild for his body. Basically, she just wanted to eat the bloke. On the other hand, she hated his dark side. The sinister side. More importantly, what would Jamie say? Maybe it *was* all over between the two of them, but it was going to look as if there might have been something going on behind Jamie's back. After all, he was *her* boyfriend. No need to guess which argument was winning . . . hands down. "But what about my job?" she asked.

"What *job?* I only asked you to get *that* job because I needed some inside information. Come over to Dublin and we'll both be working close to each other. I've a friend here who'll get you a job . . . a real good job."

"But, Tommy, I'm enjoying myself working *here*. They're really nice people."

"Nikki, do you love me?"

It was a question she wasn't expecting. She had to think. Ah, shit, "Yes, I do," she replied shyly. She did. At least, she *thought* she did.

"Well, I love you. Now, what's more important, that you work there and I stay here? That we're both apart and miserable, or that we're together and happy?"

"Happy and together, I suppose. But why is all this only coming out now, Tommy? You've always been hard pushed to smile at me, never mind telling me now that you're crazy about me."

"I suppose that's what distance does to people. I know it's made me take stock and think about what means most to me. And now I'm sure, Nikki."

Nikki looked at the phone in disbelief. If this was what going away had done to Tommy, she liked it. Maybe he should've gone away more often. Maybe he would've told her all this a lot sooner. She looked up at the bar. Frank was busy herding out the last few punters. He waved at Nikki. She wanted to say yes there and then and get the next available flight out but she didn't. "I'll have to think about it," she said quietly.

Tommy took a deep breath and bit his lip. It was important that he sounded sincere. "OK," he replied. "Look, I can understand how you feel. This must come as a bit of a shock to you. But I'll need to know tomorrow."

"Why so quickly?"

"Because," he paused, "I have a surprise for you. Before we settle down here in Dublin, I'm going to take you on a little holiday."

"Where?" Nikki asked teasingly.

"France. On a yacht."

"Tommy, I don't believe it! But where do we get the money?"

"You just leave all that to me. Actually, it's all arranged. Next Friday, you and I and a couple of friends of mine set sail by luxury yacht for the coast of Brittany. All you have to do is say *yes*." He waited. "Well?"

Nikki squeezed the receiver. "Maybe. Yes. I mean . . . I'll call you tomorrow."

"What time?"

"Tomorrow evening, half five. I'll be on my tea-break."

"OK, half five, tomorrow. Talk then."

"Tommy," Nikki shouted.

"Yeah?"

"I love you," she whispered.

Tommy sighed. "Yeah, OK, half five tomorrow." He put the phone down and clapped his hands once. Then he yelped with excitement. He was now convinced beyond any doubt that Nikki Coffey had to be the stupidest, most easily-led woman he'd ever come across in his entire life. And, more importantly, she was the ideal candidate for this very delicate, very dangerous operation. It was best that she knew as little as possible about the next few days and all they entailed. Nikki had been told all she needed to know to keep her very happy.

Frank sat at the small desk in his bedroom. He'd half-finished a letter to Jamie. It had been pushed to one side of the spacious worktop. Right now, he was poring over income tax figures. The most dreaded moment. His returns were already six weeks late and he would now have to endure the all-night task of claiming back the few quid which were rightfully his. The swivel chair squeaked as he mumbled and fidgeted to himself. Every now and then, he'd mutter a four-letter word and draw a line through figures he'd been totting up. He didn't notice Nikki standing behind him in the doorway until the door creaked. He jumped and looked around. "*Jesus* . . . Nikki, you gave me a fright!"

"Sorry. I couldn't sleep," she replied quietly. "I was wondering if you'd mind if I went downstairs and got myself a drink."

"Not at all," Frank muttered, as he stared at the figures. "You can get me one while you're at it." He looked around. She was gone. He sat back in the chair and reached across for the unfinished letter. He smiled as he read it. An hour had passed since he'd spoken to her on the phone. And here he was, trying to think of little trivialities to fill four pages. Tonight it wasn't coming to him so easily. He rubbed his eyes and left them closed, thinking of her that morning in the airport hotel. He thought of her trim body. Then he imagined her working out in the gym: lifting the weights, covered in a shimmering coat of perspiration.

Her vest wet down the back and front. Her biceps forcing her cleavage together. Her deep, heavy breathing.

"Are you asleep?" An elbow nudged him in the shoulder.

"Eh, what?" he shouted. He jumped forward in the chair, almost knocking over the two drinks that Nikki had left on the worktop.

"Careful." Nikki grabbed the toppling glass. "I thought you were asleep."

"Asleep? No. Shattered? Yes." Frank picked up the glass. It was red-hot. "Ouch!"

"Sorry. I meant to tell you it was hot. That'll put you to sleep. Hot whiskey, Nikki-style."

Frank sipped the drink. "Mmmm. Nice. What's in it?"

Nikki winked. "Secret recipe. Just shout if you want another." She made herself comfortable in the big armchair near the television. She nodded at the papers on the worktop. "What's all that?" she asked cheekily.

"VAT." Frank plunged two fingers into his mouth, showing his contempt.

"Not nice, then?"

"Like having a hot poker shoved up your . . . " Realising the company he was keeping, Frank's eyes opened wide. "Jesus, I didn't mean to be so rude."

Nikki burst out laughing. "Don't be silly."

"I'm just tired. Need a good holiday. That's all that's wrong."

Nikki cupped her glass and said nothing.

Frank looked at her carefully in the dim light. "You've something to tell me."

"How do you know?"

"Well, it's not often I get a strange woman sitting in my bedroom in a waist-length dressing-gown at twenty to two in the morning."

Nikki smiled cheekily. "*Strange* woman?"

Frank threw the pen on the table. "OK, so what is it? You want to turn the whole place into a trendy, up-market London restaurant? Or you'd like to turn the upstairs rooms into a B & B for late-night drinkers? Or . . ."

Nikki gently cut across him. "I'd like a few days off to go on a holiday with my boyfriend."

Frank raised his eyebrows. "*Boyfriend?* You've been keeping this very quiet."

Nikki nodded. "He's asked me to sail to France with him next weekend. Private yacht."

"Next weekend's out, unless Ray Flynn decides to come back. I haven't seen him for three days. And now that I've had a chance to think about it, I'm not sure that I *want* him back." Then it dawned on him what Nikki'd just said. "Private *what*? Who is this tycoon and, more importantly, does Frank McCabe know him?"

Nikki could feel her face turn red. "Well, actually, that's what I wanted to talk to you about."

Frank was suspicious. "Is there something wrong?"

Nikki shook her head. "No." She took a large sip of hot whiskey.

"Well, what do you want to talk about?"

"Tommy."

Frank froze. "*Tommy?*" He sat forward. "Tommy Barrett?"

486

Nikki bent her head.

"You're going to France with Tommy Barrett? Are you *mad*?" he shouted.

"Yes," said Nikki. "And why shouldn't I go? He was the only one who asked me. And no, I'm not mad. Anyway, I don't see why it's any of your business who I go anywhere with. I only asked for a few days off. I don't ask about your love life, do I?"

"I wouldn't mind if you *did* ask about Jamie. You *are* meant to be her best friend. Or so she thinks!"

Nikki looked at Frank.

"Nikki, look. I'm not your father. I don't want to be your father. You're old enough to make up your own mind about who you choose to hang around with. But . . . " He paused. "I just don't know. I think you're making a big mistake getting involved with this guy." He felt like telling her what he knew but he had no hard proof that any of it was true. She'd probably think that *he* was mad.

"Do you want another hot whiskey?" she asked.

Frank nodded. "Yeah, why not? They're already six bloody weeks late. Another twenty-four hours isn't going to make much difference."

"What's six weeks late?" Nikki demanded.

"The tax returns. Ah, nothing. Thanks."

Nikki quietly left the room with the two empty glasses. Frank kicked the table.

* * *

Two hours and four hot whiskeys each later they had

argued and made up, and fought and agreed to disagree dozens of time. The one thing neither could see eye to eye about was Tommy Barrett. Frank agreed to give her the time off. He said that if she'd been going on holidays with anyone else, he'd have been happy to give her two months off.

Frank lay in his bed staring into space. Their arrangement seemed strange, he thought. Here were two Irish people, a man and a woman, sharing the same house. Their partners were both in Ireland. Nikki wanted to be with a man who'd turned Jamie's life into a nightmare. She was even willing to sacrifice a week's wages so that she could go off and have a good time with that bastard! Frank thumped the mattress. He was totally confused. Jamie would go beserk if she thought that Nikki was fooling around with Tommy when her back was turned. Although, under the circumstances, she might be relieved to have him *off* her back, his desires focused on someone else. Someone with no sense.

On one hand, he felt he should tell Jamie. On the other, there was no point. It would only upset her more. And she'd probably end up murdering Nikki. She needed to forget about Tommy, not counsel his new girlfriend. He heard music coming from Nikki's room. He looked at his watch. Ten past four. He was wide awake. Obviously, so was she. He felt bad about some of the things he'd said. Maybe an apology would help.

He threw on his jacket and walked down the landing. He listened at her door for a moment before knocking. There was definitely music playing. He tapped on the door.

"Yeah?" a sleepy voice asked.

He opened the door slowly. "Are you asleep?"

"That sounds a bit Irish," she replied.

"I just wanted to say I was sorry for some of the things I said earlier," he said humbly.

"Only *some* of them?"

"Well . . . " He stood in the doorway awkwardly.

"Are you going to come in?"

Frank closed the door behind him.

"Sit down." She pointed to the side of the bed.

Frank moved nearer.

Nikki sat up in her bed.

As Frank sat down, he noticed that her dressing-gown was gone.

She was wearing a thin white vest. That seemed to be all. In the dim light, she looked sultry. Her arms and shoulders were darkly tanned.

He didn't want to get too close. Sitting at the end of the bed would do fine.

"So . . . what did you want to say that you didn't say earlier?" she asked in an alluring voice.

Frank could see the sides of her large breasts protruding from the small vest as she clasped her raised knees in her arms.

"Do you like them?"

Frank got a fright at her question. He wasn't quite sure what to say. "Sorry?"

Nikki looked down at her breasts. "I said do you like them?" She nodded. "My tits," she whispered.

"That's not what I came in for, Nikki," Frank said awkwardly. "I came in to say that whatever you want to do, you should do it and don't let anybody else ever tell you how to live your life. And . . . yes, I do like them," he spluttered. "Wouldn't any man?"

Nikki moved her legs further apart and took a deep breath. Her breasts pushed forward against the thin vest. Her enormous nipples pressed hard against the thin fabric.

Frank could feel himself getting aroused. He tried to find something else to look at. Something to take his mind off what was happening. He noticed three empty spirit glasses on the table beside her bed. Four and three, he thought. Jesus, that makes seven. "I'd better go." He coughed and stood up, trying hard to keep his jacket closed and the unmistakable swelling covered.

"What was that you said about 'doing whatever you want to do'?" Nikki crawled across the bed towards Frank.

"I'll talk to you in the morning," Frank said quickly. "Get some sleep."

"Great legs," Nikki shouted. "A jacket and no trousers. And you mean to tell me that you came in here to talk about the weather?" Nikki was standing now, between Frank and the bedroom door. Her breasts bounced about beneath the vest as she stepped towards him. "Why don't we both get some sleep . . . together?" She took hold of Frank's right hand and ran the tips of his fingers across her hardened nipples. Back and forth. Then she pressed her breast hard into his palm.

Frank took a deep breath. His huge hand just about cupped it gently. And that said something about her breasts. It was make-your-mind-up time, he thought. Stay, and it happens.

"Come on, Frank. Who's to know? You and me. For old time's sake?" She lifted the vest up over her head revealing her sleek, lustrous bust. She swayed, almost naked now, in time to the music, running her hands across her tits and down her ribs, breathing deeply so that each bone stood out firmly through her chestnut-tanned skin. She slipped her fingers inside her pants and sighed, causing her robust frame to pulsate. Her peaks were rock solid.

Frank couldn't help but admire them.

Then she forced his jacket back over his broad shoulders. Before he knew it, her hand had slipped inside his boxer shorts. She cupped his balls and played with his stiff cock. "Jesus, Frank," she moaned. "Let's get into bed, come on."

He was moaning, almost gasping to catch his breath. He wanted to. Throw caution to the wind. But then he thought of the morning in the airport hotel. Looking into Jamie's eyes while they made passionate love together. Nothing could ever match that experience. How she held him tightly as he came inside her. It was so different to anything he'd felt before. He knew nothing could ever be better than that. He wanted to finish the letter. Now there was more he needed to say in it. This would destroy everything. Or would it? "*Stop!*" he shouted. He grabbed her wrists and pushed her away from him.

Nikki looked shocked. Then embarrassed. She tried to cover her breasts with her arms. She looked around for her vest.

As she searched around the dark floor, Frank noticed she was swaying precariously. He picked up the vest which lay at his feet and handed it to her. "Here," he said softly.

Nikki grabbed the vest. There were tears in her eyes.

"Please, don't take this personally. But I can't get involved. It's not right . . . it's not meant. Do you know what I mean?" he added, desperately searching for the right words.

Nikki turned her back to him as she struggled to get the vest back over her cleavage. "Who said anything about getting involved?" she rasped. "I just thought you might fancy getting into bed with me. That's all I thought. *Involved!*" she mimicked. "You'd be so lucky!" she slurred.

Frank took a deep breath. "I'm seeing Jamie."

"*So?*"

"It's quite serious. And I just don't think it would be fair to . . . "

Nikki stared at him. "To what? Have a *bit on the side*? Is that what you're trying to say, Frank? You can tell me. I'm open-minded. Unlike you!"

"That's not what I mean. It's just that I'm upset after what has happened to her. And I'm worried that . . . "

"Oh fuck all that, Frank. Gimme a break. Heroes don't exist. Just like the tooth fairy. Speaking of fairies, maybe you're gay?"

Frank looked stunned. He shook his head. "'Course I'm not *gay*!"

"Well, I'm not talking about involvement, I'm

talking about *sex*! Anyway, what's that Jamie bitch got that I haven't?" she shouted. "Well? Answer me. She hasn't got a body like this. Her tits aren't half the size of these." She stuck her chest out. "And she's shit in bed! So don't come crawling back to me when it's too late."

"I suppose Tommy told you that."

"What?"

"That she's shit in bed?"

"Maybe."

Frank walked towards the door. He turned. "Well, you can tell Tommy for me that's she's anything but shit in bed. As for you, Nikki . . . I just want to say one thing to you. No one appreciates a beautiful woman more than me. You've got one of the most amazing bodies I've ever seen. And I think it's also fair to say that I haven't seen a pair of breasts like those since my mother refused to let us watch Marilyn Monroe on telly when we were kids. Yes, I suppose I would love to, just, as you put it, for old times sake. But, you see, Nikki, life's not that straightforward. In fact, as I think you're about to find out, life is very complicated. Anyway, as I said, nothing would give me more pleasure than getting into bed with you right now. You can see that. But what about the next time? And the next? That's when you begin to wish it wasn't all so complicated. See you in the morning. And no hard feelings . . . pardon the pun!" He closed the door behind him.

Nikki sat down on the side of the bed. All of a sudden, she felt very cold. Almost ashamed of herself.

* * *

It was twenty past five when the phone rang in the comfortable semi-detached house in Blanchardstown.

A sleepy voice answered. "Hello," the man muttered.

"Superintendent Blaney?" a crisp voice asked at the other end of the line.

"Speaking."

"Sir, it's Gerry O'Connell. I'm sorry for ringing you so late, sir, but we've just got a location on Barrett's phone call last night."

The detective leaned up on his elbow and cupped the mouthpiece with his hand. "Go on, where?" he asked eagerly.

"Well, sir, you're not going to believe this. But the woman he rang was in a pub in north London. The Clover Tap, sir. It was a public call-box, sir."

"A public call-box in the *Clover Tap?*" the inspector asked in disbelief. "*The Clover Tap?* That's an Irish pub. What the fuck would Barrett be ringing an Irish pub for?"

"I know, sir. That's what I was thinking. It doesn't make sense. But it's definitely the right number. He was chatting to a woman with a Dublin accent. He told her he loved her and that he'd take her to France on a yacht next Friday."

The inspector sat on the side of his bed. "A *yacht? This* Friday?"

"Yes sir. Along with a couple of friends of his."

"Did he mention McGrath?"

"No, sir."

"Right, that's enough over the phone, son," he said. "Get your team in for ten bells."

"Ten this morning?"

"No, *Christmas* morning. *Yes*, of course, this morning. Full conference. And O'Connell . . . "

"Yes, sir?" the young officer asked anxiously.

"Well done, son. Good work."

"Thank you, sir. Goodnight."

"Now we have you," muttered Blaney. He smiled and went back to sleep.

* * *

It seemed like the middle of the day when Frank opened his eyes. Not again, he shouted. He sat bolt upright in the bed and grabbed the small alarm clock. Twenty to ten. *"Nikki!"* he roared at the top of his voice. No answer. Come to think of it, no smell of home cooking. He ran out on to the landing. Silence. The phone was ringing in the bar. Frank grabbed his trousers and thundered downstairs. No sign of life. No sign of Nikki. The phone stopped just as he reached it. Shit, he shouted. He ran back upstairs. *"Nikki!"* he roared again. No answer. He tapped on her bedroom door and opened it slowly. Her bed was made up. The room was empty. All her belongings were gone. A note lay on the table.

Dear Frank,

This is the only way I know right now of saying sorry to you. I really didn't mean to offend you. Obviously

*seven hot whiskeys don't make me feel sleepy. Please
don't tell Jamie about what happened. Maybe sometime
I'll have the nerve to tell her about Tommy and me.
Please say a prayer that it works for the two of us because
I really do love him. And I think he really does love me.
I hope you and Jamie will be very happy together. Please
look after her because she really is one in a million. Tell
her I love her. Sorry about the short notice.*

Love,

Nikki xxx.

*P.S. It's a pity you and I didn't meet each other a
long time ago . . .*

Frank searched the small note for a phone number or a
follow-on address. Nothing. She was gone. Vanished
into thin air. He ran back down the staircase again. He
looked at the side door of the pub. Sure enough, she'd
let herself out and thrown the keys back through the
letterbox. He sat on a stool in the empty pub and
scratched his head in disbelief. He was stranded.
Everyone was gone, he thought. What the hell am I
going to do now? Just then, there was a loud knock at
the door.

"Nikki," he called. He ran to the main door.

"Frank, are you there? It's Father Duffy?"

Frank opened the door. "Howya, Father.
Everything all right?" he asked nervously.

"I should be asking you that, Frank. I was returning
from nine Mass when I noticed that pair sitting outside
the pub and no sign of life inside. I thought I'd knock
and check."

Frank looked over the priest's head and noticed a dark-blue Cavalier parked across the street. The two men inside seemed to be watching his conversation with Father Duffy.

"They're cops," he muttered.

"Come on in, Father." Frank hurried the priest inside. He closed the door quickly behind him. "How do you know they're police?"

"Because I asked them on my way to say Mass this morning." He raised his eyes to the roof. "Half seven in the morning, if you don't mind, and they're sitting outside. I thought it was a bit early to be sneaking into a public house. So I tapped on the window and said, 'Have you two no jobs or homes to be going to at this ungodly hour of the day instead of waiting for those doors to open as if youse were both in a trance?'"

"And what did they say to you, Father?"

The priest blessed himself. "The cheeky bastards told me to fuck off and mind me own business, that they were on official police business and that they'd drag me up to the station by the scapulars if I interfered any further."

Frank suppressed a smile. "You must have got a shock."

Father Duffy looked around the empty pub. "A shock? It was like a thunderbolt. I've got the shakes. Give us a double whiskey and water, Frank. No ice. For the nerves, like."

Chapter Twenty-Seven

The conference room at Harcourt Terrace, the headquarters of the Central Detective Unit for the Dublin Metropolitan Area, was packed. Rarely had the redbrick building played host to such a gathering of highly distinguished cops; the drugs squad, the Serious Crime squad and six members of the Emergency Response Unit, known as the ERU; a highly trained bunch of professionals, ready to engage in the most dangerous situations at a moment's notice. Young and superfit, this small band of elite, heavily-armed strikers provided the weaponry back-up required by other, more specialised, detectives and police officers. In the smoke-filled conference room, filled with dirty-shaven, red-eyed individuals wearing polyester suits, they were conspicuous, if only because of their trendy, sleek image. Having caused resentment and ruffled a few cosy feathers in certain key areas, they'd become known affectionately in the force as the Glory Boys.

The room was big and spacious. A large map of Ireland and a blackboard dominated the wall at the top. Desks and chairs waited to be occupied. The general feeling was one of optimistic anticipation. Despite the lousy pay, most of the officers present agreed that the overtime had been worth it.

The clock struck ten. Detective Superintendent Joe Blaney walked in through a door at the top of the room. He was known in the force as Boulder, for a number of reasons. When he took a stand on an issue, there was no changing his mind. But also because the men had always looked up to Joe Blaney as a rock of sense and encouragement. At fifty-two, he'd dedicated his entire working life to the police. He was a tough, no-shit bastard who expected total dedication in return for respect. His blotchy red, "whiskey" face was beginning to expose the toll which thirty-two years of investigative work, ten of those as a senior detective superintendent, had taken on him. He was an accessible, no-holds-barred man who hated people standing on his shadow.

His wife had left him eight years before. As she said, she'd had enough.

He came home one night, after a gruelling five-day kidnap hunt in the midlands, only to find a short note from her saying she'd gone. He later found out that she'd been having an affair with a young handyman who'd been decorating the house.

She could never understand why he'd go drinking with his men in the club in Harrington Street every evening instead of coming home to her. She just wanted to talk about the house . . . their recent holiday in Rome . . . the new conservatory he'd promised her . . . her night classes in flower-arranging.

Joe, on the other hand, was forbidden to talk to anyone, including his wife, about a lot of the top secret work that his department undertook. He tried to explain to her that he'd be in bad humour if he was to go straight home with all this hot property bottled up inside him. So he felt the logical thing to do was to blow off steam by having a few beers with the lads after work.

Joe's wife always felt that *that* was Joe's problem . . . he was too logical, all the time. And he drank too much.

He was flanked by a younger detective carrying files. He coughed as he removed his jacket. Silence fell. The Walther PPK automatic in his shoulder holster reflected the rays of sunlight streaming in through the window. A young member of the ERU nudged his partner as he spotted the gun. They both sniggered. The snub, known affectionately as the James Bond gun, had been exchanged for a more reliable weapon years ago. Typical of the Rock, he refused to give his back. Those standing near the back jostled for better positions.

"Morning, men," he said officiously.

A woman coughed repeatedly.

"And ladies," he added.

A general titter. Then silence. And business.

"I won't keep you long." He sat down at the long table and picked up a file. "Operation Motorhead, we have reason to believe, enters its final phase this week with the uncovering of important new information regarding our fishing trip. I feel I shouldn't have to repeat myself when I say this. The more experienced of you will understand why secrecy and discretion are the most important words in this room this morning, and in this operation overall, particularly at this stage. Those of you who've joined the operation for the first time this week may be tempted to discuss matters relating to its progress with your colleagues while having a drink after shift, or whatever. Let me emphasise one thing, lads. When you finish your shift, you leave *this* operation, and everything connected to *it*, behind you. Is that clear?"

A number of the younger men nodded.

Silence.

"The yacht, according to intelligence, left Howth marina last Wednesday. It hasn't been seen since. The owner is a well-known associate of our friend, Monty McGrath. He told friends that he was sailing to Blackpool. He never arrived. He flew back into Dublin airport from Manchester yesterday. We've reason to believe the yacht will return with the consignment. Possibly Thursday, more likely Friday, since a band of low pressure is moving in over the mid-Irish sea, making sailing conditions more favourable for such a vessel."

"Excuse me, sir," a voice shouted.

"Go ahead."

"Where will the consignment land?"

"Good question. Because the owner of the boat, which is more a cruiser than a yacht, I might add, is a lifelong member of the club, he should be able to get back into the country without any suspicion by arriving back at the berth he's owned for nearly fifteen years without any awkward questions being asked. So I would hazard a guess and say the smack will be brought straight into Howth."

Small groups muttered in agreement. If the Rock said Howth, it was going to be Howth.

"I'm now passing around a photograph of the vessel which I'd like you all to take a good look at. Give yourselves an idea of what you're looking for."

He paused.

"We will be backed up by the Navy and our *friends* in Customs."

Small groups booed and hissed. It was well-known that Joe Blaney didn't like the Customs people. They were too pushy. And they stood on his shadow.

"A three-man team from ERU will accompany Wylie and Flood aboard the LE Ciara. And please remember, all of you, that while on board a Navy vessel, the Navy call the shots."

Joe Blaney opened the thick file. "In the past twelve hours, I have received some very important information. There will now be a slight change in rota arangements. Detective Sergeant Bill Roly and Detective Tony Whelan . . . " He waited for acknowledgements.

"Here," they answered.

"You two will leave here before dawn on Wednesday morning and head for Wilson's guest-house overlooking the harbour. You will be checked in there by half seven, awaiting further instructions. Is that clear?"

The two men nodded. "Yes, sir."

Blaney looked back down at the notes he'd scribbled earlier.

"Detectives Wiley and Flood from the sub-aqua unit will be waiting to meet me in the St Lawrence at half two on Wednesday. Wait for me in the bar. No drinking." He looked at the two men with a wry smile.

"Yes, sir."

"McGovern, Smith, Canavan and Bell . . . you will man the communications van, known as the Terrier. It's a petrol-blue-coloured Ford Transit . . . windowless. It will be based close to the yacht club. All right?"

The men nodded.

"Brady, Gallagher and Conroy, from the traffic division. You will each be in charge of a Harley Davidson for the duration."

Some of the other officers hissed jealously at the mention of Harleys. The two female officers whistled. It broke the icy, anxious atmosphere in the room.

"Conroy."

"Yes, sir."

"I thought I asked you not to shave for the last few weeks."

"He hasn't," joked one of his colleagues. "That's four weeks' growth."

Everyone laughed.

"Quiet, Bell. Go ahead, Conroy."

"Sorry, sir. I forgot the other morning. I was half-shaved when I remembered."

Blaney ignored the laughter. "The purpose of the motor-bikes is for quick access and exiting where necessary. They'll also be easier to manoeuvre on the ramps in the marina. Bullet-proof vests are to be worn at *all* times by everyone. Is that understood?"

A general "yes".

"All local garda cars and units have been instructed to stay well away from the area. The public will be kept away also. And for God's sake, lads, don't all converge on the same spot together. OK? Right . . . any questions?"

A few hands were raised.

The inspector nodded to one. "Yes . . . Brady."

"What weapons will we carry, sir?"

"Good question. I was just about to get to that. Before I move on to that subject, any further questions based on what I've just been saying?"

"What about communicating with each other, sir?"

"I'm glad you asked that, Wiley. Now . . . no one is to try and make contact with any other group without coming through me first. Is that perfectly clear?"

Everyone nodded.

"The success of this operation could well be riding on this one crucial tactic. If you want to find out what anyone else is doing or what's going on generally, talk to *me* on the radio . . . *no one else!*"

He looked around the room again. "Conroy."

"Sir, what's this English copper like?"

Blaney shrugged his shoulders. "I've got to be honest, son, I'm not too sure. Apart from photographs and what we've been told by Scotland Yard, as well as what we've picked up on him ourselves, we don't know an awful lot, I'm afraid. He's bent *and* he's dangerous.

504

The Yard want to question him in relation to a rape incident. He was also involved in the drugs heist that went wrong in north London some weeks back. The night Jimmy Grant was murdered."

They waited for him to elaborate. He didn't.

"Any idea how many people we can expect to confront, sir?" Conroy continued.

"Well, this one's been giving me sleepless nights all week. I know, from what we've intercepted, that there'll be three people on board. Possibly a fourth, but I doubt it. How many of their people will be waiting for them, *if* they get ashore, is anyone's guess. That's something I'm hoping we won't have to deal with. They're containable while on a boat. Just remember that. I think the only word to describe our task is *vigilance*. Just keep your eyes open . . . all of you. That goes for the ones in the backs of your heads as well.

Now . . . let's talk about armoury. All of you will carry pistols. Colt model .59s and .38 Specials with the exception of ERU, Uzi sub-machineguns on semi-automatic only at all times. These must remain concealed and out of view unless I instruct you otherwise. In other words . . . no show-offs, all right? Also, on the subject of loaded weapons, I'd prefer to get this young man alive. Remember, he's no good to us on a morgue slab. We know that he's been chatting to Monty McGrath over the last few days. I've reason to believe that they're going for a big heroin haul, possibly the biggest we've ever seen. I'd like to get to it before McGrath does. He can have this stuff on the streets within a few hours of getting it. At that stage, we've lost. Without our English *friend*, McGrath will remain a pillar of our society. This bloke can lead us straight to his dirty doorstep. So, remember, this is no time to be trigger-happy. Final briefing will take place at Wilson's guest-house at half four on Friday. Any further questions before I finish?"

A hand went up.

"Yes, Larry Comerford?"

"Sir, we haven't been given our final instructions yet."

"That's right. You and Dave Mangan just stay behind for a couple of minutes. I want to have a quick chat. Everyone else all right for now? Thanks. Meeting over."

Blaney lit up a cigarette. The two detectives watched him anxiously. He inhaled and blew the smoke out in rings. "All right, lads," he started, "this is what's going to happen. And it goes no further than that door. Is that clear?"

The two young officers nodded excitedly.

"We've every reason to believe that Tommy Barrett is the mastermind behind the boat journey. Now, we expect him to talk to the boat crew before they set sail. As soon as he's closed down land-to-land communication with his crew, you'll move in swiftly and arrest him at the guest-house in town. The next time he'll be talking to his crew, he'll be in our hands telling them what *we* want them to do. Two birds with the one stone."

The two men nodded.

"Remember, this has got to be done quickly. No

press. No photographers. If his people get an inkling that something's wrong on this side, they might abort. There are promotions up for grabs if this goes well, there's grief to pay if it goes wrong."

He picked up the phone. "Garda Commissioner, please. It's Joe Blaney."

* * *

Jamie arrived home at about one. "I'm home," she shouted.

No answer.

She threw her jacket on to the end of the banister and walked into the kitchen. A small note lay on the table.

Jamie,

> *I'll be late this afternoon. Father Devereaux has left the parish mysteriously. No one seems to know where he's gone or why, so I'm busy getting a special lunch ready for the Bishop who's here for the day with Father O'Connor. If any of the neighbours are looking for me, make sure to tell them where I am. See you later.*

> *Love,*

> *Mam.*

> *PS. Don't forget to mention the Bishop if they ask.*

Jamie smiled. Her mother, in seventh heaven, serving up her favourite recipe of shepherd's pie and side salad to the Bishop. She filled the kettle. She walked back out to the phone in the hall to check for messages. Two. She pressed *play*. . . . beep . . .

"Hi, Jamie, it's Frank. Please give me a call when you get in. All hell is breaking loose here. Ray hasn't shown up for work for almost a week now. Philip is out sick. I'm on my own at the moment. I badly need some help. Maybe you'd think about flying over and giving me a dig out for a few days. I'll pay for the flight." Pause. "I love you." . . . beep . . .

. . . beep . . . "Hi, Jamie, it's Sheila. Thought you might like to come around for an undies party I'm throwing at the house tonight. Ladies only. You'll even get to try on and buy some if you like. Simpson had to fly to Nottingham this morning. Someone broke into the clinic overnight and stole five pints of prime bull's sperm. Perish the thought." She giggled. "See you later. Ring me. Bye." . . . beep . . . beep . . .

The loud ring of the doorbell almost made her jump through the roof. She could see a man wearing a cap through the frosted glass. She opened the door.

The postman stood there smiling. Then he looked surprised.

Jamie looked even more surprised.

The postman was Mr Nolan, her father's friend. The children on the road called him Finger Fucker. No one really knew why except the children who'd grown up around the area.

One day Jamie had to call to Nolan's house. She was eight. Her mother had promised to lend Mrs Nolan a special knitting pattern for an Aran sweater. She rang the doorbell. Mr Nolan opened the door. He invited her in. It was only when he closed the front door behind her that he told her Mrs Nolan was gone to the shop and would be back in a couple of minutes. He asked her to wait and have a glass of orange. He sat her on his lap. It wasn't like sitting on her daddy's lap. Mr Nolan kept moving her around. After a while he told her to leave the pattern and that he'd give it to Mrs Nolan when she got back. He made her promise that she would never tell anyone that he'd sat her on his lap. If she did, Mr Nolan's mad dog would climb in through her bedroom window some night when she was asleep and eat her up.

"Mr Nolan, I didn't know you were the postman," Jamie said.

Mr Nolan nodded and handed her a small bundle of assorted envelopes. "Ever since they made me redundant in Summerhill garage. It was either this or a lollipop man stopping traffic for the schoolkids in Malahide."

Jamie sneered. "Lollipop man. I thought you would've enjoyed that job."

"What'd you say?" he asked.

"Isn't it great you have a job, I said. Thanks." She closed the door. Her heart was thumping.

As she walked back to the kitchen, there was a tap on the window. She walked back to the door and opened it . . . this time not so hospitably. "What now?"

Mr Nolan handed her a piece of paper. "The man at the end of the street asked me to give you this."

As she took the page, he grabbed hold of her hand.

"Nice to have you home again."

Jamie slammed the door. "Dirty bastard!" she shouted.

The kettle was boiling. She was still shivering from shock. She made a mug of tea for herself and sat down to examine the post.

An envelope with the City Radio postmark and an English stamp on it. She opened it and read it quickly. Her boss, Mr Pickering, wanted her to come back, " . . . or even just call me to tell me how you are." Is this crawling or what? thought Jamie. I wonder, does his wife know how he feels about me?

A letter from Sunway Travel. She opened it dismissively and read the first couple of lines.

Dear Miss Carroll,
We would like to officially offer you the position . . .

She started to laugh. Then she threw her head back and caught her hair with her fist. *"Yes!"* she shouted. She couldn't believe the news. Despite her hotheaded departure during the interview, they still liked her enough to offer her the job. At last, it's all beginning to happen. At long last. And not a moment too soon.

As she sipped from the mug, she noticed the flimsy page lying on the worktop. She picked it up and opened it. It was written, obviously quickly, with a red biro. The handwriting was all over the place.

"Your house is being watched by the police . . . I couldn't call you because your phone is tapped . . . Use the address I gave you . . . "

She ran to the front door. No one there. A car was pulling up outside the house. Her mother climbed out of the passenger seat. She was talking in her posh accent. So, obviously, the driver must be very important.

"Oh, Jamie, you're home, pet," her mother shrilled from the footpath.

Pet, thought Jamie. She never called her or Lisa *pet* unless it was a very felicitous occasion.

"Your Grace, you'll have to come in and meet my eldest daughter, Jemima."

Jamie's face turned bright red. *Jemima!* She hadn't heard that name since her first day at school. No one called her Jemima and got away with it. Jamie, it was, since the day she learned to talk.

Sure enough, it was the bishop. Jamie recognised him from the news and from pictures in the papers. As they strolled up the small drive, Jamie's mother continued to talk at the top of her voice, alerting all of her neighbours to the visiting dignitary. "Ah, Nellie, come on over and meet Bishop Brophy," she called to her next-door neighbour. Nellie said hello and curtsied as she kissed the bishop's ring.

Jamie cringed at the sight of it. It reminded her of her Confirmation.

The bishop, however, seemed eager to get in out of the soft rainy afternoon. A small group of schoolchildren gathered around the gate.

"Your Grace," Mrs Carroll started proudly, "this is my eldest daughter, Jemima."

He smiled and extended his ring hand. "A pleasure to meet you, dear. You have a wonderful mother here. You're a very fortunate family."

Spare me, thought Jamie. "Nice to meet you too, eh, Bishop. And the name's Jamie, actually."

Her mother was not amused.

"Nicer again . . . Jamie," he enthused.

He was a big man, grossly overweight. Twenty-five stone, at least.

Jamie's mother coughed. "Actually, it's 'your Grace', Jamie."

"*My* Grace, Ma," Jamie joked. "What do you mean?"

Her mother ignored that. "Oh, children these days, your Grace."

He laughed loftily. "Ha, ha, ha . . . I know, I know."

Jamie noticed him looking down at her black tights. She crossed her legs quickly.

Her mother hurried her distinguished guest into the sitting-room. "I'm sure you know all about it."

"I'm sure he does," Jamie mumbled

"What was that?" the bishop asked in a lofty tone.

Jamie looked out the window. "Nothing. I just said here's me da."

A battered white Transit van pulled up into the drive. A man climbed out slowly and walked back to the huge, black Mercedes which was parked outside his house. Two small boys were using the passenger door as target practice for their football.

Her mother, who'd disappeared into the kitchen, was unaware of her father's imminent arrival.

The front door flew open.

"Mona," he called, as he pointed back to the big black car outside, "I hope those fuckin' politicians stay away from our house this time."

Jamie could hear her mother tripping over the chairs in the kitchen in an effort to get back to the bishop before her husband did. Mona slammed the sitting-room door, much to the bishop's surprise.

"The house is haunted," whispered Jamie. As the door opened again, Jamie could hear her father's last few words as he stamped upstairs.

" . . . if he thinks I'm going to kiss his ring, he can kiss my arse!"

The bedroom door slammed shut.

Jamie's mother arrived back. "Your Grace, you'll have to excuse us, but it seems we're completely out of tea and coffee and . . . well, everything, it seems." Her tack had changed. She wanted him to go.

There was silence.

"Ah, right," the bishop replied in his grand pulpit voice. "I'll head off, so. Nice to meet you eh, Jamie."

"Nice to meet you too, Bishop."

"*Your Grace* . . . " repeated her mother.

"Yes?" asked the bishop.

"Nothing," chirped her mother.

The bishop left. The front door closed quickly.

"Would you like a cup of tea, Ma?" Jamie asked gently.

"Something stronger, please, Jamie."

Jamie looked at her watch as her mother slumped into the armchair. "Ma, it's only half two in the afternoon."

"If you don't get me a brandy, I'll get it myself!"

"*Brandy?*"

"Yes, *Brandy*," mimicked her mother.

"Is it me da that has you upset?" Jamie asked, worried about her pale-looking mother, slumped in a heap over the arm of the chair.

"Your *father*? Me upset by *him* at this stage of me life?" She shook her head. "No, it's not your father." She stared at the papal blessing hanging over the fireplace. "It's that god-forsaken parish priest. He's destroyed my life."

Jamie looked shocked. "Why? Did he fire you?"

Jamie's mother sat forward in the chair. "Fire me?" She shook her head again. "Far worse. He's just run away with Mrs Connolly!" Tears began to stream down the woman's face.

"I'll get you that brandy, Ma."

* * *

Frank had been on the go all day, on his own, without as much as a five-minute break. He'd had to explain to the lunch-time customers that Nikki had the flu and that there'd be no food for the rest of the week. He began to realise that afternoon how popular she really was. Two cards and a bunch of flowers arrived by courier for her.

It was quiet now, thank God. As he tried to read the paper, he couldn't get his mind off what had happened the previous night. She'd obviously been pretty drunk. But to come on that heavily . . . it had never happened to him before. She'd looked gorgeous, though. Frank didn't hear the door close behind him. He heard a familiar cough. Ray was standing behind him.

"Before you even ask for an explanation, I don't have one," Ray said quietly.

"Explanation? I don't want an explanation. Maybe I

would've accepted a good one last Friday. But four days later? Do you think I'm mad?" Frank looked down at his newspaper. "You're fired," he said quietly.

Ray slumped down into a chair behind Frank. "*Fired?*" he whispered.

"Fired."

"But Frank, we're best friends."

Frank looked up and around in disbelief. "*Best friends!* What's that got to do with it? I've been breaking my fucking back in here for the guts of a week trying to do the work of two. You disappeared without any warning or reason. And you expect to walk back in here and take up where you left off. I might be mad but I'm definitely not stupid!"

Two men at the other end of the bar slipped out the side door.

"I just felt like a complete heel after those police people left here last Friday. That's all. So I had a few drinks and got into a game of poker. That didn't go too well. I ended up having another few drinks."

Frank interrupted. "What do you mean *it* didn't go too well? Were you gambling?"

Ray nodded.

"What did you lose?"

Ray sniffed a couple of times as he stared at the floor. "Enough."

"Money?"

Ray nodded.

"What else?" Frank shouted.

Ray tapped the leg of the chair with his boot.

"Ah no, Ray," Frank muttered. "The flat?"

Ray nodded. Tears rolled down his big red cheeks. "And the van," he whispered.

Frank studied him for a moment. "What did Davina say?"

"She's not talking to me." He sniffed. "Nor are the kids. And that's worse."

"Who'd you lose that flat to?"

"A little bloke who came in here one day looking for money."

"What little bloke? Do I know him?"

Ray shook his head. "It was to do with protection. I told him to shove off, that he'd get nothing out of me."

"So how'd you end up playing poker with him?"

"I got drunk. And I can't remember a lot about it. He was with a couple of his mates." His face brightened. "I was winning hands down for hours. You should have seen me, Frank, I swear. You would've been proud of me."

"So what happened?" Frank asked.

"This small guy, Ali something, pulled a fast one. I reckon he'd a couple of dud cards up his sleeve. In the space of an hour and a half he'd won everything back."

"Plus the flat and the van?"

Ray nodded.

Frank thought to himself. "Well, I suppose you could stay here for a while till we get you sorted out."

Ray looked up at Frank with an expression of relief and uncertainty. "But I can't. Nikki's here."

Frank shook his head. "Nikki left this morning."

"Nikki left. Why?"

"It's a long story." Frank walked back to the bar.

"Right, well then, we don't have any time to waste, do we?"

Ray looked puzzled. "What are you saying?"

Frank looked in the direction of the sink. "Well, there's glasses to be washed. And a couple of kegs need changing. Oh, and the brewery are collecting the empties at quarter past four. Do you think you'll have them ready?"

"Thanks," Ray said quietly.

Frank shrugged. "Some day I'll learn. Because I don't think you will."

Ray raced in behind the counter.

Frank put on his jacket. "Right. Now the bad news."

Ray stopped what he was doing and stared nervously at Frank. "What?"

"I'm taking the rest of the afternoon off. If Jamie rings, tell her not to be worrying. Just tell her that everything's fine again."

* * *

Ray had just loaded the last barrel of beer neatly in the side passage when the rain came down with a vengeance. He hopped towards the door. Back inside, he pulled off his raincoat and flung it into the kitchen. As he walked towards the main serving area, he noticed a woman standing beside the phone. She had the hood of her rain jacket pulled forward over her head.

"Are you all right there, love?" Ray shouted. Either she didn't hear him or she was ignoring him. "Excuse me." Still no reaction. Ray gently caught her arm. The hood of the jacket fell back. "Nikki?" Ray looked surprised. "I thought it was yourself."

Not half as surprised as Nikki looked.

"You're back, thanks be to God."

Just as Nikki was about to speak, the phone rang. She lunged forward. "Hello," she said cautiously.

Ray took the hint and walked back to the bar. He waved to her. "Give us a shout when you're finished."

A few minutes later, she strolled over to the bar. Ray was reading the paper. He looked up. "Well, hello, stranger," he said.

Nikki smiled. "Hi ya."

"Frank tells me you've left. A bit like me. No notice."

She nodded.

"Would you like a drink?"

She looked around. "Is Frank here?"

Ray shook his head. "Nope. I felt that after days on his own, he deserved a few hours off. He's gone to the pictures. Well, where are you off to, and, more importantly, what made you leave?"

"Nothing bad. It's just that my boyfriend asked me if I'd like to sail to France with him on his luxury yacht. That's all."

Ray's eyes opened wide. "Luxury yacht, if you don't mind. Was that Mr Loverman on the phone?"

Nikki nodded.

Ray reached under the counter. "Here, have a Heineken." He handed her a bottle and put some ice into the empty glass. "I'm sorry but we're clean out of champagne."

"Thanks." She took a sip from the glass. "So where did you get to?"

"Long story." Ray poured himself an orange.

Nikki pointed to the mineral. "I can see we all have long stories."

"So tell us more. When are you heading off to paradise?"

"Friday," she replied quietly. "From Blackpool. It's meant to be a beautiful boat."

"And when'll you be coming back?"

Nikki fiddled with the ice in her drink. "Don't know . . . don't care."

"Do I know this hunk of wealth?"

Nikki shook her head. "I don't think so."

"Where's he from?"

"Spain," she said quickly.

"Jesus, that's odd. I always thought the Spanish hated the French."

Nikki changed the conversation. "How's Davina?"

"Don't be asking. That's another day's work. Or should I say, year!"

"Does she still love you?"

"Of course." Ray patted his chest with both hands. "You see this." He punched his body. "This is like a love magnet to her soul!" He picked up a tray of drinks. "Excuse me for a moment. Big gang in this afternoon." He squeezed past a tall, neatly-dressed man sitting at the bar with his paper. The stranger stared at Nikki.

She smiled politely.

He ignored her.

Ray finished serving the drinks to the christening party at the other end of the lounge. When he came back to the bar, Nikki was gone. He hurried to the main door leading out on to Bromley Road. It was getting dark and the rain was coming down by the bucketful. No sign of her. A blue Vauxhall Cavalier was moving away from the kerbside, a few yards down from the pub.

* * *

Frank arrived back after dark. It was an hour before he stopped talking about the film he'd seen that afternoon.

"Frank," Ray hinted, "these people came out for a quiet pint, not a Power Rangers exhibition."

Frank pretended to chop Ray's neck with his wrist. "OK, quits. Any news while I was away?"

"Well, funny you should ask. You won't believe who I'd a good old chat with this afternoon."

"Davina?"

Ray wasn't amused. "No. Nikki, actually."

The smile fell off Frank's face. "What did she say?"

Ray grinned at him. "Why, Frank? What did you think she'd say?"

"Cut out the messing, Ray. What did she say?"

"Just that she's heading off to France on Friday on this big luxury yacht that her boyfriend owns."

"Did she say anything about him?"

"Nope. just that he was Spanish, and pretty rich by the sound of it."

"*Spanish?*"

"Yeah. Why?"

"He's no more Spanish than me. She's going to France with that bastard, Tommy Barrett."

"Tommy Barrett . . . where did I hear that name before?"

"Tommy Barrett. Jamie's old *boyfriend*. The bent copper. You remember the bloke Paul Flaherty told us about. He was in here a couple of times. Smug bastard. From the moment I laid eyes on him, I knew he was evil."

Frank picked up two empty glasses and began to fill them. "He's also a friend of your mate's. The bloke who now owns your house and your van." He looked at Ray who looked stunned. "What are you thinking?"

"Frank, I don't mean to scare you. Or to sound paranoid or anything like that. But there's something very weird going on around here."

"Like what?" Frank looked into the kitchen at all the redundant cooking equipment.

"I don't know. I can't quite put my finger on it. But it doesn't smell right." Ray put down the cloth he was wiping the counter with and pushed Frank into the kitchen. "Why did Nikki come back here for a phone call this evening if she left last night? Why did she tell me that this guy was Spanish, if she told you he was Tommy Barrett?" Ray walked quickly over to the window. He turned off the light and peeped out through the curtains.

"What the hell are you doing, Ray?"

"Come here," Ray urged.

Frank looked out.

521

A white Sierra was parked across the road. Two men inside were eating. Two paper cups sat on the dashboard in front of them.

Frank looked at Ray. "So?"

"*So?* Well, maybe you can tell me, then. Why is this place under police surveillance?"

"*Surveillance?* Don't be so stupid."

"Well, they're definitely not sitting out there waiting to offer you a test drive. They've been on that spot there for the last five hours, watching everyone who enters and leaves this place."

"Well, *you* go out and ask them what they're up to, if you're so bloody worried. I'm going back to work. And I suggest you do the same."

"Jesus, you're like a bear with a sore arse. What's wrong with *you*?"

"If you think something weird's going on around here, you should see what's going on in my head!"

"What do you mean?"

"I'm scared, Ray. In fact, I've never been so scared in my life. I'm beginning to think I should be in Dublin."

"Why?"

"It's a long story."

* * *

He dreamt . . . he was in Molloy's, back home in Glandore. Jamie walked back to the table with two more drinks. She bent down and kissed him. It was a quiet afternoon. An empty pub. Just the two of them and a roaring fire. Then, for some inexplicable reason, the pub was gone. So was Jamie. He was in the small graveyard beside the church. Brendan, his brother, along with the parish priest and the local sergeant were helping him to lower their mother's coffin into the deep grave. The ropes were frayed and were slowly beginning to stretch. He knew they'd snap and send the wooden box hurtling to the cold, wet earth. As he looked up for support, he called out to three other familiar faces. While they *were* there, they seemed to be somewhere else far away and out of touch. He couldn't understand it. He shouted their names over and over. They ignored him. He reached out to touch them while trying to stop himself from falling in. He squinted his eyes to see them more clearly. The tramp, Paddy Last, his face all distorted and bloody, smiled as he waved the money Frank had given him. Ray stood beside him holding his customary tea towel, his face horribly burnt. Jamie stood slightly back from them, her eyes badly bruised. She seemed to be signalling to Frank. *"Please!"* she implored. She was crying like a lost child. A sinister figure, wearing a black hood, stood behind her, slightly to her left. As he raised the knife above her head, he slowly took off the hood . . .

Frank screamed out. A howl that took his breath away. He sat up rigidly in the bed and gasped. *"Jesus!"* he choked. His T-shirt was wet through, his hair matted and stuck to his head. His arms and legs trembled violently. *"Jesus Christ!"* With all his strength, he jumped out of the bed.

Chapter Twenty-Eight

Jamie watched *Coronation Street* with the concentration
and attention to detail of a neuro-surgeon at work.
Thank God for video recorders, she thought. She'd
lost the toss of a coin with her father and sister's
boyfriend earlier on as to who'd get to watch the TV.
Premier League football won hands down. She taped
the programme and helped her mother with the
ironing. One consolation was that no one would
disturb her this late. Then the phone rang. She looked
at her watch. Quarter past one. Who the hell is that?
she wondered. She dashed to pick it up. "Hello," she
whispered sleepily.

"Jamie, it's Frank!" He was shouting.

"Frank, are you OK?"

"I'm fine, but are *you* OK?"

"Yeah, what's the panic?"

"I'm coming home later this morning. I'll be on the
twenty past ten flight. I don't know what time it gets in
at. Will you meet me?"

"Of course. But why?"

"I'll tell you when I see you. I love you."

She smiled. "I love you too." As she put the phone down, she remembered the scrappy note that Mr Nolan had given to her. Be careful what you say, it said.

* * *

Dublin Airport was quiet. Jamie told her father that he'd be all right waiting outside the arrivals terminal in the Transit van provided he didn't leave it unattended.

"What if I get fined? Or, worse still, what if they think I'm a terrorist?" he shouted as she walked towards the sliding doors.

"You, a *terrorist*?" She laughed at the top of her voice. "Jesus, the organisation would want to be hard up to give you a job. You won't get fined," she shouted back to him. "I'll be fifteen minutes. Unless you feel like parking that heap in the holiday carpark near the main road. Mind you, they might mistake it for a skip."

"That's about an hour's walk," he shouted.

"Please yourself. Tell them you're one of Rod Stewart's roadies and you're collecting all his wives for a family reunion."

"Rod *who*?" he asked.

"It doesn't matter, Da. Just wait there." The doors shut behind her. She checked the arrivals board. VS7324 was on time, at twenty-five past eleven. She looked up at the huge clock over her head. Quarter to eleven. Too early, she thought. Coffee. That'd be nice. As she stepped on to the escalator, two men stepped on behind her. They were uncomfortably close to her when she stepped off opposite the restaurant on the third floor. As she turned left towards the entrance, the two men linked her arms, one left, one right.

"Excuse me," she said nervously as she tried to pull away from their grip. "What are you doing?"

One of the men leaned nearer to her. "We'd like you to come with us, please, love." As he held her arm with one hand, he pulled a wallet out of his inside pocket with the other. It dropped open, revealing some kind of ID card.

"Who are you?"

"We'll tell you as soon as we can all sit down."

"But I have to meet someone." People were beginning to look across the restaurant at the commotion.

"This shouldn't take very long." The official put his hand around Jamie's waist.

"Get your fucking hand off my arse!" Jamie roared at the top of her voice.

Just then, the man who owned the offending hand doubled up in agony. "Oh fuck, my balls." He coughed and almost threw up. "I can't breathe." He gasped in pain.

"Jesus, what did you do that for?" asked the other official.

"Because I don't like being messed around," said Jamie. "That's why. It's called sexual harassment. Or haven't you heard?"

The remaining officer pushed Jamie through a door while his partner was helped through by an airport official.

* * *

It always felt good to be back in Ireland. But Frank didn't feel happy about this visit. Maybe he was making a mountain out of a molehill. On the other hand, Ray was right. This bad smell was turning into a stinking mudbath of strange coincidences. He wanted to get to the root of this for once and for all. Questions bounced around inside his head non-stop. Who was this Provo bloke and what did he want from Jamie? Was it a coincidence that he was at the airport the night Frank's flight had been cancelled because of the bad weather? Maybe. After all, he *was* a taxi-driver. But why did he tell her that her life was in danger? And why was he following *her*?

He stepped forward in the queue towards the passport control desk. He thought it strange that this prodecure was being carried out for domestic flights. He couldn't remember having to show his passport before. Maybe one of the transatlantic flights had arrived ahead of his. It was moving fast. Most people were instructed to file through without the need to show their passports. Two men looked on from a distance. Frank handed his passport across the counter.

The official straightened up. He turned the passport sideways and examined the photograph. He looked up at Frank.

"I'm always getting teased over the Elvis connection," he joked. "I suppose you could say I look a bit like him."

No answer.

The official handed the passport back across the counter. "Mr McCabe, please pick up the red courtesy telephone in the baggage reclaim area. You'll see it situated beside the main customs office."

"Is there a call for me?" Frank asked curiously.

The man ignored him.

Frank thought it a bit strange. He seemed to be the only passenger to have his passport checked. And the man standing in the queue behind him was black. He picked up his bag and walked with the flow towards the baggage reclaim area. It was quieter than he'd ever remembered. He looked around for the red courtesy telephone. There it was, close to the entrance to the red channel. He walked quickly across the empty floor and picked it up. "Hello," he said, hoping it would be Jamie on the other end. There was no one there.

He put the phone back and was about to look for assistance when he felt two sets of arms catch hold of him from behind.

"Here, hang on . . . what's going on?" Frank asked as he tried to stop himself from losing his balance.

"Just stay where you are, sir," a voice directed from behind.

They loosened their grip on his arms, but still held him firmly. "We'd like to ask you a few questions, sir."

All three men turned simultaneously to the right, Frank positioned between the two casually-dressed officials.

"But I'm just coming home to see my girlfriend . . . she's not well. I haven't done anything wrong. You must have the wrong person," he pleaded.

The two men ignored him as they walked him briskly towards an office with frosted glass all around it.

"Who are you?" Frank pleaded.

"Drugs squad."

Drugs squad! Frank thought. "What do you want with me?"

They ignored him and pushed him through the office door.

He could see two other men inside as he entered. They seemed to be expecting him. Just then, his heart jumped and his mouth dropped open. *"Jamie!"* he shouted. "What are you doing here?"

She sat behind a long empty table and pulled hard on a cigarette. She shook her head. "I don't know. I told them I was coming out here to meet you off the plane."

* * *

It was almost midday when they arrived at Santry police station.

They were led into a brightly-lit office. Two men and a woman sat behind a table.

"Anne!" Jamie blurted.

"Hi, Jamie," replied Detective Inspector Anne O'Brien. "Don't even ask. It's a long story."

"What are we doing here?" Jamie asked.

Anne put a finger up to her lips. "All's about to be revealed. "This is Superintendent . . . "

The stout detective coughed and cut across the pretty policewoman's introduction. "Eh, Blaney.

Detective Superintendent Joseph Blaney, Special Crime Squad. This is my assistant, Paul O'Rourke." He looked up at Jamie and Frank and then across at Anne. "I take it you've all met."

They nodded.

"Right, please . . . sit down."

The superintendent took papers from a file in front of him. "You're both probably wondering why you're here." He looked closely at the two bewildered people sitting opposite him. "Let me first of all stress that neither of you is under arrest. We're simply hoping that you might be able to help us."

Jamie looked at Frank. "Why *are* you home, anyway?"

Frank moved around uneasily in his chair. "I'll tell you later."

"Tell me now," she insisted.

Frank's glare was a warning. "Eh, my brother's not too well. Eh, he broke his leg."

"You came home because your brother broke his leg!" she shouted. "Give me a break."

"Can we get on with this, please," the superintendent urged. "I don't have all day."

"*You* don't have all day?" Jamie and Frank replied in unison.

"What about my father?" Jamie asked in a concerned voice.

"What *about* your father?" the superintendent mumbled.

"Jesus, I just remembered. He's sitting outside the arrivals building waiting on me."

Frank looked at his watch. "I doubt it."

The superintendent cleared his throat with a long phlegmy cough. "My department is currently in the throes of a major drugs seizure. We expect to apprehend the suspected traffickers by the end of this week."

"Excuse me," interrupted Jamie, "but why do all you police people talk like that."

The inspector looked puzzled. "Like what?"

"Like all those stupid police-words crap that leave us wondering what the hell you're talking about. Like, why don't you just say you're about to arrest a crowd of criminals and give them a good hiding?"

The superintendent was not amused.

"Jamie," Anne said tactfully, "I think we should all wait to hear what has to be said before saying anything ourselves."

"Oh yeah? Come to think of it, what has you in here? Holidays, my arse!"

"*Ladies, please!*" the superintendent warned.

"Now, the reason we've asked you to join the hunt, so to speak . . . "

"Didn't have much choice," Jamie muttered.

" . . . is because we have reason to believe that you may be able to assist us with important information."

Frank spoke up. "Excuse me, Superintendent, with all due respect, I think you have the wrong people. Jamie and I have just started going out together, so to speak . . . "

Jamie nudged Frank with her elbow. "What do you mean, *so to speak*? We've been going out for a good while now, actually."

Frank continued. "I run a pub in London and I can safely say, on my mother's life, that I've never been involved, even remotely, in drugs."

"I should hope not!" Jamie muttered.

"Miss Carroll, please!" the superintendent insisted.

"Sorry."

"Mr McCabe, I'm not interested in your credentials or your credibility. All I'm interested in is what you know about two suspects whose movements we are doing our utmost to follow." The superintendent stared calmly at Frank. Then at Jamie.

"Look, can I ring home?" Jamie asked.

The inspector was beginning to lose his cool. "You both obviously seem to think that I'm doing this for the good of my health. Perhaps it hasn't occurred to either of you that you both may be in serious trouble with the law, both here and in England."

Frank looked at Jamie and then back at the table.

The inspector took a number of pages from the folder in front of him. "Mr McCabe, does this look familiar?"

Frank examined it. It was the form he'd signed at Holyhead that night, in the presence of Customs officials, to get his coat back. "Yes," he said grimly.

"And this?"

It was a typed report on the conversation he'd had with the three officials that night, almost word for word. "Yes."

"Well now, it leads me to think that you know a lot more than you're actually admitting."

"That's where you're wrong. You see . . . "

The inspector cut across him. "Look, Mr McCabe, I'm not in the habit of wasting time . . . or being wrong. Your public house has been under surveillance for the past fortnight. One of our suspects who now resides here has been making regular phone calls to a young lady who appears to work for your establishment."

Frank looked confused. "I don't understand."

"Does the name Nikki Coffey ring a bell?"

"Nikki works for you?" shouted Jamie. "You told me you were talking to her all right. How long has she been working for you? Listen, I hope she hasn't been trying to get you . . . "

"Yeah, well," checked Frank, "she doesn't work for me any more. She left a couple of days ago. She's going off to France with her boyfriend . . . on a yacht if you don't mind."

"The bitch . . . no wonder she hasn't called," Jamie muttered furiously. "Some friend."

Frank decided to say no more.

"Actually, the *yacht* is coming here." The superintendent rummaged through the file again. "He held up an ID photograph of a policeman in uniform. "Does this man look familiar?"

Jamie and Frank stared at each other. They both nodded.

Anne O'Brien looked across the table at Jamie.

"He's my ex-boyfriend," Jamie said softly.

"This man," the superintendent continued, "is the prime suspect in our operation. He's staying here in Dublin at the moment, at an address we have under surveillance."

533

For a moment, Jamie thought she was going to throw up.

"Excuse me, Superintendent," interrupted Anne O'Brien, "you promised me that I would have an opportunity to talk to Jamie about this delicate business of Tommy Barrett before you briefed them on the operation. Jamie wasn't aware that this man was in Dublin. I think it's a bit unfair that you should just . . . "

"*Excuse me, Inspector O'Brien*, you have no right coming into this police station and telling me how to do my job! You offered to help out while you were here on holidays. Now I get the feeling that you're trying to take over." The superintendent placed another photograph on the table in front of Frank and Jamie. "Do you recognise him?"

"From the TV, yes."

"From your pub?"

Frank shook his head. "Can't say I do."

"That's odd. He was seen drinking in your pub a couple of weeks back. One of your employees, the red-haired lad, was questioned about this man. He confirmed that he'd been talking to him."

"Who is he?" asked Frank.

"He's *not* the man who attacked you, is he?" Anne asked Jamie.

"No."

"Who is he?" she asked softly.

"The man in the taxi," Jamie whispered, almost inaudibly.

The superintendent's eyes darted from one woman to the other. "What's all this about?"

"He's a taxi-driver here in Dublin. He gave me a lift once," Jamie replied.

"I think he can help you," added Frank.

"Oh, you think this IRA killer can *help* us, do you? *He* can help *us*? So how can this character help us?"

"Well," Frank started, "this man has been following Jamie since he arrived in Ireland some weeks back. At least, we think he's been following her."

"What do you mean, *think*?"

"Well, as Jamie just said, he gave her a lift in a taxi. And on the way into the city, he pulled over and told her all about Tommy Barrett, and about how much he hates him because he put him away in England for eight years."

"Well, Mr McCabe, with due respect to your anxieties about this character, any police officer who manages to put an IRA killer away for any amount of time deserves to be commended and promoted. I don't really see the validity of whatever petty argument you're trying to serve up here." He put the photograph into the folder.

"What are you doing?" asked Anne O'Brien.

"I'm keeping this photo on file."

"Why? You just said you're not interested in pursuing this matter."

"It's called 'for future reference', Inspector," he asserted.

"He's innocent," muttered Jamie.

"What did you say?" asked Blaney.

"I said he's innocent. He wasn't responsible for that bomb. Tommy Barrett framed him. Packed the boot of a stolen car with all kinds of shit and said it was his."

Frank butted in. "Tommy Barrett pushed a tramp on to the Euston underground line last week, right into the path of a train, because the poor old harmless skin saw him shooting his partner dead in a back alley after that drugs bust in Maida Vale."

"I beg your pardon," grunted Blaney.

"Tommy Barrett *shot* Jimmy Grant."

"How would you know?"

"Because the tramp told me," replied Frank. He stared at Anne O'Brien. "Your people found a substantial amount of money on Martin Lenane's body when they peeled him off the underground tracks. I bet they didn't find a plane ticket. Did they?"

Anne shook her head reluctantly. "No, they didn't."

"Well, that's odd. Because when he came into the pub looking for me that Sunday evening, he showed Ray a return ticket to Dublin. Where was *that* when they scraped what was left of him off the railway line?"

"Probably destroyed in the incident," Anne suggested.

"Try again, Inspector. How come no one knew Tommy Barrett was in Dublin? Well? I'll tell you why. Because, before he pushed Martin Lenane out in front of two thousand tons of screaming metal, there was a discreet scuffle. The platform was too busy for anyone else to notice. Tommy Barrett took the tramp's plane ticket. And I think if you check the airline's records, you'll find that someone flew into Dublin under the name of Martin Lenane, while Lenane's body was still warm in a London morgue."

Joe Blaney snorted. "A tramp told you that Barrett

shot his partner? You expect me to believe that? Then you advise me to trust the hunches of a convicted IRA killer?"

"Detective Blaney," Frank said forcefully, "I think you're the one who doesn't understand. This man, Paul Flaherty, can lead you to Tommy Barrett. Whether he's guilty or not doesn't really matter at the moment. All you have to do is find *him* before *he* finds Barrett."

The detective looked totally baffled. "Look, sunshine, you just let me do my job and you keep your nose clean."

Frank threw his eyes up to heaven. "Jesus Christ," he muttered.

"As for you, young lady," he nodded at Jamie, "I can't forsee anything too serious befalling you while you're under observation. What do you think? I think she's every reason in the world to feel as safe as a house."

"The three pigs' house," Anne muttered.

"That's ridiculous," Frank insisted.

Anne O'Brien walked towards the door. She looked back. "You really think you're going to catch this guy, don't you, Superintendent?"

The man looked smugly at the woman. "I don't think it, *Inspector*, I *know* it!" He looked at Frank and Jamie. "You two are free to go. The duty sergeant will show you out." Then he looked at Anne. "As for you, Inspector, I'll organise for a taxi to take you *straight* back to your hotel. Good afternoon."

You could cut the air of depression with a knife.

The three of them stood in the police station reception area. Anne waited impatiently for her taxi, Frank and Jamie were still trying to figure out what had happened to their belongings which had been confiscated at the airport.

"You know we won't get any chance to talk privately once we leave here," Anne said carefully.

Frank and Jamie nodded.

"Where are you staying?" Jamie asked quietly.

Anne checked to make sure they weren't being watched. "The Skylon Hotel on the Drumcondra Road."

Frank looked at Jamie.

"I know where it is," said Jamie. "But surely we can't meet there."

"Too right," Anne replied. "The Boot Inn," she said quietly as she watched the duty sergeant.

"The *what*?" asked Frank.

"Ssshhh." Jamie nudged him. "When?" she whispered to Anne.

"Quarter to ten tonight. Police shift changes at ten, so they're not going to hang around."

"Taxi for O'Brien," a voice shouted from behind the desk.

The courier on the huge motor-bike watched from a distance as the taxi pulled away from Santry garda station. He was deep in conversation on his two-way radio as it drove by.

Chapter Twenty-Nine

"That's nine pounds twenty-five, please," the taxi-driver pointed to the meter.

Frank rummaged in his pockets. "Jesus Christ, nine twenty-five," he whispered to Jamie. "That'd get you a tour of London." He handed the driver a tenner.

"Sorry, mate, no sterling."

"*No sterling!*" Frank gasped. "Jesus, I remember a time when you'd have slept with passengers just to get their sterling."

The driver looked around at Frank. "Trying to be funny, sham?"

Jamie leaned forward and handed him an Irish ten-pound note. They got out of the car and walked towards the house.

"Here, love," called the driver, "seventy-five pence change."

"*Keep it!*" she shouted back.

"Yeah, thanks," the driver grunted, "I'll buy a fucking house!" The car screeched as it took off down the road at high speed.

"Cheeky bastard," Jamie muttered. She looked

around. Her father's Transit was perched precariously on the kerb outside the house. "Oh Jesus, my da! What am I going to tell them?"

"Tell them the truth," replied Frank calmly.

"*The truth?* That we both got detained at the airport in connection with a drugs seizure operation? Frank, I think you need to lie down. You haven't met my mother."

Frank grinned boldly. He put his arm around Jamie. "You know, that's not a bad idea." He felt her elbow hard in the ribs. "Uuugh, Jamie." He was about to grab her arm and steal a kiss when he noticed a small, middle-aged woman standing on the doorstep. She didn't seem all that impressed.

"Ma, this is Frank. Frank, this is me ma."

She stared at Jamie. "Where were you?" She looked Frank up and down. Her mouth dropped open. "You're the breadman!" she shrieked.

"The *breadman?*" Jamie shrilled. "He told me he was a bishop."

"A *bishop? No!* He's a breadman. He was in Nolan's supermarket that day that little gurrier tried to pinch me purse. He grabbed him and gave him a thumpin'. Then he returned me purse to me. That must be years ago."

Jamie stared at Frank. Then at her mother. She seemed to have stars in her eyes. Then back at Frank. "*Breadman?*"

"Used to be . . . years ago."

"How many *years* ago?"

Frank was getting embarrassed. "Nice to meet you, Mrs Carroll."

540

"It's *Mona*, actually, Frank. And it's lovely to meet you . . . at long last. I've heard so many wonderful things about you. Well, isn't it a small world? Who ever thought that my daughter would end up dating the man who saved her mother's life?"

"Spare me," mumbled Jamie.

"Nice to meet you, Mona," Frank replied humbly.

"Jamie, you'd better have a good explanation for your father, because I've had to endure his fits for the last two and a half hours. Do you know that he refused to move that crock from the front of the airport? He thinks the police are watching him now because they questioned him at the airport about what was in the van." Her mother nodded to the car parked across the road four doors up.

Jamie looked at Frank. "If only she knew," she mumbled. "Here, come on in, Frank. I'm freezing."

They walked by her mother who was still ranting on the doorstep.

She walked behind them into the kitchen and closed the door. "Well? I'm waiting."

Jamie stared at Frank and took a deep breath. "Didn't you hear about what happened on the radio, Ma? Seemingly, there was an emergency on board the flight from London. Wasn't there, Frank?"

Frank nodded back, gobsmacked.

Her mother stood at the rickety ironing-board, her head slightly tilted to the right. "Go on, I'm listening," she said curiously. The word *gossip* seemed to light up over her head.

"Well, the pilot had a heart attack as the plane was twenty miles out."

541

"Over the sea?" her mother asked in a high voice. She put the iron down on the shirt and looked around at Frank.

Frank nodded his head nervously.

"Well, they'd no co-pilot on board because he rang in sick this morning. So one of the staff ran up and down the aisles asking if anyone could fly the plane."

Her mother swung around. Her eyeballs were touching the end of her nose by now. Her hand was firmly clasped over her mouth as she muttered as many saints' names as she could think of. "Mother of Saint Anthony, go way."

"Anyway, Frank told her that he had some flying experience from his Air Corps days in Baldonnell."

Her mother looked suspiciously at Frank. "Air Corps . . . Merciful Refuge of the Sick."

Frank nodded.

"Well, when they got the pilot out of his seat and Frank sat in, he checked all the gadgets and dials and things and realised they only had three gallons of fuel left. Isn't that right, Frank?" Jamie walked over to him and linked his arm.

"Three gallons, that's right," he mumbled.

"Three gallons . . . Blessed Son of the Holy Family," her mother whispered.

"Then he had terrible trouble getting the wheels to come down, hadn't you?" She stroked his arm with one hand and slipped her other hand into the back pocket of his jeans and squeezed his bottom.

Frank jumped forward. "*Yip!*" he squeaked.

"No wheels, no pilot and no fuel? What do the two

542

of you take me for . . . brain-dead?" she said indignantly. "Jamie, surely you know me better than to think that that'd wash with me! How long do I know you?"

Jamie threw her eyes upwards. "She says this every time . . . since before I was born, Ma."

"And how many times have you been able to fool me?"

"Never, Ma." Jamie reddened. She looked up proudly at her man. "But, I have to say, fair play. You'd make a very sexy pilot. I know you would have landed it perfectly and not one of the hundred and fifty passengers would have known any different." She reached up and kissed him on the cheek.

"And do I not make a good landlord?" he asked teasingly.

"*Landlord?*" her mother squealed. "That sounds very important and posh."

"Well, actually, I'm the landlord of a pub in London," he said modestly.

"Do you hear him, Ma? Mr Meek. He's only the landlord of the biggest and most popular Irish pub in London."

Jamie's mother stared at him with the veneration she'd normally save for members of the cloth. "A successful businessman. I love to hear of that happening to one of our own. An entre-pren-tice," she gushed. She looked at Jamie. "Your father was an entreprentice when he worked for Jaguar in Coventry."

"Ma," said Jamie, "I think you mean *entrepreneur*. Frank's an *entrepreneur*. Me da was an apprentice."

"An apprentice . . . *him*?" she shouted. "He doesn't know the meaning of a day's work. The only time he knew how to say the word was when he'd be slaggin' the Apprentice Boys' March in the North." She turned back to the ironing-board and picked up the iron. The shirt was stuck to it. "Oh, Jesus Christ, look at the good shirt. Your father was going to wear it tomorrow. What'll he do now?" she shrieked.

"He'll just have to stay in bed like he always does." As Jamie went to sit down, her mother grabbed her arm and moved her aside. She took the chair from under her. "Here, love," she said to Frank, "sit down. You must be exhausted after your long journey."

Frank started to smile.

"Long journey?" muttered Jamie. "He only came from London. If he was coming from San Francisco, that'd be a long journey."

"Speaking of San Francisco, I think he looks just like our Barry. Don't you?"

Frank looked at Jamie.

"Barry's me older brother. You're well and truly one of the Carroll family now."

"*One* of your older brothers. Seán's the eldest of the family. Then comes Barry. Then Jamie and then our youngest, Lisa. I used to think she was twenty-one years of age. But sometimes I wonder should that be twenty-one *months*." She gave up on the shirt and plugged in the kettle. "Right . . . who's for more tea? Frank? I'm sure you'd love a hot drop. You'll have to tell me all about life in London."

"She doesn't listen to me when I tell her." Jamie gave him the two fingers behind her mother's back.

544

"Behave yourself, Jamie," her mother snapped. "Open a packet of Kimberley there, will you."

"Kimberley!" Jamie sounded shocked. "This must be a *very* special occassion if the Kimberley are being brought out."

"Jamie, don't be so cheeky." The kettle began to boil. The biscuits were arranged on one of her best china plates. "So, tell me, Frank, is there much money to be made in your game?"

"Well, Mrs Carroll . . . "

"What did I tell you? Call me Mona . . . Frank." She poured the tea into the mugs and placed them on the table.

"Well . . . Mona, it's a lucrative business right now. People seem to have a few extra bob to spend. And the pub is a popular spot to spend it in."

Mona sniffed loudly. "I have to say I'm not one for pubs myself. But I'm sure if you own it, as distinct from drinking it, that's different." She walked back to the cooker to pull out the plug of the iron.

Frank looked bewildered.

"It's me da. He's an alcoholic," muttered Jamie.

Frank gently nodded his head.

"Well now, have you two any plans?" her mother asked boldly.

They stared at each other. "*Plans?*" they both stammered together. "Plans for what? Like what we're going to do while Frank's home?"

"*No!*" she piped. "Like plans for getting married, like?"

Frank and Jamie looked at each other and burst out laughing.

* * *

Within hours, the neighbours had heard that Mona Carroll's eldest daughter was going out with a wealthy Irish engineer who owned the biggest pub in London. He was also a fully-qualified pilot who loaned his Ventolin inhaler to the pilot on his journey from London when he learned that the man in charge was having an asthma attack. Neighbours called all evening to meet the male hero with the Midas touch. Lisa's friends called all night to get a good look at her sister's hunk of a boyfriend.

The two detectives in an unmarked car, parked across the street, ran out of notepaper as they wrote descriptions of everyone who visited Carroll's that evening. By quarter past nine, they'd counted twenty-four visitors. Some stayed for hours. Others just called to the door and left immediately. They couldn't understand what was going on. After a couple of hours, they'd lost count. The two men checked their watches every few minutes. Nearly clocking-off time, they agreed. They paid no great attention to the couple who left the house in slightly outgrown school uniforms at twenty past nine.

Frank waved to another taxi as it sped past.

"Jesus, I'm freezing in this uniform. Give us your pullover." Jamie shivered.

"You must be joking. This shirt is so small underneath, half the buttons won't close."

"Half *your* buttons won't close? Just be thankful you don't have a 36 B chest under a size 8 shirt. *None* of my buttons will close. And this stupid cardigan isn't helping to cover up much."

"Anyway, this was your brilliant idea, not mine," Frank added.

"Well, at least it got us past the cops, didn't it? Fair play to Lisa for getting them."

Frank nodded as he scoured the darkness and the headlights for another taxi. "I suppose all we have to do now is get into the pub," he scoffed, looking at Jamie's ridiculously short skirt and her schoolgirl tie and crested pullover. He burst out laughing. "Do you seriously think we're going to be served drink dressed like this?"

"Yeah, I do actually. I mean, we might be dressed up like sixteen-year-olds but we look about twenty years older."

Frank shook his head. "I don't know which is worse, looking like a schoolkid or looking like a pervert."

"Well, for your sake, I hope none of the teachers from Saint Paul's drink in The Boot Inn," she laughed.

"Speak for yourself," shouted Frank, as a taxi pulled up at the kerb. "Howya, Sister. I'm just having a quiet few Heinekens after me homework."

The two of them laughed and jumped into the back seat of the taxi.

"Where to?" asked the driver. His mouth dropped open.

* * *

Wednesday nights were normally quiet in the Boot
Inn. So quiet, you could count the number of planes
landing and departing at the airport next door.

Frank and Jamie raised a few eyebrows and the odd
wolf whistle when they arrived. Frank explained that
they were going to a fancy dress party in Swords and
these were the only school uniforms they could find.

"Ask your man over there what he thinks," quipped
the barman. "He's a teacher in Saint Paul's CBS."

Frank looked across at the man.

The teacher nearly choked on his beer when he
spooted the oversized pupil standing at the bar getting
stuck into a big black pint of stout.

Frank sat down and passed Jamie across her drink.

The barman walked over. "Excuse me, folks, there's
a woman over there we were just wondering about.
Maybe you know her."

Frank and Jamie stretched upright in the seat to get
a good look at the woman in the corner. They shook
their heads.

"It's just that she's not really dressed like, eh, the
way the manager insists. He's asked me to throw her
out," the barman continued. "You're sure youse don't
know her?"

"Hang on a minute," said Jamie. She stood up and
pulled at the scanty school skirt. It came down to her
thighs. "Shit," she mumbled. She walked across to the
woman in the corner.

She was dressed like a cheap hooker.

Frank heard a shriek. Then two shrieks. Then a bout of unrestrained laughter. It must be Anne, he thought. "Yeah, I think we know her," he said to the barman. He picked up the two drinks and joined the two women in the corner.

"So *this* is how you got out!" Jamie laughed, pointing to her attire.

Anne nodded. "Don't ask me how I'm going to get back into the hotel." She looked at Jamie's outfit and grinned. "How did you manage to get in here dressed like that?"

"I'm not sure. I think the manager likes a woman in uniform." She chuckled.

"Well, he definitely doesn't think much of call-girls," replied Anne nervously.

* * *

Anne leaned across the table. "I don't want to alarm you, Jamie, but . . . "

"But what?"

"Tommy Barrett was definitely your assailant. *He* raped you. We know this but I'm not sure we have enough evidence."

"What do you need?" Jamie asked reluctantly.

Anne looked around. "Keep your voice down." She paused again. "After he'd held the knife to your throat, he never wiped it clean. Mascara showed up on the serrated edge of the knife, along with skin substance. This would be dried outer skin which often crumbles away with old make-up, particularly around loose-skinned areas like the front of your neck. The skin samples we tested matched your skin substance. One of your hairs showed up knotted around one of the sharp juts. Also," she paused again and took a drink, "when his locker was searched and drug substances discovered, we also found a pair of men's Y-fronts which were obviously due for the wash." She squeezed her nose. "Forensics found pubic hair caught in the internal fabrics of his pants. They matched the pubic hairs we discovered in toilet tissue that had found its way into the bundled bed sheet. Did you use toilet tissue at any stage after the attack?"

Jamie nodded. "How do you know they were *his* underpants?" she asked quietly.

Anne smiled. "Because we found an identical pair when we searched the flat afterwards. Thankfully, they hadn't been washed either. The hairs we found on that occasion fitted the equation perfectly. We've passed the evidence on to our legal people to let them examine it for themselves. But remember, you *were* sleeping with him for three years."

There was silence for what seemed like forever.

"Did you know about this, Frank?" Anne asked compassionately.

Frank nodded. He couldn't speak.

"Yeah," Jamie added, "he's been brilliant." She looked at him and held his hand tightly. "I don't know what I would have done without you," she said softly.

"I think this is my round," Anne muttered. She stood and walked to the bar. A couple of men whistled. She looked around at Jamie and Frank. "Normally, I'd tell them where to get off. But I suppose tonight I was asking for it." She ordered and quickly sat down again.

"Do you know where he is?" Frank asked.

Anne nodded. "We've a good idea. But that's where my story comes to an abrupt end. From there on, my hands are tied."

"I don't understand," Jamie said.

"Well, I offered my services to Superintendent Blaney, the man who's heading up this drugs operation. You met him today." She smirked. "He knew that we were chasing Tommy for the last few weeks. We alerted his section to the possibilty that Tommy might hide here in Ireland because of his police background in Britain. Blaney, meanwhile, unknown to me, had been tipped off about links between Tommy and an inner-city drugs gang here. Seemingly, the gang were using Tommy's contacts to bring in small amounts of cocaine in fishing boats further up the coast. Blaney was advised last week, however, that the big one was on."

"Sorry," Jamie interrupted, "you're losing me there. The big one?"

"Yeah, a real big one! These people are planning on bringing in enough smack to fill a swimming-pool this weekend. Street value, I'd guess, one and a half million quid."

Jamie looked at Frank. His eyes were huge.

"So how's Tommy involved in this one?"

"He's organising the passage from the far side. They need him to supervise the boat's departure from somewhere in the north-west, probably in Lancashire. They're not too sure of the exact location."

"But how can he do that if he's over here?" Frank asked.

Anne grinned. "Well, see, this is what they won't hear me out on. They think he's going to return to England sometime in the next forty-eight hours but avoid the boat's exact location over there for fear of being caught. But I know him too well." She paused and looked sympathetically at Jamie. "Well, within reason. I *know* he'll head straight for the boat. I think he's so badly affected by his own addiction that he's bound to do stupid things. Blaney's people are trying to tell me that he's too clever to do something as obvious as that. If he doesn't go to the yacht, then he'll let someone on the far side go for him. Someone whom he trusts. And more importantly, someone who trusts him. Either way, it doesn't really matter if he doesn't go near the boat. At least he'll be back in Britain and catchable from our point of view. That's why it's imperative that he gets on a plane to Britain."

"And what about nailing him for Jimmy Grant's murder?" asked Frank.

Anne thought for a moment. "Well, that would be a miracle. There are people in the force, at a very high level, who suspect he's responsible for pulling the trigger. But until we can prove that the drugs yob he was chasing died before Jimmy Grant, we're barking up a dead tree. Remember, they died within seconds of each other."

"Is it possible?"

"The inquest will hopefully prove it."

Jamie coughed. "Sorry, excuse me."

552

"That's all right," Anne replied. She patted Jamie on the arm. "Do you know anyone who'd do it for him.

Jamie shook her head.

"Nikki!" Frank shouted.

Anne looked surprised. She glanced back at Jamie. "Your friend, Nikki."

Jamie shrugged her shoulders.

Anne looked at Frank. "Why Nikki?"

"Because she left the Clover Tap the other day. She'd been working part-time for me for a few weeks. She said she was going to France with Tommy on a yacht that he'd borrowed from a friend."

"Did she say where they'd sail from?"

"Blackpool."

"I thought it might be somewhere near there."

"Do you mind me asking why you're stuck in the middle of all this with a bunch of Keystone cops?" Frank asked.

"Get me another drink, *please*!" Anne laughed.

"What's your gut feeling on the whole thing, Anne?" Jamie asked quietly.

"My gut feeling?" Anne thought long and hard. "My gut feeling is that they're going to get their drugs but they won't get Tommy."

"You think he'll get away?"

Anne nodded. "Yes, I do."

"And what about what Flaherty said to Jamie; that he might try to get her out of the way first?" asked Frank, searching for change.

"I don't think he'll chance it. You're too exposed.

He's risking too much by coming out of the shadows to have a strike at you."

"So what are we supposed to do now?" Jamie asked.

"Wait, I suppose."

They all looked cluelessly at each other for a short while. The blind leading the blind. Frank got up to order another round of drinks.

"I really shouldn't have another. But, shag it," Anne muttered. "I might as well treat it as a holiday at home until *they* start treating me as one of their own."

"Unlikely . . . if today was anything to go by," replied Jamie. She finished off her drink.

Frank put fresh drinks down on the table.

Anne clicked her fingers. "We're going to have one hell of a problem keeping in touch with each other over the next few days. Our phones are more than likely bugged. And I've no doubt they're wasting huge amounts of state money keeping us all under surveillance. Can anyone think of a solution to that problem?" She looked at Jamie.

Jamie shook her head.

"Hold on a minute." Frank clapped his hands. "Yes!" he shouted.

Anne looked around the pub. It was beginning to get busy. "Keep it down, Frank. We're drawing enough attention to ourselves as it is."

They huddled closer around the small table.

"You've hired a GSM phone, Anne," Frank confirmed.

"Yes."

"And I can hire one, can't I?" He grinned.

The two girls looked at each other in dismay.

"Where's this going to get us?"

"Well, they can't put phone-tapping devices on to GSM phones if we get hold of them first, can they?" Frank continued.

Anne shook her head. "Not if they don't know you have one."

"Then that's it!" he whispered hard.

"What's *it*?" the two women asked together.

"GSM mobile phones. My brother, Brendan, that's his business: selling mobile phones!"

"What if other people can tune in and listen?" asked Anne.

"They can't . . . not on this new system."

"Brilliant." Anne shook Frank's hand. "Absolutely brilliant."

Jamie agreed. "But hang on a minute. Where are we going to get a mobile phone at quarter to eleven on a Wednesday night?"

"Problem solved." Frank stood up. "Leave that to me. I'm going to have to hire a car as well. But I can do that in the morning. Has anyone got any twenty pence pieces for the phone?"

The girls searched in their pockets and bags. A small collection of coins was made and Frank headed for the public telephone.

"Who are you ringing at this hour of the night?" Jamie asked.

He looked back and grinned. "Hello, Mr Molloy, it's Frank McCabe. Is me brother Brendan there?"

It was past one when Jamie and Frank got home to Jamie's house. The key, as usual, was under the flower-box in the neatly-kept porch. The two of them had had plenty to drink.

"I don't know why she bothers to leave one. She knows I have me own," Jamie whispered.

Just as she turned the key in the door, Frank leaned across to give her a kiss on the lips. The door flew open. Frank fell forward and knocked Jamie on to the floor of the hall. He fell on top of her. They both ended up rolling around the floor, screaming laughing.

"Who's that?" came a loud roar from upstairs.

The two drunk, over-aged schoolkids tried to stifle the laughter by holding their breaths. It didn't work. Jamie had the hiccups. She shrieked. "Jesus, I'm going to wet myself. Stop," she urged.

Frank looked up from where he was lying. He could see two fluffy slippers standing on the second step of the stairs. Frank put his hand up to his mouth.

"Jesus, Mary and Joseph, you two should be ashamed of yourselves. Look at youse, acting like schoolchildren." Mona switched on the light. Her eyes opened wide in disbelief. She put her hand up to her mouth and muttered a quick prayer. "Jamie Carroll, I hope the neighbours didn't see either of youse dressed like that." She walked back up the stairs as if she'd just seen a ghost.

* * *

Frank opened his left eye. His right eye was stuck. He

checked his watch. Quarter to five. It was pitch-dark. He felt her warm hand slipping up under his T-shirt. He closed his eye again, pretending to be asleep. Her hand moved around to his flat stomach. Then down, inside his shorts. She ran her nails through his thick bush of hair and then slowly touched his hard erection with her fingers. She pulled her hand back out and thumped him on the back. "You cheeky boy," she whispered at the top of her voice, "you were only pretending to be asleep."

Frank turned around and grabbed her quickly. "Your mother will kill us if she catches us." He planted a passionate kiss squarely on her lips and ran his hands up her bare arms. Then he noticed she was only wearing a bra and panties.

"Let me wash my teeth," she said softly. She tip-toed out to the bathroom.

Frank could hear the water running for a few seconds. Then silence. He could feel himself becoming more aroused despite the amount of alcohol in his system. He switched on the bedside light and grabbed a magazine.

" . . . He watched her, over the top of the magazine, as she slipped off her skimpy bra under her sexy, black negligee. She stood in front of the mirror for a moment and ran her fingers over the contours of her firm, large breasts. She took a sharp, deep breath as she ran her fingers beneath the thin garment and gently tweaked each nipple into a hard, bullet-like object of sexual desire.

She turned around and walked sensually towards

the naked man lying across the duvet. As she approached him, he lay up on an elbow and lifted his left knee, revealing his huge, stiff erection in all its glory. The black garment slid down her body, over her hips and on to the floor. She was completely naked. She moaned as she stood over him and ran her fingers up and down along his long, hard cock. Then, as she stroked it gently with her hand, she bent down and ran her moist tongue around his dry lips. As she moved further up to kiss his eyes and his forehead, she grabbed the back of his neck and pulled his head in between her breasts. He flicked her hard nipples with his tongue while he ran his fingers through her damp, black pubes. She groaned, urging him to explore deeper. He obliged by gently plunging his fingers into her wet crevice. She moaned louder as he bit hard on each nipple. He took hold of her hips with his hands and guided her legs, one to each side of his, and her snatch down on to his love tool. He licked the sweat from her neck as she gyrated in time to his thrusting pelvis. "Now," she screamed, as she reached for the shelf above the bed for something to hold on to.

He ran his fingers up and down her ribs while he took one of her breasts, whole, into his mouth. Then the other. Now and then, he'd stop and run his pointed tongue teasingly around each of her dark-brown nipples, while her having beasts jumped up and . . . "

"I think that's meant to be *heaving breasts*, Frank." Jamie kicked off her slippers and climbed into bed beside him. "Give me that filth. I don't want to read any more!" She grabbed the magazine out of Frank's hand. "*Hustler.* Where'd you get this?"

"It was here," he pointed, "under the bed. I swear!"

"Wait till I get Jabs. Me ma lets him stay over one night and he leaves that filth behind him." Jamie switched off the light.

Frank nuzzled up behind her. He ran his hand across her bare, warm back. "What do you say . . . just a few minutes?"

"No," she groaned, "I'm too pissed." Within seconds, she was snoring like a broken exhaust.

She woke in a panic. "Oh, my head. What time is it?" She looked around for her watch. Twenty to ten. Then she saw Frank lying beside her. "Jesus Christ, what are you doing here?" she shouted.

Frank opened one eye. "What do you mean, what am *I* doing here? This is my room."

Jamie leaped out of the bed. "Oh Jesus, if she catches us together, there'll be fucking murder. Oh, my head. Why did I have to drink so much? This is all your fault, Frank McCabe."

Just then, there was a knock on the door. "Frank, love."

Frank smiled. "Yes, Mrs Carroll?"

Jamie hid behind the wardrobe door.

"How do you like your eggs done?"

Jamie was making all sorts of signs to him not to give her away.

"Hard-boiled, please, Mrs Carroll. Thanks." He winked at Jamie.

"Right, love, they'll be ready in ten minutes. And Frank," she called.

"Yes."

"I told you to call me Mona, not Mrs Carroll. All right, love?"

"All right, Mona."

Jamie let out a deep sigh of relief.

"Oh, I nearly forgot," came the voice from beyond the door again, "Jamie."

Jamie froze and almost passed out. "Eh, yeah . . . Ma?"

"Sheila rang. She wants to know if you'd be interested in going to the national ploughing championships tomorrow. I told her I doubted it but that you'd call her anyway."

Chapter Thirty

Friday. The bright morning sunshine sent slivers of light across the bedroom. It was too bright to sleep. Jamie twisted restlessly. She looked at the clock. Quarter to nine. She heard the door closing downstairs. Her mother shouted at Nellie Fahy next door as she closed the garden gate behind her.

"Morning, Nellie. How's your piles?"

"No change," replied the small, hunched neighbour.

No shame, thought Jamie.

"I'll put in a prayer for them at the nine Mass this morning," came the heartening reply.

The phone downstairs rang once, then stopped.

That was the signal. She leaped out of bed and pulled on her jeans as she tugged at the curtains with her chin.

The police car was there all right. She took a closer look. Her eyes lit up and she smiled. The two men were there, just as they'd been there when she went to bed. But they were fast asleep. What a stroke of luck.

What a pair, she thought. She pulled a jumper on

over her nightdress and slipped her feet into a pair of trainers. She ran down the stairs taking two steps at a time, picked up the keys to Frank's hired car and ran out into the garden.

Frank had shown her how to use the mobile phone the night before. She dialled the number slowly.

"Anne?"

"Jamie?"

"This is dead handy. Any news?"

"Not yet. How are things your end, Jamie?"

"Not so bad. Our friends are still here but in spirit only, I'm afraid."

Anne sounded confused. "What do you mean?"

"I mean they're fast asleep."

"*I don't believe you!*" echoed her loud reply.

"Ssshhh," urged Jamie. "How are things your end?"

"They're crawling around here like sniffer dogs. I've never had this many men watching me in my life before. No fear of these blokes being asleep. Listen, I need to have a quick word with Frank. Is he there?"

"No. He had to go to Heuston station to pick up a parcel from the Cork train. One of his pals from home was sending him up something he said he needed badly. He wouldn't say what it was."

"How did he get to Heuston?"

"On the bus. He reckoned they probably wouldn't bother following him if he took the bus."

"Good thinking. Get him to call when he gets back. On my mobile only. Not the main hotel number. OK?"

"OK."

"Here, I'm going back inside, I'm freezing. See you later." Anne rang off. Silence again.

Jamie ran from the car to the hall-door. She took a quick look at the car across the road. The two men lay there, their seats reclined, fast asleep.

* * *

Nikki stepped down from the coach. The sea breeze made her shiver. The empty beach looked gorgeous in the early morning sunshine. Her legs ached after the long coach trip from London. But it would be worth it, she thought. She looked around the sleepy seaside resort. The harbour should be further down the narrow street. About a quarter of a mile, she guessed. She threw the small haversack up on to her right shoulder and started to walk down the steep hill.

As she got nearer the main pier, she could see the huge marina. She stopped walking and stared anxiously. Wall-to-wall yachts and cruisers . . . for as far as the eye could see, left and right, big and small . . . nothing but yachts! How the hell was she going to find her man's yacht? She walked slowly towards the marina's entrance, all the time looking from yacht to yacht. The gates were closed. She pressed the buzzer on the gate.

A voice answered. "Can I help you?"

Nikki moved up to the mouthpiece. "I'm expected on board the *Seabird*." She waited for a reply.

The huge electronic gate opened slowly. As soon as there was enough room to squeeze through, she made a dash for it. The gate closed slowly behind her. What now? she wondered. Nikki looked around for some help. She noticed a large chart on the side of what looked like the lifeboat building. It was a map of the marina. She ran her finger up the list. There it was, *Seabird*. Berth 104. She looked for 104 on the marina map. After some searching, she found it and set off in its direction. It didn't take long to find it. Nikki took a long deep breath as she checked the number again to make sure this was her man's boat. "Holy Jesus," she exclaimed as she let her backpack fall to the ground. "Wow!"

It looked like something straight out a James Bond film. It was pure majesty. Two masts stretched upwards towards the deep blue sky. Sails, carefully folded, straddled the front and back decks: decks that were so spotless, you could eat your dinner straight off them. *Seabird* was written along the side of the vessel and in bold letters across the front of the main cabin house. This is it, she muttered, as she held the rails and carefully stepped on board. It was more like a giant cabin cruiser than a yacht.

"You must be Nikki," a foreign voice said from behind.

Nikki jumped. "Jesus," she shouted, putting her hands up to her chest. "You nearly gave me a heart attack." She leaned against the ship's railing. "Don't ever do that again. Who are you?"

"I am Manuel. Your captain." He removed his skipper's cap and bowed his head in typical Spanish style. "Your friend, Thomas, he say that you come today."

He reminded Nikki of every Spanish bloke who'd ever tried to chat her up on holidays. "Where's Tommy?" she asked anxiously.

The man raised his shoulders. "There is a small problem. Thomas is in France. He has to go there at the last moment for important business. He only go last night. He waits for you there. He say he cannot call you because he is busy. But he say to me, Manuel, he say, 'Manuel, you must take good care of Nikki. She very special for me.' So, I look after you until we go to France. OK?"

His broken English was beginning to irritate her. "No, it's not OK. I'm not going to sail all the way to France with some stranger I've never laid eyes on. Do you think I'm mad?" She stormed off the boat.

He followed her. "But you are not alone. My wife, she come also."

Nikki turned around. "Have you got a phone number for Tommy?"

The Spaniard shook his head.

Just then a woman surfaced from the living quarters on the yacht.

The Spanish captain looked at her proudly. "This is Isabella, my wife. She will take care of you until France. We have food and drink. There is no need for you to worry."

Nikki looked up at the woman standing on deck, holding the railings. She wore a tiny bikini. She was stunningly beautiful.

The woman smiled down at her. "Ola," she said politely.

Nikki smiled back. Then she looked at the captain. "The cold mornings obviously don't seem to bother your wife."

"Yea . . . yea," chortled the captain, clearly misunderstanding what Nikki had just said. "Your boyfriend will be very angry with me if I do not look after you. You must come, for my sake." His smile was gone.

"What time do we sail?" Nikki sighed.

"At three . . . this afternoon." He looked relieved.

* * *

At twenty-five past nine, a blue Sierra pulled up behind the white Transit van, parked well back up the hill from the junction of Gardiner Street and Talbot Street. Two men got out and nimbly climbed into the van through the back door.

"Did you get the warrant?" the man sitting in the front seat asked.

One of the men who'd just arrived pulled the official document out of his coat pocket. "It's a green. Let's do it . . . *now*!"

Checking their weapons first, the two men got out of the van, accompanied by the man in the front seat. They huddled on the pavement, concealing their guns under the belts at the backs of their trousers. One of them carried an Uzi sub-machinegun. He tucked it into a secret compartment in the front of his long overcoat. They stood between the side of the van and the tall black railings. They nodded to each other, signalling that they were ready.

Gardiner Street was a hive of activity at that time of the morning. Commuters, rushing from Amien Street railway station towards the city centre, mixed with early morning shoppers, browsing in windows along Talbot Street. Traffic snaked through one of the busiest junctions on Dublin's northside.

No one paid any heed to the three men who dodged cars and buses as they trotted across the busy street towards the run-down guest-house. No room for errors now. They climbed the five steps to the front door in single file. Once inside, their mood changed. They walked up to reception. The man carrying the Uzi produced an official badge. "Police," he said distinctly.

The woman, behind the desk, put her hand up to her mouth with the shock of seeing the deadly Israeli sub-machinegun.

"Which room is Tommy Barrett in?" the second man asked eagerly.

The woman's hands shook as she checked the register. "Number seventeen," she answered nervously.

The three men sprinted upstairs towards the first landing.

"But . . . hold on!" she shouted.

The men stopped dead in their tracks and looked back down towards her.

" . . . he checked out this morning," she muttered timidly.

The officers looked at each other in disbelief.

"Why the fuck didn't you see him leaving?" the tall man with the machinegun shouted at the officer who'd been sitting in the front of the Transit, as he thumped his shoulder with the butt of his rifle.

"But we were watching everything he was doing . . ."

They didn't wait for his answer. The two officers, who'd arrived with the warrant for Tommy Barrett's arrest, were already on their way down the main steps back to their dilapidated, blue Sierra patrol car.

"Check the fucking room for anything you can find," the driver roared from across the street at the small man who stood on the top step. "Your head's on the block for this one, sonny."

The Sierra sped off into the busy traffic, its siren wailing. The small blue light was already flashing as the driver affixed it to the roof.

The passenger waved his hand at motorists in front to get out of their way. "Sierra Bravo to control . . . over," he shouted into the radio.

"Control to Sierra Bravo, go ahead . . . over," the voice crackled.

"Inform the Rock that Barrett has checked out of his lodgings. We're *en route* for Dublin airport . . . over."

There was a long crackly silence. The two men looked nervously at each other. They knew what was coming next.

The radio crackled back into life. "Sierra Bravo," a deep, enraged voice shouted.

The two men recognised the voice instantly. "Go ahead, sir," golloped the passenger.

"What the fuck's going on with you lot? I sent you two down there to arrest this man and you let him slip away? What am I paying you two fucking wankers for? Why didn't I just look after this myself? Wait till the commissioner hears about this one? I'll drag the two of you fairies down with me . . . *that* you can be sure of!"

The two men squirmed in their seats at the mention of the word "commissioner".

"Jesus wept!" he continued. "Wait till the papers get hold of this! Await further instructions. Don't do anything till you hear from me," the loud voice ordered.

The line went dead.

* * *

Frank almost tripped over the porch steps in his effort to get inside quickly. He slammed the front door behind him.

Jamie came running to the top of the stairs. "Frank, are you all right? What happened you? Did they follow you?" She ran down the stairs and grabbed his hands.

"They've lost him," Frank gasped, out of breath.

"Lost what? Who's lost what?"

"They've lost Tommy. They must have been trying to arrest him. Two of them have just got a verbal hiding from Blaney."

"Frank, what are you talking about?" Jamie tried to get him to sit down at the kitchen table.

Frank paced up and down.

"What's that you're holding?" Jamie asked. She stared at the device with the huge rubber aerial in Frank's hand.

"He's on his way to the airport, I know it," he ranted.

"*Frank!*" Jamie shouted.

That got his attention.

Jamie nodded to the transistor-like device in his hand.

"This?" he gasped. "Oh . . . it's a scanner. One of the lads from home gave me a lend of it. He sent it up by FastTrack this morning. Here, listen to this . . . " He fiddled with a knob under the frequency dial.

The scanner came to life. Jumbled voices. Police-talk. That was obvious from the coded language.

"We can listen to the cops with this." He waved the radio and turned and headed back to the front door.

"Where are you going?" Jamie asked.

"To talk to Anne," he replied. "Get her on the phone. I want to listen to this . . . find out what's going on."

Jamie called Anne's mobile number. No reply. Either she couldn't hear it ringing or she was otherwise engaged.

* * *

"This is all your fault, *Inspector* O'Brien," Blaney roared down the phone. "I bet any money you *knew* he was going to leave that guest-house this morning."

"Superintendent Blaney." Anne held the phone away from her ear. "With due respect, you messed up big-time on this one. Why would I be interested in concealing important information from you? And anyway, it would be a bit difficult trying to plan a conspiracy from my hotel bedroom with half the Irish police force breathing down my neck, listening to every phone call I make. Don't you agree?"

"I beg your pardon, *Inspector*," he sneered, "my men are doing a commendable job when one considers the petty resources we're expected to work with. We mightn't have the same budget as the London Metropolitan police force. In fact, I think I could safely say that our entire budget for this operation is smaller than the budget Rod Stewart has to have his hair styled. But I will say one thing for my men . . . they *are* dedicated to their work. And I think you've been planning this little plot for a lot longer than the last few weeks. You want that boy back on British soil. That way, you can arrest him. Let me tell you, Inspector, if you think for a moment that you're going to walk away from this leaving the egg on *my* face, you've got it wrong. He's mine. We'll have that tosser in cuffs before he can set foot on a flight out of here this morning. And if you don't believe it, get your pretty arse out to the airport and watch us!"

The phone line went dead.

The phone rang once in Jamie's house and stopped.

Frank started the engine and called to Jamie to hurry up. As the little red Fiesta drove quickly up Church Avenue, the two men in the blue Ford Orion pulled their seats into the upright position and followed closely behind.

"Whereabouts are you?" Jamie asked as they swung out on to Santry Avenue.

"I'm just coming past Ballymun flats," replied Anne.

"We must be close to you then . . . the reception is perfect. Anyone behind you?"

"I'm not sure, but I'd guess half the city's police force," she shrilled nervously. "When I arrive at the airport, don't come near me, OK? Frank, you should be able to hear what's going on on that scanner. By law, I should confiscate it and arrest you for having one. But we'll let it go this once, OK?" she joked.

Frank smiled as he pointed to the airport buildings on his left.

"I suppose where you come from, you never get to see airports," Jamie muttered sarcastically.

"I beg your pardon. It's probably been years since you've seen green fields," he replied. He turned to look at Jamie. "What are you thinking?"

She stared out the window. "I suppose that at long last they're going to catch him and lock him up."

"Is that what you want?"

"Of course that's what I want," said Jamie angrily. "The bastard's an animal. Prison isn't good enough for him. With a bit of luck, he'll do something stupid and they'll shoot him dead. Do us all a favour."

Just then, the police scanner exploded into life.

"He's already gone through, we think," a voice shouted.

They recognised the next voice as that of Inspector Blaney. "What do you mean, he's gone through, we *think*? Find out what flight he's on and follow him . . . force your way on to the flight if you have to. In fact, *stop* the flight if you have to. I'm on my way."

A unmarked patrol car with a flashing blue light and a wailing siren shot passed them on the other side of the road. The siren was partly broken. It only gave out a one-sided *meep . . . meeep . . . meeep* yowl. A man was hanging out the back window waving at traffic to clear a route up the middle of the main Belfast road towards the airport.

"There's our friend . . . Blaney," muttered Jamie.

* * *

Inspector Anne O'Brien was one of the first of the top brass to arrive at the departures gate. She flashed her badge and was admitted without question.

Uniformed police officers stood about conspicuously. The scene was one of utter confusion. Passengers were being instructed to stand to one side so that police back-up could get through to the departures area. An announcement over the intercom informed those travelling that all flights had been delayed due to a security alert.

Anne showed her badge again to a uniformed officer. "Which flight is Barrett booked on to?"

"It's the 11.45am flight to Manchester, we suspect. It's the only flight departing for the UK between now and one."

Anne smiled. So he *is* going to meet the boat. Suddenly she looked puzzled. "Is his name down as Barrett?"

"No. We've checked. He may have booked in under a false name," the garda replied.

Anne remembered what Frank had told herself and Blaney. She racked her brain for a minute. Jesus, what was the name again? Lenihan . . . or something like that. "Check for a name like Lenihan. Or something that sounds like that," she urged the policeman.

He nodded and walked briskly towards the reservations desk.

Just then, Inspector Blaney rushed by her with his badge above his head.

They were heading for Gate A6, she thought. She decided to follow them. She looked at her watch. It was 11.45am. *Go on!* she willed out loud. *Take off . . . now!*

Frank and Jamie sipped their cups of coffee as they stared in disbelief at the scanner sitting, partially covered by a newspaper, on the table in front of them. It sounded as if five people were talking at any one time.

From where they were sitting, high about the departures area, they could see the flurry of military activity down below.

Frank stretched his head over the glass partition to get a closer look. "I don't believe it!" he exclaimed. "They've brought in the *army*!"

Men in khaki-green uniforms, armed with rifles, were now standing close to entrances and exits keeping a close eye on everyone's movements.

"Ssshhh," urged Jamie.

They pressed their ears close to the crackly radio. "There's no sign of him here in the departures' lounge," a voice echoed.

"Well, there has to be," replied Blaney. "He can't just have vanished into thin air, for God's sake! Anybody on board the plane yet?" he shouted anxiously.

"Almost half full, sir," another voice answered. "He's not on board. At least, not yet, sir."

"Jesus Christ," roared Blaney, "He has to be somewhere in there. Could he have gone through another gate?"

"Negative, Inspector," came the reply. "Airport authorities have thoroughly checked every passenger through in the past hour, sir. They say he couldn't have got on board any other plane without their knowing it. Not without the right boarding pass."

"I don't believe it," Blaney bellowed.

Frank was beginning to knock great fun out of the major cock-up. He grinned at the radio. "This is brilliant, isn't it? I mean, where would you get it?" He looked up at Jamie. She looked petrified. He changed his tone. "Are you all right?" he asked gently.

She shook her head. "He got away," she whispered. "He has . . . hasn't he?"

"No, he *hasn't*!" Frank tried to reassure her. "That place in there is huge. *You* know that. It takes about twenty minutes to walk down to the A departure section. They'll find him, I promise." He reached across the table and took her hands. "I love you. Don't be worrying."

The scanner crackled. "Everyone's on board now, sir," a worried voice said.

"Well, check them all again, for Christ's sake. And

again if you have too. He has to be in there somewhere. Don't leave that plane before I get there," roared Blaney frantically.

Then an excited voice shouted. "There's one empty seat, sir. We reckon it's his!"

The public intercom rang. *Bing bong.* " . . . would passenger Lenane, flying to Manchester, please report to Gate A6 in the departures area, as this flight is now ready for departure . . . " The announcer sounded so laid-back that Frank burst out laughing. He slapped the table. "What did I tell you? He's using Michael Lenane's ticket. They have him sussed. Now they'll catch him."

"*Frank!*" urged Jamie. "Quiet. Everyone's looking at you."

Frank winked. "If only they knew what we knew."

Jamie looked across the table, above the ear-piercing battle which continued to rage on the scanner. "He's done it again," she whispered in a resigned voice. "He's not anywhere, is he?"

Frank looked awkwardly at her. "What do you mean, not anywhere?"

"Well, now *no one* knows where he is. Do they? He knows where *we* are but no one knows where *he* is or *where* he's gone. Or, worse still . . . where he's going to turn up next." She stood up from the table.

"Where are you going?" Frank asked.

"Give me the keys. I'll wait for you in the car."

"Are you OK on your own?"

"I'm a big girl now. I'm well able to look after myself."

Jamie wasn't aware that she was being followed. Her heart was heavy. Her mind was racing. She walked lethargically back towards the car on the ground floor level of the short-term car park. As she opened the passenger door of the red Fiesta, an arm went round her throat from behind, grabbing her forcefully. She instantly sensed the gun being held to the side of her head. "Not *one* word. There's a highly sophisticated silencer on this. No one's going to hear it except you. And that might feel rather unpleasant. Just do as I say. Get into the car."

She found it difficult to breathe. She gasped and spluttered. "*Please* don't kill me," she begged.

Tommy looked different, she thought. He wasn't the cool, calm individual she'd known for so long. He was agitated. Flustered. Nervous. "Start the fucking car and get out of here."

He held the gun low. "You're hurting me, Tommy. I can't breathe with it sticking into me."

"Fucking bitch. You always had something to whinge about, you stupid cow!" He watched excitably as a uniformed police officer directed them into an exit lane.

"Use the pay-booth on the left only," the cop said to Jamie.

She nodded nervously and drove past.

"No silly moves," rasped Tommy.

"The ticket," she whimpered.

"What *ticket*?"

"The ticket for getting out of the carpark. I don't have it!"

577

"Jesus Christ, where is it?"

"Frank has it. He was driving." She tried hard to remain calm, anything to stop the tears and stay in control . . . and alive.

"Fucking great. What are we going to do now?" Tommy looked around at the other lanes of traffic. "Here, stay close to him," he said, pointing to the car in front. "The minute the barrier lifts and he goes under, get right up his arse and stay with him all the way through."

Jamie did what he told her. Unfortunately, the car spluttered and hesitated as it snaked under the barrier. They weren't fast enough. It came down hard on the roof, activating an alarm in the carpark cash office.

"*Move . . . fast!*" ordered Tommy.

Jamie accelerated. She looked in the rear view mirror. An attendant was signalling to a nearby patrol car. Jamie prayed they'd follow. They didn't. "Where are we going?"

"Howth."

Frank scratched his head. He stood on a step and checked again. It was definitely here, he swore to himself. Now the car was gone. And so was Jamie. He walked down the slope to the exit. An attendant was talking to a policeman.

"Excuse me, did a red Fiesta go past here in the last ten minutes?" asked Frank.

The two men's eyes lit up. "Bloody hell, did it what? Through the barrier, damaging the mechanism, and not bothering to stop. It'll need a bit of panel-beating to the roof."

"Did you see who was in it?" Frank asked.

"Nope, driving too fast."

A passing car honked at Frank. It was Anne O'Brien. "Where's Jamie?" she shouted.

Frank sat into the passenger seat. "Good question. I've got an horrible feeling that Tommy's in the car."

"So have I?"

"Why?"

"The taxi-driver who dropped him to the airport rang 999 when he'd dropped him off. Seemingly, when Tommy got into the taxi earlier in town, he was wearing a blond wig. He took it off until he arrived at the departures building, where he put it on again."

"So that's how he managed to get on board the plane unnoticed?"

"He didn't get on a plane, Frank. The wig was discovered in the gents' toilets in the arrivals hall. Tommy went through departures all right, but then took a left and walked downstairs back into arrivals. We've lost him again. Only this time, I've got a horrible feeling that he's got Jamie."

The small red Fiesta pulled up outside the car rental office in Swords, three miles north of the airport.

"Right, now, we're going to walk in here calmly. We're here on our honeymoon for a week and we're hiring a car to tour the west of Ireland. Have you got that?" he said.

Jamie nodded nervously. Her voice twittered. "Yeah."

"Then you hand over your credit card and

complete the transaction. No funny moves, do you hear me?"

She agreed.

He kept the gun hidden in his leather jacket pocket, his hand permanently on the trigger. As he turned the handle on the showroom door, he looked around the quiet street apprehensively. He failed to notice a leather-clad biker talking to a red-haired taxi-driver. Every now and then, they'd stop talking and observe the couple standing inside the showroom window.

Ten minutes later, Jamie Carroll and Tommy Barrett left Swords in the direction of Howth, driving a sleek black BMW 318is. A taxi and motor-bike followed closely, alternating positions so as not to give Tommy any idea that he was being followed.

Chapter Thirty-One

Nikki staggered up the few steep steps and out on to the deck. Her head was spinning. Each time she tried to focus on the horizon, she felt twice as bad. She barely made it to the side of the ship. This must be the fifth time she'd thrown up. Or was it fifteenth? She'd lost count. She slumped back against the cold cabin wall. Her stomach was still retching. Anything solid for support. She looked up at the captain. She just wanted to die. In fact, if someone had shown her a gun, she'd have happily held it to the side of her head and pulled the trigger. She'd never been so sick in her entire life.

The captain gabbled something in Spanish and laughed to himself. "I thought you Irish were used to the sea," he shouted, above the noise of the engine.

"You'd want to be a duck to get used to this," she muttered. The sea seemed to be getting nastier by the hour. She looked up at the sky. Dark grey. Then it occurred to her that the boat didn't seemed to be going anywhere. It climbed each huge swell and dropped down the other side. She threw her head forward and hugged herself. "Jesus . . . how long more?" she groaned.

"Four hours . . . maybe five, depending on the swell," he replied.

"Jesus," she sighed. "I'm going to die."

"My wife Isabella will look after you. She has some nice paella and shrimps for our dinner. It is a traditional dish she learns from her mother."

Nikki lunged towards the railings again. "I need something to take for this," she cried, in between the retching.

"Check the first-aid box underneath my bunk."

Nikki groped her way towards the small door which led to the comfortable living quarters below. As she stepped on to the small staircase, the yacht lurched forward over a wave sending her flying down the four steps. She landed hard on her knees. The pain was excrutiating. Crying, she crawled into the small cabin and ran her hand under the bed. The smell of salt water and engine diesel made her feel wretched. She pulled the small box, marked with a red cross, on to her lap and opened it. Bandages, flares, bottles of pills. She held each bottle carefully up to the small light bulb by the sink.

Ponstan Forte . . . DF 118s . . . pain-killers, she thought. Augmentin 500s . . . antibiotics to kill flu infections, no doubt.

She picked up the second bottle again. Nikki had heard of DF 118s somewhere. She reckoned they were pain-killers. She remembered Jamie telling her that they were great for bad period pains even though the doctor freaked every time she asked for them. She opened the plastic top and shook three of them into her hand. Make it four, she thought. Why not? Maybe they'd help to knock her out for the rest of the trip. Anything to stop the awful vomiting. As she placed the bottles back in the box, she noticed the trigger and froze. She slowly moved the giant roll of cotton wool aside. It was a gun. Just like the guns in all the films she'd seen. It looked real. Maybe it was for letting off flares. She picked it up, careful to avoid putting her finger near the trigger.

This wasn't for flares . . . this was for *bullets*. It was heavier than she'd imagined.

She ran her fingers down along the cold, smooth barrel and gently, nervously, felt the tip. She remembered the thought that had crossed her mind only minutes earlier. The notion of ending her misery this way didn't seem so appealing now. She heard someone coming. Quickly, she stuffed the weapon back under the roll of cotton wool and put the lid back tightly on.

"Are you all right?" the captain asked.

Nikki stood up slowly, rubbing her knees. She nodded. "Have you got a glass of water so I can take these?"

The captain took hold of her hand and examined the tablets. He frowned at her. "*Four* of these?" He tutted under his breath. "Very strong," he urged. "Four is too many. You sleep for many days. You may not wake up. Two is OK. No more. You hear me?" He filled a mug with water and handed it to her. He hopped back up the stairs.

As soon as the two tablets were down, Nikki lowered the other two and gulped down the water. She held her breath and her stomach for a minute while the concoction settled. She sat down on the side of the bunk bed and rubbed her forehead. Hot and cold sweats. Probably caused by all the vomiting, she thought. She felt as though she might have a mild temperature. She sat back on to the bed and rested her head against the life-jacket which had fallen off the wall during the heavy swell and on to the pillows. It felt hard but supportive. As she pushed the jacket to make it more comfortable, her hand came across a magazine. She pulled it out from underneath. It was a copy of *Mayfair*. A soft-porn girlie magazine for men. She'd never really bothered with sexy magazines before. The girl on the cover was naked, apart for a Manchester United football flag which she'd loosely draped across her ample cleavage. Nikki opened the magazine and slowly turned the pages. There seemed to be a naked woman on every second page. On page twelve, there was a nude shot of a black-haired college student called Loretta. She lay across a large armchair with her hands over her head and her legs wide apart. Not a very convincing smile, thought Nikki. She turned the page. Then the next page. Eleven pages of Loretta. By page eleven, Loretta appeared to have two heads and four breasts. Nikki tried to focus. She was losing her grip on the magazine. It slid slowly across her shoulder and dropped on to the floor. Nikki didn't notice. She was fast asleep.

Tommy went up through the gears. The engine revved out to its limit as he climbed. Third. He checked the clock. Eighty-five . . . not bad. Fourth. Touching a hundred. Not a budge out of the steering wheel. Into fifth. Then he saw the flashing blue lights up ahead. The taxi and motor-bike slowed down and pulled in. Too late, thought Tommy. A speed trap . . . and they'd caught him. He was already sixty miles per hour faster than the legal limit. This speed meant an instant arrest. Possibly prison. But not in his case. No way! Quick thinking was called for. Fuck it. He passed the patrol car like an express train. And kept going. Jamie screamed. *"Please let me go!"* she pleaded above the blaring radio. He ignored her and laughed.

The young officer who'd been holding the speed-gun ran around to the passenger seat and climbed in. *"Go on,"* he roared enthusiastically to his partner, *"get this heap moving. That fucker's right off the clock!"*

By the time the driver had started the small White Astra, Tommy was long gone.

"I got his reg!" the officer shouted eagerly. He grabbed the radio to inform control.

Tommy Barrett pulled into the hotel carpark at ten to three that afternoon. The powerful Kawasaki motor-bike sat on the other side of the level-crossing, the passing train obscuring the view, its rider talking frantically into his two-way radio.

* * *

Howth marina was quiet. Normal for a wet, windswept afternoon. Three men huddled for shelter close to the giant, greyish ice plant, used by local trawlers and private fishing crews for preserving catches while at sea for long durations. Two more carried refills of coffee from the small, cosy coffee shop across the street. The marina itself sounded like a giant jangling tambourine, as millions of steel rings, used for holding sails in postion, rattled against the yachts' aluminium masts in the chilling breeze coming in off the Irish sea. The men chatted, while trying to stay warm.

"They won't come in in this," one muttered, as he nodded to the sky.

"This'd be the very day they *would* try to come in, when no one's expecting them," muttered another.

The giant, grey Navy patrol vessel was just about visible, three miles out, in bleak conditions. Two other men strolled slowly down a giant wooden ramp which led to a cluster of luxury yachts and cruisers. And an empty berth.

* * *

The curtains in room 27 were pulled. Quarter past four. It was a grim afternoon and beginning to get dark, usually early. Tommy Barrett checked the knots in the rope again. He pulled hard, causing the hard back of the teak chair to dig into her arms. Jamie squealed through the large strip of sticking-plaster which stretched across her mouth. She mumbled incoherently. Tears streamed down her red cheeks, bloated now because of her efforts to plead with Tommy. A long length of fishing-line, tied around her neck, was attached to the trigger of the .38 Special which sat bolted between her knees pointing directly at her chin. Her knees were tightly bound together with yards of sticking-tape to prevent the gun from becoming unbalanced. The wooden handle of the weapon dug into the sides of her knees. The pain was horrible. But she couldn't move or she'd lose her head.

"You've a couple of inches to play around with. But don't sneeze or fall asleep," he mocked. "And whatever you do, don't rock the chair. I suggest you relax. Because you could end up in a right mess if you work yourself into one of your chesty states again." He opened the door. "If anyone rings, I'll be back in half an hour. Fancy some fish for dinner?" he teased. He turned the key in the door.

Jamie could hear him getting further and further away. Then silence, apart from the sound of her heart beating. Now she was staring down the barrel of a loaded gun.

* * *

He noticed heads turn as the powerful sports car cruised slowly up the main street. Maybe it wasn't such a good idea hiring a car like this. He reckoned the police had his number for speeding and failing to stop at a checkpoint. He was about as conspicuous as a circus clown. He steered slowly on to the garage forecourt. Best get it off the street for a few hours. At least until after dark. He was sure the cops would be looking for him. No point in testing fate. "Can I leave it in for a full service?" he asked the young mechanic.

The mechanic looked at his watch. "Bit on the late side. We won't have it for you today. Can you collect it tomorrow?"

"No problem. What time?"

"Lunch-time?"

"Perfect. I'll fix up with you then. Here's the keys, mate. Cheers."

Tommy glanced back at the marina as he strolled out along the road towards the hotel. Not a lot of activity. Possibly one or two Special Branch. He could spot them a mile away. Or was he just being paranoid? Don't bother me, he mumbled. Then he remembered that the gun was back in the hotel. He sharpened his pace. He'd had a hunch all day that this plan wasn't going to go as smoothly as he'd hoped. Look on the good side, he thought. The bad weather would surely keep any troublemakers away. The cops wouldn't expect to nab anyone on a day like this. Not here. A drink seemed like a good idea.

* * *

The phone rang in Carroll's. There'd been no word all evening of Jamie's whereabouts. Frank had called the police and told them he thought she'd been kidnapped. They were now treating the possibility seriously.

"Frank, it's for you," called Mona.

"Jamie?" he asked hopefully.

Mona shook her head. "It's a man." She blew her nose.

"Would you like another cup of tea?" asked Anne O'Brien.

"No thanks, love," sighed Mona. "I'm beginning to feel like the little red teapot, I've drunk so much. You've been very good to stay so long. I'll sit up for a bit longer. Just in case . . . "

Frank closed the sitting-room door behind him. He picked up the receiver. "Hello."

"Frank McCabe?" the northern voice asked.

"Yes?" Frank replied anxiously.

"I'm a friend of the family. I think you might have an idea who I am. We must meet."

"Anything you say. Where?"

* * *

Nikki woke up in a cold sweat. She was shivering violently. She sat up quickly and banged her head off the upper bunk. Her fingers felt numb and her legs ached from her knees down to her toes. A dull, dead agonising pain. Then she remembered the tablets. She rubbed her watery eyes and rolled sideways until she was able to sit on the side of the lower bunk. Her head was spinning. But her stomach didn't feel so bad any more.

Then, it dawned on her. Everything was still. Motionless. Silence, apart from an occasional gurgling sound which seemed to be coming from above her bunk. That unnerved her. Were they sinking? She relaxed. Her cabin was obviously below the waterline, she thought, and it hadn't flooded.

Then it started again. The banging sound which she now remembered had woken her up only minutes before. It sounded like a hammer against the wall of the neighbouring cabin. Maybe the captain was doing some repairs. She walked over to the wall and listened carefully. It was a rhythmic knocking sound. A bang every second. She opened the cabin door. It wasn't coming from the deck area. It was definitely next door. Just then, a loud, terrifying scream echoed throughout the ship. Without a second thought, Nikki dived through the door.

"What's wrong?" she shouted. "Is everyone all right . . . " Her words stopped short as her mouth dropped open.

Isabella was lying across the bed, completely naked. Black nylon stockings tied her wrists and feet to the four corners of the bed. She was moaning and mouthing the occasional Spanish expression, which meant nothing to Nikki.

Manuel, the captain, meanwhile, rocked backwards and forwards, urging his partner underneath to shout louder. His gangly body moved like a set of well-oiled pistons.

Jesus, thought Nikki, a bull on steroids.

They were happy. Just as Nikki backed out of the small room, the woman looked up and saw her.

Nikki froze.

The woman smiled. She nodded at the man who towered over her and then at the door.

The captain glanced quickly across at Nikki.

If there was ever a perfect case of being in the wrong place at the wrong time, thought Nikki, then this was *it*!

His rocking movement slowed. He smiled at Nikki. "You come in if you like . . . " He gestured with his hand and patted the side of the small bed.

Nikki looked at the two bodies on the bed. The thought of getting passionate after puking all night was beginning to make her feel quite ill again. "No, thanks." She put her hand to her mouth as she shook her head and banged the door. She stood in the tiny corridor area, between the two cabins, and took a deep breath. What have I got myself into? she asked.

"*Jesus!*" she muttered, "Who's steering the boat?" The smell of paella turned her stomach again, as she walked past the littered dinner table. Filthy pigs, she mumbled.

Up onto the deck. The fresh sea air felt wonderful. Exhilarating. She checked her watch. Shit! It was full of greenish water. A wave must have hit it when she was vomiting earlier on. She looked around the control panels for a clock. All sorts of gadgets and dials but no clock. What time was it? She looked up at the sky. Plenty of stars but not really pitch-dark yet. Probably about seven, or thereabouts. She looked around the yacht. The sails were folded up. Bare masts climbed into the moonstone-blue darkness. The boat was silent apart from the gentle lapping of the sea against its sides, and the occassional crackle of activity on the radio. And, of course, that awful knocking.

Nikki moved carefully to the front of the yacht and sat down against the base of the giant wooden mast. She looked around the blackness in front of her. As her eyes adjusted to the increasing darkness, she was able to pick out small lights, bobbing up and down, here and there. There seemed to be five or six of them. She noticed one boat, very near. But she couldn't hear a sound. She held her hand up to her eyes. They were stinging her. She looked up at the sky again. The stars were everywhere. Millions of them in giant clusters. All sorts of different shapes and sizes. Just then, a shooting star shot across the sky directly overhead. She watched it as it cut a path through the other stars and dropped into the sea. She'd heard that wishing on a shooting star would bring luck. She'd no time for all that bullshit, usually. Tonight she felt she needed it. She looked out over the sea. Then she saw them. Lights. Small lights. They seemed to be at different levels some distance from the side of the boat. Dotted up and down hills by the look of it. She climbed up on to her knees and held the railing at the front of the yacht. That's land, she shouted.

The knocking downstairs stopped.

"France!" she shouted.

A man's voice muttered downstairs. The two Spaniards laughed. The knocking started again.

Nikki hated them by now. Soon, though, she'd be with Tommy. She wouldn't have to endure them any more. She wondered if the boat was drifting. Surely not, she thought. It must be anchored. Why aren't we moving? she wondered. Maybe it's something to do with the tide. She sat back down again. She felt relieved that land was so close. Nikki's stomach gurgled. She was hungry. It was a good sign. What she'd have given now for a mug of tea and a couple of slices of hot, buttered toast . . . the way that Ray made it in the mornings for her. Her mouth watered at the thought.

"*Seabird . . . Seabird!*" the ship's radio crackled to life.

Nikki almost lost her balance with the fright of hearing the voice. She made her way back along the side of the narrow yacht into the cabin. She waited for the voice again. Maybe she'd just been imagining it. She'd been very sick and the tablets might've been playing games on her mind.

"*Mayday . . . mayday!*" the voice shouted more impatiently. "*Can anyone hear us? Over.*" It was an Irish accent. Nikki's heart was beating so fast it felt as if it would burst. Instinctively, she grabbed the radio's mouthpiece. "Hello, hello," she shouted. "I can hear you. Who are you?"

There was no reply for what seemed like ages. "*Seabird . . .* we are receiving you, loud and clear. What is your position . . . over?"

Nikki hadn't a clue what he meant. Or, for that matter, where she was. "I'm not the captain. He's . . . well, he's busy at the moment. Are you in trouble?" she asked eagerly.

"We seem to be. Our engines have cut out and won't start. We're in danger of taking on water if the storm blows up again. Over . . . "

"I don't know where we are. All I know is that we must be close to the coast of France. Can you see the lights on land?"

This time there was a long delay before the stranger's voice answered, "Yes, we can. You say we're near the coast of France. Are you sure?"

"I think we must be. That's where we're heading for." She thought about her next question for a moment. "You're Irish, aren't you?" She waited.

"Yes. We were fishing. We've been drifting for hours. What's your name?"

"Nikki Coffey. I'm from Dublin." She was delighted to hear a familiar accent. "What's your name?"

"Derek," replied the stranger. "There's five of us on board. We haven't eaten since yesterday morning. Can you help us?"

Nikki looked anxiously at the radio set. "I don't know. Where are *you*? And maybe we'll try and get to where you are?" Nikki thought to herself for a moment. "How did you know this is the *Seabird* . . . over?"

"The coastguard was able to tell us. Your captain must have been talking with them earlier on." Another delay. "Nikki, I think we're only a couple of hundred yards from you. Look to your left."

Nikki stuck her head out from behind the controls into the breezy darkness. A small light was flashing a short distance away. "Is that you flashing the light?" she asked.

"Yes," came the reply. "Who've you got on board with you?"

"You wouldn't believe it. A couple of rabbits diguised as Spaniards." She laughed. She have given anything just to see the Irish crew right now.

"Only two?"

"Only two, I'm afraid," Nikki replied.

"Are they men or women?"

"One of each."

"Big or small?"

Nikki seemed puzzled. "Why do you ask . . . big or small?"

"It's just that we were hoping they might be able to help us get our engines going again. That's all. Can they swim?"

Nikki was now totally confused. "*Swim?*"

"Just in case we need to check the propeller . . . no one here can swim, I'm afraid!"

Nikki looked out into the pitch-black darkness again. Maybe it *was* just her imagination, but if that was the small trawler that the stranger on the radio was talking about, it was much closer to her now. Couldn't be, she thought. The lights were playing games with her eyes.

A hand grabbed the mouthpiece forcibly from her. "What do you think you are doing?" the captain shouted. "You have no permission to be talking!" he roared, pointing to the two-way radio.

"Nikki . . . Nikki. Are you still there?" the now-familiar voice asked.

"You have to help him," Nikki urged. "They're afraid they'll sink if the weather gets bad again."

The captain started up the cruiser's engines.

It was only then that Nikki realised he was only wearing a small pair of underpants.

As the boat veered away in the opposite direction, Nikki realised that Manuel had no intention of going near the stricken trawler.

The desperate voice kept calling out Nikki's name over the radio.

She put out her hand to pick up the receiver.

Manuel hit it so hard that Nikki cried out in pain. "For God's sake, they're Irish. We've got to help them," she shouted, as the wind picked up and blew hard against the cruiser's path.

The small trawler slipped further away.

"What's wrong with you?" Nikki shouted.

The captain ignored her. He muttered some things to himself in Spanish.

"We've got to help them, Manuel!"

The captain's wife appeared at the top of the small staircase and shouted something to her ranting husband.

He shouted back at her.

She disappeared back downstairs.

The radio squawked. "Nikki, please answer if you're all right. Give us your position."

The captain shouted at the radio and pushed the throttle further forward.

Nikki ran to the back of the yacht. She held one hand up to her eyes to shield them from the spray. It was difficult to keep her eyes focused on the trawler for long. The swell was building again. Every few seconds, the fishing trawler would disappear from view. Nikki noticed something strange.

As the boat came back into view, it wasn't alone.

She squinted her eyes again to get a better look. She counted three boats. Maybe they were coming to help the trawler. It didn't make sense. They all seemed to be going in the same direction. Even the boat that was having problems was following *Seabird*.

Nikki was about to go back to the captain and plead with him again when the sea was lit up by a blaze of white light.

Nikki stood rooted to the spot, blinded by the crushing brightness. She closed her eyes and bowed her head down into her jacket to stop her from losing her balance. With her head buried, she was able to open her eyes slowly. She'd never seen anything like this. But what was it? Lightning? Not for this length of time. Something from outer space? At this stage of the evening, after all that had happened, she couldn't rule anything out. Her eyes slowly adjusted to the light, but it was still far too bright to see clearly. Then she heard a loud siren and a booming loudspeaker.

"*Seabird* . . . this is the Irish Navy. We are accompanied by Customs officers and armed detectives. Switch off your engines and prepare to be boarded . . . "

All hell broke loose on board the *Seabird*.

"*Irish police?*" Nikki shouted. She ran towards the captain. He had his back towards her. She grabbed his arm and spun him around. "What the fuck is going on? Why are the Irish police following us this far from home?" she demanded.

He shoved her backwards.

She held out her arm and grabbed the railings.

"Fuck you . . . Irish bitch!" he screamed at the top of his voice. *"This is all your fault. You fucking stupid bitch!"*

The engines accelerated. As the cruiser picked up more speed, the waves came crashing in over the sides. She fought to hold back the tears. She tried to look for the stars again. They were gone, blocked out by the giant spotlight of a deafening helicopter which whirred directly overhead.

"Switch off your engine. Repeat . . . switch off your engine, now. Prepare to be boarded. You are surrounded by armed detectives. You cannot escape . . . " The voice was getting louder.

Nikki could just about make out the shape of a huge ship, close to the yacht on the starboard side. It looked like a big battleship. Three boats following from behind were closing in on them rapidly. *"Give yourself up, for God's sake!"* she pleaded with Manuel. "Why are you doing this?"

He stared into her eyes. "Drugs," he replied.

Nikki's lips took the shape of the word he'd just said. Drugs. *"Drugs?"* she shouted. She thumped his shoulder. "Why are we going to France?"

Manuel looked at her in disbelief. *"France?"* he laughed. "We are going home to Ireland. Or maybe," he paused as he looked across the starboard bow at the huge naval frigate which thundered alongside, " . . . maybe, we are all going to hell . . . together!"

Then she remembered. She groped her way towards the staircase as the boat crashed through the swell. Through the dining area and into the small cabin. She pulled out the first-aid box and ripped off the lid. Her hand folded around the cold, wooden handle of the Smith and Wesson. It felt like a ton weight in her hands. Almost like something you'd work out with in a gymnasium. Her small hands gripped it tightly. Her fingers were barely able to reach the trigger. Nikki had no idea if it was loaded. Or, for that matter, how to fire it properly *or* accurately. She'd just have to take a chance.

" . . . For the final time," boomed the voice from the big ship. As she climbed back out on to the wet, windy deck, she saw a smaller boat speeding towards theirs from the big frigate.

"Stop the engines," she roared at the captain.

He ignored her. Then he felt the cold barrel against the nape of his neck. He turned his head slowly. First he looked at the gun. Then at Nikki. She was holding it with both hands, inches from his chin.

"Please, put it down," he said calmly.

"Turn off the engine," Nikki said.

"We can't turn off the engines, or we're in very big trouble," he explained.

"Turn off the fucking engines . . . now," she roared, *"or, so help me, I'll blow your fucking head into the water!"*

Manuel turned away again as if to pull the throttle back and drop the speed. Suddenly, unexpectedly, he lunged at Nikki and grabbed her arm.

She fought to keep hold of the gun but he head-butted her in the face. She cried out in pain. As she fell to the ground, he grabbed the gun from her.

The detectives in the small dinghy jumped with fright when they heard the gunfire. They ducked for cover. *"Jesus Christ. Gunfire!"* one of them shouted into the two-way radio. *"They're armed. Be careful!"*

Tommy sat in the corner of the comfortable lounge. He was curious to know what was causing all the commotion. The bar began to fill up very quickly. "Excuse me." He nodded to the stout barman. "What's all the excitement about?"

"The police have seized a huge drugs haul just off the coast tonight. Hundreds of thousands worth, they reckon. Fair play to them. They shot dead a couple of the bastards that were bringing in the drugs." He winked at Tommy and then nodded. "They reckon there's a few of them around the town tonight. Like waiting for the boat to come in. I hope they catch them and drown the miserable bastards. Nothing less than they're good for ... "

Tommy didn't wait for him to finish the sentence. He left the lounge and walked briskly back to the hotel. He kicked a discarded can along the pavement, muttering obscenities with each forceful blow. He had to think fast. The deal was now obviously off. He'd have to meet Monty McGrath before the monster came looking for him. What would Nikki tell the police, provided, that is, she wasn't one of the casualties? And what would he do with Jamie? He shrugged. That plan was in place. It would simply take its own course in its own good time. As he passed the garage lock-up where he'd left the BMW earlier that day, he heard the clanking sound of a tool hitting the ground. Tommy thought he saw a dim glow through a skylight in the low, slanted roof. He slowed down to take a closer look. Maybe they're working late, he thought. Maybe just a reflection from the lights of the marina. He walked quickly. Too much police presence for comfort.

The two men worked silently, almost with a sense of *déjà vu*. One lay in under the driver's compartment of the huge German chassis. He held a torch in one hand and worked feverishly on the jackshaft with the other, gently tapping and prodding. Occasionally he'd put down the light to test the parts with both hands. Adjusting and testing. Then readjusting and tightening. His accomplice handed him the appropriate part each time he tapped on the bottom of the door panel. As soon as the parts were securely in place, he slid out silently from under the vehicle. Within seconds the jack was gone and all four wheels were back on terra firma. The second man gently squeezed the car door shut with gloved hands. They gathered up their tools in a hold-all. Then, while one checked the area they'd worked in for any unaccounted-for tools, the other stood quietly for a moment, almost admiring a job well done. "That should do it grand," he muttered. "Let's go home."

Chapter Thirty-Two

Frank felt a warm hand on his shoulder. It seemed to be gently shaking him awake. "Lower," he moaned in a dull voice. "Lower . . . down my back, please." He groaned. He could feel himself getting aroused. "Oh, Jamie, no more shaking. Here, give me your hand . . . "

"*Frank!*" the voice became more commanding, "can you hear me? Wake up, for God's sake!"

Frank looked around in the half-darkness. He leapt up in the bed with an enormous fright. "Oh, Jesus, Mona, I didn't think . . . eh, I mean, I thought that . . . sorry, I shouldn't have been . . . sorry. What's wrong?" Frank put his hand up to his eyes and squeezed them shut with embarassment.

"You must have been having a nightmare, Frank. There seemed to be hands all over you. I'm sorry for waking you, son, but there's a Ray Flynn on the phone for you. He says it's very urgent." She stood back from the bed.

"Ray?" Frank said, still adjusting to the rude awakening. "*Ray?*" He dived out of bed. Then he suddenly remembered that he wasn't wearing any underpants. Mona let out a mild gasp and turned her back.

Frank pulled the global orange lampshade off the top of the bedside reading-lamp and covered his dignity as best he could.

Mona reached the bedroom door just as the wire frame on the inside of the lampshade touched a sore point. "Careful, son, I find that shade gets very hot very quickly." She shut the door.

Frank dressed quickly and ran down the stairs. He grabbed the phone. "Ray?"

"Jesus, Frank, what the fuck's going on there?"

"I'm sorry. I thought Jamie was in bed beside me and she was rubbing my shoulder. Then I turned around and discovered it was her mother . . . and when I leapt out of the bed, I wasn't wearing any . . . "

"I'm not talking about what kept you," Ray shouted. "What's going on with Nikki?"

Frank thought for a moment. He was lost. Then he looked at his watch. Quarter past one in the morning. Suddenly he was wide awake.

"Is everything all right?" a soft voice asked.

Mona was slowly making her way down towards him, adjusting her dressing-gown.

"It's all right. It's just Ray . . . in the pub," he said.

"It's not *all right*!" Ray snapped. "You obviously haven't seen the news this evening, have you . . . well?" he shouted.

"No," Frank replied. "Why?"

"Well, go in and switch on *Sky News* and I'll call you back in fifteen minutes."

"I hope you haven't been serving drinks until now, Ray," Frank said, looking at the clock over the phone.

The phone went dead.

"Is everything all right?" Mona asked again.

"Something must have gone wrong in the pub. Nikki must have had an accident. See . . . I told you she wouldn't be embarking on wild sailing excursions. I bet you she came back full of apologies and Ray needed the extra help. She's probably had a run-in with one of the customers for leering at her." Frank stood up and walked quickly into the sitting-room, confident that things were looking up for a change. He plugged in the television and switched it on. "Where's the zapper?" he asked impatiently.

Mona pointed to the mantlepiece.

He trawled through the channels until he found the one with the logo and the timepiece in the bottom, left-hand corner. *Sky News*.

The newscaster had that ominous look on her face which spelt *serious*. "We go back to our main story again this morning, the massive drugs haul off the Irish coast tonight. We can return live now to our southern Irish correspondent, David Bell, who's in Howth, a small fishing village close to Dublin and the centre of tonight's unfolding drama. Good morning again, David . . . "

"Good morning, Kay."

"Any more developments there tonight?"

Frank looked at Mona Carroll. He reached out and put his arm around her.

The newscaster continued. "Any further news on

604

the man police want to question and how he may have been connected to this operation tonight?"

"Well, we know that Irish police were on the point of arresting him when they *lost* him at Dublin airport yesterday morning just as he was about to board a flight to Manchester. Apparently, they want to talk to him about the disappearance of his former girlfriend yesterday. Her red Fiesta was found abandoned not far from here. Police are refusing to say whether she may have been kidnapped or not. *He* appears to have *disappeared*, the only word to describe his movements, somewhere between the boarding gate and the steps of the plane at Dublin Airport . . . that's according to unofficial sources. Now it's still a mystery how he was able to hire a car three miles from the airport less than an hour later. Police are refusing to be drawn on any conclusions. Nor are they ruling out the possibility of kidnapping in relation to his former girlfriend."

"So where do they think the missing man is tonight, David?"

"It's anyone's guess, Kay. The Irish police can only assume that he's still somewhere in Dublin. We also know now that British police want to question him in relation to the drugs haul in Maida Vale last January in which a detective was shot dead. And also in relation to the recent escape from Brixton prison of IRA bomber, Paul Canice Flaherty, who was spotted here in Dublin during the week."

"Are police saying how this man may be connected to these two cases?"

"Not at the moment. All we know about this

mystery man is that he's a detective police officer assigned to the London drug squad."

"Thank you, David. That was David Bell, talking live to us on *Sky News* this morning from the scene of one of the biggest ever heroin seizures in southern Ireland earlier tonight. Just to recap for you . . . one man is dead, it appears, and two other people, both women, are being questioned by police. The drugs haul, estimated to be worth four and a half million pounds, was made just after half eight last night when Irish police and Customs officials, assisted by the Irish Air Corps and Navy, boarded a yacht en route for a destination in County Dublin. When armed detectives eventually managed to board the craft, they discovered the drugs packed neatly into virtually every available space on the cruiser. Shortly before police boarded the vessel, a burst of gunfire was heard on board. It's alleged that the Spanish captain was shot dead during a struggle. The dead man has been named as Manuel Cartega, aged forty-three, with an address in Bilbao. Two women, twenty-eight-year-old Nicola Coffey, with an address in Artane, Dublin, along with Cartega's wife, were arrested, when police boarded the yacht."

Jamie's mother sat down on the arm of the couch beside Lisa and Jabs. "Mother of Divine Strength," she muttered, "I always told you that girl would get herself into serious trouble." She tapped her chest after she made the sign of the Cross.

"Shut up, Ma," Lisa shouted indignantly. "That's Jamie's best friend you're talking about."

"Sorry, love. I didn't mean that." Mona sighed. Then she started to sob. "Oh, my Jamie. Where is she? Why isn't she coming home?" She put her head in her hands and sat still for a few moments. Silence. Then she blew her nose and stood up. "Who'd like a nice cup of tea?"

Everyone nodded.

"I wouldn't mind one," muttered Jabs.

"Neither would I, love," she said, as she squeezed his ear. "Go and stick the kettle on. And keep the place tidy, will you?" Then it suddenly dawned on her as he left the room. She looked down at Lisa. "What's *he* still doing here at quarter to two in the morning? And why is he wearing one of your T-shirts?"

Lisa went out to help Jabs make the tea.

She sighed again. "Always bad news . . . never any good." Mona closed her eyes.

Frank comforted her.

"Oh, Frank," whispered Mona. "Why has all this happened? And now, Nikki."

Frank rocked her soothingly. They were questions he couldn't answer. Then he felt the tears on the inside of his shirt. "Don't cry," he whispered. "Everything's going to be all right . . . I promise."

"So that's what he's up to when he's not a policeman," muttered Mona. "I always got the feeling he was a bad apple. He even sounds like a criminal. I'm glad she has you, Frank."

Jabs handed Mrs Carroll a mug of tea. "Here you go, Mona."

"Mrs Carroll to you, son. Does your mother know

where you are at this hour of the night? Come to think of it, does your mother even remember what you look like? I'd say she's forgotten she has a son since you met my Lisa." She took a mouthful of her tea and swallowed it quickly. Her eyes bulged as she grabbed her throat, making a choking sound. "*Sugar!*" she gasped. "*There's sugar in it!*" She jumped up and ran out of the room.

No one noticed.

The phone rang. "Hello," said Frank carefully. No one there.

Then the doorbell rang. Frank opened the door quickly. The porch was empty. "What the hell?" He stepped out and looked up and down the quiet, sleepy avenue. No one. Then he heard the quiet rumbling of an engine, gently ticking over.

"Who is it, Frank?" called Mona.

"I'm not sure. I'll be back in a minute." Frank walked slowly to the gate. A stocky, well-built man, straddling a huge motor-bike, sat by the kerb. "Paul?"

"Yes. We don't have a lot of time. You've probably heard the news."

Frank nodded. "Where's Jamie?"

"Look, I can't tell you. It's all too delicate." He seemed nervous, almost fearful, as he cowered down on the chest of the huge bike. "I know you feel strongly for Jamie. But I can't have you involved more than you have to be. There's only going to be one way to deal with this . . . to get her out safely, I mean. You'll just have to trust me." He revved the engine impatiently.

"Has Tommy got Jamie?"

"Yes. But after what's happened, he's not going to want her around for long."

"So what'll he do?"

Paul hesitated. "*I* don't even want to think about the consequences of anything else going wrong."

"Will he . . . " Frank couldn't say it.

"*Kill* her? Is that what you were going to ask?"

Frank nodded.

"Hopefully not. If I can get to her, there's a chance."

"Why haven't you got to her already?" Frank shouted impatiently. His feet were fidgety, moving and kicking the stone pillar unconsciously.

"Ssshhh. Keep your voice down. I can't just go in and grab her. I have to wait for the right moment. Timing is everything."

"Yeah, you'd know all about timing," Frank muttered snidely.

"I'm sorry?"

"Nothing. *I'm* sorry."

"Barrett's goin' to try and make a break for it. He's not goin' to want Jamie hangin' out of him. Too much baggage for a man on the run. I'd say he'll leave her behind."

"What about the police?"

Paul stared at Frank. His look was indignant. "*No police!*" he grounded.

"But what if . . . "

"*I said no police!*"

"Why not?"

609

"Because I don't trust them. Anyway I don't get on too well with them. Remember who we're dealing with here."

Frank nodded. "A policeman," he acknowledged.

"Yes."

"Is he mad?"

Paul smiled. "A complete fruitcake."

"So what can we do?"

"Nothing, tonight."

"But what if he's already . . . "

Paul cut across him forcefully. "I said there's *nothing* any of us can do tonight. Get some sleep. You look as if you could do with it."

"What do you need from me?" Frank asked nervously.

"Firstly . . . that you're available if I need you. You're lucky in that the police aren't looking for you. Secondly, and more importantly . . . that you stay alive on me."

Frank gulped. "Will she be OK?"

"I hope so. I've still got a couple of interesting people to see tonight. So I'll have to split. I'll be in touch." He nodded and put his full-face helmet on. "Remember . . . no police!" He gently revved the huge engine and was gone.

It was almost half past four before Lisa settled down. Frank peeped through the open door. She appeared to be sound asleep. Jabs was stretched out across the settee, unconscious.

Mona Carroll sat silently at the kitchen table. Every

couple of minutes, she'd shake her head and mutter a line from the Litany.

"Would you like another cup of tea, Mona?" Frank asked politely.

"Ah, sure, I might as well, love . . . if you're having one yourself," she muttered in a forlorn voice. "The whole world's gone mad, Frank. Do you know that? Stark raving mad!" She shook her head again. "Nikki's poor mother is distraught tonight. And I've known Mrs Coffey since Nikki and Jamie started school together over twenty-five years ago. She's above in her house tonight refusing to believe the news about her daughter. Up to her eyeballs in the biggest drugs swoop in history. God love her . . . she's a basket-case!" She looked up at Frank as he filled the teapot. "What's going on, Frank?"

He shrugged his shoulders. "I don't know." The less Mona knew the better, he reckoned. "We'll get over it. Don't worry." He smiled at her as he placed the tea cosy over the pot.

Mona's worried look gave way to a half-smile. "I'm glad she has you," she whispered.

* * *

Frank tried to sleep on that morning. Not a sound in the house. Mona had gone to Mass to pray for them all and, in her own words, "ask the good Lord for my daughter back safely". Every few minutes, the phone would ring. After two rings, the answering machine took over. Most of the callers left messages. That way, he could pick it up if it was important. From where Frank was lying, he could hear the voices quite clearly.

Anne O'Brien . . . to say that she'd been called back to London. A serious case needed her attention. She'd be flying out that afternoon.

Ray Flynn . . . to say that Davina's two kids were in Great Ormond Street children's hospital with scarlet fever, asking Frank to call as soon as he'd got a chance.

Sheila Hoey-Langer . . . to say that she was devastated to hear about Nikki. However, Simpson, her influential husband, was a personal friend of a man who knew someone important and she'd enquire if he was able to "do anything" for her.

Frank pulled the quilt up over his head and groaned. The phone rang. And rang. And rang.

Then he heard noises from the kitchen. He walked out on to the landing. "Lisa?" he shouted.

"She's gone out for a while, son," a croaky voice answered. Her father walked to the end of the stairs. "Would you like a beer?"

Frank shook his head. "At *this* hour?"

"Ah, fuck that. Anyway, there's one there if you fancy it." He wobbled back into the kitchen.

Frank raced back to the bedroom and threw on a pair of jeans and a shirt. He walked casually down the stairs and into the kitchen, trying to give the impression that he saw nothing wrong with having a few beers at . . . he looked at his watch, *"Jesus Christ, it's only twenty to nine in the morning!"*

Jamie's father tried to focus on his watch. "Jesus, you know you're right. So it is." He pointed to the fridge behind him. "There's a pound of sausages and some bacon in there. The Duchess bought them yesterday. Throw them on to the pan, like a good lad." He steered the half-pint glass up to his lips and gulped it down.

"The *Duchess*?" Frank asked sensitively. The expression reminded him of Paddy Last.

"Yeah," he belched. "Your mother-in-law. She who must be obeyed."

"My *mother-in-law*?" Frank thought.

"Yeah," he muttered. "I bet you're glad you married my daughter and not that Nikki Coffey young one. Amn't I right?"

"Have you had much to drink, Mister Carroll?"

Mr Carroll reacted slightly indignantly to the question. "You didn't answer the question, son."

"Jamie and I are not married . . . yet."

The drunken man smiled as he swayed with his glass. "Fair play to you. And if you take my advice, you won't let her get that ring on your finger for at least another twenty years. Tie you up and rob you . . . that's all they do. Glorified doormats . . . that's all us men are. If I'd known how that old cow was going to treat me, I'd have legged it long ago. But no. And sure you only have to look at me now. I've aged about thirty years since I married that old cross-grained sow."

Frank stared at him. "Do you mind me asking how long you're married?"

He had to think for a minute. "Eh, thirty years." He burped again and broke wind.

"Do you go to the early-house every morning?" Frank asked.

"Only when there's been a tragedy or a bereavement." He finished off his glass. "If you ask me, life's been one long bereavement since I met that old bull-headed yapper. If it wasn't for that backbiting doggess . . . "

The front door slammed.

Mr Carroll sat bolt upright in the seat. He slipped the empty pint bottle into his jacket pocket. Then he pulled a couple of fresh tulips out of a large vase on the worktop and stuck them into the empty glass. He placed it niftily beside the window. "You do the talking, son."

The kitchen door flew open. Mona Carroll stared at her husband who obviously thought he was making a damn good job of concealing the crapulent state he was in.

"Where were you?" She forced her lower jaw forward. "Or do I need to ask?"

"Ah, my sweet, I bought you a little something on my way . . . "

"Get out of here and take the dog for a walk, you shameless *tosspot*!" she shouted.

"Yes, mavourneen," he muttered.

"And don't you dare *mavourneen* me, you tanked-up sponge!" she roared.

"Whatever you say, poppet," he mumbled. He closed the door quietly behind him. A moment later, the front door banged.

Frank wasn't sure where to look.

"Are these for you, love?" she asked, pointing to the sausages and bacon on the worktop.

Frank felt embarrassed. "I was going to stick a couple of them on for Mr Carroll, actually."

"*Mr* Carroll? Don't you worry your head about *Mr* Carroll, love. We've enough to be worrying about without that good-for-nothing giving me a headache. Anyway, good food would only spoil forty quid's worth of shameless drinking for him right now. I'll do it for you, love. After all, you're still the guest."

Frank scratched his head. "I didn't know you had a dog."

Mona slapped four rashers and four sausages on to the pan. She looked around at Frank. "We don't!"

* * *

"Hello, Ray . . . it's Frank. You were looking for me."

"Jesus, Frank. You don't know how relieved I am to hear your voice. When are you coming back?"

"Jaysus, Ray, what sort of a question is that? I'm up to me bollock in shit over here at the moment. Jamie's missing. An ex-Provo's convinced he can save her life before the psycho that kidnapped her does her in. And to cap it all, I've been told to do nothing. And *you* want to know when am I coming *back*?" Frank held his breath for a moment. "I don't know, right now."

"*You don't know?*" Ray roared. "Frank, I can't keep this up on my own. Did you get my message?"

"Yeah, I did. How are the children?"

"Well, they're a bit like the way kids *are* with scarlet fever . . . *sick!*" he shouted. "I didn't think they'd end up in hospital, but the doctor said they'd be better off there for a few days. Seemingly, there's complications with their bowels, or something. Davina's been down there for the last two days. I'm going to give her a night off tonight. I'll go down there until they fall asleep. She can get a good night's sleep. It'll be her first in over a week. Listen to me, why can't you find someone to help me? I need someone who knows the ropes," Ray shouted. "Jamie wasn't involved in the drugs business, was she?"

"No. Well, not directly. Nikki was."

"I know. Nikki was about to bunk off to France with her boyfriend. We'd already worked that out . . . sorry, Frank, I didn't mean that. It's just that . . . "

"I know. You're under pressure," replied Frank. "No one wants to be back in the pub more than I do, Ray. It's my business. It's just that I . . . love Jamie. I'd die if anything happened to her. It'd kill me if . . . " He stopped. "Look, I'll be back in a couple of days. At least I know the pub's being well looked-after while I'm over here."

"Will you get a chance to get home to Cork?"

"Are you joking me? I'm afraid to leave the house here because of . . . "

"Because of what?" Ray asked curiously.

"Ah, nothing. Listen, are the police still watching the pub?"

"I'm not sure. They were up to the time Nikki left. And I have noticed an odd-looking car around the place now and again. But not at regular times. To be honest, I've been so busy, I haven't had time to scratch me arse!"

"What do you mean, *odd*-looking?"

"Well, it doesn't seem to be cops. A small, tidy, red

car. Too old, I'd say. Maybe I'm just imagining things. After the few days we've had over here, I'm surprised we're not in the loony bin." Ray laughed.

"Ray, you'd ring me if anything was wrong, wouldn't you?"

"What do you mean? Sure, I'm grand here. Nothing's going to go wrong. Come here, listen to me, I managed to get us two tickets for the Portugal game next month. What d'ya say? Just you and me on a wild weekend in the sun?"

Frank smiled. "Sounds brilliant. We'll definitely go for that."

"*Great!*" Ray cheered. "I'm going to tell Davina that we won them in a draw I entered us in down in The Pig and Whistle, all right. So, you tell your judy the same. That way, we don't get our lines crossed. Listen, I'll have to go. Give us a call when you have some news. And listen, Frank, I never thought I'd have to say it, but . . . I miss you. We all do. Good luck, see ya soon." The line went dead.

"Good luck, ya big softie," Frank muttered.

The key turned in the front door as Frank put down the phone. It was Lisa.

"Mam, will you ever get my father indoors before he makes a show of us all! He's fast asleep in the porch next door with his arm around Nellie Ryan's dog."

* * *

Jamie's lips were numb. Her tongue felt dry and swollen. She hadn't been able to breathe through her mouth for nearly twelve hours now. She was parched and aching all over from the tight cords that bound her. She squealed as Tommy Barrett forcefully ripped the gun from between her knees, dragging large strips of the sticking-plaster with it, tearing away her skin. He then bound her knees quickly with fresh tape. He yanked the plaster from across her mouth. She gasped a lungful of the cold night air. It felt as if her lips had been torn off in the process. "Not a word," he muttered. "I got you a burger and chips."

Jamie shook her head. "I don't want a *burger*!" she croaked.

He held a cup of tea to her lips. "Drink this," he commanded.

Jamie spluttered and coughed. "Too hot," she cried. She wanted to call out for help. But she had to keep her cool. What was it that her English teacher called it? Imperturbability. That was it. How could she forget? She'd ended up having to write it out five hundred times! "Why are you feeding me if you're going to kill me?" she asked.

He grabbed her by the throat. He was choking her. His grip was so tight, she started to retch.

Someone will come along, she kept thinking. *Please*.

He released his grip. His fingers wandered across her shoulder. He pulled at her jacket until the top buttons opened. "I bet he's fucked you. *Hasn't he?*" He started to shake her violently by the throat. *"Tell me!"* he exploded. *"I'm going to kill you either way!"* He let go of her and held the cold nozzle of the gun to the side of her head. She was afraid to move. Then he took it away.

"Why?" she whispered. She was weak from hunger . . . shock . . . fear.

"What?" he shouted.

"Why did you do it? I need to know."

"Do what?"

"Why did you rape me?"

He hesitated. For a moment, he seemed nervous. Unsure. "It doesn't matter why. It's done. Anyway, no one will ever be able to tell what really happened, will they? Because there won't be anybody left to tell. Will there?"

"I know why you raped me," she said quietly.

"Shut up!" he shouted.

"You raped me because you were jealous of me. Jealous of everything I stood for. Everything I had. Friends. Family. A job I enjoyed. Other men's attention. Isn't that right, Tommy? All the things you never had."

"*Shut up!*" He kicked the leg of the chair. Jamie gasped. She tried to catch her breath. "The only way you could feel like a real man was to put a black hood over your head and attack me at knifepoint. That was the only way you were ever going to prove to yourself that you were a *man*. Is that the right word, Tommy?" she goaded. "Just like you're doing now."

"*Shut up, shut up!*" he roared.

"In the three years that I've known you, you've always been an inadequate little wimp. You only wanted sex when you were half-pissed. That way you'd never know how much of a jerk you really were. 'Little willy' is what the *boys* in the station used to call you. Isn't that right?"

"No!"

"*Yes!*" she gloated. "You never could handle someone who was stronger than you, could you? Someone who had the guts to say *no*!"

"You're not stronger than *me*!"

"Maybe I'm not," she said quietly. "If what you mean by 'stronger' is holding a knife to my throat and violating me. That's not being strong. That's being a fucking monster. A *bastard*!"

"I'm not," he bayed.

"I bet you feel like crying now, don't you? Look at you. Shaking. Dribbling like a small child. That's exactly all you are, Tommy . . . a small child. A juvenile skiver. You never wanted a wife. You wanted a mother. Someone who'd put you to bed when you came in drunk. Someone who'd lie down and take the insults and the hurt. Your problem was that you picked the wrong person. When I said no, you couldn't understand why. Could you? So the only way you could prove to yourself that you were still the iron hand was to subject me to the most crushing, degrading form of abuse you could imagine. You *raped* me!"

Tommy fidgeted with his pockets. He kicked the leg of the chair again, this time almost causing it to collapse.

"You hurt me more than you'll ever know. But that's it. It's all over. You can't hurt me any more. You can kill me, but what's that going to do? Make you feel like a *real* man of the world?" She stared into his weakening eyes. "I'll tell you what you are, Tommy. You're a man of straw . . . a nobody. A selfish, miserable bully. You're just a pathetic, worthless little motherfucker living in your own squalid shithole!" She barely got the words out when a fresh strip of tape was stretched from ear to ear, preventing her from saying any more. This time he made it worse. Far worse. Her eyes bulged as she watched him cut off a longer strip. She'd barely time to close them, shield them. Then everything went dark.

Chapter Thirty-Three

" . . . she was remanded in custody on all five charges until June the twenty-third next," the newsreader continued. "And now, today's other main story. In the Dáil this morning . . . "

Frank switched off the radio.

The carpark outside the prison was full. Frank and Lisa sat quietly in the car.

"What are you thinking?" Frank asked Lisa.

She shrugged her shoulders and sniffed. "I still can't believe it. Five charges, including murder. *Murder*, Frank. Do you know anyone who's committed murder?"

Frank shook his head.

"Neither do I. At least, I didn't until today. And now it turns out that my sister's best friend is a murderer. It doesn't add up."

"What do you mean, *add up*?" he asked.

"Well, ask yourself, why did she do it? Why did she shoot him? She could have just as easily jumped overboard. She's a qualified lifeguard. I mean, it's not like she couldn't swim."

"Well, maybe *she'll* tell me why." Frank looked up at the high wall opposite the car. It looked grim and uninviting. "Are you sure we're doing the right thing?"

"I don't know. We didn't drive over here to start asking questions like that. Fair play to Sheila for getting her husband to pull a few strokes with that bloke . . . what's he called?"

"Can't tell you that."

"Yeah. Anyway, go on. I'll wait here for you," said Lisa.

"No. I'm not going into a woman's prison on my own, Lisa."

"Well, I'm not going into a woman's prison, full stop. I hardly know the girl!"

"Please?"

Lisa grimaced. "Oh, all right!"

A small crowd huddled outside the huge, grey door. No one spoke. A couple of young-looking women smoked impatiently.

"Excuse me," Frank said to a girl with a tattoo on her neck. "Why are you standing here?"

The girl looked at her friend. "Because someone robbed all the fucking deckchairs and beer tables." The two women roared laughing. "What does it look like?"

The other girl seemed friendlier. "Depends on who you've got inside. We're here early 'cos her fella's being transferred. Have you someone inside?"

"Yeah," Frank answered quietly.

"How long is she in for?"

"I don't know. She's on remand until the end of June."

The cheeky girl nudged her friend. "That's yer one who murdered the spik on the boat."

They both looked at Frank. "He's gorgeous," one of them mumbled. "Only one of youse is allowed in at a time," she nodded to Lisa, "so you can wait out here with me," she said to Frank.

"Ring on the bell, love," the other girl said.

Frank pressed the large red button and heard a bell ringing inside.

A few seconds passed. Then a large, steel hatch slid back halfway up the door.

Two big eyes peered out at the crowd. "Who rang?" a deep voice asked in a Dublin accent.

"I did," Frank answered nervously. "I'm here to see Nicola Coffey."

"Are you on your own?" the voice asked.

"No, why?"

"Only one visitor allowed at a time," he shouted.

"I'll wait in the car." Lisa seemed relieved. She gave Frank a peck on the cheek for luck.

The watching crowd shouted and whistled. One of the girls standing close to them was shouting. "Ah, go on, love . . . give him the tongue an' give us all a thrill! I won't be getting any of that for another three years!"

The crowd roared laughing.

"That's not what you were saying to me last night, Siobhán Shorthall. That Cork bloke in the pub couldn't keep his hands off ye. Siobhán yer knickers, more like it!"

The jeering faded to a distant echo as the huge door

closed behind Frank. He looked around. He was in a long dark tunnel. Just him and a big, burly uniformed officer. He pointed to a small window hatch. "Over there," he muttered.

Frank walked over to the window.

"Name?" shouted a small uniformed man inside.

"Frank McCabe."

"Here to see?"

Frank didn't catch what he'd said. "Sorry?"

"*Here to see?*" he shouted impatiently.

"Nicola Coffey."

"Thank you. Leave all valuables, including money and jewellery, in this envelope. Place your shoes and socks, and any belts or buckles you may be wearing, in this box. Collect them on your way out."

Frank was horrified at the notion of walking around this awful place in his bare feet. He tucked his socks into his shoes and put them, with his jeans belt, in the box.

"Wait there. A prison officer will take you to a meeting room." The hatch slammed shut.

He looked around at the cold, grey brick walls. It was the first time he'd ever been inside a prison. With the exception of Kilmainham Jail, which he'd visited years ago as part of a school history trip.

"*Nicola Coffey,*" the high-pitched voice shouted.

Frank looked. "Yes," he answered.

"This way," the uniformed woman called. "Hold on," she said, stopping Frank in his tracks. "Arms out, legs apart," she ordered. She searched Frank.

Frank felt humiliated.

"This way."

He was told to sit at a small table. Two chairs faced each other. No refinements, he thought as she looked around the room. Plain tables and cold, hard wooden chairs. There must have been a dozen tables. Huge, steel bars criss-crossed every window. The room was empty.

He was sitting barely a minute when there was a loud, clanking noise. Nikki came in slowly. A uniformed woman followed her. The door clunked shut behind them.

Nikki was crying. She looked as if she'd been crying for days. She swayed from side to side. She looked as if she was on drugs.

Frank swallowed and bit hard.

Nikki walked faster towards the table.

They were about to hug when the observing officer cautioned them. "No touching, hugging or holding hands," she intoned.

Frank stood up. He sat down as soon as Nikki did. He couldn't think of anything to say. Anything that was remotely relevant. He looked up at the screw who was staring at them, watching their every movement. "Did you have your breakfast?"

Nikki shook her head. "I can't eat."

"Nikki, you have to eat or you'll get run down."

Nikki was panting. "I'm sorry, Frank," she whispered, "I'm so sorry."

Frank was about to grab her hand when he remembered. "Don't say that. There's no need to be sorry. Are they treating you well?"

Nikki shook her head. "They hate me. The place is full of drug addicts, pushers, pimps and prostitutes. They're the dregs of the earth." Then she smiled. "But then, I suppose I'm no different if you believe everything you read." She put her hand up to her mouth and shuddered.

"What happened?" Frank asked.

Nikki signalled to the pair of ears standing close by.

Frank acknowledged. "Did *you* kill the man on the boat?" he whispered.

Nikki clutched her stomach and winced. "It was an accident. I swear. I didn't mean to kill him. I just wanted to go to the Irish people on the boat I'd been talking to. He hit me and I fell. Whatever way he tried to grab the gun, it just went off. It was an *accident*, really . . . it was. I swear. I've never seen a real gun in my life, never mind use one."

Frank was confused. "But wasn't there someone else on board who'll vouch for the fact that it was an accident? That he hit you and the gun went off accidentally?"

"His *wife*?" asked Nikki. "Oh yeah, I can see that happening all right. Ten minutes before, they're screwing like rabbits, and then I blow his head off. Yeah, I could see her trying to explain to the judge that it was all one big accident and that none of it was my fault." She wiped her eyes. "Still, my da's solicitor is trying to get me out on bail. I'll know before lunch. Say a prayer . . . please?"

Frank nodded. He took a deep breath before asking what he had to know. "Was Tommy on the boat with you?"

626

Nikki straightened up. Her face contorted. "That *bastard* set me up!" she screamed at the top of her voice. She stood up and kicked the chair to one side. "*Bastard!*" she wailed. "*This is all his fault!*" She thumped the table.

"*Right, time up!*" the officer yelled. Within seconds, four prison officers thundered through the security door.

Nikki had gone beserk. She was screaming and punching at everything that could move: chairs . . . tables . . . benches. All the time screaming one word . . . "*Bastard!*"

Frank was petrified. He jumped backwards, out of Nikki's path.

It took three prison officers to pacify her. A fourth led Frank quickly from the meeting-room back to the main entrance.

* * *

The whirring windscreen wipers were starting to annoy Tommy Barrett. He was tired and tetchy. He asked the taxi-driver to wait. "I'll be five minutes, maximum."

It was after closing time. Grady's was ready to close for the night. The stout barman fiddled with the television zapper, jumping from channel to channel, waiting for the last few drinkers to vacate the premises. Monty McGrath sat in a dark corner of the pub. He chewed a matchstick as he listened to details of the foiled drugs-run two nights before.

He looked up as a tall figure obscured his view of the TV. He cackled. "Barrett, my favourite cop. You fucked up again, you pillock." He looked away and sipped his mineral water. "I hope you've brought my money back." He belched.

"Ulcer bothering you again, Monty?" muttered Barrett. He placed the black carrier bag on the table. "I want to talk to you."

"Then talk to me. I don't waste precious time on losers."

Tommy Barrett nodded to the two men sitting at the table.

McGrath nodded back. "Well, gentleman, you heard what the policeman said. So fuck off and let me hear what this asshole has to say for himself! And it had better be good."

The two men left quickly.

"Here's your money."

"All of it?"

"Of course."

"And my gun?"

"I need to hold on to it."

"I need it back. It's booked . . . popular make."

"You obviously didn't hear me the first time."

McGrath looked at him suspiciously. "No? *You* obviously didn't fuckin' hear *me*! No one, not even some small time cop-maggot like you, Barrett, talks to me like that. Get out of here before I break every fuckin' bone in your body. And don't ever set foot in this part of town again, do you hear me?"

As McGrath went to stand up, Tommy Barrett's

arm was outstretched in an instant. He looked at the barman. "Turn up the TV," he shouted.

The barman froze. He looked at Monty, then at the gun.

"Turn up the fuckin' TV!"

He pressed the volume control on the zapper.

"Higher . . . all the way!" he rasped.

Monty McGrath looked bemused. Then confused. Then frightened.

The double crack from the .38 Special was almost simultaneous. Monty McGrath's eyeballs were practically facing each other as he fell backwards, breaking the three-legged wooden table in pieces, two gaping holes in his head; a small discreet entry point between his eyes and a larger exit, a hole the size of a large orange, directly behind. Crimson brain tissue, mixed with sharp shards of bone, was spattered all over the dirty whitewashed wall. A pool of dark red blood fused with a puddle of urine. Tommy Barrett didn't notice the barman ducking behind the bar as he shot at Monty once more. He was more interested in making sure that Monty McGrath would never stand up and humiliate him again. He walked to the door and turned. He waited silently.

The barman's head appeared above the counter. "Please . . . *no!*" he begged. He raised his trembling hands.

"Who's a frightened little puppy now?" Tommy aimed quickly and fired once. The bullet smashed through the barman's forehead. It exited, almost simultaneously, demolishing a large bottle of vodka directly behind its target. He knew the single blast was accurate enough to ensure permanent silence. He turned the *closed* sign outwards, unclipped the safety catch and pulled it shut behind him. "Goodnight," he shouted.

Barrett was back in the taxi in less than five minutes.

"That was a quick one," the taxi-driver remarked.

"Quickest yet. Howth, please."

Chapter Thirty-Four

Frank sat at the back of the church.

Sunlight lit the stained glass windows throwing lozenges of different colours across the empty, shiny seats.

He was all alone in this huge building. He tried to think of the last time he'd been inside a church. It must have been ten years ago, at least. He peeped into his pocket at the mobile phone. It was powered and switched on. Why hadn't Paul Flaherty called? Even just to let him know that Jamie was alive. The notion made him tremble. Would he ever see her again? He'd made up his mind to ask her to marry him the minute he saw her. But would he see her . . . alive? He'd never felt so alone before.

"Well, miracles will never cease," a voice muttered from behind.

Frank looked around to see Mona Carroll dragging the church polisher through one of the back doors. He nearly died of embarrassment. She was after finding him in the church on his own.

"Mass is over, love. Almost three hours now," Mona said. She walked over and sat down beside him.

"Ah, I just needed somewhere to be on my own for a while, that's all."

Mona smiled and gave him a hug. "Well, you couldn't have picked a better place, love. I always tell the girls that. There's always someone willing to listen to you inside of these four walls."

"Is there?" muttered Frank.

"Well, most times."

"Don't go, Ma. Sit down."

Mona looked at Frank. "Ah, thanks, love. It's nice to hear a man calling me Ma. I do rarely hear from the boys in America these days. Although they've been on the phone non-stop since Jamie . . . " She started to cry.

Frank tried hard to control his own emotions. He reached across and hugged Mona. "Come on, don't be worrying. It's early days."

"It's *three* days, Frank. *Three* too many. Not a blink. All the police can say is that they're looking."

"Just be careful what you tell the police if they call."

"Why?"

"Just a hunch, that's all. Tell them to talk to me," Frank whispered. He remembered what Paul Flaherty had told him. Frank had no intention of telling the police anything.

"And then that bloke, that druggie they murdered last night, *he* was involved with . . . " She couldn't bring herself to say his name.

"You should be resting, Mona. Taking it easy," urged Frank.

"Takin' it easy. I'm goin' around the twist sitting in

that house on me own. I have to do something to try and take me mind off Jamie. Them neighbours . . . I know they mean well, but they're calling to the door like as if she was d . . . " She sobbed into her tissue. "Oh Jesus, Frank. Where's the good Lord now that we need him most?"

"Good question," mumbled Frank. He stared at the altar.

Mona sniffed and took a deep breath. "I was out doing a bit of gardening yesterday, and do you know what I was just thinking?"

"What?"

"I was looking at the apple tree that we planted when Jamie was six. She brought it home from her grandad's plot and she asked me to plant it for her?"

Frank smiled and hugged her tighter.

"And I'd no sooner planted it, when she started asking me when the apples would grow on it, and this thing no bigger than a nettle, an' I only after planting it ten minutes beforehand. Every hour of the day and night, she'd be running up the back garden to see if there were any apples hanging on it yet. Well, I knew it'd be years and years before she'd see a blossom on those tiny little branches, never mind an apple, but I knew she'd never able to understand that in *her* small head then. So I said, 'Maybe tomorrow'. And every day she'd asked me that question, I'd say, 'Maybe tomorrow', and before she knew it, there were loads of apples all over the branches. Problem was, they were cooking apples. But how was her grandad to know that . . . God rest him. Anyway, those little brats from next door stole them one day and Nellie ended up having to get the doctor for them that evening. Served them right."

They both laughed. Just for a fleeting moment, everything seemed all right.

Mona blessed herself and stared silently up the empty church. "There's a long story in that little tree. Every time I look out the kitchen window at it, I think of Jamie. I remember the day her brother Dermot hit her over the head with his champion conker, and that thing was after being in a jar of vinegar all winter. I swear to God it was hard as cement. She had to go to Temple Street hospital for the night. I remember sitting up crying beside the tree that night."

Frank smiled.

"I remember when I'd be missing her and her away in England, and I'd ask her on the phone when was she coming home to me, and she'd say, 'Maybe tomorrow'. Sometimes I wish we were back then, all those years ago. All of us. Instead of scattered all over the world."

"Well, you still have Lisa . . . and Jamie."

"Lisa's too scattered to go anywhere. And as for that Jabs fella. She won't go outside the door without that yoke. Bloody brains like wet brown bread, he has. Still, I suppose she's happy, God love her. No, I'm talking about years and years ago . . . when all of them were children. Then we'd have all those 'maybe tomorrows' to look forward to all over again."

"But we do, Mona. There'll be loads of tomorrows."

"Still," her mother breezed. "I believe that if you

really want something badly enough, you'll be given it."

"And Mr Carroll?"

Mona gave Frank a funny look. "What about *Mr* Carroll?"

"Do you love *him*?"

"Of course I love him. He *is* my husband." She thought to herself for a moment. "The thing is that sometimes I do think that he's lost his way in life, but if your question is, 'would I do it all again?' my answer would have to be . . . *yes*!" She looked seriously at Frank. Then her look softened into a smile. "I know who *you* love."

Frank blushed. "Right from the moment I laid eyes on her."

Her mother put down the cable of the polisher. "Tell me, when was that?"

"The night I went back to England on the boat."

"My God, the two of youse didn't waste any time," she joked.

"Oh, I don't know about that," he sighed. "I'll tell you the whole story the next time I take you all out for a celebration . . . I hope."

"I knew from the moment I heard about this Frank McCabe that he was the man for my daughter. I'm always very wary when it comes to dodgy fellas. You only have to look at Jamie's sister to see why. I don't know where Jabs was when looks and brains were being handed out. Probably queuing outside one of them rave nightclubs. I do worry about them two." She stopped talking and pinched Frank's cheek. "But not about *you* two. That's one day I'm definitely looking forward to."

"Maybe tomorrow," whispered Frank.

"Please God, as me poor mother still says."

"Speaking of your mother, she left a message on the machine. It didn't make much sense."

Mona's hand shot up to her mouth. "Oh, God love dear Gran. She's not all with it any more."

"Why?"

"She thought she was going to the toilet the other afternoon. It took the staff above in the home nearly half an hour to coax her out of the wardrobe." She stood up. "Anyway, that's all I have to say. Maybe you don't see it right now, but you have all those tomorrows staring you in the face. Go out and make them yours." Mona dragged the long cable across towards the socket. "Dickie Rock's playing in the Abbey Tavern on Saturday night. I got us four tickets..," she tried hard to maintain the enthusiastic smile, " . . . for when, like, Jamie gets back." She sniffed.

"Sounds great," whispered Frank. "See you back home."

He pushed open the church door.

"Oh, Frank," called Mona.

"Yeah?"

"Thanks, love. I needed that bit of cheering up." Mona smiled as she started to hum "Candystore on the Corner". The electric polisher whirred into action and dragged her up the shiny aisle. For a while, she was in seventh heaven.

Chapter Thirty-Five

Teatime in Carroll's was normally a chatty affair, gossip and slander being the usual order of the day. Not that any of *us* are ones for gossip, Mona Carroll would regularly warn her family as she dished out the sausages and scrambled eggs, before destroying the good character of one of her neighbours.

This evening was different, though. No one spoke. A large sliced pan sat proud and tall in the spot normally taken up by a large bowl of steaming hot shepherd's pie.

"This *is* Monday, isn't it?" mumbled Jamie's father.

Lisa nodded. "Shut up, Da. Ma, I swear, it was an accident. We all just forgot."

"But how could you all forget . . . and it me sixtieth birthday?" she wailed from the cooker as she kept an eye on a boiling egg. "Jamie wouldn't have forgot." She scooped it out of the pot and sat down at the top of the table.

"And what are we going to do?" muttered the old man.

"*And what are we going to do?*" mimicked his wife.

"You can do what you do every bloody night of the week . . . you can go to the pub and give out about me."

Jamie's father stood up and put his cap on.

"And just where do you think you're going?" roared Mona.

"Where you told me to go . . . the pub!" he mumbled.

"Oh, did I now? Well that'd be too easy, wouldn't it? No, *precious*, you're not going to the pub tonight. Our daughter is missing. *Missing*, I said. And all you can think of is going to the pub and drinking with all your old cronies. Well, *not* tonight! You're going to stay here and wait for word."

Frank stood up and excused himself. No one heard him. He walked slowly up the stairs. The phone rang. He picked it up. "Hello, Carroll's," he said politely.

"The big, bad wolf said, 'I'll huff and I'll puff and I'll burn your pub down'. Play with fire and get burnt, McCabe. I'll get you . . . " There was a click and the line went dead.

What the hell was that about? Frank wondered. "The pub," he shouted.

"What?" Mona called from the kitchen.

"He's going to do something to the pub. I know it."

"Who?"

"*Him!*"

"*Who's* going to do what, Frank?"

"*The pub . . . the pub! He'll burn it down. Or something! I just know it,*" he shouted. He dialled the number of the Clover Tap. "Come on. Answer the

638

bloody phone." He slammed it down. "*Engaged!*" he shouted.

Everyone took turns to try and calm Frank down.

"I'll get you a drink, son. That'll help to calm you," Jamie's father suggested. Within seconds, there was another loud roar, this time from the fridge. "Who took the Guinness that I was chilling in here?"

"Probably the Angel Gabriel, if he'd any sense," Mona muttered under her breath. "Come in and have a cup of tea, Frank."

Frank pressed the redial button continuously. "Shaggin' phone's off the hook, I'll bet you," he said angrily.

"Maybe, it was just a hoax, love," Mona suggested.

"A *hoax*? This week?" He paced frantically up and down the narrow hall. "He's going to do something to the pub. That's what he told me," he repeated. He grabbed the phone. "Get the airline number in the directory."

"Frank, it's twenty to eight. There's no more flights tonight."

"There must be some company that's got a late-night flight. Or the car ferry. That wouldn't have left yet, would it? I've got to get back there *now*!"

"Maybe not, but you won't get to London before breakfast-time tomorrow morning. What good is that?"

"Jesus," he muttered nervously. "I don't like this. I don't like this at all. I know something's going to happen."

"But what can he do to the pub? Sure, isn't Ray

there? He'd notice if something was wrong." Lisa tried to comfort him. "Come on. We'll all go out for a couple of hours. Have a nice drink and relax." She smiled up at him.

He smiled in return. It didn't last long. He knew in his heart that something was terribly wrong. It was too sinister to be a joke. At least, if Barrett was still in Dublin, the chances were slim that anything serious would happen. But what if he wasn't? He'd managed to con the top police investigators in the country. But how could he get at the pub if he was still here? Maybe Flaherty had got it all wrong. Maybe Jamie *was* back in London. Alone with that monster. Maybe he should call the police. Whatever made him trust Flaherty in the first place? A hunch. And his hunches had never been wrong. But then, there was always a first time for everything. Maybe it was a hoax. What if it wasn't? The words haunted him all night . . . "and I'll burn your pub down."

* * *

Lisa woke him from a deep sleep.

He felt as if he'd been out cold for days.

"There's a call for you," she whispered.

Frank looked at her. She looked worried. "Who is it?"

"The police."

Frank didn't bother with clothes. He ran across the landing into Jamie and Lisa's room and grabbed the phone. "Hello," he said anxiously.

"Mr McCabe?"

"Yes?"

"Can you hold for Detective Inspector Anne O'Brien?"

"Yes," muttered Frank. The wait seemed to last for hours.

Lisa handed him a pullover. He shivered. Yet, he didn't feel cold.

"Hello, Frank?"

Anne's voice told him that something was badly wrong. "Hi, Anne."

"Frank, any news on Jamie?"

"No. Why?"

"Frank, I'm sorry but you'll have to get an early flight back to London. There's been an awful accident." Her voice faltered.

Frank closed his eyes tightly and swallowed. "The pub," he whispered. "What happened?"

"We got a call at about two this morning from a couple of people who'd noticed smoke coming from a window downstairs. They told us later they'd been afraid to ring the police because they'd had a lot to drink and they were driving. They were afraid of being arrested. They walked back to the pub from their house to take a look half an hour later."

"And?"

"The pub was on fire. By that time the fire brigade had arrived."

There was a long silence.

Frank was terrified to ask. "Is everyone all right?"

Another long pause. "No," she replied. "Davina." She stopped.

" . . . was burnt?" Frank blurted.

"Firemen . . . recovered her body shortly after three o'clock."

The news came like an electric shock. "And Ray?" he asked gently.

"Ray risked his life to save her. He was extremely brave. Seemingly, he was visiting Davina's two young children in Great Ormond Street. He arrived back around quarter past two, we think. From what we can gather, he got in through a window. We found him unconscious on the stairs."

"Is *he* all right?"

"He's in intensive care at Saint Raphael's right now. He suffered a broken leg and a broken pelvis in the fall. He's also suffering from smoke inhalation."

"Does he know about . . . Davina?"

"Not yet."

Frank bit hard on his bottom lip. "Will he be OK?" he asked again.

"The doctors won't be able to tell for a couple of days. He's been very badly burnt." She paused. "Frank," she said softly, "I mean *really* badly. From what I've been told, he's very, very sick. Apparently, he was asking where you were in the ambulance this morning. After that, he passed out. Frank? Are you there?"

Frank let the phone slip. He put his two hands up to his face.

Mona picked up the receiver. "Hello . . . this is Mona Carroll," she whispered.

"Hello, Mrs Carroll, this is Inspector Anne O'Brien," she replied softly. "It's not good news, Mrs Carroll."

Mona started to shiver. "Is it Jamie? Please tell me she's all right. Is it my Jamie?"

"No, it's not Jamie. It's the Clover Tap. There's been a terrible accident. Frank will have to come back to London. I just wanted to be the one to tell him. They have a habit in here sometimes of making it a bit too matter-of-fact when they call to tell you these things. Particularly long-distance. He'll have to come over later this morning."

"So he *was* right all along," Mona muttered.

"Right about what?"

"The three little . . . eh, nothing. When is it all going to end?"

"Frank has my home number if you need me. Let me know what flight he's on and I'll send a car to collect him."

Mona put the phone down slowly. She walked across and rubbed Frank's back.

Chapter Thirty-Six

Frank's immediate instinct on walking into the Intensive Care Unit was to turn around and walk back out. He tugged angrily at the long green gown he was wearing and cursed. Then he leaned against a radiator in the long corridor and thumped it.

The nurse walked slowly up to him. "Are you all right?" she asked.

Frank nodded without looking up. He straightened up and went for another stab.

The door was on strong swing-hinges and was difficult to open. The room was bright but chilling. The only noise to break the silence was the loud intermittent beeping of the machines that stood beside each bed.

"The sister will help you," the nurse whispered. She pointed to the small kiosk in the corner.

Frank looked around anxiously.

There were five patients in the unit. But they weren't placed side by side like in a normal ward. Each seemed to have a different-sized portion of the large room. One or two had more equipment than the others. It was almost impossible to see their faces. They all seemed to be covered in bandages. Sticky tape held big wide plastic tubes to their mouths and noses.

Jesus Christ, he whispered. Being kept alive by machines. Frank had never been inside an Intensive Care Unit before. He looked over to his left, just behind the door.

A young boy lay still. Tubes, coming out of three different machines, were connected to his mouth and nose. Other tubes disappeared under the bedclothes on one side. Others seemed to be coming out the other side. The huge gash on the front of his forehead had turned purple. He must have had thirty stiches to keep the wound closed.

"Are you family?" a soft voice enquired.

Frank spun around. A small woman in a green gown and face-mask stood between him and the door. A stethoscope hung loosely around her neck. He couldn't make out if she was young or old. "Sorry?" he replied nervously.

"Dermot . . . " She nodded to the young boy in the bed.

Frank shook his head as he watched the lad's ribs rise and expand in time to the whooshing sound of the ventilator beside him. Then they'd settle for a moment. The process seemed to take about three seconds. Then a couple of seconds of silence and it would repeat itself. "What happened him?" he asked.

"Motor-bike crash. He skidded and hit the front of a bus. His girlfriend was killed instantly. She was found half an hour later down a steep embankment. She'd been thrown nearly fifty feet clear of the bike. That was almost a month ago."

Frank swallowed hard.

The nurse seemed perfectly composed as she related the horrific details. Almost deadpan. "Who are you looking for?" she asked in the same tone.

"Ray Flynn," Frank replied emotionally.

The nurse put her arm around Frank's waist as she led him to the far corner of the room. "Are you a member of the family?"

"I'm his boss, actually." He wavered. "He's . . . my best friend." As they reached the large bed, more like a slab than a bed, Frank could just make out the big, familiar shoulders.

Ray's head and face were wrapped tightly in white bandages. Here and there, a small moist patch had appeared. His eyes and mouth and nose were uncovered. His lips were burnt and cut, his nose swollen and red. Two small tubes were connected, one to each nostril. "What's that?" Frank pointed to the huge tent-like frame covered by blankets. It seemed to cover the full length of his body.

"It's a burns-aid. A bit like the frame of a tent. We use it in very serious burns cases. It prevents the bedclothes from sticking to the patient's skin . . . or what's left of their skin," she explained.

Then Frank saw the red, swollen stretch marks on Ray's shoulders and neck, covered here and there in a whitish calomine-type lotion.

Frank's eyes watered up, tears were beginning to run down his face, on to the gauze mask covering his nose and mouth. "Is he conscious?" he mumbled.

"Now and again. He's only been here for four hours. We're watching him constantly." She tapped Frank on the elbow. She signalled him towards her desk. "Come over here and sit down."

Frank followed her, looking back, now and again, at the still figure of the giant he loved.

"Here, sit down," she said quietly.

"I hate to even have to ask, but . . . is he going to be all right?"

The nurse opened a file in front of her and studied the charts inside. "Ray has been very seriously burnt. Many of the burns are third-degree which means the outer layers of skin, along with some flesh and muscle, have been irrevocably damaged. Completely burnt away in some places," she whispered. "The burns cover forty per cent of his body. He's also broken his leg in two places . . . we think. We haven't been able to examine that in much detail so far, because of the discomfort it would cause him."

Frank listened attentively. "You haven't answered my question."

"If he *was* to recover, he'd be in intensive care for a long, long time . . . maybe a year. After that, he'd remain in hospital under constant supervision for a further six months."

Frank placed his hands between his knees to stop the shaking. "Why so long?"

"Because in order to treat the burns, he'd require a huge number of skin grafts. Unfortunately, in his present condition, there are very few areas of his body where healthy skin could be taken from."

"Is he in pain?"

"No. He's not. He's been heavily sedated and we're administering a morphine pain-killer directly, along with a general antibiotic called claforin. That's used to ward off the kind of infections that his body might pick up in its present condition. Many of the blood cells that fight infection have been destroyed, leaving his immune system very low and his body wide open to attack."

Frank looked around the room. Then he studied the corner of the room that he reckoned was going to become a daily part of life for a long time to come. "Can I sit with him?" he asked.

The nurse seemed to smile behind her protective mask. "Yes. I'd be delighted if you would. But I'll have to ask you not to talk to him. I know it's tempting but, right now, Ray needs rest more than anything else."

Frank was slightly relieved on hearing the word rest. It spelt hope. It was a word his mother always used when he was too sick to go to school. Rest will have you right as rain in no time, she'd say. Maybe he would be all right.

He sat down on the small school-like wooden chair beside the bed. He looked at Ray's eyes. His eyelashes and eyebrows were gone. His lips were chapped and ragged raw. He breathed unevenly. Every now and then, he'd groan as if he was trying to say something.

Frank reached out and took his huge hand in his.

Bandages covered his wrists and palms. His fingers were free, though.

He'd never held a man's hand before. Shook them

plenty of times . . . but never held one. He squeezed Ray's hand gently.

Ray's eyes flickered. Maybe it was just a reflex action. His eyes opened slowly.

Frank moved closer. He squeezed his hand again. He knew he shouldn't be doing this but he didn't care. "Ray," he whispered. "It's Frank. Can you hear me?"

Ray's eyes opened wider.

Frank squeezed his hand a little tighter.

Ray groaned, as if trying to say something. Then he was overcome by a frightening, nauseating cough. Rasping and spluttering. It sounded as if there was a gallon of phlegm in his lungs. Then he relaxed and closed his eyes.

It scared Frank. He'd never heard anything like it before. Thank God he's got none of those hoses running down his throat, Frank thought. Maybe *that's* a sign that he's not as serious as the others. It must have been a horrible fire, he thought to himself. Then he thought of Davina. Ray didn't know. Frank hadn't been to the pub yet. He tried to imagine the scene. If this was the way the fire left his best friend and *his* fiancée, what state was the pub in? he wondered. He blew the breath he'd been holding out through the gauze mask. He didn't care about the pub. All he wanted now was for Ray to sit up and talk to him. Frank could smuggle him in the odd bottle of brown stout and some good tips for the horses. He turned around. The smell of phenol almost overpowered him. "Excuse me, sister," Frank called.

The nurse dropped her pen and hurried over to the

649

bed. "Is he all right?" she asked anxiously. She started to check that each of Ray's drip bags were functioning properly.

"I'm sorry, I didn't mean to give you a fright. I was just wondering why he's got no tubes like the rest of them." He waited, hoping to be told that Ray wasn't as sick as the others.

The nurse seemed reluctant. "It's because of the burns. His throat, particularly. It would be far too painful." She left it at that. "Call me if you need anything."

Frank now knew that Ray was a seriously sick man. Maybe his optimism was a bit like a one-armed man hanging off the side of a cliff with an itchy arse, hoping to feel better. He wiped his forehead. The heat in the unit was unbearable. He yawned and looked at his watch. He wondered about Jamie. Was she OK? Was she in pain too? Keeping his eyes open in these conditions was proving to be difficult. Jesus, the heat! Impossible. Eventually they closed.

* * *

The room seemed darker when Frank opened his eyes. He checked his watch. Quarter to one. He'd been asleep for nearly an hour and a half. It dawned on him that these patients wouldn't be sitting up in their beds to enjoy their mashed parsnips and chips. These bags of clear liquid were all they'd be getting for a long time to come. It was then that Frank noticed Ray's gaze.

He was staring straight up at Frank.

At first, Frank got a terrible fright. Then a huge wave of relief ran through him. *"Ray!"* he hinted.

The nurse looked across from her desk disapprovingly.

"Sorry," whispered Frank. He smiled at her and nodded his head.

Then Ray tried to nod his head. He coughed again. Frank quickly took hold of his hand.

This time, Ray squeezed it. He seemed to be trying to say something. Then, as quickly as he'd opened them, he closed his eyes again.

Frank sat back in the chair and wondered what it'd meant.

Ray was a fighter. This was a positive sign that he wasn't going to take this lying down for too long. Frank knew Ray. He knew he could tolerate pain. Please God, he muttered, let him be all right. Frank closed his eyes again. He had a good feeling about all this now.

"Mr McCabe," the voice called. The hand was shaking him by the shoulder. Softly first, then a little firmer. "Mr McCabe," she repeated.

Frank opened his eyes.

The corner of the room was lit up. Two tall spotlights seemed to be trained on the bed which was surrounded by a long curtain.

Frank couldn't see what was going on behind it. As he sat up in the chair, the bright lights were switched off and the curtain pulled back.

A middle-aged man in a white coat stood

respectfully silent as Fr Duffy made the sign of the cross on Ray's forehead and muttered a prayer in Latin close to his ear.

Frank lunged forward in the chair.

The bed was silent. Inactive. The beeping noises had stopped. There wasn't as much sunlight coming into the unit any more.

Frank rubbed his eyes and looked closely at Ray.

He lay very still, his hands across his chest.

Frank stood up and then sat down again. He looked up at the nurse.

She wasn't wearing her gauze mask any more.

"How is he?" Frank asked urgently.

She placed the chart she was holding in a case and closed it. "I'm afraid that . . . Ray died about twenty minutes ago." She paused. "I'd have woken you up if . . . " She cut the explanation short. It didn't really matter now. "I think it was a merciful release that he went in his sleep. From what we know about the extent of his injuries, he'd never have fully recovered. He'd most likely have required hospital attention for the rest of his life."

The man in the white coat returned and beckoned to the nurse. He whispered something in her ear.

Frank stared at his best friend. He was dead. He wasn't here any more. He remembered Ray telling him about after-death experiences. About how the spirit leaves the body and hovers around the room for a while before it heads off down a long dark tunnel towards a bright light to meet its maker.

Frank looked up at the ceiling and across the room

at the top of the television. He looked back at the still figure lying on the bed. He reached out and touched his hand.

This time it was colder than before.

He looked at his chest and his neck and mouth. Not a move.

"Excuse me, Mr McCabe," the nurse called politely. Frank was in another world. The doctor spoke quietly with Fr Duffy. "Yes," he muttered.

"Mr Flynn's mother and sister have just arrived. They . . . don't know yet. If you like, this priest can inform them but he thought that, maybe, it might be nicer . . . easier, if it came from you."

Frank was numb. He stood up. "Of course," he mumbled.

"You can stay for another few minutes if you want to. We're just making arrangements to have the remains transferred."

Remains? thought Frank. He's only dead half an hour. And already he's *remains*. He sighed. At least he was spared the news about Davina. That would have really finished him. Now he knows and they're together, he thought.

* * *

A police officer stated that they weren't ruling out arson. "Nor are we ruling out involvement from terrorist groups."

The reporter continued, "A suggestion that this is the work of the Neofascist group, Combat 18, is also being seriously considered. The pub was a popular drinking haunt and meeting place for many of London's Irish. An anti-Irish plot, according to police investigators, is thought to be the most likely cause of this horrific blaze in which two young Irish people lost their lives."

* * *

It rained all night.

Eventually, Frank had to cover his nose and mouth with a scarf. The rancid smell of wet, charred furnishings and fabrics made him sick. He walked carefully through the burnt-out shell, kicking the incinerated leftovers of familiar items which were strewn about. Debris lay everywhere. Small gullies of water poured down on top of him.

He held the scarf tightly to his nose and looked up.

The roof was practically gone. The late morning sunshine threw streaks of bright light on to the remains of months of hard work. The bar was still intact, though badly scorched. That was about it. Even the new cooking equipment had warped in the unbearable heat of the fire. Small artefacts, broken and twisted, lay everywhere.

Frank bent down and picked up a picture-frame. He carefully rubbed the mucky gunge off the shattered glass. It was the photo of himself and the lads at their old Friday night darts tournament. He could barely make out the familiar faces. Winners in The Clover Tap's Dart League. Mossy, Paddy, Bilbo, Colin, Decco,

Joe, Ray. And Frank. His mind wandered back to that Friday night.

* * *

"Howya, Frank? What can I get for you?"

"Howya, Mr Mulligan. A pint of Bass, please."

"There you go, son. A pound and fifteen to yourself. A bitter evening. How's your mother?"

"Thanks, yeah, she's in great form. Hopefully coming over with Brendan and his missus for Paddy's Day. She hates the boat, though. So I'm trying to get a few bob back to her so she can fly. She's hoping to come for a full week."

"That'll be great. Someone to look after you for a change. And, more importantly, keep an eye on you. Well, listen, I may be looking for someone part-time in a couple of weeks. Gimme a shout if you fancy a shot."

"Jesus, I will, Mr Mulligan, thanks. Any sign of the lads?"

"Need you ask? Can't you hear them in the snug? Bilbo's just in. Colin and Mossy are on their third at this stage. Tell us, when is Ray due back from Leeds?"

"Eh, this evening, I think. He said the train should be in about six. Why?"

"Ah, sure, the place isn't the same without him. As true as me mother's in heaven, I'm down about five per cent since he went away a month ago. God bless his appetite. What has him up north for so long, Frank?"

"Job interviews and some part-time work."

"What? So he might be leaving us for good?"

"Yeah, it looks that way. If he gets something more permanent. Money's great up there. Question is, how long will they put up with him?"

"He *is* coming tonight, isn't he?"

"I hope so. Sure we don't stand a chance against that team from The Queen's Arse if he doesn't."

"The Queen's *Arch*, Frank."

"Sorry?"

"Arch, not ar . . . nothing."

Half six. The door of the pub opened so hard that it almost came away from its hinges.

"Make way for the prodigal son. I'm back from the wilderness. Me tongue's like sandpaper and me throat's like a whore's fanny doin' overtime. How are you, Mr Mulligan?"

"Holy God, Ray. We're all delighted you're back but will y'ever give up the huggin' and cursin'?"

"What's your fuckin' problem, Mr Mulligan? You have a face on you like a bulldog lickin' piss off a nettle. Have you got a wasp up your arse?"

"A pint, son?"

"To start with, Mr Mulligan."

"Anything strange up north?"

"Well, while you're there pullin' me a few pints, I'll tell youse all the good news." There was a deafening silence. "Well, who's going to ask big Ray Flynn did he get the interview?"

"Did you get the interview, Ray?"

"I did. I got loads of interviews. But I didn't get one fuckin' job!"

There was a loud cheer and sighs of relief all round. The darts team was safe for another year.

"How are you, Mary O'Keefe? Jesus, you should leave that brassière off more often."

* * *

Frank stared at the characters in the photograph. It seemed like yesterday. He wished, for a moment, it was. Bilbo married the daughter of a construction tycoon who dropped dead at the wedding reception. Bilbo and his new wife inherited the lot. They moved back to Ireland and bought a pub in the west which Bilbo proceeded to drink dry in six months. Mossy was killed in a construction accident when he fell out of a crane. Something which affected Ray for a long time afterwards. Colin suffered from bouts of depression. During one such bout, he was spotted getting on the Dover to Calais car ferry. He was never seen again. Decco got a job building swimming-pools for the rich and famous in the south of Spain. When last heard of, he was doing well for himself. And Joe and Paddy? They sprang the most astonishing news of all. They announced they were both gay and were setting up home together on the Dingle peninsula. They opened a small tea room which was still thriving, the last Frank heard.

That left Frank and Ray. Now Ray was gone.

"What the hell happened, Ray?" he whispered as he pushed the scarf further up his face and wiped his eye.

The police officers and the forensics people

watched him as he examined the damage. Two of them nodded to him sympathetically.

Frank squeezed in, sideways, behind the bar. Everything was charred-black and soaking wet. He wasn't too sure how much damage the fire hose water had done. Not much, he thought. They deserved a medal for fighting something this bad.

The door to the stairs and upstairs quarters was closed and had a *Police. Do not enter* tape running across it. He was about to open the door.

"Sorry, sir, excuse me," a voice said politely.

Frank looked around.

A police officer stood behind him. "I'm going to have to ask you not to go upstairs, sir. Since the structure of the building is now unsound and considered dangerous, we can't vouch for your safety. Insurance assessors are due any time. Also, our forensics people would like to take one last look up there when it dries out." The police officer smiled and directed Frank back towards the centre of the pub.

"But this is . . . was *my* pub," Frank said indignantly.

"I understand, sir. But I'm simply passing on a police regulation. I'd appreciate it if you'd comply."

Frank shrugged his shoulders. "Time to get out of here before I throw up," he mumbled. He picked up the photograph and shoved it inside his jacket.

"Hello," said a soft voice. "I was hoping I'd run into you."

It was Anne O'Brien. "Hello, there," Frank muttered. "Funny how we always meet just as all hell breaks loose."

Anne looked him straight in the eyes. "Frank, I don't know what to say."

"That makes two of us."

"I was talking to Ray's mother and sister. They're very upset."

"Why wouldn't they be? What happened to him and Davina is as good as murder. The thing that really scares me is that it could've been me. In fact, I'd say it was meant for me." He put his hands in his deep coat pockets and shivered. He kicked bits of broken wood and slashed carpet around the filthy, soaking carpet.

"Why do you say that?"

"Because I'm the manager. He was only an employee. She didn't even work here. Why would anyone want to kill Ray and Davina?"

"What if they didn't want to kill *anyone*? What if this was just a statement. A political statement?"

"Ah, for God's sake," Frank shouted, "can you not come up with anything better than that? Are you trying to tell me that this was a sectarian attack by Loyalist terrorists? I might have believed that a few years ago. But not today. Some of my best drinkers were Protestants. No one gave that a second thought."

Silence.

"I'm not trying to tell you what happened, Frank. For a start, I don't know *what* happened. I'm as much in the dark as you are."

"Oh yeah? Well, now, I'm also out of work. Two of my best friends are dead. One of my *ex*-employees is looking at a fifteen-year stretch in prison for something she knew nothing about, and there's a lunatic out there holding my girlfriend and neither of us knows whether she's dead or alive! And you're telling me we're *both* in the dark?"

Anne sighed. "I'm sorry. There's nothing else I can say . . . for now, anyway."

Frank shrugged. "I better be getting back to the airport. I'm flying back this afternoon. We're really worried about Jamie."

"I know. Any word?"

"No. That Detective Blaney seems to be in charge again. He said he'd keep in touch."

"Can I buy you a cup of coffee?"

"Something stronger than coffee," he muttered.

"It's on me," she whispered. She linked his arm as they carefully followed a small, clear path out of the smouldering ruin.

* * *

4.45pm. Tommy Barrett packed his toilet bag into his neat hold-all. He stroked his chin. "Nice shave, eh?" He turned away from the mirror and walked over to the chair which stood alone in the dead centre of the small bedroom. "What do you think?" He bent down and rubbed his cheek against the side of Jamie's face. The tape which covered her eyes was gone, along with small clumps of her pretty eyebrows. She whimpered and muttered something. It was inaudible. She was barely conscious by now. He picked up the milkshake and held it in front of her. She shook her head.

He stood up again. "Time to say goodbye . . .

farewell . . . it's been so nice to know you . . . " He danced in front of her, whirling around, pretending to waltz. Then he froze. "Whoops . . . better not touch that cord." He hissed and pointed to the tight nylon filament leading first to the bathroom door, then to the main bedroom door. The gun sat nestled between her knees again, the barrel pointing directly at her chin. "What a clever boy," he remarked. "It's a pity I'm not gonna be around to see this because I think I deserve a reward for being such a genius." He squatted down beside the chair and linked Jamie's arm. She was afraid to breathe. "You see, what's goin' to happen . . . because obviously you're going to miss a considerable chunk of the show once it gets rollin' . . . I'm going to leave here in a few minutes and hang the *Please clean this room* sign on the outside of the door. Then I'm going to go down the fire escape really quietly and leave you here on your own. Problem is the door's going to be locked from the inside, so they ain't goin' to able to get in. They'll then break down the door to find out what's going on and . . . *bang*! There'll be bits of poor Jamie all over the carpark." He patted her sharply on the back, almost causing her to lose her balance. He stood up and squeezed his nose tightly. "What a horrible smell, Jamie. Have you been wetting yourself again? You should have told me you wanted to visit the bathroom. Anyway, you should really save that for when the gun goes off." He laughed.

Jamie screamed and pleaded behind the tight plaster covering her mouth. All Tommy could hear was babbling nonsense. He pulled a fresh length of plaster and cut it with the sharp knife. "Goodnight," he muttered. He stretched it across her eyes.

He glanced out into the carpark to see if his car had been dropped back to the hotel from the garage. "Fuckin' dickheads . . . what's keepin' them?"

* * *

5.40 pm. "Keep all local units well away. Is that clear?"

"Roger." The police radio crackled.

"Whereabouts are ERU?" he shouted.

"They should be right behind you, sir."

"Tell them, no sirens!"

Joe Blaney had overseen four kidnappings in twelve years. He had a nasty feeling about this one. More of a hunch. He wasn't sure if Jamie Carroll was in that room. But everything was pointing in that direction. The hotel reception had called the emergency services at five o'clock that afternoon, and asked for police. The occupant of room 27, a Michael Lenane, according to the hotel register, was seen carrying two long lengths of binding twine through reception shortly after his arrival. The young lady who accompanied him hadn't been seen for four days. Hotel staff tried on a number of occasions to enter the room but a *Do not disturb* sign hung permanently outside. Michael Lenane had told them he'd only intended staying overnight. Now, a cleaner had heard ferocious shouting between a man and a woman in the room. She reported this to the duty manager. He became concerned and notified the police.

Joe Blaney was uneasy, if only about the name of the guest. He remembered what Frank McCabe had told him about the tramp's plane ticket. If Tommy Barrett *was* in room 27, this could turn out to be a lot nastier than even he'd bargained for.

* * *

6.00 pm. Frank turned the key in the front door. Mona Carroll ran out to meet him. "Frank, a man called Paul with a northern accent's been looking for you all day. I'd no number for him to contact you. But he said it was about Jamie."

"What did he say?" Frank asked quickly.

"He wouldn't tell me anything. Just that if you got in early to go to a hotel in Howth. Does that make sense?" Her voice was shaking. "Frank!"

He was gone before she could call him a second time. He ran as hard as he could towards the main road. No taxis in sight. Typical. Then he saw one. "*Taxi!*" he screamed. It was almost as if the driver saw him before he even had a chance to wave.

The driver had turned the car and was speeding towards the coast road before he bothered to ask Frank where he was going.

"Howth," called Frank.

"I know, I know," the red-haired driver butted in. "Where *were* you? Paul's been trying to contact you since ten this morning. He asked you to be ready to dig out. He's had to go and look himself. If he gets tied up in that battle, he could get whacked."

"What *battle*?"

"Jamie's in the hotel in Howth. What state she's in, we're not sure. We're sure that Barrett's also still there. But not for long, I'd say. I think he'll leave her behind."

"Oh, thank God!" muttered Frank.

The man looked at Frank in the mirror. "I hope, for my brother's sake, God is on *your* side."

* * *

6.05pm. Tommy Barrett snaked out on to the fire escape. He quickly, but carefully, hopped down the twenty or so cast-iron steps to the rear carpark, clutching the well-worn briefcase securely under his arm. Its contents would guarantee him anonymity. All he had to do now was get away untraced, as far away as possible. Paul Flaherty stood behind an open tradesman's entrance leading to the hotel kitchens. He watched Barrett. As soon as he was out on the main road, Flaherty scaled the metal steps of the fire escape. The curtains in room 27 were closed, except for an inch or so, allowing a narrow streak of light to enter the room. He squeezed his face against the window, trying to block out the light with his cupped hands. He held his breath which was fogging up his view. He was looking at the back of a woman's head. She was tied to a wooden chair. Her hands were bound tightly behind her back. He could see a length of string stretching away from her. He could only assume it was a booby-trap. He had to think fast. Preferably a gun, he thought. If it was a bomb, there could be real problems. The entire room could be primed. He tried to see if there were cables on the floor. He couldn't see any. Then again, it was difficult to see anything. If he burst through the window, he might set off whatever it was that threatened her. If it was an automatic pistol, he could get killed himself. He sighed. His breathing was heavy. Risks would have to be taken.

* * *

6.10 pm. Tommy Barrett arrived at the garage. "Excuse me, is my car ready?"

"Oh yeah, you left that BMW in a couple of days ago."

"That's right. It's just that I need it fairly urgently."

"You could have had it the day before yesterday. We thought you'd forgotten to come back. I was tempted to take it home myself." The young lad laughed as he wiped oil off his hands. "Another five minutes and we were shut up for the night."

"Right, yeah. Is it ready?"

"Yeah, I'll just get you to sign for it. How would you like to pay?"

"Credit card?"

"No problem. That's, eh, let's see . . . a hundred and forty-three pounds exactly."

Tommy tried not to look surprised. Why should I pay the little bastard? he thought. I'm not coming back. "No problem. Would it all right if I took it for a quick spin up the road?"

The young apprentice mechanic didn't seem too impressed. "Well, garage rules, I'll have to go with you. Anything you're not happy with, you can tell me there and then."

Tommy was getting fidgety. He noticed the detective car pull into the hotel carpark. "Come on then, let's go."

The black car headed for Howth Summit.

* * *

Paul Flaherty strolled around the front of the hotel to see if there was a discreet access to the second floor which might allow him take a look at the problem through the keyhole. Just then, his mouth dropped open. "Fuck," he muttered. Superintendent Joe Blaney was walking towards the hotel entrance, accompanied by two detectives brandishing automatic machineguns. Paul knew there was no time to waste. He had less than sixty seconds to free Jamie from whatever it was she was hooked up to. He hotfooted it back up the fire escape until he stood outside the window. "Please don't let her move," he prayed. He put his leather-clad elbow sharply through the pane of glass. He was standing in the room behind her in seconds. His eyes whizzed about. Then he saw it, the .38 Special, jammed between her knees. Jamie was trembling violently, almost swaying. Another inch and she was dead. He walked around in front of her. Her eyes were covered. He held her head firmly and ripped the tape clean off. He signalled to her that everything was going to be OK. He could see that she was on the verge of blacking out. "I'll have you out of here in minutes."

There was a loud bang on the door. "Open up . . . armed police!"

A strong vibration against the door was all it would take to make the pistol trigger itself, blowing Jamie's face and most of her head clean off.

"*Don't open the door!*" shouted Paul. "The room's wired!" He gently tried to remove the sticking-plaster from across her mouth to help her breathing. But it was bound right around the back of her head, twice over. He'd have to disarm the loaded weapon first. He needed a knife. "Have you a nail-file?" he asked Jamie calmly but insistently.

She mumbled through the tight tape.

Paul searched for her handbag. He had to stay calm. No time for a frenzy, he thought.

"Open the door or we're comin' in!"

"I can't. It's booby-trapped. Break it down and you'll kill her." He reefed open her small handbag and threw its contents across the bed. There it was. A nail-file. "*Yes!*" he grunted.

"I'll count to three, Barrett, then we're coming in!"

"*This isn't Barrett!*" He held his breath while he carefully carved away at the tight twine. "I'm not armed!" he shouted. It seemed impenetrable. "*Come on!*" he begged. He could see it fraying. His leg leaned against Jamie's thigh for support. She was shaking. One last stroke. "*Got it!*" The door burst open. The gun, now loose between her knees, discharged a bullet into the ceiling. The detectives crouched and fired.

Paul Flaherty lay on top of Jamie to shield her from the erratic gunfire. She could hear him shouting at them to stop. *"I'm not armed!"* he screamed, over and over. *"Jesus Christ, stop!"* he implored. He shook violently for what seemed like minutes, while gripping Jamie's arm tightly, almost protectively. Then a weak shudder. He went limp, then silent. Jamie could feel blood trickling down her face on to the floor. She started to cry silently.

* * *

The taxi-driver, hearing the gunfire, spun the car around in the carpark. He jammed on the brakes beside a discarded police motor-cycle. A helmet rested on the petrol tank. His face was red with anger. His eyes were racing. "No more time!" he muttered.

"For what?" asked Frank.

He didn't answer. He reached into the glove compartment and took out a small device, similar to a walkie-talkie. He climbed out of the car quickly. "I think you'll find your girlfriend's upstairs. Paul was trying to get her out. I hope they're both all right," he told Frank compassionately. He straddled the bike and kicked it into power. "I've still got some business to look after before it's too late." Then, with a quick reassuring glance around, he put on the helmet and sped off.

His first stop was the garage. To all intents and purposes, he looked like the real thing. He took off the helmet. "Where's the bloke in the BMW?" he shouted at the foreman.

"Gone out for a quick run. Up to the Summit. Right at the end of the seafront, past the big church and left, on up the steep hill. The lads always take them up there. He should be back any minute."

He handed the helmet to the foreman and sped off, racing up through the gears, like only an experienced biker could do. Past the affluent, sleepy hamlets, and up the steep incline. On his way towards the summit, he noticed a greasy looking kid in overalls heading down in the direction of the village. He slowed down and pulled in. *"Where is he?"* he demanded.

The young man looked nervous and disturbed. "He pulled a knife on me and told me to get out of the car." He pointed towards the Summit.

The biker didn't wait for a full explanation. He raced up the winding road towards the Summit. Within seconds, he had the BMW in sight. "Bastard!" he shouted. "Why not?" He glanced down to familiarise himself with the controls. On went the siren. And the flashing blue lights.

Tommy heard the two-tone first, then saw the lights in his mirror. *"Shit!"* He had no choice but to pull in. He kept the knife buried between his left thigh and the black leather seat. The officer didn't bother to alight. He rode up alongside the car to the driver's window. He raised his visor. "Bit fast for my liking," the uniformed man shouted through the full-face helmet. Tommy was about to reply politely when the man grinned at him. It was an evil, menacing snigger. But then you always *were* too fast for my liking."

Tommy froze.

"Driving that fast on unfamiliar roads can kill. But then, you always liked a *dare*. Didn't you . . . *Tommy Barrett!* You detroyed my family eight years ago. You made my mother ill. You deprived my brother of a normal life, and all of us of a member of the family. Your sick, bastardly mind never knew when to say *enough*. Did it? Everyone you've ever touched, you've destroyed. Well, no more."

Tommy was speechless. He put his foot down hard on the accelerator. The car lunged forward and sped off. He'd no time to check the map for directions. He'd just have to rely on intuition. If he took left turns, he reckoned he'd stay close to the coastline. Hopefully, this would take him to the main coast road. Daylight was slowly losing its sharp edge. A foggy dusk was making it more difficult to see ahead now. He wiped the windscreen with the back of his fingers. His hand was shaking. Come on, man, he thought. Get a grip. You're almost there. Another few minutes and you'll just be another motorist in the dark. He spotted a busy pub on his left. The Summit Inn. He looked in his mirror. No sign of the biker. He slowed down to study the options. Three roads fanned out ahead of him. One seemed to lead to a housing estate. Another swept away downwards to the left. It seemed too narrow to be a main route. He edged forward and meditated the other, sharper, left turn. It was a wide road that continued to rise, just like the one he'd taken. Seemed like the right choice, he thought. Into first gear. The front wheels spun as the car screeched forward. A small group of bikers drinking outside the pub cheered as the car screamed up the hill. Then they booed and hissed as the police motorcycle slowed down and stopped. One of the group remarked that the policeman wasn't wearing a helmet. The others took no notice.

The man on the bike didn't seem too perturbed at the sudden departure. He slowly turned left and stopped, parking the bike dead centre in the road, facing the hill. He held out the remote control. He pressed a small gadget and checked to make sure the red light was flashing. Then he casually looked around at the terrain, ignoring the slagging behind him. Seemed safe enough. Now all he had to do was wait.

Tommy Barrett was in trouble. He looked around at the barren landscape. One or two new luxury houses, set back in from the road. Apart from that, nothing. A carpark overlooking Dublin bay. A dead-end. He could feel himself panicking. No way, he thought. He took a moment to unwind. Then he remembered. He took out his wallet. He carefully removed the small red tissue inside. He opened it and poured a small line of white powder on to the back of his hand. He held it up to one of his nostrils and sniffed hard. Then the other. That felt much better. Time to think. He'd have to turn around and head back down the hill. Take the other left turn. Why didn't he think of that in the first place? That would surely lead him back onto the coast road. Yes. He turned the powerful car around and drove to the edge of the carpark. He stopped again. There he was, in the middle of the road, at the bottom of the hill. The man on the bike. It was dark now, but he could still see him. Flashing blue lights. It was definitely *him*. But what was he playing at? A 750cc-powered, two-wheel machine would undoubtedly catch most cars on the open road, but not when the car is racing towards you head-on and you're parked right in its path! He'd just drive straight through him if he refused to get out of the way. He'd probably kill him, but who cared? He revved the engine three times and took his foot off the clutch. The car lunged forward. He kept his eyes peeled on the blue lights as he accelerated down the bumpy hill. Then, without any warning, they disappeared. Gone. It was pitch-dark. He was no longer able to see the motor-bike. Yet something was telling him that *he* was still there, dead ahead.

The biker stretched out his arm and pointed the small handset at the car, which was now nearly two hundred metres away, he reckoned. He waited until he was sure that it was within range, but beyond the house on the right. Dare I die, he murmured. He pressed a second button and kept his thumb firmly down.

Tommy Barrett laughed as the car went into fourth gear. There was no way he'd catch him. Jamie was dead by now. He felt a great sense of relief as he eagerly slapped the steering wheel three times. He'd dump the car at the border and fly out of Belfast. He patted the briefcase on the seat beside him. Fifty grand. Thanks, Monty! He sniggered. Where to? he wondered smugly. Tenerife sounded nice. Three months on a quiet, sun-soaked beach. He might even take on some part-time work. Just to prevent boredom. Who knows who I'll bump into? he thought. Vinny Weight owned a sports and leisure complex in Playa de las Americas . . . financed by a giant swoop on a Wembly high-street bank eight years before. He'd done his time and stockpiled the money safely. Weight wasn't his real name. It was an affectionate reference to the methods he employed to dispose of threatening tell-tale merchants. He'd bury their feet in cement and throw them into the Thames, downriver. Tommy could almost smell the suntan lotion. Three months. The furore would have died down by then. Then again, he might get to like the island lifestyle. London was such a dump.

The man stood in the centre of the dark, lonely road. Tommy could see him now with his full headlights. He wondered what the stranger was holding. He could just about make out the flashing light. Whatever it was, he seemed to be pointing it at him. Tommy stopped smiling. Then he thought . . .

The bomb, strapped to the half-shaft on the driver's side, directly beneath the chassis under Tommy Barrett's feet, contained ten pounds of Semtex, a very powerful plastic explosive. Enough to destroy a ten-storey building. The car lifted thirty feet into the air, as it was being ripped to shreds, panel from panel, bolt by bolt. The horrific blast lit up the night-time sky. The thrust of the explosion shook the ground, throwing the biker backwards. Windows in the pub, close by, shattered. Drinkers dived for cover. Within seconds, a peaceful silence began to settle on the picturesque hillside again, as burning debris and twisted metal fragments littered the surrounding fields. Thousands of crisp twenty-pound notes fluttered in the soft sea breeze, like a light snowfall. Birds squawked. A dog barked. Then came the wail of police sirens. The biker threw the device into a grassy ditch and climbed on to the motor-bike.

* * *

Two weeks later. They walked hand in hand, oblivious to the water which lapped against their sodden shoes. Neither said a word. They had the entire beach to themselves.

Now and again, Frank looked at her.

It was uncannily quiet. Eerie. Almost as if it had been expected. Predicted.

"Was it a big funeral?" asked Jamie.

"Very big. Ray wasn't home in years and yet half the town turned out," Frank replied pensively.

"It was nice that the two of them were buried together."

"Yeah."

Jamie stared out at the lonely sea. "What are you thinking?" she asked softly.

Frank jumped slightly. "What am *I* thinking?"

She still didn't look at him.

"Maybe this isn't the right place to come to."

Jamie shrugged her shoulders and looked back out at the sea. "Do you think he deserved it?" she asked quietly.

"Who, Tommy?"

She nodded.

Frank thought carefully for a moment. "I suppose it was the only way to stop him. He was mad. He wouldn't have stopped until . . . " He paused. "I'm sorry. What are you thinking?"

Jamie shrugged. "That I never got a chance to thank him."

"Paul?"

"Yeah. All the time, people were pointing the finger at *him*. He saved my life."

"I know. Did you ever . . . "

Jamie cut him short. She turned and ran her warm hands up and down his freezing cold cheeks.

"That's nice," he whispered.

"So's this." She nodded at the quiet beach. Then she reached up and kissed him.

"Did Blaney get back to you?"

"Yeah."

"What did he say?"

"Not much. Just that there was no way they could prove that Paul Flaherty had any sort of kind-hearted intentions when it came to saving my life. Blaney maintained it was just his way of getting to Tommy."

Frank sneered. "Funny how he wouldn't believe a word I said to him in the police station that day, isn't it? What did he say about the car bomb?"

"Nothing. Apart from the structural damage it did to the surrounding area, which was pretty small anyway." She looked at Frank. "I told him I wouldn't be here today if it wasn't for Paul Flaherty. That *they*

675

would have been responsible for shooting me if they'd come through that door."

"What did he say to that?"

"He refused to accept it. He said that Tommy would've been responsible because he set up the trap."

"What a load of bullshit."

Jamie slowed down and pulled at Frank's arm. "What now?"

Frank smiled. "Now? Or . . . now?"

"I mean now."

"Well, I thought that maybe I could tempt you to a drink somewhere nice and quiet and away from all the madness now that you're out of hospital." He waited for a moment. "I have to talk to you."

Jamie looked serious for a moment. "Oh, that sounds ominous."

"Have you seen Nikki?"

"Yeah. She called up yesterday afternoon. The hearing's been set for September. She's in OK form . . . considering."

"And how's your ma?"

"Oh, you know my ma. Still holding press conferences. Still telling everyone the gory details." Jamie shrugged. "Glad to have me home."

Frank turned to Jamie and kissed her. "Not half as glad as me. When do you start work?"

"Tuesday. Why?"

"Well, since *you* have a good job here, I think I'd go mad if I had to travel backwards and forwards to see you every weekend. And in my job, weekends would be out anyway. So . . . "

"So?"

"So, I thought I'd look for a manager's job here. Then we could see a lot more of each other."

"A lot more?"

"Yeah, like getting out a bit more together like normal couples."

"Normal couples?"

"Jesus, Jamie, you're beginning to sound like a parrot!"

"A parrot?"

They walked back towards the small row of steps which led on to the beach.

Frank put his arm around her and pulled her close to him. "I saw some gorgeous new houses when I was coming in from the airport this morning. Would you like to take a look?"

"Gorgeous new houses?" Jamie slipped her arm around Frank's waist and squeezed him. "I don't mind."

He thought carefully again for a while.

"Go on," she urged, "say it."

Frank hesitated. "Well, it's just that . . . I promised myself when Ray was in the hospital, when I was sitting with him, that we'd look after the kids . . . just for a while. I can't think of anywhere else they could go . . . apart from foster-homes."

Jamie stopped him in his tracks. "A ready-made family?"

"Well, only if you're up to it. You'd obviously have to agree to the whole idea. Your mother said you had to go to the doctor last night because you were run down. So this might be the last thing you'd need."

"Run down?" she giggled. "Run over would be more like it." She took Frank's hands in hers. Then she looked up into his face with the most gorgeous smile he'd ever seen in his life. "I love you," she whispered.

"What?" he asked.

"I'm not run down, Frank. I'm pregnant." She reached up and kissed him. "Daddy!"

Frank was speechless. "How long?"

"Nearly seven weeks . . . remember?" Jamie gently thumped his shoulder. "Stop grinning." She dragged him along behind her as they walked towards the end of the beach. "So, tell me all about this house you say you've been looking at . . . I hope it's a big house."

Frank said nothing.

"What are you thinking?" asked Jamie.

"Just that . . . maybe Elvis might play at the wedding. That's all."